BY JANET EVANOVICH

ONE FOR THE MONEY
TWO FOR THE DOUGH
THREE TO GET DEADLY
FOUR TO SCORE
HIGH FIVE
HOT SIX
SEVEN UP
HARD EIGHT

TO THE NINES
TEN BIG ONES
ELEVEN ON TOP
TWELVE SHARP
LEAN MEAN THIRTEEN
FEARLESS FOURTEEN
FINGER LICKIN' FIFTEEN
SIZZLING SIXTEEN

VISIONS OF SUGAR PLUMS
PLUM LOVIN'
PLUM LUCKY
PLUM SPOOKY

WICKED APPETITE

FULL HOUSE

WITH DORIEN KELLY

LOVE IN A NUTSHELL

THE HUSBAND LIST

WITH CHARLOTTE HUGHES

FULL TILT
FULL SPEED
FULL BLAST

FULL BLOOM
FULL SCOOP

WITH LEANNE BANKS

HOT STUFF

WITH INA YALOF

HOW I WRITE

AVAILABLE FROM HARPERCOLLINS

HERO AT LARGE
MOTOR MOUTH
METRO GIRL

HARD EIGHT

&

TO THE NINES

TWO NOVELS IN ONE

JANET EVANOVICH

St. Martin's Paperbacks

This is a work of fiction. All of the characters, organizations, and events portrayed in this novel are either products of the author's imagination or are used fictitiously.

Published in the United States by St. Martin's Paperbacks, an imprint of St. Martin's Publishing Group.

HARD EIGHT & TO THE NINES: HARD EIGHT copyright © 2002 by Evanovich, Inc. and TO THE NINES copyright © 2003 by Evanovich, Inc.

For information, address St. Martin's Publishing Group, 120 Broadway, New York, NY 10271.

www.stmartins.com

ISBN: 978-1-250-62076-7

Our books may be purchased in bulk for promotional, educational, or business use. Please contact your local bookseller or the Macmillan Corporate and Premium Sales Department at 1-800-221-7945, ext. 5442, or by email at MacmillanSpecialMarkets@macmillan.com.

Printed in the United States of America

St. Martin's Paperbacks edition / June 2020

10 9 8 7 6 5 4 3 2 1

HARD EIGHT

Here's to the great teams of the world:
Betty and Veronica, Stephanie and Lula, Ralph and
Alice, and me and Jennifer Enderlin,
my St. Martin's editor.
Thanks Jen . . . you're the greatest.

Thanks to Ree Mancini
for suggesting the title for this book.

Chapter
ONE

Lately, I've been spending a lot of time rolling on the ground with men who think a stiffy represents personal growth. The rolling around has nothing to do with my sex life. The rolling around is what happens when a bust goes crapola and there's a last ditch effort to hog-tie a big, dumb bad guy possessing a congenitally defective frontal lobe.

My name is Stephanie Plum, and I'm in the fugitive apprehension business . . . bond enforcement, to be exact, working for my cousin Vincent Plum. It wouldn't be such a bad job except the direct result of bond enforcement is usually incarceration—and fugitives tend to not like this. Go figure. To encourage fugitive cooperation on the way back to the pokey I usually persuade the guys I capture to wear handcuffs and leg shackles. This works pretty good most of the time. And, if done right, cuts back on the rolling around on the ground stuff.

Unfortunately, today wasn't most of the time. Martin Paulson, weighing in at 297 pounds and standing five feet, eight inches tall, was arrested for credit card fraud and for being a genuinely obnoxious person. He failed to show for his court appearance last week, and this put Martin on my Most Wanted List. Since Martin is not too bright, he hadn't been too hard to find. Martin had, in fact, been at home engaged in what he does best . . . stealing merchandise off the Internet. I'd managed to get Martin into cuffs and leg shackles and into my car. I'd even managed to drive Martin to the police station on North Clinton Avenue. Unfortunately, when I attempted to get Martin *out* of my car he tipped over and was now rolling around on his belly, trussed up like a Christmas goose, unable to right himself.

We were in the parking lot adjacent to the municipal building. The back door leading to the docket lieutenant was less than fifty feet away. I could call for help, but I'd be the brunt of cop humor for days. I could unlock the cuffs or ankle shackles, but I didn't trust Paulson. He was royally pissed off, red-faced and swearing, making obscene threats and horrifying animal sounds.

I was standing there, watching Paulson struggle, wondering what the hell I was going to do, because anything short of a forklift wasn't going to get Paulson up off the pavement. And just then, Joe Juniak pulled into the lot. Juniak is a former police chief and is now mayor of Trenton. He's a bunch of years older than me and about a foot taller. Juniak's second cousin, Ziggy, is married to my cousin-in-law Gloria Jean. So we're sort of family . . . in a remote way.

The driver's side window slid down, and Juniak grinned at me, cutting his eyes to Paulson. "Is he yours?"

"Yep."

"He's illegally parked. His ass is over the white line."

I toed Paulson, causing him to start rocking again. "He's stuck."

Juniak got out of his car and hauled Paulson up by his armpits. "You don't mind if I embellish this story when I spread it all over town, do you?"

"I do mind! Remember, I voted for you," I said. "And we're almost related."

"Not gonna help you, cutie. Cops live for stuff like this."

"You're not a cop anymore."

"Once a cop, always a cop."

Paulson and I watched Juniak get back into his car and drive away.

"I can't walk in these things," Paulson said, looking down at the shackles. "I'm gonna fall over again. I haven't got a good sense of balance."

"Have you ever heard the bounty hunter slogan, Bring 'em back—dead or alive?"

"Sure."

"Don't tempt me."

Actually, bringing someone back dead is a big no-no, but this seemed like a good time to make an empty threat. It was late afternoon. It was spring. And I wanted to get on with my life. Spending another hour coaxing Paulson to walk across the parking lot wasn't high on my list of favored things to do.

I wanted to be on a beach somewhere with the sun blistering my skin until I looked like a fried pork rind. Okay, truth is at this time of year that might have to be Cancún, and Cancún didn't figure into my budget. Still, the point was, I didn't want to be *here* in this stupid parking lot with Paulson.

"You probably don't even have a gun," Paulson said.

"Hey, give me a break. I haven't got all day for this. I have other things to do."

"Like what?"

"None of your business."

"Hah! You haven't got anything better to do."

I was wearing jeans and a T-shirt and black Caterpillar boots, and I had a real urge to kick him in the back of his leg with my size-seven CAT.

"Tell me," he said.

"I promised my parents I'd be home for dinner at six."

Paulson burst out laughing. "That's pathetic. That's fucking pathetic." The laughter turned into a coughing fit. Paulson leaned forward, wobbled side to side, and fell over. I reached for him, but it was too late. He was back on his belly, doing his beached whale imitation.

My parents live in a narrow duplex in a chunk of Trenton called the Burg. If the Burg was a food, it would be pasta—penne rigate, ziti, fettuccine, spaghetti, and elbow macaroni, swimming in marinara, cheese sauce, or mayo. Good, dependable, all-occasion food that puts a smile on your face and fat on your butt. The Burg is a solid neighborhood where people buy houses and live in them until death kicks them out. Backyards are used to run a clothesline, store the garbage can, and give the dog a place to poop. No fancy backyard decks and gazebos for Burgers. Burgers sit on their small front porches and cement stoops. The better to see the world go by.

I rolled in just as my mother was pulling the roast chicken out of the oven. My father was already in his seat at the head of the table. He stared straight ahead, eyes glazed, thoughts in limbo, knife and fork in hand. My sister, Valerie, who had recently moved back home after leaving her husband, was at work whipping potatoes in the kitchen. When we were kids Valerie was the perfect daughter. And I was the daughter who stepped in dog poo, sat on gum, and constantly fell off the garage roof in an attempt to fly. As a last ditch effort to preserve her marriage, Valerie had traded in her Italian-Hungarian genes and turned herself into Meg Ryan. The marriage failed, but the blonde Meg-shag persists.

Valerie's kids were at the table with my dad. The nine-year-old, Angie, was sitting primly with her hands folded, resigned to enduring the meal, an almost perfect clone of Valerie at that age. The seven-year-old, Mary Alice, the kid from hell, had two sticks poked into her brown hair.

"What's with the sticks?" I asked.

"They not sticks. They're antlers. I'm a reindeer."

This was a surprise because usually she's a horse.

"How was your day?" Grandma asked me, setting a bowl of green beans on the table. "Did you shoot any-body? Did you capture any bad guys?"

Grandma Mazur moved in with my parents shortly after Grandpa Mazur took his fat clogged arteries to the all-you-can-eat buffet in the sky. Grandma's in her midseventies and doesn't look a day over ninety. Her body is aging, but her mind seems to be going in the opposite direction. She was wearing white tennis shoes and a lavender polyester warm-up suit. Her steel gray hair was cut short and permed to within an inch of its life. Her nails were painted lavender to match the suit.

"I didn't shoot anybody today," I said, "but I brought in a guy wanted for credit card fraud."

There was a knock at the front door, and Mabel Mar-kowitz stuck her head in and called, "Yoohoo."

My parents live in a two-family duplex. They own the south half, and Mabel Markowitz owns the north half, the house divided by a common wall and years of dis-agreement over house paint. Out of necessity, Mabel's made thrift a religious experience, getting by on Social Security and government-surplus peanut butter. Her husband, Izzy, was a good man but drank himself into an early grave. Mabel's only daughter died of uterine cancer a year ago. The son-in-law died a month later in a car crash.

All forward progress stopped at the table, and every-one looked to the front door, because in all the years Mabel had lived next door, she'd never once *yoohoo*ed while we were eating.

"I hate to disturb your meal," Mabel said. "I just wanted to ask Stephanie if she'd have a minute to stop over, later. I have a question about this bond business. It's for a friend."

"Sure," I said. "I'll be over after dinner." I imagined it would be a short conversation since everything I knew about bond could be said in two sentences.

Mabel left and Grandma leaned forward, elbows on the table. "I bet that's a lot of hooey about wanting advice for a friend. I bet Mabel's been busted."

Everyone simultaneously rolled their eyes at Grandma.

"Okay then," she said. "Maybe she wants a job. Maybe she wants to be a bounty hunter. You know how she's always squeaking by."

My father shoveled food into his mouth, keeping his head down. He reached for the potatoes and spooned seconds onto his plate. "Christ," he mumbled.

"If there's anyone in that family who would need a bail bond, it would be Mabel's ex-grandson-in-law," my mother said. "He's mixed up with some bad people these days. Evelyn was smart to divorce him."

"Yeah, and that divorce was real nasty," Grandma said to me. "Almost as nasty as yours."

"I set a high standard."

"You were a pip," Grandma said.

My mother did another eye roll. "It was a disgrace."

Mabel Markowitz lives in a museum. She married in 1943 and still has her first table lamp, her first pot, her first chrome-and-Formica kitchen table. Her living room was newly wallpapered in 1957. The flowers have faded but the paste has held. The carpet is dark Oriental. The upholstered pieces sag slightly in the middle, imprinted with asses that have since moved on . . . either to God or Hamilton Township.

Certainly the furniture doesn't bear the imprint of

Mabel's ass as Mabel is a walking skeleton who never sits. Mabel bakes and cleans and paces while she talks on the phone. Her eyes are bright, and she laughs easily, slapping her thigh, wiping her hands on her apron. Her hair is thin and gray, cut short and curled. Her face is powdered first thing in the morning to a chalky white. Her lipstick is pink and applied hourly, feathering out into the deep crevices that line her mouth.

"Stephanie," she said, "how nice to see you. Come in. I have a coffee cake."

Mrs. Markowitz *always* has a coffee cake. That's the way it is in the Burg. Windows are clean, cars are big, and there's always a coffee cake.

I took a seat at the kitchen table. "The truth is, I don't know very much about bond. My cousin Vinnie is the bond expert."

"It's not so much about bond," Mabel said. "It's more about finding someone. And I fibbed about it being for a friend. I was embarrassed. I just don't know how to even begin telling you this."

Mabel's eyes filled with tears. She cut a piece of coffee cake and shoved it into her mouth. Angry. Mabel wasn't the sort of woman to comfortably fall victim to emotion. She washed the coffee cake down with coffee that was strong enough to dissolve a spoon if you let it sit in the cup too long. *Never* accept coffee from Mrs. Markowitz.

"I guess you know Evelyn's marriage didn't work out. She and Steven got a divorce a while back, and it was pretty bitter," Mabel finally said.

Evelyn is Mabel's granddaughter. I've known Evelyn all my life, but we were never close friends. She lived several blocks away, and she went to Catholic school. Our paths only intersected on Sundays when she'd come to dinner at Mabel's house. Valerie and I called her the Giggler because she giggled at everything. She'd come

over to play board games in her Sunday clothes, and
she'd giggle when she rolled the dice, giggle when she
moved her piece, giggle when she lost. She giggled so
much she got dimples. And when she got older, she was
one of those girls that boys love. Evelyn was all round
softness and dimples and vivacious energy.

I hardly ever saw Evelyn anymore, but when I did
there wasn't much vivacious energy left in her.

Mabel pressed her thin lips together. "There was so
much arguing and hard feelings over the divorce that
the judge made Evelyn take out one of these new child
custody bonds. I guess he was afraid Evelyn wouldn't
let Steven see Annie. Anyway, Evelyn didn't have any
money to put up for the bond. Steven took the money
that Evelyn got when my daughter died, and he never
gave Evelyn anything. Evelyn was like a prisoner in that
house on Key Street. I'm almost the only relative left
for Evelyn and Annie now, so I put my house here up
for collateral. Evelyn wouldn't have gotten custody if I
didn't do that."

This was all new to me. I'd never heard of a *custody*
bond. The people I tracked down were in violation of
a *bail* bond.

Mabel wiped the table clean of crumbs and dumped
the crumbs in the sink. Mabel wasn't good at sitting.
"It was all just fine until last week when I got a note
from Evelyn, saying she and Annie were going away
for a while. I didn't think much of it, but all of a sudden everyone is looking for Annie. Steven came to my
house a couple days ago, raising his voice and saying
terrible things about Evelyn. He said she had no business taking Annie off like she did, taking her away from
him and taking her out of first grade. And he said he
was invoking the custody bond. And then this morning
I got a phone call from the bond company telling me

they were going to take my house if I didn't help them get Annie back."

Mabel looked around her kitchen. "I don't know what I'd do without the house. Can they really take it from me?"

"I don't know," I told Mabel. "I've never been involved in anything like this."

"And now they all got me worried. How do I know if Evelyn and Annie are okay? I don't have any way of getting in touch. And it was just a note. It wasn't even like I talked to Evelyn."

Mabel's eyes filled up again, and I was really hoping she wasn't going to flat-out cry because I wasn't great with big displays of emotion. My mother and I expressed affection through veiled compliments about gravy.

"I feel just terrible," Mabel said. "I don't know what to do. I thought maybe you could find Evelyn and talk to her . . . make sure her and Annie are all right. I could put up with losing the house, but I don't want to lose Evelyn and Annie. I've got some money set aside. I don't know how much you charge for this sort of thing."

"I don't charge anything. I'm not a private investigator. I don't take on private cases like this." Hell, I'm not even a very good bounty hunter!

Mabel picked at her apron, tears rolling down her cheeks now. "I don't know who else to ask."

Oh man, I don't believe this. Mabel Markowitz, crying! This was at about the same comfort level as getting a gyno exam in the middle of Main Street at high noon.

"Okay," I said. "I'll see what I can do . . . as a neighbor."

Mabel nodded and wiped her eyes. "I'd appreciate it." She took an envelope from the sideboard. "I have a picture for you. It's Annie and Evelyn. It was taken last year when Annie turned seven. And I wrote Evelyn's

address on a piece of paper for you, too. And her car
and license plate."

"Do you have a key to her house?"

"No," Mabel said. "She never gave me one."

"Do you have any ideas about where Evelyn might
have gone? Anything at all?"

Mabel shook her head. "I can't imagine where she's
taken off to. She grew up here in the Burg. Never lived
anyplace else. Didn't go away to college. Most all our
relatives are right here."

"Did Vinnie write the bond?"

"No. It's some other company. I wrote it down." She
reached into her apron pocket and pulled out a folded
piece of paper. "It's True Blue Bonds, and the man's
name is Les Sebring."

My cousin Vinnie owns Vincent Plum Bail Bonds
and runs his business out of a small storefront office on
Hamilton Avenue. A while back when I'd been desperate for a job, I'd sort of blackmailed Vinnie into taking
me on. The Trenton economy has since improved, and
I'm not sure why I'm still working for Vinnie, except
that the office is across from a bakery.

Sebring has offices downtown, and his operation
makes Vinnie's look like chump change. I've never met
Sebring but I've heard stories. He's supposed to be ex-
tremely professional. And he's rumored to have legs
second only to Tina Turner's.

I gave Mabel an awkward hug, told her I'd look into
things for her, and I left.

My mother and my grandmother were waiting for
me. They were at my parents' front door with the door
cracked an inch, their noses pressed to the glass.

"*Pssst,*" my grandmother said. "Hurry up over here.
We're dying."

"I can't tell you," I said.

Both women sucked in air. This went against the

code of the Burg. In the Burg, blood was *always* thicker than water. Professional ethics didn't count for much when held up to a juicy piece of gossip among family members.

"Okay," I said, ducking inside. "I might as well tell you. You'll find out anyway." We rationalize a lot in the Burg, too. "When Evelyn got divorced she had to take out something called a child custody bond. Mabel put her house up as collateral. Now Evelyn and Annie are off somewhere, and Mabel is getting pressured by the bond company."

"Oh my goodness," my mother said. "I had no idea."

"Mabel is worried about Evelyn and Annie. Evelyn sent her a note and said she and Annie were going away for a while, but Mabel hasn't heard from them since."

"If I was Mabel I'd be worried about her *house*," Grandma said. "Sounds to me like she could be living in a cardboard box under the railroad bridge."

"I told her I'd help her, but this isn't really my thing. I'm not a private investigator."

"Maybe you could get your friend Ranger to help her," Grandma said. "That might be better anyway, on account of he's hot. I wouldn't mind having him hang around the neighborhood."

Ranger is more associate than friend, although I guess friendship is mixed in there somehow, too. Plus a scary sexual attraction. A few months ago we made a deal that has haunted me. Another one of those jumping-off-the-garage-roof things, except this deal involved my bedroom. Ranger is Cuban-American with skin the color of a mocha latte, heavy on the mocha, and a body that can best be described as *yum*. He's got a big-time stock portfolio, an endless, inexplicable supply of expensive black cars, and skills that make Rambo look like an amateur. I'm pretty sure he only kills bad guys, and I think he might be able to fly like Superman, although the flying part has never been confirmed. Ranger works in bond enforcement, among other things. And Ranger always gets his man.

My black Honda CR-V was parked curbside. Grandma walked me to the car. "Just let me know if there's anything I can do to help," she said. "I always thought I'd make a good detective, on account of I'm so nosy."

"Maybe you could ask around the neighborhood."

"You bet. And I could go to Stiva's tomorrow. Charlie Shleckner is laid out. I hear Stiva did a real good job on him."

New York has Lincoln Center. Florida has Disney World. The Burg has Stiva's Funeral Home. Not only is Stiva's the premier entertainment facility for the Burg, it's also the nerve center of the news network. If you can't get the dirt on someone at Stiva's, then there isn't any dirt to get.

It was still early when I left Mabel's, so I drove past Evelyn's house on Key Street. It was a two-family house very much like my parents'. Small front yard, small front porch, small two-story house. No sign of life in Evelyn's half. No car parked in front. No lights shining behind drawn drapes. According to Grandma Mazur, Evelyn had lived in the house when she'd been married to Steven Soder and had stayed there with Annie when Soder moved out. Eddie Abruzzi owns the property and rents out both units. Abruzzi owns several houses in the Burg and a couple large office buildings in downtown Trenton. I don't know him personally, but I've heard he's not the world's nicest guy.

I parked and walked to Evelyn's front porch. I rapped lightly on her door. No answer. I tried to peek in the front window, but the drapes were drawn tight. I walked around the side of the house and stood on tippy toes, looking in. No luck with the side windows in the front room and dining room, but my snoopiness paid off with the kitchen. No curtains drawn in the kitchen. There were two cereal bowls and two glasses on the counter next to the sink. Everything else seemed tidy. No sign of Evelyn or Annie. I returned to the front and knocked on the neighbor's door.

The door opened, and Carol Nadich looked out at me.

"Stephanie!" she said. "How the hell are you?"

I went to school with Carol. She got a job at the button factory when we graduated and two months later married Lenny Nadich. Once in a while I run into her at Giovichinni's Meat Market, but beyond that we've lost touch.

"I didn't realize you were living here," I said. "I was looking for Evelyn."

Carol did an eye roll. "Everyone's looking for Evelyn. And to tell you the truth, I hope no one finds her. Except for you, of course. Those other jerks I wouldn't wish on anyone."

"What other jerks?"

"Her ex-husband and his friends. And the landlord, Abruzzi, and his goons."

"You and Evelyn were close?"

"As close as anyone could get to Evelyn. We moved here two years ago, before the divorce. She'd spend all day popping pills and then drink herself into a stupor at night."

"What kind of pills?"

"Prescription. For depression, I think. Understandable, since she was married to Soder. Do you know him?"

"Not well." I met Steven Soder for the first time at Evelyn's wedding nine years ago, and I took an instant dislike to him. In my brief dealings with him over the following years I found nothing to change my original bad impression.

"He's a real manipulative bastard. And abusive," Carol said.

"He'd hit her?"

"Not that I know. Just mental abuse. I could hear him yelling at her all the time. Telling her she was stupid. She was kind of heavy, and he used to call her 'the cow.' Then one day he moved out and moved in with some other woman. Joanne Something. Evelyn's lucky day."

"Do you think Evelyn and Annie are safe?"

"God, I hope so. Those two deserve a break."

I looked over at Evelyn's front door. "I don't suppose you have a key?"

Carol shook her head. "Evelyn didn't trust anyone. She was real paranoid. I don't think her grandma even has a key. And she didn't tell me where she was going, if that's your next question. One day she just loaded a bunch of bags into her car and took off."

I gave Carol my card and headed for home. I live in a three-story brick apartment building about ten minutes from the Burg . . . five, if I'm late for dinner and I hit the lights right. The building was constructed at a time when energy was cheap and architecture was inspired by economy. My bathroom is orange and brown, my refrigerator is avocado green, and my windows were born before Thermopane. Fine by me. The rent is reasonable, and the other tenants are okay. Mostly the building is inhabited by seniors on fixed incomes. The seniors are, for the most part, nice people . . . as long as you don't let them get behind the wheel of a car.

I parked in the lot and pushed through the double glass door that led to the small lobby. I was filled with chicken and potatoes and gravy and chocolate layer cake and Mabel's coffee cake, so I bypassed the elevator and took the stairs as penance. All right, so I'm only one flight up, but it's a start, right?

My hamster, Rex, was waiting for me when I opened the door to my apartment. Rex lives in a soup can in a glass aquarium in my kitchen. He stopped running on his wheel when I switched the light on and blinked out at me, whiskers whirring. I like to think it was *welcome home* but probably it was *who put the damn light on?* I gave him a raisin and a small piece of cheese. He stuffed the food into his cheeks and disappeared into his soup can. So much for roommate interaction.

In the past, Rex has sometimes shared his roommate status with a Trenton cop named Joe Morelli. Morelli's two years older than I am, half a foot taller, and his gun is bigger than mine. Morelli started looking up my skirt when I was six, and he's just never gotten out of the habit. We've had some differences of opinion lately, and Morelli's toothbrush is not currently in my bathroom. Unfortunately, it's a lot harder to get Morelli out of my heart and my mind than out of my bathroom. Nevertheless, I'm making an effort.

I got a beer from the fridge and settled in front of the television. I flipped through the stations, hitting the high points, not finding much. I had the photo of Evelyn and Annie in front of me. They were standing together, looking happy. Annie had curly red hair and the pale skin of a natural redhead. Evelyn had her brown hair pulled back. Conservative makeup. She was smiling, but not enough to bring out the dimples.

A mom and her kid . . . and I was supposed to find them.

Connie Rosolli had a doughnut in one hand and a cup of coffee in the other when I walked into the bail bonds office the next morning. She pushed the doughnut box across the top of her desk with her elbow and white powdered sugar sifted off her doughnut, down onto her boobs. "Have a doughnut," she said. "You look like you need one."

Connie is the office manager. She's in charge of petty cash and she uses it wisely, buying doughnuts and file folders, and financing the occasional gaming trip to Atlantic City. It was a little after eight, and Connie was ready for the day, eyes lined, lashes mascara-ed, lips painted bright red, hair curled into a big bush around her face. I, on the other hand, was letting the day creep up on me. I had my hair pulled into a half-assed ponytail and was wearing my usual stretchy little T-shirt, jeans, and boots. Waving a mascara wand in the vicinity of my eye seemed like a dangerous maneuver this morning, so I was au naturel.

I took a doughnut and looked around. "Where's Lula?"

"She's late. She's been late all week. Not that it matters."

Lula was hired to do filing, but mostly she does what she wants.

"Hey, I heard that," Lula said, swinging through the door. "You better not be talking about me. I'm late on account of I'm going to night school now."

"You go one day a week," Connie said.

"Yeah, but I gotta study. It's not like this shit comes easy. It's not like my former occupation as a ho helps me out, you know. I don't think my final exam's gonna be about hand jobs."

Lula is a couple inches shorter and a lot of pounds heavier than me. She buys her clothes in the petite department and then shoehorns herself into them. This wouldn't work for most people, but it seems right for Lula. Lula shoehorns herself into *life*.

"So what's up?" Lula said. "I miss anything?"

I gave Connie the body receipt for Paulson. "Do you guys know anything about child custody bonds?"

"They're relatively new," Connie said. "Vinnie isn't doing them yet. They're high-risk bonds. Sebring is the only one in the area taking them on."

"Sebring," Lula said. "Isn't he the guy with the good legs? I hear he's got legs like Tina Turner." She looked down at her own legs. "My legs are the right color but I just got more of them."

"Sebring's legs are white," Connie said. "And I hear they're good at running down blondes."

I swallowed the last of my doughnut and wiped my hands on my jeans. "I need to talk to him."

"You'll be safe today," Lula said. "Not only aren't you blonde, but you aren't exactly decked out. You have a hard night?"

"I'm not a morning person."

"It's your love life," Lula said. "You aren't getting any, and you got nothing to put a smile on your face. You're letting yourself go, is what you're doing."

"I could get plenty if I wanted."

"Well, then?"

"It's complicated."

Connie gave me a check for the Paulson capture. "You aren't thinking about going to work for Sebring, are you?"

I told them about Evelyn and Annie.

"Maybe I should talk to Sebring with you," Lula said. "Maybe we can get him to show us his legs."

"Not necessary," I said. "I can manage this myself." And I didn't especially want to see Les Sebring's legs.

"Look here. I didn't even put my bag down," Lula said. "I'm ready to go."

Lula and I stared at each other for a beat. I was going to lose. I could see it coming. Lula had it in her mind to go with me. Probably didn't want to file. "Okay," I said, "but no shooting, no shoving, no asking him to roll up his pants leg."

"You got a lot of rules," Lula said.

We took the CR-V across town and parked in a lot next to Sebring's building. The bonds office was on the ground floor, and Sebring had a suite of offices above it.

"Just like Vinnie," Lula said, eyeballing the carpeted floor and freshly painted walls. "Only it looks like humans work here. And check out these chairs for people to sit in . . . they don't even have stains on them. And his receptionist don't have a mustache, either."

Sebring escorted us into his private office. "Stephanie Plum. I've heard of you," he said.

"It wasn't my fault that the funeral parlor burned down," I told him. "And I almost never shoot people."

"We heard of you, too," Lula said to Sebring. "We heard you got great legs."

Sebring was wearing a silver gray suit, white shirt, and red, white, and blue tie. He reeked of respectability, from the tips of his shined black shoes to the top of his perfectly trimmed white hair. And behind the polite politician smile he looked like he didn't take a lot of shit. There was a moment of silence while he considered Lula. Then he hiked his pants leg up. "Get a load of these wheels," he said.

"You must work out," Lula said. "You got excellent legs."

"I wanted to speak to you about Mabel Markowitz," I said to Sebring. "You called her on a child custody bond."

He nodded. "I remember. I have someone scheduled to visit her again today. So far, she hasn't been helpful."

"She lives next door to my parents, and I don't think she knows where her granddaughter or her great-granddaughter have gone."

"That's too bad," Sebring said. "Do you know about child custody bonds?"

"Not a lot."

"PBUS, which as you know is a professional bail agents association, worked with the Center for Missing and Exploited Children to get legislation going that would discourage parents from kidnapping their own kids.

"It's a pretty simple idea. If it looks like there's a good chance either or both parents will take off with the child for parts unknown, the court can impose a cash bond."

"So this is like a criminal bail bond, but it's a child who's at risk," I said.

"With one big difference," Sebring said. "When a criminal bond is posted by a bail bondsman and the accused fails to appear in court, the bondsman forfeits the bond amount to the *court*. Then the bondsman can hunt down the accused, return him to the system, and hopefully be reimbursed by the court. In the case of a child custody bond, the bondsman forfeits the bond to the wronged *parent*. The money is then supposed to be used to find the missing child."

"So if the bond isn't enough of a deterrent to kidnapping, at least there's money to hire a professional to search for the missing child," I said.

"Exactly. Problem is, unlike a criminal bond, the child custody bondsman doesn't have the legal right to hunt down the child. The only recourse the child custody bondsman has to recoup his loss is to foreclose on property or cash collateral posted at the time the bond is written.

"In this case, Evelyn Soder didn't have the cash on hand for the bond. So she came to us and used her grandmother's house as collateral for a surety bond. The hope is that when you call up the grandmother and tell her to start packing, she'll divulge the location of the missing child."

"Have you already released the money to Steven Soder?"

"The money gets released in three weeks."

So I had three weeks to find Annie.

Chapter
TWO

"That Les Sebring seemed like a nice guy," Lula said when we were back in my CR-V. "I bet he don't even do it with barnyard animals."

Lula was referring to the rumor that my cousin Vinnie had once been involved in a romantic relationship with a duck. The rumor's never been officially confirmed or denied.

"Now what?" Lula asked. "What's next on the list?"

It was a little after ten. Soder's bar and grill, The Foxhole, should be opening for the lunch trade. "Next we visit Steven Soder," I said. "Probably it'll be a waste of time, but it seems like something we should do anyway."

"No stone unturned," Lula said.

Steven Soder's bar wasn't far from Sebring's office. It was tucked between Carmine's Cut-rate Appliances and a tattoo parlor. The door to The Foxhole was open. The interior was dark and uninviting at this hour. Still, two souls had found their way in and were sitting at the polished wood bar.

"I've been here before," Lula said. "It's an okay place. The burgers aren't bad. And if you get here early, before the grease goes rancid, the onion rings are good, too."

We stepped inside and paused while our eyes adjusted. Soder was behind the bar. He looked up when we entered and nodded an acknowledgment. He was just under six foot. Chunky build. Reddish blond hair. Blue eyes. Ruddy complexion. Looked like he drank a lot of his own beer.

We bellied up to the bar, and he found his way over to us. "Stephanie Plum," he said. "Haven't seen you in a while. What'll it be?"

"Mabel is worried about Annie. I told her I'd ask around."

"Worried about losing that wreck of a house is more like it."

"She won't lose the house. She has money to cover the bond." Sometimes I fib just for practice. It's my one really good bounty hunter skill.

"Too bad," Soder said. "I'd like to see her sitting on the curb. That whole family is a car crash."

"So you think Evelyn and Annie just took off?"

"I know they did. She left me a fucking letter. I went over there to pick the kid up and there was a letter for me on the kitchen counter."

"What did the letter say?"

"It said she was taking off and next time I saw the kid would be never."

"Guess she don't like you, hunh?" Lula said.

"She's nuts," Soder said. "A drunk and a nut. She gets up in the morning and can't figure out how to button her sweater. I hope you find the kid fast because Evelyn isn't capable of taking care of her."

"Do you have any idea where she might have gone?"

He made a derisive grunt. "Not a clue. She didn't have any friends, and she was dumb as a box of nails. So far as I can figure she didn't have much money. They're probably living out of the car somewhere in the Pine Barrens, eating from Dumpsters."

Not a pretty thought.

I left my card on the bar. "In case you think of something helpful."

He took the card and winked at me.

"Hey," Lula said. "I don't like that wink. You wink at her again, and I'll rip your eye outta your head."

"What's with the fat chick?" Soder asked me. "The two of you going steady?"

"She's my bodyguard," I told him.

"I'm not no *fat chick*," Lula said. "I'm a big woman. Big enough to kick your nasty white ass around this room."

Soder locked eyes with her. "Something to look forward to."

I dragged Lula out of the bar, and we stood blinking on the sidewalk in the sunlight.

"I didn't like him," Lula said.

"No kidding."

"I didn't like the way he kept calling his little girl *the kid*. And it wasn't nice that he wanted an old lady kicked out of her house."

I called Connie on my cell phone and asked her to get me Soder's home address and car information.

"You think he got Annie in his cellar?" Lula asked.

"No, but it wouldn't hurt to look."

"What's next?"

"Next we visit Soder's divorce lawyer. There had to be some justification for setting the bond. I'd like to know the details."

"You know Soder's divorce lawyer?"

I got in the car and looked over at Lula. "Dickie Orr."

Lula grinned. "Your ex? Every time we visit him he throws you out of the office. You think he's going to talk to you about a client?"

I had had the shortest marriage in the history of the Burg. I'd barely finished unpacking my wedding

presents when I caught the jerk on the dining room
table with my arch-enemy, Joyce Barnhardt. Looking
at it in retrospect I can't imagine why I married Orr in
the first place. I suppose I was in love with the idea of
being in love.

There are certain expectations of girls from the Burg.
You grow up, you get married, you have children, you
spread out some in the beam, and you learn how to set
a buffet for forty. My *dream* was that I would get irradi-
ated like Spiderman and be able to fly like Superman.
My *expectation* had been that I'd marry. I did the best
I could to live up to the expectation, but it didn't work
out. Guess I was stupid. Swayed by Dickie's good looks
and education. My head turned by the fact that he was
a lawyer.

I didn't see the flaws. The low opinion Dickie has of
women. The way he can lie without remorse. I guess
I shouldn't fault him so much for that since I'm pretty
good at lying myself. Still, I don't lie about personal
things . . . like love and fidelity.

"Maybe Dickie's having a good day," I said to Lula.
"Maybe he'll be feeling chatty."

"Yeah, and it might help if you don't leap across the
desk and try to choke him like you did last time."

Dickie's office was on the other side of town. He'd
left a large firm and gone off on his own. From what
I could tell he was having some success. He was now
located in a two-room suite in the Carter Building. I'd
been there, briefly, once before and had sort of lost control.

"I'll be better this time," I said to Lula.

Lula rolled her eyes and got into the CR-V.

I took State Street to Warren and turned onto Som-
merset. I found a parking space directly across from
Dickie's building and took it as a sign.

"Unh-uh," Lula said. "You just got good parking

karma. It don't count for interpersonal relationships. You read your horoscope today?"

I looked over at her. "No. Was it bad?"

"It said your moons weren't in a good spot, and you need to be careful about making money decisions. And not only that, you're going to have man trouble."

"I always have man trouble." I had two men in my life, and I didn't know what to do with either of them. Ranger scared the bejeezus out of me, and Morelli had pretty much decided that unless I changed my ways I was more trouble than I was worth. I hadn't heard from Morelli in *weeks*.

"Yeah, but this is going to be *big* trouble," Lula said.

"You're making that up."

"Am not."

"You *are*."

"Well, okay, maybe I made some of it up, but not the part about the man trouble."

I fed the meter a quarter and crossed the street. Lula and I entered the building and took the elevator to the third floor. Dickie's office was at the end of the hall. The sign beside the door read *Richard Orr, Attorney*. I resisted the urge to write *asshole* below the sign. I was, after all, a woman scorned, and that carried certain responsibilities. Still, best to write *asshole* on the way out.

The reception area of Dickie's office was tastefully done up in industrial chic. Blacks and grays and the occasional purple upholstered chair. If the Jetsons had hired Tim Burton to decorate, it would have turned out like this. Dickie's secretary was seated behind a large mahogany desk. Caroline Sawyer. I recognized her from my last visit. She looked up when Lula and I entered. Her eyes widened in alarm, and she reached for the phone.

"If you come any closer I'm calling the police," she said.

"I want to talk to Dickie."

"He isn't here."

"I bet she's fibbing," Lula said. "I got a knack for knowing when people are fibbing." Lula shook her finger at Sawyer. "The Lord don't like when people fib."

"Honest to God, he isn't here."

"Now you're blaspheming," Lula said. "You're in big trouble now."

The door to Dickie's inner office opened, and Dickie stuck his head out. "Oh shit," he said, spotting Lula and me. He pulled his head back and slammed his door shut.

"I need to talk to you," I yelled.

"No. Go away. Caroline, call the police."

Lula leaned on Caroline's desk. "You call the police and I'll break one of your fingernails. You'll need a new manicure."

Caroline looked down at her nails. "I just got them done yesterday."

"They did a good job," Lula said. "Where'd you go?"

"Kim's Nails on Second Street."

"They're the best. I go there, too," Lula said. "I got mine detailed this time. See, I got little-bitty stars painted on them."

Caroline looked over at Lula's nails. "Awesome," she said.

I scooted around Sawyer and knocked on Dickie's door. "Open up. I promise I won't try to choke you. I need to talk to you about Annie Soder. She's missing."

The door opened a crack. "What do you mean . . . missing?"

"Evelyn apparently took off with her, and Les Sebring is enforcing the child custody bond."

The door opened all the way. "I was afraid this would happen."

"I'm trying to help find Annie. I was hoping you could give me some background information."

"I don't know how helpful I can be. I was Soder's attorney. Evelyn was represented by Albert Kloughn. There was so much acrimony during the divorce process, and so many threats were made on both sides, that the judge imposed the bonds."

"Soder had to post a bond, too?"

"Yes, although Soder's was relatively meaningless. Soder owns a local business and isn't likely to flee. Evelyn, on the other hand, had nothing holding her here."

"What do you think of Soder?"

"He was a decent client. Paid his bill on time. Got a little hot under the collar in court. There's no love lost between him and Evelyn."

"Do you think he's a good father?"

Dickie did a palms-up. "Don't know."

"What about Evelyn?"

"She never looked like she was totally with the program. A real space cadet. Probably in the kid's best interest to get found. Evelyn might misplace her and not realize it for days."

"Anything else?" I asked him.

"No, but it doesn't seem right that you haven't gone for my throat," Dickie said.

"Disappointed?"

"Yeah," he said. "I bought pepper spray."

It would have been funny if it had been casual banter, but I suspected Dickie was serious. "Maybe next time."

"You know where to find me."

Lula and I sashayed out of the office, down the hall, and into the elevator.

"That wasn't as much fun as last time," Lula said. "You didn't even threaten him. You didn't chase him around the desk, or anything."

"I don't think I hate him as much as I used to."

"Bummer."

We crossed the street and stared at my car. It had a parking ticket on the window.

"See this," Lula said. "It's your moons. You made a bad money decision when you picked this busted meter."

I stuffed the ticket into my bag and wrenched the door open.

"You better watch out," Lula said. "The man trouble's gonna come next."

I called Connie and asked for an address for Albert Kloughn. In minutes I had Kloughn's business address and Soder's home address. Both were in Hamilton Township.

We drove past Soder's home first. He lived in a complex of garden apartments. The buildings were two-story brick, decked out to be colonial style with white window shutters and white columns at the front doors. Soder's apartment was on the ground floor.

"Guess he hasn't got the little girl in his cellar," Lula said. "Since he hasn't got a cellar."

We sat and watched the apartment for a few minutes, but nothing happened, so we moved on to Kloughn.

Albert Kloughn had a two-room office, next to a Laundromat, in a strip mall. There was a desk for a secretary but no secretary was in residence. Instead, Kloughn was at the desk, typing at the computer. He was my height and looked like he was approaching puberty. He had sandy-colored hair, a face like a cherub, and the body of the Pillsbury Doughboy.

He looked up and smiled tentatively when we entered. Probably thought we were scrounging quarters to do our laundry. I could feel my feet vibrating from the drums tumbling next door, and there was a distant rumble from the large commercial washers.

"Albert Kloughn?" I asked.

He was wearing a white shirt, red-and-green striped tie, and khakis. He stood and self-consciously smoothed out his tie. "I'm Albert Kloughn," he said.

"Well, this is a big disappointment," Lula said. "Where's the red nose that goes *beep beep*? And where're your big clown feet?"

"I'm not that kind of clown. Yeesh. Everybody says that. Ever since kindergarten I've been hearing that. It's spelled 'K-l-o-u-g-h-n.' Kloughn!"

"Could be worse," Lula said. "You could be Albert Fuch."

I gave Kloughn my card. "I'm Stephanie Plum and this is my associate, Lula. I understand you represented Evelyn Soder in her divorce case."

"Wow," he said, "are you really a bounty hunter?"

"Bond enforcement," I told him.

"Yeah, that's a bounty hunter, right?"

"About Evelyn Soder . . ."

"Sure. What do you want to know? Is she in trouble?"

"Evelyn and Annie are missing. And it looks like Evelyn took Annie away so she wouldn't have to visit her father. She left a couple notes."

"She must have had a good reason to leave," Kloughn said. "She really didn't want to jeopardize her grandmother's house. She just didn't have any choice. She had no place to turn for the bond money."

"Any ideas where Evelyn and Annie might have gone?"

Kloughn shook his head. "No. Evelyn didn't talk much. From what I could tell, her entire family lived in the Burg. I don't want to be mean or anything, but she didn't impress me as being real bright. I'm not even sure she could drive. She always had someone bring her to the office."

"Where's your secretary?" Lula asked him.

"I don't have a secretary right now. I used to have someone who came in part-time, but she said the lint blowing around from the dryers bothered her sinuses. Probably I should put an ad in the paper, but I'm not real organized. I only opened this office a couple months ago. Evelyn was one of my first clients. That's why I remember her."

Probably Evelyn was his *only* client.

"Did she pay her bill?"

"She's paying it off monthly."

"If she mails in a check, I'd appreciate it if you'd let me know where it was postmarked."

"I was just gonna suggest that," Lula said. "I thought of that, too."

"Yeah, me, too," Kloughn said. "I was thinking the same thing."

A woman rapped on Kloughn's open door and stuck her head in. "The dryer at the far end don't work. It took all my quarters, and now it's just doing nothing. And on top of that, I can't get the door open."

"Hey," Lula said, "do we look like we care? This man's an attorney-at-law. He don't give a rat's ass about your quarters."

"This happens all the time," Kloughn said. He pulled a form from his top desk drawer. "Here," he said to the woman. "Fill this out and the management will refund your money."

"They gonna comp your rent for that?" Lula asked Kloughn.

"No. They'll probably evict me." He looked around the room. "This is my third office in six months. I had an accidental wastebasket fire in my first office that sort of spread throughout the building. And the office after that got condemned when there was a toilet incident above it and the roof caved in."

"Public restroom?" Lula asked.

"Yes. But I swear it wasn't me. I'm almost positive."

Lula looked at her watch. "It's my lunchtime."

"Hey, how about if I go to lunch with you guys," Kloughn said. "I have some ideas on this case. We could talk about it over lunch."

Lula cut her eyes to him. "Haven't got anybody to eat lunch with, hunh?"

"Sure, I've got lots of people to eat lunch with. Everybody wants to eat lunch with me. I didn't make any plans for today, though."

"You're an accident waiting to happen," Lula said. "We eat lunch with you we'll probably get food poisoning."

"If you were really sick I could get you some money," he said. "And if you died it would be *big* money."

"We're only getting fast food," I said.

His eyes lit up. "I *love* fast food. It's always the same. You can count on it. No surprises."

"And it's cheap," Lula said.

"Exactly!"

He put a small *out to lunch* sign in his office window and locked the door behind himself. He climbed into the backseat of the CR-V and leaned forward.

"What are you, part golden retriever?" Lula asked. "You're breathing on me. Sit back in your seat. Put your seat belt on. And if you start drooling, you're outta here."

"Boy, this is fun," he said. "What are we going to eat? Fried chicken? Fish sandwich? Cheeseburger?"

Ten minutes later, we pulled out of the McDonald's drive-thru, loaded with burgers and shakes and fries.

"Okay, here's what I think," Kloughn said. "I think Evelyn isn't far away. She's nice but she's a mouse, right? I mean, where's she gonna go? How do we know she's not at her grandma's?"

"Her grandmother is the one who hired me! She's going to lose her house."

"Oh yeah. I forgot."

Lula looked at him in the rearview mirror. "What'd you do, go to one of them offshore law schools?"

"Very funny." He did another tie-smoothing thing. "It was a correspondence course."

"Is that legal?"

"Sure, you take tests and everything."

I pulled into the Laundromat parking lot and stopped. "Here we are, back from lunch," I said.

"Already? But it's too short. I didn't even finish my fries," he said. "And after that I have a pie to eat."

"Sorry. We have work to do."

"Yeah? What kind of work? Are you going out after someone dangerous? I bet I could help."

"Don't you have lawyer things to do?"

"It's my lunch hour."

"You wouldn't want to tag along," I said. "We're not doing anything interesting. I was going back to Evelyn's house and maybe talk to some of her neighbors."

"I'm good at talking to people," he said. "That was one of my best courses . . . talking to people."

"Don't seem right to kick him out before he eats his pie," Lula said. She looked over the seatback at him. "You gonna eat that whole thing?"

"Alright, he can stay," I said. "But no talking to people. He has to stay in the car."

"Like I'm the wheel guy, right?" he said. "In case you have to make a fast getaway."

"*No.* There will be no fast getaways. And you're not the wheel guy. You don't drive. *I* drive."

"Sure. I know that," he said.

I rolled out of the lot, found Hamilton Avenue, and took it to the Burg, left-turning at St. Francis Hospital. I wound my way through the maze of streets and came to an idle in front of Evelyn's house. The neighborhood was quiet at midday. No kids on bikes. No porch sitters. No traffic to speak of.

I wanted to talk to Evelyn's neighbors, but I didn't want to do it with Lula and Kloughn tagging along. Lula scared the hell out of people. And Kloughn made us look like religious missionaries. I parked the car at the curb, Lula and I got out, and I pocketed the key. "Let's just take a look around," I said to Lula.

She cut her eyes to Kloughn, sitting in the backseat. "You think we should crack a window for him? Isn't there a law about that sort of thing?"

"I think the law applies to dogs."

"Seems like he fits in there, somehow," Lula said. "Actually, he's kind of cute, in a white bread kind of way."

I didn't want to go back to the car and open the door. I was afraid Kloughn would bound out. "He'll be okay," I said. "We won't be that long."

We walked to the porch, and I rang the bell. No answer. Still couldn't see in the front window.

Lula put her ear to the door. "I don't hear anything going on in there," she said.

We walked around the house and looked in the kitchen window. The same two cereal bowls and glasses were on the counter next to the sink.

"We need to look around inside," Lula said. "I bet the house is lousy with clues."

"No one has a key."

Lula tried the window. "Locked." She gave the door the once-over. "Of course, we're bounty hunters and if we think there's some bad guy in there we have the right to bust the door apart."

I've been known to bend the law a little from time to time, but this was a multiple fracture. "I don't want to ruin Evelyn's door," I said.

I saw Lula eye the window.

"And I don't want to break her window. We're not act-ing as bond enforcement here, and we have no ground for forced entry."

"Yeah, but if the window broke by accident it would be neighborly of us to investigate it. Like, maybe we could fix it from the inside." Lula swung her big black leather shoulder bag in an arc and smashed the window. "Oops," she said.

I closed my eyes and rested my forehead against the door. I took a deep breath and told myself to stay calm. Sure, I'd like to yell at Lula and maybe choke her, but what would that accomplish? "You're going to pay to have that window fixed," I told her.

"The hell I am. This here's a rental. They got insur-ance on stuff like this." She knocked out a few remain-ing pieces of glass, stuck her arm through the open window, and unlocked the door.

I pulled some disposable rubber gloves out of my bag and we snapped them on. No point leaving prints all over since this was sort of an illegal entry. With the kind of luck I had, someone would come in and burgle the place and the police would find my prints.

Lula and I slipped into the kitchen and closed the door behind us. It was a small kitchen, and with Lula next to me we were wall-to-wall people.

"Maybe you should do lookout in the front room," I said. "Make sure no one walks in on us."

"Lookout is my middle name," Lula said. "No one will get by me."

I started with the countertop, going through the usual kitchen clutter. There were no messages written on the pad by the phone. I rifled through a pile of junk mail. Aside from some nice towels on sale in the Martha Stewart line, there wasn't anything of interest. A drawing of a house done in red and green crayon was taped to the refrigerator. Annie's, I thought. The dishes were neatly stacked in over-the-counter cupboards. Glasses were spotless and lined by threes on the shelves. The refrigerator was filled with condiments but empty of food that might spoil. No milk or orange juice. No fresh vegetables or fruit.

I drew some conclusions from the kitchen. Evelyn's cupboard was better stocked than mine. She left quickly but still took the time to get rid of the milk. If she was a drunk or on drugs or loony tunes, she was a *responsible* drunk or druggie or loony.

I didn't find anything of help in the kitchen, so I moved on to the dining room and living room. I opened drawers and checked under cushions.

"You know where I'd go if I had to hide out?" Lula said. "I'd go to Disney World. Have you ever been to Disney World? I'd especially go there if I had a problem, because everybody's happy at Disney World."

"I've been to Disney World seven times," Kloughn said.

Lula and I both jumped at his voice.

"Hey," Lula said, "you're supposed to be in the car."

"I got tired of waiting."

I gave Lula the evil eye.

"I was watching," Lula said. "I don't know how he got past me." She turned to Kloughn. "How'd you get in here?"

"The back door was open. And the window was broken. You didn't break the window, did you? You could get into big trouble for something like that. That's breaking and entering."

"We found the window like that," Lula said. "That's how come we're wearing gloves. We don't want to screw up the evidence if anything's been stolen."

"Good thinking," Kloughn said, his eyes getting bright, his voice up an octave. "Do you really think stuff has been stolen? You think anybody got roughed up?"

Lula looked at him like she'd never seen anybody that dumb before.

"I'm checking upstairs," I said. "You two stay down here and don't touch anything."

"What are you looking for upstairs?" Kloughn wanted to know, following me up the stairs. "I bet you're looking for clues that'll lead you to Evelyn and Annie. You know where I'd look? I'd look—"

I whirled around, almost knocking him off his feet. "*Down*," I said, pointing stiff-armed, shouting at him nose to nose. "Go sit on the couch and don't get up until I tell you."

"Yeesh," he said. "You don't have to yell at me. Just tell me, okay? Boy, it must be one of those days for you, hunh?"

I narrowed my eyes. "One of *what* days?"

"You know."

"It is *not* one of those days," I said.

"Yeah, she's like this on a good day," Lula said. "You don't want to know what she's like on one of *those* days."

I left Lula and Kloughn downstairs, and I poked through the bedrooms on my own.

There were still clothes hanging in the closets and folded in dresser drawers. Evelyn must have only taken essentials. Either her disappearance was temporary or else she was in a rush to leave. Maybe both.

As far as I could tell there was no sign of Steven. Evelyn had sanitized the house of him. There were no leftover men's toiletries in the bathroom, no forgotten men's belts lurking in the closet, no family photo in a silver frame. I'd done a similar house cleaning when I'd divorced Dickie. Still, for months after our breakup

I'd get bushwhacked by an overlooked item . . . a man's sock that had dropped behind the washing machine, a set of car keys that had gotten kicked under the couch and been given up for lost.

The medicine chest contained the usual . . . a bottle of Tylenol, a bottle of kids' cough syrup, dental floss, nail scissors, mouthwash, box of Band-Aids, talcum powder. No uppers or downers. No hallucinogens. No happy pills. Also, conspicuously missing was anything alcoholic. No wine or gin stashed in kitchen cupboards. No beer in the fridge. Could be Carol was mistaken about the booze and pills. Or could be Evelyn took it all with her.

Kloughn popped his head around the bathroom door-jamb. "You don't mind if I look, too, do you?"

"Yes! I mind. I told you to stay on the couch. And what's Lula doing? She was supposed to keep her eye on you."

"Lula's doing watch out. That doesn't take two people, so I decided to help you search. Did you already look in Annie's room? I just looked in there, and I didn't find any clues, but her drawings were real scary. Did you look at her drawings? I'm telling you, that's a messed-up kid. It's television. All that violence."

"The only picture I saw was of a red-and-green house."

"Did the red look like blood?"

"No. It looked like windows."

"Uh-oh," Lula said from the front room.

Damn. I hate *uh-oh*. "What?" I yelled down at her.

"There's a car pulled up behind your CR-V."

I peeked out Evelyn's bedroom window. It was a black Lincoln Towncar. Two guys got out and started walking toward Evelyn's front door. I grabbed Kloughn's hand and pulled him down the stairs after me. Don't panic, I thought. The door's locked. And they can't see in. I made a sign for everyone to be quiet, and we all stood still as statues, barely breathing, while one of the men rapped on the door.

"Nobody home," he said.

I carefully exhaled. They'd leave now, right? Wrong. There was the sound of a key being inserted in the lock. The lock clicked, and the door swung open.

Lula and Kloughn lined up behind me. The two men stood their ground on the front porch.

"Yes?" I asked, trying to look like I belonged to the house.

The men were late forties, early fifties. Medium height. Built solid. Dressed in business suits. Both Caucasian. Didn't look especially happy to see the Three Stooges in Evelyn's house.

"We're looking for Evelyn," one of the men said.

"Not here," I told him. "And you would be?"

"Eddie Abruzzi. And this is my associate, Melvin Darrow."

Chapter
THREE

Oh boy. Eddie Abruzzi. Talk about a day going into the toilet.

"It's been brought to my attention that Evelyn moved out," Abruzzi said. "You wouldn't happen to know where she is, would you?"

"No," I said. "But as you can see, she hasn't moved out."

Abruzzi looked around. "Her furniture's here. That doesn't mean she hasn't moved out."

"Well, technically . . ." Kloughn said.

Abruzzi squinted at Kloughn. "Who are you?"

"I'm Albert Kloughn. I'm Evelyn's lawyer."

This got a smile out of Abruzzi. "Evelyn hired a clown for a lawyer. Perfect."

"K-l-o-u-g-h-n," Albert Kloughn said.

"And I'm Stephanie Plum," I said.

"I know who you are," Abruzzi said. His voice was eerily quiet, and his pupils were shrunk to the size of pinpricks. "You killed Benito Ramirez."

Benito Ramirez was a heavyweight boxer who tried to kill me on several occasions and finally was shot on my fire escape, poised to break through my window. He was criminally insane and flat-out evil, taking pleasure and finding strength through other people's pain.

"I owned Ramirez," Abruzzi said. "I had a lot of time and money invested in him. And I understood him. We enjoyed many of the same pursuits."

"I didn't kill him," I said. "You know that, don't you?"

"You didn't pull the trigger . . . but you killed him all the same." He turned his attention to Lula. "I know who you are, too. You're one of Benito's whores. How did it feel to spend time with Benito? Did you enjoy it? Did you feel privileged? Did you learn anything?"

"I don't feel so good," Lula said. And she fainted dead away, crashing into Kloughn, taking him down with her.

Lula had been brutalized by Ramirez. He'd tortured her and left her for dead. But Lula hadn't died. Turns out, it's not so easy to kill Lula.

Unlike Kloughn, who looked like he might be ready to cash in his chips any minute. Kloughn was squashed under Lula with only his feet showing, doing a good imitation of the Wicked Witch of the East when Dorothy's house fell on her. He made a sound that was half squeak, half death rattle. "Help," he whispered. "I can't breathe."

Darrow grabbed one of Lula's legs and I grabbed an arm, and we rolled Lula off Kloughn.

Kloughn lay there for a moment, eyes glazed, breath shallow. "Does anything look broken?" he asked. "Did I mess myself?"

"What are you doing here?" Abruzzi asked. "And how did you get in?"

"We came to visit Evelyn," I said. "The back door was open."

"You and your fat whore friend always wear rubber gloves?"

Lula opened an eye. "Who you calling fat?" She opened the other eye. "What happened? What am I doing on the floor?"

"You fainted," I told her.

"That's a lie," she said, getting to her feet. "I don't faint. I never fainted once in my life." She looked over at Kloughn, who was still on his back. "What's with him?"

"You landed on him."

"Squashed me like a bug," Kloughn said, struggling to stand. "I'm lucky I'm alive."

Abruzzi considered us all for a moment. "This is my property," he said. "Don't break in again. I don't care if you're friends of the family or lawyers, or murdering bitches. Got that?"

I pressed my lips tight together and said nothing. Lula shifted her weight foot to foot. "Hunh," she said.

And Kloughn vigorously nodded his head. "Yes-sir," he said, "we understand. No problemo. We only came in this time on account of—"

Lula gave him a kick in the back of his calf.

"*Yow!*" Kloughn said, bending at the waist, grabbing his leg.

"Get out of this house," Abruzzi said to me. "And don't return."

"I've been employed by Evelyn's family to look after her interests. That includes stopping by here from time to time."

"You're not listening," Abruzzi said. "I'm telling you to stay out. Stay out of this house and stay out of Evelyn's affairs."

Bells and whistles were going off in my head. Why did Abruzzi care about Evelyn and her house? He was her landlord. My understanding of his business was that this wasn't even an important piece of real estate to him.

"And if I don't?"

"I'll make your life very unpleasant. I know how to make women uncomfortable. Benito and I had that in

common. We knew how to make women pay attention. Tell me," Abruzzi said, "what were Benito's last
moments like? Was he in pain? Was he afraid? Did he
know he was going to die?"

"I don't know," I said. "He was on the other side
of the glass. I don't know what he was feeling." Aside
from insane rage.

Abruzzi stared at me for a moment. "Fate is a funny
thing, isn't it? Here you are back in my life. And you're,
once again, on the wrong side. It will be interesting to
see how this campaign unfolds."

"Campaign?"

"I'm a student of military history. And, this is to some
extent a war." He made a small hand gesture. "Maybe
not a war. More of a skirmish, I think. Whatever we
call it, it's a contest, of sorts. Because I'm feeling gener-
ous today, I'll give you an option. You can walk away
from Evelyn and this house, and I'll let you go. You'll
have bought amnesty. If you continue to participate, I'll
consider you to be enemy troops. And the war game
will begin."

Oh boy. This guy is a total fruitcake. I held my
hand up in a stop gesture. "I'm not playing war games.
I'm just a friend of the family, checking on things for
Evelyn. We're going now. And I think you should do
the same." And I think you should take a pill. A *big*
pill.

I ushered Lula and Kloughn past Abruzzi and Darrow and through the door. I hustled them into the car,
and we took off.

"Holy crap," Lula said. "What was that? I'm totally
creeped out. Eddie Abruzzi has eyes like Ramirez. And
Ramirez had no soul. I thought I put all that behind me,
but I looked into those eyes just now and everything
went black. It was like being with Ramirez all over

again. I'm telling you, I'm freaked. I got the sweats. I'm hyperventilating is what I'm doing. I need a burger. No, wait a minute, I just had a burger. I need something else. I need . . . I need . . . I need to go shopping. I need shoes."

Kloughn's eyes brightened. "So Ramirez and Abruzzi are bad guys, right? And Ramirez is dead, right? What was he, a professional killer?"

"He was a professional boxer."

"Holy cow. *That* Ramirez. I remember reading about him in the paper. Holy cow, you're the one who killed Benito Ramirez."

"I didn't kill him," I said. "He was on my fire escape, trying to break in, and someone else shot him."

"Yeah, she almost never shoots anyone," Lula said. "And I don't care anyway. I'm getting out of here. I need mall air. I could breathe better if I had mall air."

I took Kloughn back to the Laundromat and dropped Lula at the office. Lula roared off in her red Trans Am, and I went in to visit with Connie.

"You know that guy you picked up yesterday," Connie said to me, "Martin Paulson? He's back on the street. There was something wrong with his original arrest, and the case has been dismissed."

"He should be locked up just for living."

"Apparently, when he was released his first words as a freed man were some unflattering references to you."

"Great." I slouched onto the couch. "Did you know Eddie Abruzzi owned Benito Ramirez? We ran into him at Evelyn's house. And speaking of Evelyn's house, she has a broken window that we need to repair. It's in the back."

"It was a kid with a baseball, right?" Connie said. "And after you saw him break the window, he ran away, and you don't know who he is. Wait, even better, you *never* saw him. You got there and the window was broken."

"On the nose. So, what do you know about Abruzzi?"

Connie punched the name into her computer. In less than a minute, information started coming in. Home address, previous address, work history, wives, children, arrest history. She printed it out and handed it over to me. "We can find out his toothpaste brand and the size of his right nut, but it'll take a little longer."

"Tempting, but I don't think I need to know his nut size just yet."

"I bet they're big."

I clapped my hands over my ears. "I'm not listening!" I looked sideways at Connie. "What else do you know about him?"

"I don't know much. Just that he owns a bunch of real estate in the Burg and downtown. I've heard he's not a nice guy, but I don't know any details. A while back he was arrested on a minor racketeering charge. The charge was dropped due to lack of *live* witnesses. Why do you want to know about Abruzzi?" Connie asked.

"Morbid curiosity."

"I got two skips in today. Laura Minello got picked up for shoplifting a couple weeks ago and was a no-show for her court appearance yesterday."

"What did she shoplift?"

"A brand-new BMW. Red. Took it right off the lot in broad daylight."

"Test drive?"

"Yeah, only she didn't tell anyone she was taking it, and she tested it for four days before they caught her."

"You've got to respect a woman with that kind of initiative."

Connie passed me two files. "The second failure to appear is Andy Bender. He's a repeat for domestic violence. I think you might have picked him up on a previous charge. He's probably home, drunk as a skunk, without a clue if it's Monday or Friday."

I flipped through Bender's file. Connie was right. I'd tangled with him before. He was a scrawny wasteoid of a man. And he was a nasty drunk.

"This is the guy who came after me with a chain saw," I said.

"Yes, but look on the bright side," Connie said. "He didn't have a gun."

I tucked the two files into my bag. "Maybe you could run Evelyn Soder through the computer and see if you could pull out her innermost secrets."

"Innermost secrets is a forty-eight-hour search."

"Put it on my tab. I have to take off. I need to talk to the Wizard."

"The Wizard hasn't been answering his page," Connie said. "Tell him to call me."

The Wizard is Ranger. He's the Wizard because he's magic. He mysteriously passes through locked doors. He seems to read minds. He's able to refuse dessert. And he can give me a hot flash with the touch of a fingertip. I had mixed feelings about calling him. We were currently in a strange place, filled with double entendre and unresolved sexual tension. But we were also partners, of sorts, and he had contacts I'd never have. The Annie search would go much faster if I brought Ranger in.

I got into my car and dialed Ranger on my cell phone. I left a message on his machine and read through Bender's file. Didn't sound like much new had happened since I last saw Andy Bender. He was still unemployed. He was still beating on his wife. And he still lived in the projects on the other side of town. It wasn't going to be hard to find Bender. The hard part was going to be wrestling him into the CR-V.

Hey, I thought, no sense being negative right from the start. Look on the bright side, right? Be a cup-is-half-full person. Maybe Mr. Bender will be sorry he missed his court date. Maybe he'll be happy to see me. Maybe he won't have any gas in his chain saw.

I put the car in gear and headed across town. It was a pleasant afternoon, and the projects looked habitable. There was a hopefulness to the dirt front yards that suggested perhaps this year some grass might grow. Perhaps the junkers at the curb would stop leaking oil. Perhaps a Lotto ticket would pay out big. But then again, perhaps not.

I parked in front of Bender's unit and watched for a while. For lack of a better word, this part of the complex would be described as garden apartments. Bender lived on the ground floor. He had a battered wife and, thankfully, no kids.

An open-air bazaar, of sorts, was operating a short distance away. The bazaar consisted of two cars, an old Caddy and a new Oldsmobile. The owners had parked the cars at the curb and were selling handbags, T-shirts, DVDs, and God knows what else from their trunks. A few people milled around the cars.

I rooted around in my bag and found a purse-size cylinder of pepper spray. I shook it to make sure it was active and stuffed it into my pants pocket for easy access. I took a pair of cuffs out of the glove compartment and slipped them into the back of my jeans, under the waistband. Okay, now I was all dressed up like a bounty hunter. I walked to Bender's door, took a deep breath, and knocked.

The door opened and Bender looked out at me. "What?"

"Andy Bender?"

He leaned forward and squinted. "Do I know you?"

Get right to it, I thought, reaching behind my back for the cuffs. Move fast and catch him by surprise. "Stephanie Plum," I said, whipping the cuffs out, clapping one on his left wrist. "Bond enforcement. We need to go to the station and reschedule your court date." I put my hand to his shoulder and spun him around, so I could cuff his right wrist.

"Hey, hold on here," he said, jerking away. "What the hell is this? I'm not going nowhere."

He took a swing at me, lost his balance, and listed sideways, knocking into an end table. A lamp and an ashtray crashed to the floor. Bender looked at them, dumbfounded. "You broke my lamp," he said. His face got red and his eyes narrowed. "I don't like that you broke my lamp."

"I didn't break your lamp!"

"I said you broke it. You hard of hearing?" He picked the lamp up from the floor and threw it at me. I sidestepped, and the lamp sailed past me and hit the wall.

I rammed my hand into my pocket, but Bender tackled me before I could grab hold of the spray. He was a couple inches taller than me, thin and wiry. He wasn't especially strong, but he was mean as a snake. And he was motivated by hate and beer. We scrabbled around on the floor for a while, kicking and scratching. He was trying to do damage, and I was trying to get clear, and neither of us was having much luck.

The room was a mess of clutter with stacks of newspapers, dirty dishes, and empty beer cans. We were bumping into tables and chairs, dumping the dishes and cans on the floor, then rolling over it all. A floor lamp went down, followed by a pizza box.

I managed to slither from his grasp and get to my feet. He lunged after me and came up with a ten-inch chef's knife. I suppose it had been buried in the garbage heap in his living room. I yelped and bolted. No time for the pepper spray.

He was surprisingly fast, considering he was shit-faced drunk. I ran flat-out, up the street. And he ran close at my heels. I skidded to a stop when I got to the boosted goods market, putting the Cadillac between me and Bender while I caught my breath.

One of the vendors approached me. "I got some nice T-shirts," he said. "Exactly like what you'd see at the Gap. Got them in all sizes."

"Not interested," I said.

"Selling them for a good price."

Bender and I were doing a dance around the car. He'd move, then I'd move, then he'd move, then I'd move. Meanwhile, I was trying to get the pepper spray out of my pocket. Trouble was, my pants were tight, the spray was shoved to the bottom of my pocket, and my hands were sweating and shaking.

There was a guy sitting on the Oldsmobile's hood. "Andy," he called, "why're you going after this girl with a knife?"

"She ruined my lunch. I was just sitting down to eat my pizza, and she came and ruined it all."

"I can see that," the guy on the Oldsmobile said. "She got pizza all over her. Looks like she rolled in it."

There was a second guy sitting on the Olds. "Kinky," he said.

"How about one of you guys giving me a hand here," I said. "Get him to drop the knife. Call the police. Do something!"

"Hey, Andy," one of the men said, "she wants you to drop the knife."

"I'm gonna gut her like a fish," Bender said. "I'm gonna filet her like a trout. No bitch just walks in and ruins *my* lunch."

The two guys on the Olds were smiling. "Andy needs some anger management courses," one of them said.

The T-shirt salesman was next to me. "Yeah, and he don't know much about fishing, either. That ain't no filet knife."

I finally pried the pepper spray loose from my pocket. I shook it and aimed it at Bender.

The three men mobilized into action, slamming the trunks shut, putting some distance between us.

"Hey, you want to watch which way the wind is blowing," one of them said. "I don't need my sinuses cleaned. And I don't want my merchandise ruined, either. I'm a businessman, you see what I'm saying? We got inventory here."

"That stuff doesn't scare me," Bender said, inching his way around the Caddy, waving the knife at me. "I love it. Bring it on. I've had so much pepper spray I got an addiction."

"What you got on your wrist?" one of the men asked Bender. "Looks like you got a bracelet on. You and the old lady doing S and M shit now?"

"Those are my cuffs," I said. "He's in violation of his bail bond agreement."

"Hey, I know you," one of the men said. "I remember seeing your picture in the paper. You burned down a funeral home and set your eyebrows on fire."

"It wasn't my fault!"

They were all smiling again. "Didn't Andy go after you with a chain saw last year? And all you got now is this puny girlie-size pepper spray? Where's your gun? You're probably the only one in the whole project not got a gun."

"Gimme the keys," Bender said to the T-shirt guy. "I'm getting out of here. This is turning into a real downer."

"I'm not done selling."

"Sell some other time."

"Shit," the guy said, and flipped him the keys.

Bender got into the Cadillac and roared away.

"What was that?" I asked. "Why did you give him the keys?"

The T-shirt guy shrugged. "It's his car."

"He doesn't have a car listed on his bond agreement," I said.

"Guess ol' Andy don't tell everything. Anyways, it's a recent acquisition."

Recent acquisition. Probably stole it last night along with the T-shirts.

"You sure you don't want a T-shirt? We got more in the Oldsmobile," the guy said. He opened the trunk and took a couple shirts out. "Look at this. This here's the V-neck model. Even got some spandex in it. You'd look fine in this shirt. Show off your boobies."

"How much?" I asked.

"How much you got?"

I shoved my hand back into my pocket and pulled out two dollars.

"This here's your lucky day," the guy said, "on account of this shirt is on sale for two bucks."

I gave him the two dollars, took the shirt, and trudged back to my CR-V.

There was a sleek black car parked just in front of mine. A man leaned against the car, watching me, smiling. Ranger. His black hair was pulled back from his face, tied into a ponytail. He was dressed in black cargo pants, black Bates boots, and a black T-shirt that stretched taut over muscles he'd acquired when he was in Special Forces.

"Looks like you've been shopping," he said.

I tossed the shirt into the CR-V. "I need some help."

"Again?"

A while ago I'd asked Ranger to help me capture a guy named Eddie DeChooch. DeChooch had been accused of trafficking contraband cigarettes and had been causing all kinds of problems for me. Ranger, being of mercenary mentality, had quoted his price for assistance as a night of his choosing, spent together. The *whole* night. And he got to pick the night's *activities*. Not exactly a hardship, since I'm attracted to Ranger in a moth-to-the-flame sort of way. Still, the idea was scary. I mean, he's the Wizard, right? I practically have an orgasm standing next to him. What would happen with actual penetration? My God, my entire vagina might go up in flames. Not to mention, I can't figure out if I'm still attached to Morelli.

As it turns out, I'd needed Ranger for the takedown. And it had been an okay takedown except for a couple small hitches . . . like DeChooch getting his ear shot off. Ranger had hauled DeChooch off to the lockdown prison ward of St. Francis Hospital, and I had retreated to my apartment and crawled into bed, not wanting to think too hard about the day's events.

What happened after that is still vivid in my mind. At one o'clock the lock tumbled on my front door, and I heard the security chain swing free. I knew a lot of people who could pick a lock. I only knew one man who could release a security chain from the outside.

Ranger stepped into the doorway to my bedroom and knocked softly on the jamb. "Are you awake?"

"I am now. You scared the hell out of me. You ever think about ringing a doorbell?"

"Didn't want to get you out of bed."

"So what's going on?" I asked. "Is DeChooch okay?"

Ranger removed his gun belt and dropped it on the

floor. "DeChooch is fine, but *we* have unfinished business."

Unfinished business? Omigod, was he talking about his price for the takedown? The room whirled in front of my eyes, and I involuntarily clutched the sheet to my breast.

"This is sort of sudden," I said. "I mean, I didn't think it would be tonight. I didn't even know if it would be *any* night. I wasn't sure you were serious. Not that I'd go back on a deal, but, um, what I'm trying to say is . . ."

Ranger raised an eyebrow. "I make you nervous?"

"Yes." Damn.

He sat in the rocker in the corner. He slouched slightly, elbows on the arms of the chair, fingers steepled against each other.

"Well?" I asked.

"You can relax. I'm not here to collect on the deal."

I blinked. "You're not? Then why did you drop your gun belt?"

"I'm tired. I wanted to sit and the belt is uncomfortable."

"Oh."

He smiled. "Disappointed?"

"No." Liar, liar, pants on fire.

The smile widened.

"So what's the unfinished business?"

"The hospital is holding DeChooch overnight. He'll be transferred out first thing tomorrow morning. Someone should be present during the transfer to make sure the paperwork is handled correctly."

"And that would be me?"

Ranger looked at me over his steepled fingers. "That would be you."

"You could have called with this information."

He picked the gun belt off the floor and stood. "I

could have, but it wouldn't have been as interesting."
He kissed me lightly on the lips and walked to the
doorway.

"Hey," I said, ". . . about the deal. You were kidding,
right?"

It was the second time I'd asked, and I got the same
answer. A smile.

And now, here we were weeks later. Ranger still
hadn't collected his fee, and I was in the undesirable position of negotiating more assistance. "Do you know
about child custody bonds?" I asked him.

He inclined his head a fraction of an inch. This was
the equivalent to intense nodding for Ranger. "Yes."

"I'm looking for a mother and a little girl."

"How old is the little girl?"

"Seven."

"From the Burg?"

"Yes."

"It's difficult to hide a seven-year-old," Ranger said.
"They peek out windows and stand in open doorways.
If the child is in the Burg, word will get around. The
Burg isn't good at keeping a secret."

"I haven't heard anything. I have no leads. I have
Connie running a computer check, but I won't get that
back for a day or two."

"Give me whatever information you have, and I'll ask
around."

I looked past Ranger and saw the Cadillac in the
distance, cruising toward us. Bender was still behind
the wheel. He slowed when he reached us, gave me
the finger, and rolled away around the corner, out of
sight.

"A friend of yours?" Ranger asked.

I opened the driver's side door to the CR-V. "I'm supposed to be capturing him."

"And?"

"Tomorrow."

"I could help you with that, too. We could run a tab for you."

I sent him a grimace. "Do you know Eddie Abruzzi?"

Ranger removed a slice of pepperoni from my hair and picked some crushed potato chip crumbs off my T-shirt. "Abruzzi's not a nice guy. You want to stay away from Abruzzi."

I was trying to ignore Ranger's hands on my chest. On the surface it seemed like innocent grooming. In the pit of my stomach it felt like sex. "Stop fondling me," I said.

"Maybe you should get used to it, considering what you owe me."

"I'm trying to have a conversation here! The missing mother is renting a house owned by Abruzzi. I sort of ran into him this morning."

"Let me guess—you rolled on his lunch?"

I looked down at my shirt. "No. Lunch belongs to the guy who gave me the finger."

"Where did you meet up with Abruzzi?"

"At the rental house. This is the weird thing . . . Abruzzi didn't want me in the house, and he didn't want me involved with Evelyn. I mean, what's it to him? This isn't even a significant property for him. And then he got really freaky about this being a military campaign and a war game."

"Abruzzi makes his money primarily through loan sharking," Ranger said. "Then he invests it in legitimate ventures like real estate. His hobby is war gaming. Do you know what that is?"

"No."

"A war gamer studies military strategy. When it first started it was a bunch of guys in a room, pushing toy soldiers around on a map on the table. Like the board game Risk, or Axis and Allies. Imaginary battles are constructed and fought. A lot of war gamers play by computer now. It's Dungeons and Dragons for adults. I'm told Abruzzi takes it seriously."

"He's crazy."

"That's the general consensus. Anything else?" Ranger asked.

"Nope. That's about it."

Ranger angled into his car and drove away.

So much for the part of my day where I actually tried to earn some money. I still had Laura Minello, grand theft auto, but I was feeling discouraged and I didn't have any handcuffs. Probably I needed to get back to the kid search, anyway. If I went back to the house now chances were good that Abruzzi wouldn't be there. He probably left in a huff after threatening me and went home to shove some toy soldiers around.

I drove back to Key Street and parked in front of Carol Nadich's half of the house. I rang her bell and scraped some pizza cheese off my breast while I waited.

"Hey," Carol said, opening the door. "Now what?"

"Did Annie play with any kids in the neighborhood? Did she seem to have a best friend?"

"Most of the kids on this street are older, and Annie stayed inside a lot. Is that pizza in your hair?"

I put my hand to my head and felt around. "Any pepperoni?"

"No. Just cheese and tomato sauce."

"Well," I said, "as long as there aren't any pepperonis."

"Hold on," Carol said. "I remember Evelyn telling me that Annie had a new friend at school. Evelyn was worried about it because the little girl thought she was a horse."

Mental head slap. My niece, Mary Alice.

"Sorry, I don't know the horse kid's name," Carol said.

I left Carol and drove two blocks to my parents' house. It was midafternoon. School would be out, and Mary Alice and Angie would be in the kitchen, eating cookies, getting grilled by my mother. One of my early lessons was that everything has a price. If you want an after-school cookie, you have to tell my mother about your day.

When we were kids, Valerie always had lots to report. She made glee club. She won the spelling contest. She was chosen for the Christmas pageant. Susan Marrone told her Jimmy Wizneski thought she was pretty.

I had lots to report, too. I didn't make glee club. I didn't win the spelling contest. I wasn't chosen for the Christmas pageant. And I accidentally knocked Billy Bartolucci down the stairs, and he ripped the knee out of his pants.

Grandma met me at the door. "Just in time to have a cookie and tell us about your day," she said. "I bet it was a pip. You've got food all over you. Were you after a killer?"

"I was after a guy wanted for domestic violence."

"I hope you kicked him where it hurt."

"I didn't actually get to kick him, but I ruined his pizza." I sat down at the table with Angie and Mary Alice. "How's it going?" I asked.

"I made the glee club," Angie said.

I stifled the urge to scream and took a cookie. "How about you?" I asked Mary Alice.

Mary Alice took a drink of milk and wiped her mouth with the back of her hand. "I'm not a reindeer anymore on account of I lost my antlers."

"They fell off on the way home from school, and a dog went to the bathroom on them," Angie said.

"I didn't want to be a reindeer anyway," Mary Alice said. "Reindeers don't got nice tails like horses."

"Do you know Annie Soder?"

"Sure," Mary Alice said, "she's in my class. She's my best friend, except she's never in school lately."

"I went to see her today, but she wasn't home. Do you know where she is?"

"Nope," Mary Alice said. "I guess she's gone. That happens when you get divorced."

"If Annie could go anywhere she wanted . . . where would she go?"

"Disney World."

"Where else?"

"Her grandma's."

"Where else?"

Mary Alice shrugged.

"How about her mom? Where would her mom want to go?"

Another shrug.

"Help me out here," I said. "I'm trying to find Annie."

"Annie is a horse, too," Mary Alice said. "Annie is a brown horse, only thing, she can't gallop as fast as me."

Grandma moved to the front door, driven there by Burg radar. A good Burg housewife never missed anything happening on the street. A good Burg housewife could pick up street sounds not ordinarily heard by the human ear.

"Look at this," Grandma said, "Mabel's got company. Somebody I never saw before."

My mother and I joined Grandma at the door.

"Fancy car," my mother said.

It was a black Jaguar. Brand new. Not a splatter of mud or a speck of dust on it. A woman emerged from behind the wheel. She was dressed in black leather pants, high-heeled black leather boots, and a short form-fitting black leather jacket. I knew who she was. I'd run into her once before. She was the female equivalent of Ranger. My understanding was that, like Ranger, she did a variety of things including but not limited to body-guarding, bounty hunting, and private investigating. Her name was Jeanne Ellen Burrows.

Chapter
FOUR

"Mabel's visitor looks like Catwoman," Grandma said. "Except she hasn't got pointy cat ears and whiskers."

And the cat suit was by Donna Karan.

"I know her," I said. "Her name is Jeanne Ellen Burrows, and she's probably connected to the child custody bond, somehow. I need to talk to her."

"Me, too," Grandma said.

"*No.* Not a good idea. Stay here. I'll be right back."

Jeanne Ellen saw me approach and paused on the sidewalk. I extended my hand to her. "Stephanie Plum," I said.

She had a firm handshake. "I remember."

"I assume you've been hired by someone connected to the bond."

"Steven Soder."

"I've been hired by Mabel."

"I hope we won't have an adversarial relationship."

"That would be my hope, too," I said.

"Would you like to share any information with me?"

I took a beat to think about it and decided I didn't have any information to share. "No."

Her mouth curved into a small, polite smile. "Well, then."

Mabel opened her door and peered out at us.

"This is Jeanne Ellen Burrows," I told Mabel. "She's working for Steven Soder. She'd like to ask you some questions. I'd prefer you didn't answer them." I was getting strange vibes on Evelyn and Annie's disappearance, and I didn't want Annie given up to Steven until I heard Evelyn's reason for leaving.

"It would be in your best interest to talk to me," Jeanne Ellen said to Mabel. "Your great-granddaughter could be in danger. I could help find her. I'm very good at finding people."

"Stephanie's good at finding people, too," Mabel said.

Again, the small smile returned to Jeanne Ellen's mouth. "I'm better," she said.

It was true. Jeanne Ellen was better at finding people. I relied more on dumb luck and blind persistence.

"I don't know," Mabel said. "I don't feel comfortable going against Stephanie. You look like a perfectly nice young woman, but I'd rather not talk to you about this."

Jeanne Ellen gave Mabel her card. "If you change you mind, you can reach me at one of these numbers."

Mabel and I watched Jeanne Ellen get into her car and drive off.

"She reminds me of someone," Mabel said. "I can't put my finger on it."

"Catwoman," I said.

"*Yes!* That's it, except for the ears."

I left Mabel, filled my mother and grandmother in on Jeanne Ellen, took a cookie for the road, and headed for home, making a fast stop at the office first.

Lula pulled in behind me. "Wait until you see the boots I got. I got myself a pair of biker boots." She tossed her bag and her jacket on the couch and opened the shoe box. "Look at this. Are these hot, or what?"

They were black with a high stacked heel with an eagle stitched onto the side. Connie and I agreed. The boots were hot.

"So what have you been up to?" Lula asked me. "I miss anything interesting?"

"I ran into Jeanne Ellen Burrows," I said.

Connie and Lula did a double mouth drop. Jeanne Ellen wasn't seen a lot. She mostly worked at night and was as elusive as smoke.

"Tell me," Lula said. "I gotta know everything."

"Steven Soder hired her to find Evelyn and Annie."

Connie and Lula exchanged glances. "Does Ranger know about this?" Connie asked.

There were a lot of rumors about Ranger and Jeanne Ellen. One rumor had them secretly living together. One rumor had them as mentor and mentee. Clearly there'd been some sort of relationship at some point. And I was pretty sure it no longer existed, although it was hard to know anything for sure with Ranger.

"This is going to be good," Lula said. "You and Ranger and Jeanne Ellen Burrows. If I was you, I'd go home and do my hair and put some mascara on. And I'd stop at the Harley store and get a pair of these cool boots. You need a pair of these boots just in case you need to walk over Jeanne Ellen."

My cousin Vinnie stuck his head out of his office. "Are you talking about Jeanne Ellen Burrows?"

"Stephanie ran into her today," Connie said. "They're working a case together, from opposite sides."

Vinnie grinned at me. "You're going up against Jeanne Ellen? Are you nuts? This isn't one of *my* FTAs, is it?"

"Child custody bond," I said. "Mabel's great-granddaughter."

"The Mabel next door to your parents? The old-as-dirt Mabel?"

"That's the one. Evelyn and Steven got a divorce and Evelyn took off with Annie."

"So Jeanne Ellen is working for Soder. That makes

sense. Sebring probably wrote the bond, right? Jeanne
Ellen works for Sebring. Sebring can't go after Evelyn,
but he can recommend that Soder hires Jeanne Ellen.
Just the sort of case Jeanne Ellen would take, too. A
missing kid. Jeanne Ellen loves to have a cause."

"How do you know so much about Jeanne Ellen?"

"Everybody knows about Jeanne Ellen," Vinnie
said. "She's a legend. Cripes, you're gonna get your ass
kicked."

This Jeanne Ellen thing was starting to annoy me.

"Gotta go," I said. "Things to do. I just stopped in to
borrow a pair of cuffs."

Everyone's eyebrows rose a couple inches.

"You need another pair of cuffs?" Vinnie asked.

I gave him my PMS look. "You got a problem with
that?"

"Hell no," Vinnie said. "I'm gonna go with S and
M. I'm gonna pretend you got a man chained up naked somewhere. It's more comforting than thinking
one of my FTAs is running around with your bracelet
attached."

I parked in the back of the lot, next to the Dumpster, and
walked the short distance to my apartment building's
rear entrance. Mr. Spiga had just docked his twenty-
year-old Oldsmobile in one of the coveted handicapped
slots, close to the door, his handicapped sign proudly
affixed to his windshield. He was in his seventies, retired from his job at the button factory and, with the exception of his addiction to Metamucil, was in perfect
health. Lucky for him, his wife is legally blind and
lame from a hip replacement gone bad. Not that it cuts
a lot of slack in this lot. Half the people in the building have poked out an eye and run over their foot to get
handicapped status. In Jersey, parking is often more
important than sight.

"Nice day," I said to Mr. Spiga.

He grabbed a grocery bag from the backseat. "Have you bought ground chuck lately? Who decides these prices? How can people afford to eat? And why is the meat so red? You ever notice it's only red on the outside? They spray it with something, so you think it's fresh. The food industry's going to hell."

I opened the door for him.

"Another thing," he said, "half the men in this country have breasts. I'm telling you, it's from those hormones they feed the cows. You drink the milk from the cows and you grow breasts."

Ah, I thought, if only it was that easy.

The elevator doors opened and Mrs. Bestler peeked out. "Going up," she said.

Mrs. Bestler was about two hundred years old and liked to play elevator operator.

"Second floor," I told her.

"Second floor, ladies handbags and better dresses," she sang out, punching the button.

"Cripes," Mr. Spiga said. "This place is filled with loonies."

First thing I did when I entered my apartment was check my messages. I work with a mysterious bounty hunter guy who turns me to jelly and makes sexual innuendoes and never follows through. And I'm in the off-again phase of an off-again-on-again relationship with a cop guy I think I might want to marry . . . someday, but not now. That's my love life. In other words, my love life is a big zero. I can't remember the last time I had a date. An orgasm is nothing more than a distant memory. And there were no messages on my machine.

I flopped onto my couch and closed my eyes. My life was in the toilet. I did about a half hour of self-pity and was about to get up and take a shower when my doorbell rang. I went to the door and looked out my security peephole. Nobody there. I turned to walk away and heard rustling on the other side of the door. I looked out again. Still no one there.

I called my neighbor across the hall and asked him to look out his door and tell me if anyone was there. Okay, so this is a little despicable on my part, but no one ever wants to kill Mr. Wolesky and from time to time people want to kill me. Doesn't hurt to be careful, right?

"What are you crazy?" Mr. Wolesky said. "I'm watching *The Brady Bunch*. You called right in the middle of *The Brady Bunch*."

And he hung up.

I was still hearing the rustling sounds, so I got my gun out of the cookie jar, found a bullet in the bottom of my purse, put the bullet in the gun, and opened the door. There was a dark green canvas bag hanging from my doorknob. The bag had a drawstring pulled tight at the top and something was moving in the bag. My first thought was an abandoned kitten. I removed the bag from the doorknob, opened the drawstring, and looked inside.

Snakes. The bag was filled with big black snakes.

I shrieked and dropped the bag on the floor, and the snakes slid out. I jumped back into my apartment and slammed my door shut. I looked out my peephole. The snakes were scattering. Shit. I opened the door and shot a snake. Now I was out of bullets. Shit again.

Mr. Wolesky opened his door and looked out. "What the . . . ?" he said, and slammed his door shut.

I ran into my kitchen to look for more bullets, and a snake followed me in. Another shriek and I climbed onto my kitchen counter.

I was still on the counter when the police arrived. Carl Costanza and his partner, Big Dog. I'd gone to school with Carl, and we were friends, in a strange, distant sort of way.

"We got a weird call from your neighbor about snakes," Carl said. "Since there's one shot to shit on your doorstep, and you're up there on the counter, I suppose the call isn't a hoax."

"I ran out of bullets," I said.

"So by a rough estimate, how many snakes do you think we got here?"

"I'm pretty sure there were four in the bag. I shot one. I saw one go down the hall. I saw one head for my bedroom. And one is God knows where."

Carl and Big Dog grinned up at me. "Is the big, bad bounty hunter afraid of snakes?"

"Just *find* them, okay?" *Yeesh.*

Carl adjusted his gun belt and swaggered off with Big Dog a step behind him.

"Here, snakey, snakey, snakey," Carl crooned.

"I think we should look in her panties drawer," Big Dog said. "That's where I'd go if I was a snake."

"Pervert!" I yelled.

"I don't see any snakes here," Carl said.

"They go under things, and they hide in corners," I told him. "Did you check under the couch? Did you look in my closet? Under my bed?"

"I'm not looking under your bed," Carl said. "I'm afraid I'll find some knuckle dragger hiding there."

This got a laugh out of Big Dog. I didn't think it was funny since it was one of my constant fears.

"Listen, Steph," Carl called from the bedroom, "we really have searched everywhere, but we're not seeing any snakes. Are you sure there's one in here?"

"Yes!"

"How about her closet?" Big Dog said. "Did you look in the closet?"

"The door's closed. A snake couldn't get in there."

I heard one of them pull the closet door open, and then they both started shouting.

"Jesus *Christ*."

"Holy *shit!*"

"Shoot it. *Shoot it!*" Carl yelled. "Kill the mother-fucker!"

There was a lot of gunshot and more shouting.

"We didn't get it. It's coming out," Carl said. "God-damn, there are two of them."

I heard the door to my bedroom slam shut.

"Stay here and watch the door," Carl told Big Dog. "Make sure they don't come out."

Carl stormed into my kitchen and started going through my cupboards. He found a half-empty bottle of gin and drank two fingers from the bottle.

"Jesus," he said, capping the bottle, returning it to the cupboard shelf.

"I thought you weren't supposed to drink on duty."

"Yeah, except when you find snakes in closets. I'm calling Animal Control."

I was still on the counter when two Animal Control guys arrived. Carl and Big Dog were in my living room, guns drawn, eyes trained on my bedroom door.

"They're in the bedroom," Carl told the Animal Control officers. "Two of them."

Joe Morelli showed up a couple minutes later. Morelli wears his hair short but always needs a cut. Today was no exception. His dark hair curled over his ears and his collar and fell onto his forehead. His eyes were melted-chocolate brown. He wore jeans and running shoes and a gray-green thermal Henley. Under the shirt his body was hard and perfect. Fortunately, at this particular moment, under the jeans he was *just perfect*. Although I'd seen that part of him hard, and it was pretty damn fantastic. His gun and his badge were also under the Henley.

Morelli grinned when he saw me on the counter. "What's going on?"

"Someone left a bag of snakes on my doorknob."

"And you let them loose?"

"They took me by surprise."

He looked back at the one I'd shot, still untouched on the hall floor. "Is that the one *you* shot?"

"I ran out of bullets."

"How many bullets did you start with?"

"One."

The grin widened.

The Animal Control officers came out of the bedroom with the two snakes in a bag. "Racers," they said. "Harmless." One of them toed the dead snake in the hall. "You want us to take this one, too?"

"Yes!" I said. "And there's another snake somewhere."

Someone screamed at the far end of the hall.

"Guess we know where to look for snake number four," Joe said.

The Animal Control guys took off with the snakes, and Carl and Big Dog shuffled out of my living room, into my foyer.

"Guess we're done here," Carl said. "You might want to check out your closet. I think Big Dog killed a pair of shoes."

Joe closed the door behind them. "You can get off the counter now."

"It was scary."

"Cupcake, your *life* is scary."

"What's that supposed to mean?"

"Your job sucks."

"It's no suckier than yours."

"I don't have people leaving snakes on my doorknob."

"Animal Control said they were harmless."

He threw his hands into the air. "You're impossible."

"What are you doing here, anyway? I haven't heard from you in weeks."

"I heard the call go out on the radio and had a misguided urge to make sure you were okay. You haven't heard from me because we broke up, remember?"

"Yes, but there's all kinds of broken up."

"Oh yeah? What kind is this? First you decide you don't want to marry me . . ."

"That was a mutual agreement."

"Then you go off with Ranger . . ."

"That was work-related."

He had his hands planted on his hips. "Let's get back to the snakes, okay? You have any idea who left them?"

"I guess I could make a list."

"Jesus," he said, "you've got a list. Not one or two people. A whole list. You have a whole list of people who might want to leave snakes on your doorknob."

"The last couple days have been sort of busy."

"Is that pizza in your hair?"

"I accidentally rolled on Andy Bender's lunch. He would be on the list. A guy named Martin Paulson isn't too happy with me. There's my ex-husband. Then I had an unfortunate encounter with Eddie Abruzzi."

That caught Morelli's attention. "Eddie Abruzzi?" I told him about Evelyn and Annie and the Abruzzi connection.

"I don't suppose you'd listen to me if I told you to stay away from Abruzzi," Morelli said.

"I'm *trying* to stay away from Abruzzi."

Morelli grabbed me by the front of my shirt, pulled me to him, and kissed me. His tongue touched mine, and I felt liquid fire slide through my stomach and head south. He released me and turned to go.

"Hey!" I said. "What was that?"

"Temporary insanity. You drive me nuts."

And he stalked off down the hall and disappeared into the elevator.

I took a shower and dressed in clean jeans and T-shirt. I did the makeup thing this time and put some gel in my hair. Sort of like locking the barn after the horses have escaped.

I went into the kitchen and stared into the refrigerator for a while, but nothing materialized. No cake. No hot sausage sandwich. No macaroni and cheese magically appeared. I took a bag of chocolate chip cookies out of the freezer and ate one. You were supposed to bake them first, but that seemed like unnecessary effort.

I'd talked to Annie's best friend and that hadn't given me a lot. Okay, so what would I do if I needed to protect my daughter from her father? Where would I go?

I wouldn't have a lot of money, so I'd need to rely on a friend or relative. I'd need to go far enough that my car wouldn't be recognized, and I wouldn't run the risk of bumping into Soder or one of his friends. This narrowed the search down to the entire world, except for the Burg.

I was contemplating the world when my doorbell rang. I wasn't expecting anyone, and I'd just received a bag of snakes, so I wasn't all that crazy about answering the door. I looked out my peephole and grimaced. It was Albert Kloughn. But wait a minute, he was holding a pizza box. *Hello.*

I opened the door and gave a quick look up and down the hall. I was pretty sure there'd been four snakes in the bag . . . still, doesn't hurt to keep your eyes open for renegade reptiles.

"Hope I'm not disturbing anything," Kloughn said, stretching his neck out to look around me into my apartment. "You aren't entertaining or anything, are you? I didn't know if you were living with anyone."

"What's up?"

"I've been thinking about the Soder case, and I have some ideas. I thought we could, like, brainstorm."

I looked down at the box he was holding.

"I brought a pizza," he said. "I didn't know if you'd eaten yet. Do you like pizza? If you don't like pizza I could get something else. I could get Mexican or Chinese or Thai . . ."

Please, Lord, tell me this isn't a date. "I'm sort of engaged."

He vigorously nodded his head. Up and down, up and down, like one of those dogs people put in their back car windows. "Absolutely. I knew you would be. Understood. I'm almost engaged, too. I have a girlfriend."

"Really?"

He took a deep breath. "No. I just made that up."

I took the pizza box from him and dragged him into my apartment. I got some napkins and a couple beers, and we sat at my small dining room table and ate pizza.

"What are these ideas you have about Evelyn Soder?"

"I figure she's with a friend, right? So she had to get in touch with the friend somehow. She had to tell her she was coming to stay. I figure she did this on the phone. So what we need is a phone bill."

"And?"

"That's it."

"Good thing you brought a pizza."

"Actually, it's a tomato pie. In the Burg they call it a tomato pie."

"Sometimes. You know anyone at the phone company? Anyone in the billing department?"

"I figured *you'd* have the contacts. See, that's why we're such a good team. I have the ideas. And you have the contacts. Bounty hunters have contacts, right?"

"Right." Unfortunately, not in the phone company.

We finished the pizza, and I brought out the bag of frozen cookies for dessert.

"I heard you get cancer from eating raw cookie dough," Kloughn said. "Don't you think you should bake this?"

I ate a bag of raw dough a week. I considered it to be one of the four major food groups. "I always eat raw cookie dough," I said.

"Me, too," Kloughn said. "I eat raw cookie dough all the time. I don't believe that stuff about the cancer." He looked into the bag and tentatively took out a frozen lump of dough. "So what do you do here? Do you, like, nibble on it? Or do you put it all in your mouth at once?"

"You've never had raw cookie dough, have you?"

"No." He took a bite and chewed. "I like it," he said. "Very good."

I glanced down at my watch. "You're going to have to go now. I have some unfinished business to take care of."

"Is it bounty hunter business? You can tell me. I won't tell anybody, I swear. What are you doing? I bet you're going after someone. You were waiting for nighttime, right?"

"Right."

"So who are you going after? Is it anyone I know? Is it, like, a high-profile case? A killer?"

"It's no one you know. It's domestic abuse. A repeat offender. I'm waiting until he passes out in a drunken stupor, and then I'm going to capture him when he's unconscious."

"I could help you—"

"No!"

"You didn't let me finish. I could help you drag him to the car. How are you going to get him to the car? You're going to need help, right?"

"Lula will help me."

"Lula has class tonight. Remember she said she had to go to school tonight. Do you have anyone else who helps you? I bet you don't have anyone else, right?"

I was getting an eye twitch. Tiny, annoying muscle contractions below my right lower lid. "Okay," I said, "you can come with me, but you can't talk. *No talking*."

"Sure. No talking. My lips are sealed. Look at me, I'm locking my lips and throwing the key away."

I parked half a block from Andy Bender's apartment, positioning my car between pools of light thrown by overhead halogens. Traffic was minimal. Vendors had closed up shop for the day, switching to nighttime pursuits of hijacking and shoplifting. Residents were locked behind closed doors, beer can in hand, watching reality television. A nice break from their own reality, which wasn't all that terrific.

Kloughn gave me a look that said *now what?*

"Now we wait," I told him. "We make sure nothing unusual is going on."

Kloughn nodded and made the zippered mouth sign again. If he made the zippered mouth sign one more time I was going to smack him in the head.

After a half hour of sitting and waiting I was convinced that I didn't want to sit and wait anymore. "Let's take a closer look," I said to Kloughn. "Follow me."

"Shouldn't I have a gun or something? What if there's a shoot-out? Do you have a gun? Where's your gun?"

"I left my gun home. We don't need guns. Andy Bender has never been known to carry a gun." Best not to mention he prefers chain saws and kitchen knives.

I approached Bender's unit as if I owned it. Bounty hunter rule number seventeen—don't look sneaky. Lights were on inside. The windows were curtained, but the curtains were a skimpy fit, and it was possible to look around the fabric. I put my nose to the window and stared in at the Benders. Andy was in a big, overstuffed recliner, feet up, open bag of chips on his chest, dead to the world. His wife sat on the tattered couch, eyes glued to the television.

"I'm pretty sure we're doing something illegal," Kloughn whispered.

"There's all kinds of illegal. This is one of those things that's only a little illegal."

"I guess it's okay if you're a bounty hunter. There are special rules for bounty hunters, right?"

Right. And there really *is* an Easter bunny.

I wanted to get into the apartment, but I didn't want to wake Bender. I walked around the building and carefully tried Bender's back door. Locked. I returned to the front and found that door locked, too. I gave a couple light raps on the door with my knuckles, hoping to get the wife's attention without waking Bender.

Kloughn was looking in the window. He shook his head. No one was getting up to answer the door. I rapped louder. Nothing. Bender's wife was concentrating on the television show. Damn. I rang the bell.

Kloughn jumped away from the window and rushed to my side. "She's coming!"

The door opened, and Bender's wife stood flat-footed in front of us. She was a large woman with pale skin, and a dagger tattooed on her arm. Her eyes were red-rimmed and dull. Her face expressionless. She wasn't as wasted as her husband, but she was well on the way. She took a step back when I introduced myself.

"Andy don't like to be disturbed," she said. "He gets in a real bad mood when he's disturbed."

"Maybe you should go to a friend's house, so you're not here if Andy gets disturbed." Last thing I wanted was for Andy to beat on his wife because she let us *disturb* him.

She looked at her husband, still asleep in his chair. Then she looked at us. And then she took off, out the door, disappearing into the darkness.

Kloughn and I tiptoed up to Bender and took a closer look.

"Maybe he's dead," Kloughn said.

"I don't think so."

"He smells dead."

"He always smells like that." I was prepared this time. I had my stun gun with me. I leaned forward, pressed my stun gun to Bender, and hit the juice button. Nothing happened. I examined the stun gun. It looked okay. I put it to Bender again. Nothing. Goddamn electronic piece of shit. Okay, go to backup plan. I grabbed the cuffs I had tucked into my back pocket and quietly clicked a bracelet on Bender's right wrist.

Bender's eyes flew open. "What the hell?"

I pulled his cuffed hand across his body and secured the second bracelet onto his left wrist.

"Goddamn," he yelled. "I hate being disturbed when I'm watching television! What the fuck are you doing in my house?"

"The same thing I was doing in your house yesterday. Bond enforcement," I said. "You're in violation of your bond. You need to reschedule."

He glared at Kloughn. "What's with the dough boy?"

Kloughn handed Bender his business card. "Albert Kloughn, attorney at law."

"I hate clowns. They creep me out."

Kloughn pointed to his name on the card. "K-l-o-u-g-h-n," he said. "If you ever need a lawyer, I'm real good."

"Oh yeah?" Bender said. "Well, I hate lawyers even more than clowns." He jumped forward and knocked Kloughn on his ass with a head butt to Kloughn's face. "And I hate *you,*" he said, lunging at me, head down.

I sidestepped and tried the stun gun on him again. No effect. I ran after him and made another stab. He never broke stride. He was across the room, through the open front door. I threw the stun gun at him. It bounced off his head, he yelled *ouch,* and he was gone, into the darkness.

I was torn between following after him and helping Kloughn. Kloughn was on his back, blood trickling from his nose, mouth open, eyes glazed. Hard to tell if he was just stunned or in a genuine coma.

"Are you okay?" I yelled at Kloughn.

Kloughn didn't say anything. His arms were in motion, but he wasn't making any progress at getting up. I went to his side and dropped to one knee.

"Are you okay?" I asked again.

His eyes focused, and he reached for me, grabbing a handful of shirt. "Did I hit him?"

"Yeah. You hit him with your face."

"I knew it. I knew I'd be good under pressure. I'm pretty tough, right?"

"Right." God help me, I was starting to like him.

I dragged him up and got him some paper towels from the kitchen. Bender was long gone, along with my cuffs. Again.

I retrieved the useless stun gun, packed Kloughn into the CR-V, and took off. It was a cloudy, moonless night. The projects were dark. Lights burned behind drawn shades but did nothing to illuminate lawns. I drove along the streets surrounding the projects, searching the shadows for movement, staring into the occasional uncurtained window.

Kloughn had his head tipped back with the towels stuffed up his nose. "Does this happen a lot?" he asked. "I thought it would be different. I mean, this was pretty fun, but he got away. And he didn't smell good. I didn't expect him to smell that bad."

I looked over at Kloughn. He seemed different. Crooked, somehow. "Has your nose always curved to the left?" I asked him.

He gingerly touched his nose. "It feels funny. You don't think it's broken, do you? I've never had anything broken before."

It was just about the most broken nose I'd ever seen. "It doesn't look broken to me," I said. "Still, it wouldn't hurt to have a doctor look at it. Maybe we should make a quick stop-off at the emergency room."

Chapter
FIVE

I opened my eyes and looked at the clock: 8:30. Not exactly an early start to the day. I could hear rain spattering on my fire escape and on my windowpane. My feeling on rain is that it should only occur at night when people are sleeping. At night, rain is cozy. During the day, rain is a pain in the gumpy. Another screwup on the part of creation. Like waste management. When you're planning a universe you have to think ahead.

I rolled out of bed and sleepwalked to the kitchen. Rex was done running for the night, sound asleep in his soup can. I got coffee going and shuffled to the bathroom. An hour later I was in my car, ready to start the day, not sure what to do first. Probably I should pay a condolence visit on Kloughn. I'd gotten his nose broken. By the time I'd dropped him at his car, his eyes were black and his nose was being held straight by a Band-Aid. Problem is, if I go see him now, I run the risk of having him latch onto me for the day. And I really didn't want Kloughn tagging along. I was fairly inept when left to my own devices. With Kloughn tagging along, I was a disaster waiting to happen.

I was sitting in my lot, staring out the rain-smeared window, and I realized there was a plastic sandwich bag attached to my windshield wiper. I opened the door and snatched the bag off the wiper. There was a note-size piece of white paper folded four times inside the bag. The message on the paper was written in black marker.

Did you like the snakes?

Wonderful. Just the way I wanted to start my day. I returned the note to the bag and put the bag in the glove compartment. On the seat beside me were the two FTA folders Connie had given me. Andrew Bender, still at large. And Laura Minello. I'd go out and capture one of them this morning, but I didn't have any handcuffs. And I'd rather poke myself in the eye with a fork than get another pair of cuffs from the office. That left Annie Soder.

I put the CR-V in gear and drove to the Burg. I parked in front of my parents' house, but I knocked on Mabel's door.

"Who did Evelyn hang out with when she was a kid?" I asked Mabel. "Did she have a best friend?"

"Dotty Palowski. They went all through grade school together. High school, too. Then Evelyn got married and Dotty moved away."

"Did they stay friends?"

"I think they lost touch. Evelyn kept more and more to herself after she married."

"Do you know where Dotty is now?"

"I don't know where Dotty's living but her folks are still here in the Burg."

I knew the family. Dotty's parents lived on Roebling. There were some aunts and uncles and cousins in the Burg, too. "I need one more thing," I said to Mabel. "I need a list of Evelyn's relatives. All of them."

I had the list in my hand when I left. It wasn't a long list. An aunt and an uncle in the Burg. Three cousins, all in the Trenton area. A cousin in Delaware.

I jumped the railing that divided the porches and went next door to see Grandma Mazur.

"I went to the Shleckner viewing," Grandma said. "I'm telling you, that Stiva is a genius. When it comes to morticians, you can't beat Stiva. You know how old Shleckner had all those big scabby things on his face? Well, Stiva covered them all somehow. And you couldn't even tell Shleckner had a glass eye. They both look just the same. It was a miracle."

"How do you know about the glass eye? Didn't they have his eyes closed?"

"Yeah, but they might have come open for a second while I was standing there. It might have happened when I accidentally dropped my reading glasses into the casket."

"Hmmm," I said to Grandma.

"Well, you can't blame a person for wondering about those things. Wasn't my fault, either. If they'd left his eyes open I wouldn't have had to wonder."

"Did anyone see you prying Shleckner's eyes open?"

"No. I was real sneaky."

"Did you hear anything useful about Evelyn or Annie?"

"No, but I got an earful about Steven Soder. He likes to drink. And he likes to gamble. The rumor is that he's lost a lot of money, and that he lost the bar. The story goes that he lost the bar in a card game a while back, and now he's got *partners*."

"I've heard some of those same rumors. Anyone give names to the partners?"

"Eddie Abruzzi is what I heard."

Oh boy. Why am I not surprised at this?

I was in my car, ready to roll, when my cell phone rang. It was Kloughn.

"Boy, you should see me," he said. "I've got two black

eyes. And my nose is swollen. At least it's straight now.
I was real careful how I slept on it."

"I'm sorry. Really, really sorry."

"Hey, no biggie. I guess you have to expect stuff like
this when you're a crime fighter. So what are we doing
today? Are we going after Bender again? I have some
ideas. Maybe I could meet you for lunch."

"See, here's the thing . . . I usually work alone."

"Sure, but once in a while you work with a partner,
right? And I could be that partner sometimes, right? I
got myself all prepared. I got a black hat with BOND
ENFORCEMENT printed on it this morning. And I got
pepper spray and handcuffs . . ."

Handcuffs? Be still, my fast-beating heart. "Are these
regulation handcuffs with a key and everything?"

"Yeah. I got them at that gun store on Rider Street. I
would have gotten a gun, too, but I didn't have enough
money."

"I'll pick you up at twelve."

"Oh boy, this is going to be great. I'll be all ready.
I'll be at my office. Maybe we can get fried chicken this
time. Unless you don't want fried chicken. If you don't
want fried chicken, we could get a burrito, or we could
get a burger, or we could—"

I made crackling sounds into the phone. "Can't hear
you," I yelled. "You're breaking up. See you at twelve."
And I disconnected.

I cruised out of the Burg and turned onto Hamilton.
In a few minutes I was at the office. I parked at the
curb behind a new black Porsche, which I suspected belonged to Ranger.

Everyone looked over when I swung through the
door. Ranger was at Connie's desk. He was dressed in
SWAT black, again. He caught my eye, and I felt my
stomach do a nervous roll.

"I had a friend working the emergency room last

night, and she told me you came in with a little guy who was all busted up," Lula said.

"Kloughn. And he wasn't *all* busted up. He just had a broken nose. Don't ask."

Vinnie was lounging in the doorway to his inner office. "Who's this clown?" Vinnie asked.

"Albert Kloughn," Ranger said. "He's an attorney."

I stopped short of asking how Ranger knew Kloughn. The answer was obvious. Ranger knew everything.

"Let me guess," Vinnie said to me. "You need another pair of cuffs."

"Wrong. I need an address. I need to talk to Dotty Palowski."

Connie fed the name to the search system. A minute later the information started coming in. "She's Dotty Rheinhold now. And she's living in South River." Connie printed the page and handed it over to me. "She's divorced with two kids, and she works for the Turnpike Authority in East Brunswick."

Ordinarily I'd stay to chat, but I was afraid someone would ask about Kloughn's nose.

"Gotta run," I said. "Things to do."

I paused just outside the office door. I was sheltered by a small overhead awning. Beyond the awning, the rain fell in a relentless drizzle that didn't measure up to downpour status but was enough to ruin my hair and soak into my jeans.

Ranger followed me out. "It might be good to keep more than one bullet in your gun, babe."

"You heard about the snakes?"

"I ran into Costanza. He was looking at life through the bottom of a beer glass."

"I'm not having much luck finding Annie Soder."

"You're not the only one."

"Jeanne Ellen can't find her, either?"

"Not yet."

Our eyes held for a moment. "Which team are you on?" I asked.

He tucked my hair behind my ear, his fingertips brushing feather light across my temple, his thumb at the line of my jaw. "I have my own team."

"Tell me about Jeanne Ellen."

Ranger smiled. "The information would have a price."

"And the price would be what?"

The smile widened. "Try not to get too wet today," he said. And he was gone.

Damn. What's with the men in my life? Why do they always leave first? Why don't *I* ever walk away and leave first? Because I'm a dope, that's why. I'm a big dope.

I picked Kloughn up at the Laundromat. He was dressed in a black T-shirt and black jeans, wearing his new bond enforcement hat. And he had brown tassel loafers on his feet. The pepper spray was clipped to his belt. The cuffs had been shoved into his back pocket. His eyes and nose were an alarming shade of black, blue, and green.

"Wow," I said. "You look awful."

"It's the tassels, right? I wasn't sure if the tassels went with the outfit. I could go home and change. I could have worn black shoes, but I thought they were too dressy."

"It's not the tassels, it's your eyes and nose." Okay, and it's the tassels.

Kloughn got in and buckled his seat belt. "I guess that's all part of the job. Gotta get physical sometimes, right? Goes with the territory, you know what I mean?"

"Your territory is law."

"Yeah, but I'm an assistant bond enforcer, too, right? I'm walking the mean streets with you, right?"

You see, Stephanie, I told myself, this is what happens when you run your credit card up buying nonessentials like shoes and underwear and then can't afford to buy handcuffs.

"I was going to get a stun gun," Kloughn said, "but yours didn't work last night. What's with that? You pay good money for these things and then they don't work. That's always the way, isn't it? You know what you need? You need a lawyer. You were misled by product promises."

I stopped for a light and pulled the stun gun out of my bag and checked it over. "I don't understand this," I said to Kloughn. "It's always worked just fine."

He took the stun gun from me and turned it around in his hand. "Maybe it needs batteries."

"No. They're new. They test out okay."

"Maybe you were doing it wrong?"

"Hardly. It's not that complicated. You press the prongs against someone's skin and push the button."

"Like this?" Kloughn said, pressing the prongs against his arm, pushing the button. He gave a tiny squeak and slumped in his seat.

I took the stun gun from his inert hand and studied it. It seemed to work okay now.

I dropped the stun gun back into my bag, drove back to the Burg, and stopped at Corner Hardware. Corner Hardware was a ramshackle affair that had been in existence for as long as I could remember. The store itself occupied two adjoining buildings with a door carved into the common wall. The floor was unvarnished wood and cracked linoleum. The shelves were dusty, and the air smelled of fertilizer and socket wrenches. Everything you might need could be found in the store at a price higher than could be found elsewhere. The advantage to Corner Hardware was the location. It was in the Burg. No need to drive down Route 1 or go to Hamilton Township. The additional advantage for me today was the fact that no one at Corner Hardware would think it odd that I was schlepping around with a guy with two black eyes. Everyone in the Burg would have heard about Kloughn.

By the time I got to the hardware store, Kloughn was starting to come around. His fingers were twitching, and he had one eye open. I left Kloughn in the car while I ran into the store and bought twenty feet of medium-weight chain and a padlock. I had a plan for capturing Bender.

I dumped the twenty feet of chain onto the street behind the CR-V. I got the cuffs from Kloughn's back pocket, and I attached one end of the chain to one of the bracelets. Then I padlocked the other end of the chain to the tow hitch on my car. I tossed the remaining chain and cuffs into the back window and got behind the wheel. I was soaked, but it was worth it. No way was Bender going to run off with my cuffs this time. The instant I cuffed Bender, he'd be attached to my car.

I drove across town, idled one block over from Bender's apartment, and dialed his number. When he answered I hung up.

"He's home," I told Kloughn. "Let's roll."

Kloughn was examining his hand, wiggling his fingers. "I feel kind of tingly."

"That's because you zapped yourself with my stun gun."

"I thought it didn't work."

"I guess you fixed it."

"I'm real handy," Kloughn said. "I'm good at all kinds of things like that."

I jumped the curb in front of Bender's apartment, drove across the mud yard, and parked with my rear bumper pressed to Bender's front stoop. I leaped out of the car, ran to Bender's door, and barged into his living room.

Bender was in his chair, watching television. He saw me enter and went bug-eyed and slack-jawed. "You!" he said. "What the fuck?" A second later he was out of his chair, bolting for the back door.

"Grab him," I yelled to Kloughn. "Gas him. Trip him. *Do something!*"

Kloughn took a flying leap and caught Bender by the pants leg. Both men went down to the floor. I threw myself on Bender and cuffed him. I rolled off, elated.

Bender scrambled to his feet and ran for the door, dragging the chain behind him.

Kloughn and I did a high five.

"Boy, you're smart," Kloughn said. "I would never have thought of hooking him up to the bumper. I gotta hand it to you. You're good. You're really good."

"Make sure the back door is locked," I said to Kloughn. "I don't want the apartment burgled." I clicked the television off, and Kloughn and I walked to the door just in time to see Bender drive off in my CR-V.

Shit.

"Hey," Kloughn yelled to Bender, "you've got my handcuffs!"

Bender had his arm out the window, holding the door on the driver's side closed. The chain snaked from the door to the back bumper, a loop of chain dragging on the ground, sending up sparks. Bender raised his arm and gave us the finger just before turning the corner and disappearing from view.

"I bet you left the key in the ignition," Kloughn said. "I think that might be illegal. I bet you didn't lock your door, either. You should always take the key and lock the door."

I gave Kloughn my bitch look.

"Of course, these were special circumstances," he added.

Kloughn huddled under the small overhang that protected the front stoop to Bender's apartment. I was at curbside, in the rain, sopping wet, waiting for the blue-and-white. You reach a point with rain where it just doesn't matter anymore.

I'd hoped to get Costanza or my pal Eddie Gazarra when I'd put the call in for a stolen vehicle. The car that responded wasn't either.

"So you're the famous Stephanie Plum?" the cop said.

"I almost never shoot people," I said, sliding onto the backseat of the cruiser. "And the fire in the funeral parlor wasn't my fault." I leaned forward and water dripped from the tip of my nose onto the floor of the car. "Usually Costanza answers my calls," I said.

"He didn't win the pool."

"There's a pool?"

"Yeah. Participation really dropped after that thing with the snakes."

Fifteen minutes later the blue-and-white left, and Morelli showed up.

"Listening to your radio again?" I asked.

"I don't have to listen to my radio anymore. As soon as your name pops up somewhere in the system, I get forty-five phone calls."

I did a small grimace, which I hoped was endearing. "Sorry."

"Let me get this straight," Morelli said. "Bender drove away chained to the car."

"It seemed like a good idea at the time."

"And your handbag was in the car?"

"Yep."

Morelli looked over at Kloughn. "Who's the little guy in the tassel loafers and black eyes?"

"Albert Kloughn."

"And you brought him along because . . . ?"

"He had the handcuffs."

Morelli struggled not to smile and lost. "Get in the truck. I'll take you home."

We dropped Kloughn off first.

"Hey, you know what?" Kloughn said. "We never had lunch. Do you think we should all go to lunch? There's Mexican just down the street. Or we could catch a burger, or an egg roll. I know a place that makes good egg rolls."

"I'll call you," I said.

He waved us out of sight. "That'll be great. Call me. Do you have my number? You can call anytime. I hardly ever sleep, even."

Morelli stopped for a light, looked at me, and shook his head.

"Okay, so I'm wet," I said.

"Albert thinks you're cute."

"He just wants to be part of the gang." I brushed a clump of hair from my face. "How about you? Do you think I'm cute?"

"I think you're crazy."

"Yes. But besides that, you think I'm cute, right?" I gave him my Miss America smile and fluttered my lashes.

He glanced over at me, stone-faced.

I was feeling a little like Scarlett O'Hara at the end of *Gone with the Wind* when she's determined to get Rhett Butler back. Problem was, if I got Morelli back, I wasn't sure what I'd do with him.

"Life is complicated," I said to Morelli.

"No shit, cupcake."

I waved good-bye to Morelli and dripped through the lobby to my building. I dripped in the elevator, and I dripped down the hall to my next-door neighbor, Mrs. Karwatt. I got my spare key from Mrs. Karwatt and then I dripped into my apartment. I stood in the middle of my kitchen floor and peeled my clothes off. I toweled my hair until it stopped dripping. I checked my messages. None. Rex popped out of his soup can, gave me a startled look, and rushed back into the can. Not the sort of reaction that makes a naked woman feel great . . . even from a hamster.

An hour later I was dressed in dry clothes, and I was downstairs waiting for Lula.

"Okay, let me get this straight," Lula said when I settled into her Trans Am. "You need to do surveillance and you don't got a car."

I held my hand up to ward off the next question. "Don't ask."

"I'm hearing 'don't ask' a lot lately."

"It was stolen. My car was stolen."

"Get out!"

"I'm sure the police will find it. In the meantime, I want to take a look at Dotty Palowski Rheinhold. She's living in South River."

"And South River is *where*?"

"I've got a map. Turn left out of the lot."

South River jug-handles off Route 18. It's a small town squashed between strip malls and clay pits and has more bars per square mile than any other town in the state. The entrance provides a scenic overlook of the landfill. The exit crosses the river into Sayreville, famous for the great dirt swindle of 1957 and Jon Bon Jovi.

Dotty Rheinhold lived in a neighborhood of tract houses built in the sixties. Yards were small. Houses were smaller. Cars were large and plentiful.

"You ever see so many cars?" Lula said. "Every house has at least three cars. They're everywhere."

It was an easy neighborhood for surveillance. It had reached an age where houses were filled with teenagers. The teenagers had cars of their own, and the teenagers had friends who had cars. One more car on the street would never be noticed. Even better, this was suburbia.

There were no front-porch-stoop sitters. Everyone migrated to the postage stamp–size backyards, which were crammed full of outdoor grills, above-ground pools, and herds of lawn chairs.

Lula parked the Trans Am one house down and across the street from Dotty. "Do you think Annie and her mom are living with Dotty?"

"If they are, we'll know right away. You can't hide two people in your cellar with kids underfoot. It's too weird. And kids talk. If Annie and Evelyn are here, they're coming and going like normal house guests."

"And we're going to sit here until we figure this out? This sounds like it could take a long time. I don't know if I'm prepared to sit here for a long time. I mean, what about food? And I have to go to the bathroom. I had a super-size soda before I picked you up. You didn't say anything about a long time."

I gave Lula the squinty eye.

"Well, I gotta go," Lula said. "I can't help it. I gotta wee."

"Okay, how about this. We passed a mall on the way in. How about if I drop you at the mall, and then I take the car and do the surveillance."

Half an hour later, I was back at the curb, alone, snooping on Dotty. The drizzle had turned to rain and lights were on in some of the houses. Dotty's house was dark. A blue Honda Civic rolled past me and pulled into Dotty's driveway. A woman got out and unbuckled two kids from kiddie seats in the back. The woman was shrouded in a hooded raincoat, but I caught a look at her face in the gloom, and I was certain it was Dotty. Or, to be more precise, I was certain it wasn't Evelyn. The kids were young. Maybe two and seven. Not that I'm an expert on kids. My entire kid knowledge is based on my two nieces.

The little family entered the house and lights went

on. I put the Trans Am into gear and inched my way up until I was directly across from the Rheinholds'. I could clearly see Dotty now. She had the raincoat off, and she was moving around. The living room was in the front of the house. A television was switched on in the living room. A door opened off the living room, and the room beyond was obviously the kitchen. Dotty was traveling back and forth across the doorway, from refrigerator to table. No other adult appeared. Dotty made no move to draw the living room curtains.

The kids were in bed and their bedroom lights were out by 9:00. At 9:15 Dotty got a phone call. At 9:30 Dotty was still on the phone, and I left to pick Lula up at the mall. A block and a half from Dotty's house, a sleek black car slid by me, traveling in the opposite direction. I caught a glimpse of the driver. Jeanne Ellen Burrows. I almost took the curb and ran across a lawn.

Lula was waiting at the mall entrance when I got there.

"Get in!" I yelled. "I have to get back to Dotty's house. I passed Jeanne Ellen Burrows when I was leaving the neighborhood."

"What about Evelyn and Annie?"

"No sign of them."

The house was dark when we returned. The car was in the driveway. Jeanne Ellen was nowhere to be found.

"You sure it was Jeanne Ellen?" Lula asked.

"Positive. All the hair stood up on my arm, and I got an ice-cream headache."

"Yep. That would be Jeanne Ellen."

Lula dropped me at the door to my apartment building. "Anytime you want to do surveillance, you just let me know," Lula said. "Surveillance is one of my favorite things."

Rex was in his wheel when I came into the kitchen. He stopped running and looked at me, eyes bright.

"Good news, big guy," I said. "I stopped at the store on the way home and got supper."

I dumped the contents of the bag on the counter. Seven Tastykakes. Two Butterscotch Krimpets, a Coconut Junior, two Peanut Butter KandyKakes, Creme-filled Cupcakes, and a Chocolate Junior. Life doesn't get much better than this. Tastykakes are just another of the many advantages of living in Jersey. They're made in Philly and shipped to Trenton in all their fresh squishiness. I read once that 439,000 Butterscotch Krimpets are baked every day. And not a heck of a lot of them find their way to New Hampshire. All that snow and scenery and what good does it do you without Tastykakes?

I ate the Coconut Junior, a Butterscotch Krimpet, and a KandyKake. Rex had part of the Butterscotch Krimpet.

Things haven't been going too great for me lately. In the past week I've lost three pairs of handcuffs, a car, and I've had a bag of snakes delivered to my door. On the other hand, things aren't *all* bad. In fact, things could be a lot worse. I could be living in New Hampshire, where I would be forced to mail order Tastykakes.

It was close to twelve when I crawled into bed. The rain had stopped and the moon was shining between the broken cloud cover. My curtains were drawn, and my room was dark.

An old-fashioned fire escape attached to my bedroom window. The fire escape was good for catching a cool breeze on a hot night. It could be used to dry clothes, quarantine house plants with aphids, and chill beer when the weather turned cold. Unfortunately, it was also a place where bad things happened. Benito

Ramirez had been shot to death on my fire escape. As it happens, it isn't easy to climb up my fire escape, but it isn't impossible, either.

I was laying in the dark, debating the merits of the Coconut Junior over the Butterscotch Krimpet, when I heard scraping sounds beyond the closed bedroom curtains. Someone was on my fire escape. I felt a shot of adrenaline burn into my heart and flash into my gut. I jumped out of bed, ran into the kitchen, and called the police. Then I took the gun out of the cookie jar. No bullets. *Damn.* Think, Stephanie—where did you put the bullets? There used to be some in the sugar bowl. Not anymore. The sugar bowl was empty. I rummaged through the junk drawer and came up with four bullets. I shoved them into my Smith & Wesson five-shot .38 and ran back into my bedroom.

I stood in the dark and listened. No more scraping sounds. My heart was pounding, and the gun was shaking in my hand. Get a grip, I told myself. It was probably a bird. An owl. They fly at night, right? Silly Stephanie, freaked out by an owl.

I crept to the window and listened again. Silence. I opened the curtain a fraction of an inch and peeked out.

Yikes!

There was a huge guy on my fire escape. I only saw him for an instant, but he looked like Benito Ramirez. How could that be? Ramirez was dead.

There was a lot of noise, and I realized I'd fired all four rounds through my window, into the guy on my fire escape.

Rats! This isn't a good thing. First off, I might have killed someone. I *hate* when that happens. Second, I haven't a clue if the guy had a gun, and the law frowns on shooting unarmed people. The law isn't even all that fond of citizens shooting *armed* people. Even worse, my window was trashed.

I ripped the curtain aside, and pressed my nose to the window pane. No one out there. I looked more closely and saw that I'd blasted a life-size cardboard cutout. It was laying flat on the fire escape and there were a bunch of holes in it.

I was standing there dumbfounded, breathing heavy with the gun still in my hand, when I heard the police siren whining in the distance. Good going, Stephanie. The one time I call the police, and it turns out to be an embarrassing false alarm. An evil prank. Like the snakes.

So who would do something like this? Someone who knew about Ramirez getting killed on my fire escape. I gave up a sigh. The entire state knew about Ramirez. It was in all the papers. Okay, someone who had access to a life-size cutout. There had been a lot of the cutouts floating around when Ramirez was fighting. Not many of them floating around now. One person came to mind. Eddie Abruzzi.

A blue-and-white pulled into my parking lot, lights flashing, and a uniform got out.

I opened my window and leaned out. "False alarm," I yelled down. "Nobody here. It must have been a bird."

He looked up at me. "A bird?"

"I think it was an owl. A real big owl. Sorry you got called out."

He waved, got back into the car, and drove off.

I closed and locked the window, but it was an empty gesture since a lot of the glass was missing. I ran into the kitchen and ate the Chocolate Junior.

I was half-asleep, contemplating the nutritional value of a Creme-filled Cupcake for breakfast, when there was a knock at my door.

It was Tank, Ranger's right-hand man. "Your car turned up at a chop shop," he said. He handed my bag over to me. "This was on the floor in the back."

"And my car?"

"In your parking lot." He gave me my keys. "The car's fine except for a chain attached to the tow. We didn't know what the chain was all about."

I closed and locked the door after Tank, stumbled into the kitchen, and ate the package of cupcakes. I told myself it was okay to eat the cupcakes because it was a celebration. I had my car back. Calories don't count if they're connected to a celebration. Everyone knows this.

Coffee would taste good, but it seemed like a lot of work this morning. I had to change the filter, add the coffee and water, and push the button. Not to mention, if I had coffee I might wake up, and I didn't think I was ready to face the day. Better to go back to bed.

I'd just crawled into bed when the doorbell rang again. I put the pillow over my head and closed my eyes. The doorbell kept ringing. "Go away," I yelled. "Nobody's home!" Now there was knocking. And more ringing. I threw the pillow off and heaved myself out of bed. I stomped to the door, wrenched it open, and glared out. "What?"

It was Kloughn. "It's Saturday," he said. "I brought doughnuts. I always have doughnuts on Saturday morning." He looked more closely. "Did I wake you up? Boy, you don't look all that good when you wake up, do you? No wonder you're not married. Do you always sleep in sweats? How'd you get your hair to stick out like that?"

"How'd you like to have your nose broken a second time?" I asked.

Kloughn pushed past me, into my apartment. "I saw the car in the parking lot. Did the police find it? Do you have my handcuffs?"

"I don't have your handcuffs. And get out of my apartment. Go away."

"You just need some coffee," Kloughn said. "Where do you keep the filters? I'm always a cranky pants in the morning, too. And then I have my coffee, and I'm a new person."

Why me? I thought.

Kloughn got the coffee out of the refrigerator and started the machine. "I didn't know if bounty hunters worked on Saturday," he said. "But I thought better safe than sorry. So here I am."

I was speechless.

The front door was still open, and there was a rap on the doorjamb behind me.

It was Morelli. "Am I interrupting something?" he asked.

"It's not what it looks like," Kloughn said. "I just brought jelly doughnuts."

Morelli gave me the once-over. "Frightening," he said.

I narrowed my eyes at him. "I had a bad night."

"That's what they tell me. I understand you were visited by a large bird. An owl?"

"So?"

"The owl do any damage?"

"Nothing worth mentioning."

"I'm seeing more of you now than I did when we were living together," Morelli said. "You aren't doing all this stuff just to have me stop around, are you?"

Chapter

SIX

"Oh jeez, I didn't know you two used to live together," Kloughn said. "Hey, I'm not trying to cut in on anything. We just work together, right?"

"Right," I said.

"So, is this the guy you're engaged to?" Kloughn asked.

A smile twitched at the corner of Morelli's mouth. "You're engaged?"

"Sort of," I said. "I don't want to talk about it."

Morelli reached into the bag and selected a doughnut. "I don't see a ring on your finger."

"I *don't* want to *talk* about it."

Kloughn's voice was apologetic. "She hasn't had any coffee yet."

Morelli took a bite of doughnut. "You think coffee will help?"

They both looked at me.

I pointed stiff-armed to the door. *"Out."*

I slammed the door after them and slid the security bolt. I leaned against the door and closed my eyes. Morelli had looked great. T-shirt and jeans and a red flannel shirt worn open like a jacket. And he'd smelled good, too. The scent still lingered in my foyer, mingling with

jelly doughnuts. I took a deep breath and had a lust attack. The lust attack was followed by a mental head
slap. I sent him away! What was I thinking? Oh yeah,
now I remember. I was thinking he'd just said I was
frightening. *Frightening!* I'm having a hot flash over a
guy who thinks I'm frightening. On the other hand, he
did stop by to see if I was okay.

I was running this through while I walked to the
bathroom. I was up and awake now. Might as well get
on with the day. I switched the light on and caught a
glimpse of myself in the mirror. *Eeeek!* Frightening.

I thought Saturday would be a good day to follow Dotty
around. I had no real reason to think she was helping
Evelyn. Only instinct. But sometimes instinct is all you
need. There's something special about childhood friend-
ships. They might be set aside for reasons of convenience, but they're seldom forgotten.

Mary Lou Molnar has been my best friend for as long
as I can remember. Truth is, we haven't got a whole lot
in common anymore. She's Mary Lou Stankovik now.
She's married and has a couple kids. And I'm living
with a hamster. Still, if I had to tell someone a secret,
it would be Mary Lou. And if I was Evelyn, I'd turn to
Dotty Palowski.

It was close to ten by the time I reached South River.
I cruised past Dotty's house and parked a short distance down the street. Dotty's car was in the driveway.
A red Jeep was parked curbside. Not Evelyn's car. Evelyn drove a nine-year-old gray Sentra. I pushed my
seat back and stretched my legs. If I was a man lurking
in front of a house, I'd be suspect. Fortunately, no one
paid much attention to a woman.

Dotty's front door opened, and a man stepped out.
Dotty's two kids jumped out after him and ran around

him in circles. He took them by the hand, and they all walked to the Jeep and got in.

The ex-husband on visitation day.

The Jeep pulled away and five minutes later Dotty locked the house up and got into her Honda. I followed her easily, out of the neighborhood, onto the highway. She wasn't looking for a tail. Never picked me up in her rearview mirror.

We went straight to one of the strip malls on Route 18 and parked in front of a chain bookstore. I watched Dotty get out of her car and cross the lot to the store. She was barelegged, wearing a sundress with a sweater. I would have been cold in the outfit. The sun was shining but the air was cool. I guess Dotty had run out of patience for warm weather. She pushed through the doors and went straight for the coffee bar. I could see her through the plate glass window. She ordered a coffee and took it to a table. She sat with her back to the window and looked around. She checked her watch and sipped her coffee. She was waiting for someone.

Please let it be Evelyn. It would make everything so easy.

I left my car and walked the short distance to the store. I browsed the section to the rear of the coffee bar, staying hidden behind racks of books. I didn't know Dotty personally, but I worried that she might recognize me, all the same. I scanned the store for Evelyn and Annie. I didn't want them to see me, either.

Dotty looked up from her coffee and focused. I followed her line of sight, but I didn't see Annie or Evelyn. I was looking so intently for Annie and Evelyn that I almost missed the red-haired guy making his way toward Dotty. It was Steven Soder. My first reaction was to intercept him. I didn't know what he was doing here, but he was going to ruin everything. Evelyn would run when she saw him. And then it hit me, brain surgeon that I am. Dotty was waiting for Soder.

Soder got a coffee and took it to Dotty's table. He sat across from her and slouched in his chair. An arrogant posture. I could see his face, and he didn't look friendly.

Dotty leaned forward and said something to Soder. He made a crooked smile that was close to a snarl and nodded his head. They had a brief conversation. Soder stuck his finger in Dotty's face and said something that turned Dotty white. He stood, made one last parting remark, and left. His coffee remained, untouched, on the table. Dotty collected herself, made certain Soder was out of sight, and then she left, too.

I followed Dotty to the parking lot. She got into her car, and I ran for mine. Hold the phone. No car. Okay, I know I'm a little dingy sometimes, but I usually remember where I've parked the car. I trotted up and down the aisle. I tried one aisle over. No car.

Dotty pulled out of her space and headed for the exit. A sleek black car followed a short distance behind Dotty. Jeanne Ellen.

"Damn!"

I rammed my hand into my bag, found my cell phone, and pounded out Ranger's number.

"Call Jeanne Ellen and find out what she did with my car," I said to Ranger. *"Now!"*

A minute later Jeanne Ellen called me. "I might have seen a black CR-V in front of the deli," she said.

I punched the end button so hard I broke a nail. I dropped the phone back into my bag and stomped off, down the strip mall to the deli. I found my car and checked it over. There were no scratch marks from where Jeanne Ellen had popped the lock. No loose wires from hot-wiring. Somehow she'd gotten into the car and moved it without leaving a trace of herself. This was a trick Ranger could easily accomplish, and I couldn't hope to pull off. The fact that Jeanne Ellen could do it really grated on me.

I left the strip mall and returned to Dotty's house. No one was home. No car in the driveway. Probably Dotty had taken Jeanne Ellen straight to Evelyn. Fine. Who cares. I'm not even making any money on this. I did an eye roll. It wasn't fine. If I go back to Mabel with nothing, she'll start bawling again. I'd walk on molten lava and shards of glass before I'd face more of Mabel crying.

I hung around until early afternoon. I read the paper, filed my nails, organized my shoulder bag, and talked on my cell phone with Mary Lou Stankovik for a half hour. My legs were twitchy from the confinement, and my butt was asleep. I'd had a lot of time to think about Jeanne Ellen Burrows, and none of the thoughts were friendly. In fact, after about an hour of Jeanne Ellen Burrows thinking I was darn cranky, and I'm not sure, but I think steam might have started escaping from the top of my head. Jeanne Ellen had bigger boobs and a smaller ass than me. She was a better bounty hunter. She had a nicer car. And she had leather pants. I could deal with this. What I couldn't deal with was her involvement with Ranger. I'd thought their relationship had ended, but clearly I was wrong. He knew where she was every minute of the day.

While *she* had a relationship, *I* had the threat of a single night of gorilla sex hanging over my head. Okay, so I'd made the deal during a moment of professional desperation. His aid in exchange for my body. And yes, maybe it had been flirty and fun, in a scary sort of way. And true, I'm attracted to him. I mean, I'm only human, for crying out loud. A woman would have to be *dead* not to be attracted to Ranger. And it's not like I'm having any luck getting Morelli into my bed these days.

So here I am with my one night. And there's Jeanne Ellen with some sort of relationship. Well, forget it. I'm not fooling around with a man who's possibly in a relationship.

I dialed Ranger and drummed my fingers on the steering wheel while I waited for the connection.

"Yo," Ranger said.

"I owe you *nothing*," I said. "The deal is off."

Ranger was silent for a couple beats. Probably wondering why he ever made the deal in the first place. "Having a bad day?" he finally asked.

"My bad day has nothing to do with this," I said. And I hung up.

My cell phone chirped, and I debated answering. Curiosity ultimately won out over cowardice. Pretty much the story of my life.

"I've been under a lot of stress," I said. "I might even be sick with a fever."

"And?"

"And what?"

"I thought you might want to retract the part where you tell me the deal is off," Ranger said.

There was a long silence on the phone.

"Well?" Ranger asked.

"I'm thinking."

"That's always dangerous," Ranger said. And he hung up.

I was still contemplating the retraction when Dotty rolled in. She parked in her driveway, took two grocery bags from the backseat, and let herself into the house.

My phone rang again. I did an eye roll and snapped my phone open. "Yes."

"Have you been waiting long?" It was Jeanne Ellen.

I whipped my head around, looking up and down the street. "Where are you?"

"Behind the blue van. You'll be happy to know you didn't miss anything this afternoon. Dotty had a full day of housewifey things to do."

"Did she know you were following her?"

There was a pause where I assumed Jeanne Ellen was stunned that I might think she'd ever get made. "Of course not," Jeanne Ellen said. "She didn't have Evelyn in her day planner today."

"Well, cheer up," I said. "The day's not over."

"True. I thought I'd stay here a bit longer, but the street feels crowded with both of us sitting here."

"And?"

"And I thought it would be a good idea for you to leave."

"No way. *You* should leave."

"If anything happens I'll call you," Jeanne Ellen said.

"That's a big fib."

"True, again. Let me tell you something that isn't a fib. If you don't leave, I'll put a bullet hole in your car."

I knew from past experience that bullet holes were very bad for resale. I disconnected, put the car in gear, and drove away. I drove exactly two blocks and parked in front of a small white ranch. I locked up and walked around the block until I was directly behind Dotty's house, one street over. There was no activity on the street. Not a lot of life visible from Dotty's neighbors. Everyone was still at the mall, the soccer game, the Little League game, the car wash. I cut between two houses and straddled the white picket fence that enclosed Dotty's backyard. I crossed the small yard, and knocked on Dotty's back door.

Dotty opened the door and stared out at me, surprised to find a strange woman on her property, "I'm Stephanie Plum," I said. "I hope I didn't startle you by showing up at your back door like this."

Relief replaced surprise. "Of course, your parents live next to Mabel Markowitz. I went to school with your sister."

"I'd like to talk to you about Evelyn. Mabel is worried about her, and I said I'd do some inquiring around. I came to the back door because the front of your house is under surveillance."

Dotty's mouth dropped and her eyes widened. "Someone's watching me?"

"Steven Soder has hired a private detective to find Annie. The detective's name is Jeanne Ellen Burrows, and she's in a black Jaguar, behind the blue van. I spotted her when I drove up, and I didn't want her to see me, so I came through the back." Take that, Jeanne Ellen Burrows. Direct hit. *Kapow!*

"Omigod," Dotty said. "What should I do?"

"Do you know where Evelyn is?"

"No. Sorry. Evelyn and I sort of lost touch."

She was lying. She'd waited too long to say no. And now spots of color were blooming on her cheeks. She was possibly the worst liar I'd ever seen. She was a disgrace to Burg women. Burg women were *great* liars. No wonder Dotty had to move to South River.

I let myself into her kitchen and closed the door. "Listen," I said, "don't worry about Jeanne Ellen. She's not dangerous. You just don't want to lead her to Evelyn."

"You mean *if* I knew where Evelyn was then I should be careful about going there."

"Careful isn't good enough. Jeanne Ellen will follow you, and you'll never see her. Don't go anywhere near Evelyn. Stay away from her."

Dotty wasn't liking this advice. "Hmmm," she said. "Maybe we should talk about Evelyn."

She shook her head. "I can't talk about Evelyn."

I gave her my card. "Call me if you change your mind. If Evelyn gets in touch with you, and you need to go see her, please consider letting me help you. You can call Mabel and check me out."

Dotty looked at the card and nodded. "Okay."

I let myself out the back door and slipped through the yards to the street. I walked the half block back to my car and took off for home.

I stepped out of the elevator and felt my heart sink at the sight of Kloughn camping in my hall. He was sitting with his back to the wall, legs outstretched, arms crossed over his chest. His face brightened when he saw me, and he scrambled to his feet.

"Boy," he said, "you've been gone all afternoon. Where were you? You didn't catch Bender, did you? You wouldn't catch him without me, would you? I mean, we're a team, right?"

"Right," I said. "We're a team." A team without handcuffs.

I let us into my apartment, and we both migrated to the kitchen. I slid a look at the answering machine. Nothing was blinking. No message from Morelli, pleading for a date. Not that Morelli ever pleaded for anything. Still, a girl could hope. Large mental sigh. I was going to spend Saturday night with Albert Kloughn. It felt like doomsday.

Kloughn was looking at me expectantly. He was like a puppy, eyes bright, tail wagging, waiting to be taken for a walk. Endearing . . . in an incredibly annoying sort of way.

"Now what?" he asked. "What do we do now?"

I needed to think about this. Usually the problem is *finding* the FTA. I never had a problem finding Bender. I had a problem hanging on to him.

I opened the refrigerator and stared inside. My motto

has always been, When all else fails, eat something. "Let's make dinner," I said.

"Oh boy, a home-cooked meal. That would really hit the spot. I haven't eaten in hours. Okay, I had a candy bar just before you got here, but that doesn't count, does it? I mean, it's not like real food. And I'm still hungry. It's not like it's a meal, right?"

"Right."

"What should we cook? Pasta? You got some fish? We could have fish. Or a nice steak. I still eat meat. Lots of people don't eat meat anymore, but I still eat it. I eat everything."

"Do you eat peanut butter?"

"Sure. I love peanut butter. Peanut butter is a staple, right?"

"Right." I ate a lot of peanut butter. You don't have to cook it. You only dirty one knife in the preparation. And you can count on it. It's always the same. As opposed to picking out a piece of fish, which in my experience is risky.

I made us peanut butter and bread-and-butter pickle sandwiches. And because I had company, I added a layer of potato chips.

"This is very creative," Kloughn said. "You get a lot of textures this way. And you don't get your fingers greasy by eating the potato chips separately. I'll have to remember this. I'm always looking for new recipes."

Alright, I was going to take another shot at capturing Bender. I was going to break into his house, one more time. As soon as I located a pair of handcuffs.

I dialed Lula's number.

"So," I said to Lula, "what's going on tonight?"

"I'm just trying to figure out what to wear, on account of it's Saturday. And it's not like I'm some loser who can't get a date. I'd be out of the house by now, but I can't make up my mind between two dresses."

"Do you have handcuffs?"

"Sure. I got handcuffs. You never know when you need handcuffs."

"Maybe I could borrow them. Just for a couple hours. I need to bring Bender in."

"You're gonna go get Bender tonight? You need help? I could cancel my date. Then I wouldn't have to decide on a dress. You have to come over here to get the cuffs anyway. You might as well take me with."

"You don't actually have a date, do you?"

"I could if I wanted."

"I'll pick you up in a half hour."

Lula was in the front seat, and Kloughn was in the backseat. We were parked in front of Bender's apartment, trying to decide on the best approach.

"You watch the back door," I said to Lula. "And Albert and I will go in the front door."

"I don't like that plan," Lula said. "I want to go in the front door. And I want to be the one holding the cuffs."

"I think Stephanie should hold the cuffs," Kloughn said. "She's the bounty hunter."

"Hunh," Lula said. "What am I, chopped liver? And besides, they're my cuffs. I should get to hold them. Either I hold them, or you haven't got no cuffs."

"Fine!" I said to Lula. "*You* go in the front door, and *you* hold the cuffs. Just make sure you get them on Bender."

"What about me?" Kloughn wanted to know. "Where do I go? Do I take the back door? What do I do back there? Do I bust in the door?"

"No! No door busting. You stand there and wait. Your job is to make sure Bender doesn't escape from the back door. So if the back door opens and Bender runs out, you have to stop him."

"You can count on me. He won't get past me. I know I look pretty tough, but I'm even tougher than that. I'm *real* tough."

"Right," Lula and I said in unison.

Kloughn went around back, and Lula and I marched up to the front door. I rapped on the door and Lula and I stood to either side. There was the unmistakable sound of a shotgun ratcheting back, Lula and I gave each other an *oh shit* look, and Bender blasted a two-foot hole in his front door.

Lula and I took off, running. We dove into the car headfirst, there was another shotgun blast, I scrambled behind the wheel and took off, tires smoking. I whipped the car around the side of the building, jumped the curb, and skidded to a stop inches from Kloughn. Lula grabbed Kloughn by the front of his shirt, pulled him into the car, and I rocketed away.

"What happened?" Kloughn asked. "Why are we leaving? Wasn't he home?"

"We changed our mind about getting him tonight," Lula said. "We could have got him if we really wanted, but we changed our mind."

"We changed our mind because he shot at us," I said to Kloughn.

"I'm pretty sure that's illegal," Kloughn said. "Did you shoot back?"

"I was thinking about it," Lula said, "but you gotta fill out a lot of papers when you shoot someone. I didn't want to take the time tonight."

"At least you got to hold the cuffs," Kloughn said.

Lula looked down at her hands. No cuffs. "Uh-oh," Lula said. "I must have dropped the cuffs in the excitement of the moment. It wasn't that I was scared, you know. I just got excited."

On the way through town I stopped at Soder's bar.

"This will only take a minute," I told everyone. "I need to talk to Steven Soder."

"Fine by me," Lula said. "I could use a drink." She looked over at Kloughn. "How about you, Pufnstuf?"

"Sure, I could use a drink, too. It's Saturday night, right? You gotta go out and have a drink on Saturday night."

"I could have had a date," Lula said.

"Me, too," Kloughn said. "There are lots of women who want to go out with me. I just didn't feel like being bothered. Sometimes it's good to take a night off from all that stuff."

"Last time I was in this bar I sort of got thrown out," Lula said. "You don't suppose they're gonna hold a grudge, do you?"

Soder saw me when I walked in. "Hey, it's Little Miss Loser," he said. "And her two loser friends."

"Sticks and stones," I said.

"Have you found my kid yet?" A taunt, not a question.

I shrugged. The shrug said *maybe I have, but then again maybe I haven't.*

"*Looooser,*" Soder sang.

"You should learn some people skills," I said to him. "You should be more civil to me. And you should have been nicer to Dotty earlier today."

That got him standing up straighter. "How do you know about Dotty?"

Another shrug.

"Don't give me another one of them shrugs," he said. "That birdbrain ex-wife of mine is a kidnapper. And you better tell me if you know anything."

I had him wondering. about the extent of my knowledge. Probably not smart, but definitely satisfying.

"I've changed my mind about wanting a drink," I said to Lula and Kloughn.

"Okay by me," Lula said. "I don't like the atmosphere in this bar anyway."

Soder took another look at Kloughn. "Hey, I remember you. You're the jerk-off lawyer who represented Evelyn."

Kloughn beamed. "You remember me? I didn't think anyone would remember. Boy, how about that."

"Evelyn got control of the kid because of you," Soder said. "You made a big issue about this bar. You put my kid with a drugged-up moron, you incompetent fuck."

"She didn't look drugged-up to me," Kloughn said. "Maybe a little . . . distracted."

"How about if I distract my foot up your ass," Soder said, making for the end of the long oak bar.

Lula shoved her hand into her big leather shoulder bag. "I got Mace in here, somewhere. I got a gun."

I turned Kloughn around and pushed him toward the door. "*Go,*" I yelled in his ear. "Run for the car!"

Lula still had her head down, rummaging in her bag. "I *know* I've got a gun in here."

"Forget the gun!" I said to Lula. "Let's just get out of here."

"The hell," Lula said. "This guy deserves to get shot. And I'd do it if I could just find my gun."

Soder rounded the bar and charged after Kloughn. I stepped in front of Soder, and he gave me a two-handed shove.

"Hey, you can't shove her like that," Lula said. And she smacked Soder in the back of his head with her bag. He whirled around, and she hit him again, this time catching him in the face, knocking him back a couple feet.

"What?" Soder said, dazed and blinking, swaying slightly.

Two goons started at us from the other end of the bar, and half the room had guns drawn.

"Uh-oh," Lula said. "Guess I left my gun in my other handbag."

I grabbed Lula by the sleeve and gave her a yank toward the door, and we both took off running. I beeped the car open with my remote, we all jumped in, and I zoomed away.

"Soon as I find my gun, I've got a mind to go back there and pop a cap up his ass," Lula said.

In all the time I've known Lula, I've never known her to pop a cap up anyone's ass. Unjustified bravado was high on our list of bounty hunter talents.

"I need a day off," I said. "I especially need a day without Bender."

One of the good things about hamsters is that you can tell them anything. Hamsters are nonjudgmental as long as you feed them.

"I have no life," I said to Rex. "How did it come to this? I used to be such an interesting person. I used to be fun. And now look at me. It's two o'clock on a Sunday afternoon, and I've watched *Ghostbusters* twice. It's not even raining. There's no excuse, except that I'm boring."

I glanced over at the answering machine. Maybe it was broken. I lifted the phone receiver and got a dial tone. I pushed the message button and the voice told me I had no messages. Stupid invention.

"I need a hobby," I said.

Rex sent me a *yeah, right* look. Knitting? Gardening? Decoupage? I don't think so.

"Okay, then how about sports? I could play tennis." No, wait a minute, I'd tried tennis and I sucked. What about golf? Nope, I sucked at golf, too.

I was wearing jeans and a T-shirt and the top button was open on my jeans. Too many cupcakes. I got to

thinking about Steven Soder calling me a loser. Maybe
he was right. I scrinched my eyes closed to see if I could
pop out a pity tear for myself. No luck. I sucked my
stomach in and buttoned my pants. Pain. And there was
a roll of fat hanging over the waistband. Not attractive.

I stomped into my bedroom and changed into running
shorts and shoes. I was *not* a loser. I had a small roll of
fat hanging over my waistband. No big deal. A little
exercise and the fat would disappear. And there'd be
the added benefit of endorphins. I didn't exactly know
what endorphins were but I knew they were good and
you got them from exercise.

I got into the CR-V and drove to the park in Hamilton Township. I could have gone running from my back
door but where's the fun in that? In Jersey we never miss
an opportunity for a car trip. Besides, the driving gave
me prep time. I needed to psych myself up for this exercise stuff. I was going to really get into it this time. I
was going to run. I was going to sweat. I was going to
look great. I was going to *feel* great. Maybe I'd actually
take up running.

It was a glorious blue-sky day, and the park was
crowded. I got a spot toward the back of the lot, locked
the CR-V up, and walked to the jogging path. I did some
warm-up stretches and took off at a slow run. After
a quarter mile I remembered why I never did this. I
hated it. I hated running. I hated sweating. I hated the
big, ugly running shoes I was wearing.

I pushed through to the half-mile mark where I had
to stop, thank God, for a stitch in my side. I looked down
at the fat roll. It was still there.

I made it to a mile and collapsed onto a bench. The
bench looked out over the lake where people were row-
ing around in boats. A family of ducks floated close to
the shore. Across the lake, I could see the parking lot

and a concession stand. There was water at the concession stand. There was no water by my bench. Hell, who was I kidding? I didn't want water, anyway. I wanted a Coke. And a box of Cracker Jacks.

I was looking out at the ducks, thinking there were times in history when fat rolls were considered sexy, and wasn't it too bad I didn't live during one of those times. A huge, shaggy, prehistoric, orange beast bounded over to me and buried his nose in my crotch. Yipes. It was Morelli's dog, Bob. Bob had originally come to live at my house but after some shifting around had decided he preferred living with Morelli.

"He's excited to see you," Morelli said, settling next to me.

"I thought you were taking him to obedience school."

"I did. He learned how to sit and stay and heel. The course didn't address crotch sniffing." He looked me over. "Flushed face, the hint of sweat at the hairline, hair pulled into a ponytail, running shoes. Let me take a guess here. You've been exercising."

"And?"

"Hey, I think it's great. I'm just surprised. Last time I went running with you, you took a detour into a bakery."

"I'm turning over a new leaf."

"Can't button your jeans?"

"Not if I want to breathe at the same time."

Bob spotted a duck on the bank and raced after it. The duck took to the water, and Bob splashed in up to his eyeballs. He turned and looked at us, panic stricken. He was possibly the only retriever in the entire world who couldn't swim.

Morelli waded into the lake and dragged Bob back to the shore. Bob slogged onto the grass, gave himself a shake, and immediately ran off, chasing a squirrel.

"You're such a hero," I said to Morelli.

He kicked his shoes off and rolled his slacks to his knees. "I hear you've been up to some heroics, too. Butch Dziewisz and Frankie Burlew were in Soder's bar last night."

"It wasn't my fault."

"Of course it was your fault," Morelli said. "It's always your fault."

I did an eye roll.

"Bob misses you."

"Bob should call me sometime. Leave a message on my machine."

Morelli slouched back on the bench. "What were you doing in Soder's bar?"

"I wanted to talk to him about Evelyn and Annie, but he wasn't in a good mood."

"Did his mood take a downturn before or after he got clocked with the shoulder bag?"

"He was actually more mellow after Lula hit him."

"*Dazed,* was the word Butch used."

"Dazed could be accurate. We didn't stay around long enough to find out."

Bob returned from the squirrel chase and woofed at Morelli.

"Bob's restless," Morelli said. "I promised him we'd walk around the lake. Which direction are you headed?"

It was one mile if I retraced my steps and three miles if I continued around the lake with Morelli. Morelli looked very fine with his pants rolled up, and I was sorely tempted. Unfortunately, I had a blister on my heel, I still had a cramp in my side, and I suspected I wasn't at my most attractive. "I'm headed for the lot," I said.

There was an awkward moment where I waited for Morelli to prolong our time together. I would have liked him to walk back to the car with me. Truth is, I missed Morelli. I missed the passion, and I missed the affectionate teasing. He never tugged at my hair anymore. He didn't try to look down my shirt or up my skirt. We were at an impasse, and I was at a loss as to how to end it.

"Try to be careful," Morelli said. We stared at each other for a moment, and we each went our own way.

Chapter
SEVEN

I limped back to the concession stand and got a Coke and a box of Cracker Jacks. Cracker Jacks don't count as junk food because they're corn and peanuts, which we know to be high in nutrition. And they have a prize inside.

I walked the short distance to the water's edge, opened the box of Cracker Jacks, and a goose rushed up to me and pecked me in the knee. I jumped back, but he kept coming at me, honking and pecking. I threw a Cracker Jack as far as I could, and the goose scrambled after it. Big mistake. Turns out, tossing a Cracker Jack is the goose equivalent to a party invitation. Suddenly geese were rushing at me from every corner of the park, running on their stupid goose webbed feet, waggling their fat goose asses, flapping their big goose wings, their beady, black goose eyes fixed on my Cracker Jacks. They fought among themselves as they charged me, squawking, honking, viciously snapping, jockeying for position.

"Run for your life, honey! Give them the Cracker Jacks," an old lady yelled from a nearby bench. "Throw them the box, or those honkers'll eat you alive!"

I held tight to my box. "I didn't get to the prize. The prize is still in the box."

"Forget the prize!"

There were geese flying in from across the lake. Hell, for all I knew they could have been flying in from Canada. One of them hit me square in the chest and sent me sprawling. I let out a shriek and lost my grip on the box. The geese attacked with no regard for human or goose life. The noise was deafening. Goose wings beat against me, and goose toenails ripped holes in my T-shirt.

It seemed like the feeding frenzy lasted for hours, but in fact it was maybe a minute. The geese departed as quickly as they came, and all that was left were goose feathers and goose poop. Huge, gelatinous gobs of goose poop . . . as far as the eye could see.

An old man was on the bench with the old woman. "You don't know much, do you?" he said to me.

I picked myself up, crept to my car, opened the door with the remote, and numbly wedged myself behind the wheel. So much for exercise. I drove on autopilot out of the lot and somehow found my way to Hamilton Avenue. I was a couple blocks from my apartment building when I sensed movement on the seat next to me. I turned my head to look, and a spider the size of a dinner plate jumped at me.

"*Eeeeyow!* Holy shit! *HOLY SHIT!*" I sideswiped a parked car, took the curb, and came to a stop on a patch of lawn. I threw my door open and hurled myself out of the car. I was still jumping around, shaking my hair out, when the first cops arrived.

"Let me get this straight," one of the cops said. "You almost totaled the Toyota that's parked at the curb, not to mention major damage on your CR-V, because you were attacked by a spider?"

"Not just *a* spider. We're talking more than one. And big. Possibly *mutant* spiders. A herd of mutant spiders."

"You look familiar," he said. "Aren't you a bounty hunter?"

"Yes, and I'm very brave. Except for spiders." And except for Eddie Abruzzi. Abruzzi knew how to frighten a woman. He knew all the creepy crawly things that were demoralizing and irrationally frightening. Snakes and spiders and ghosts on fire escapes.

The cops exchanged a glance that said *girls* . . . and swaggered off to the CR-V. They poked their heads inside and a moment later there was a double shriek, and the car door was slammed shut.

"Jesus freaking Christ," one of them yelled. "Holy crap!"

After a brief discussion it was decided this was beyond the ability of a simple exterminator and, once again, Animal Control was called. An hour later, the CR-V was pronounced spider-free, I possessed a ticket for reckless driving, and I'd exchanged insurance information with the owner of the parked car.

I drove the remaining couple blocks, parked the CR-V, and stumbled into my building. Mr. Kleinschmidt was in the lobby.

"You look terrible," Mr. Kleinschmidt said. "What happened to you? Are those goose feathers stuck to your shirt? And how'd your shirt get all ripped and grass stained?"

"You don't want to know," I told him. "It's really ugly."

"I bet you were feeding the geese at the park," he said. "You never want to do that. Those geese are animals."

I gave up a sigh and stepped into the elevator. When I let myself into my apartment I realized something was different. My message light was blinking. *Yes*. Finally! I punched the button and leaned forward to listen.

"Did you like the spiders?" the voice asked.

I was still standing in the kitchen, sort of dumbstruck by the day, when Morelli showed up. He rapped once on the front door, and the unlocked door swung open. Bob bounded in and began running around, investigating.

"I understand you had a spider problem," Morelli said.

"That's an understatement."

"I saw your CR-V in the lot. You trashed the whole right side."

I played the phone message for him.

"It's Abruzzi," I said. "It's not his voice on the tape, but he's behind this. He thinks this is some *war game*. And someone must have followed me to the park. Then they unlocked my car and dumped a load of spiders into it while I was running."

"How many spiders?"

"Five large tarantulas."

"I could talk to Abruzzi."

"Thanks, but I can handle it." Yeah, right. That's why I ripped the door off a parked car. Truth is, I'd love to have Morelli step in and make Abruzzi go away. Unfortunately, it would send a bad message: Dopey, helpless female needs big strong man to get her out of unfortunate mess.

Morelli gave me the once-over, taking in the grass stains, goose feathers, and rips in my shirt. "I got Bob a hot dog after we walked around the lake, and there was a lot of talk at the concession stand about a woman who'd been attacked by a flock of geese."

"Hmm. Imagine that."

"They said she provoked the attack by feeding one of the geese a Cracker Jack."

"It wasn't my fault," I said. "Damn stupid geese."

Bob had been roaming the apartment. He came into the kitchen and smiled up at us. A piece of toilet paper dangled from his lips. He opened his mouth and stuck his tongue out. *"Kack!"* His mouth opened wider, and he horked up a hot dog, a bunch of grass, a lot of slime, and a wad of toilet paper.

We both stared at the steaming pile of dog barf. "Well, I guess I should be going now," Morelli said, looking to the door. "I just wanted to make sure you were okay."

"Wait a minute. Who's going to clean this up?"

"I'd like to help, but . . . oh man, that smells really bad." He had his hand over his nose and mouth. "Gotta go," he said. "Late. Something to do." He was in the hall. "Maybe you should just leave and rent a new apartment."

Another opportunity to use the bitch look.

I didn't sleep well . . . which I'm sure is normal after you've been attacked by killer geese and mutant spiders. At six o'clock I finally hauled myself out of bed, took a shower, and got dressed. I decided I needed a treat after the crappy night, so I packed myself off in the CR-V and drove into town to Barry's Coffees. There was always a line at Barry's but it was worth it because he had forty-two different kinds of coffee, plus all the exotic espresso drinks.

I ordered a double skinny caramel mochaccino and took my drink to the window bar. I squeezed in next to an old lady with chopped-off, spikey hair dyed flame red. She was short and round, with apple cheeks and an apple shape. She was wearing large turquoise and silver earrings, elaborate rings on every gnarled finger, a white polyester warm-up suit, and platform Skechers. Her eyes were heavily gunked with mascara. Her dark red lipstick had been transferred to her cappuccino cup.

"Hey, honey," she said in a two-pack-a-day voice. "Is that a caramel mochaccino? I used to drink them but they gave me the shakes. Too much sugar. You keep drinking them you're gonna get diabetes. My brother has diabetes and they had to cut his foot off.

It was real ugly. First his toes turned black, and then the whole foot, and then his skin started falling off in big clumps. It was like a shark had got hold of him and ripped off chunks of meat."

I looked around for another place to stand while I drank my coffee, but the place was packed.

"He's in a nursing home now on account of he can't get around so good," she said. "I visit him when I can, but I got things to do. You get to be my age and you don't want to sit around wasting time. I could wake up any morning and be dead. Of course I keep myself in real good shape. How old do you think I am?"

"Eighty?"

"Seventy-four. I look better some days than others," she said. "What's your name, honey?"

"Stephanie."

"My name's Laura. Laura Minello."

"Laura Minello. That sounds familiar. Are you from the Burg?"

"Nope. I've lived all my life in North Trenton. Cherry Street. I used to work at the Social Security office. Worked there for twenty-three years, but you wouldn't remember me from there. You're too young."

Laura Minello. I knew her from somewhere, but I couldn't place it.

Laura Minello gestured at a red Corvette parked in front of Barry's. "See that fancy red car? That's my car. Pretty slick, hunh?"

I looked at the car. And then I looked at Laura Minello. Then I looked at the car again. Holy cow. I dug around in my shoulder bag, searching for the papers Connie had given me.

"Have you had the car long?" I asked Laura.

"Couple days."

I pulled the papers out of my bag and scanned the top page. Laura Minello, accused of grand theft auto, age seventy-four. Residence on Cherry Street.

God works in mysterious ways.

"You stole that Corvette, didn't you?" I asked Minello.

"I borrowed it. Old people are allowed to do things like that so they can go for the gusto before they croak."

Oh boy. I should have looked at the bond agreement before I accepted the file from Connie. Never take on old people. It's always a disaster. Old people think conveniently. And you look like a jerk when you apprehend them.

"This is a strange coincidence," I said. "I work for Vincent Plum, your bail bondsman. You missed a court date, and you need to reschedule."

"Okay, but not today. I'm going to Atlantic City. Just pencil something in for me next week."

"It doesn't work that way."

A blue-and-white cruised by Barry's. It stopped just beyond the red Vette and two cops got out.

"Uh-oh," Laura said. "This don't look good."

One of the cops was Eddie Gazarra. Gazarra was married to my cousin, Shirley the Whiner. Gazarra checked the plate on the Vette, and then he walked around the car. He went back to the blue-and-white and made a call.

"Damn cops," Laura said. "Haven't got anything better to do than to go around and bust senior citizens. There should be a law against it."

I rapped on the coffeehouse window and caught Gazarra's attention. I pointed to Laura sitting next to me and smiled. *Here she is,* I mouthed to Gazarra.

It was close to noon, and I was parked in front of Vinnie's office, trying to muster the courage to go inside. I'd followed Gazarra and Laura Minello back to the station, and I'd gotten a body receipt for Minello. The body receipt would get me fifteen percent of Minello's bond. And the fifteen percent would make an essential contribution toward this month's rent. Ordinarily the delivery of a body receipt is a happy occasion. Today it would be marred by the fact that in the pursuit of Andrew Bender I'd lost four pairs of cuffs. Not to mention that on all occasions I'd looked like a complete idiot. And Vinnie was in residence, lurking in his lair, anxious to remind me of all this.

I set my teeth, grabbed my bag, and headed for the door.

Lula stopped filing when I walked in. "Hey, jelly-bean," Lula said. "What's new?"

Connie looked up from her computer. "Vinnie's in his office. Break out the garlic and crosses."

"What kind of mood is he in?"

"Are you here to tell me you captured Bender?" Vinnie yelled from the other side of his closed door.

"No."

"Then I'm in a *bad* mood."

"How can he hear with the door closed?" I asked Connie.

She raised her hand, middle finger extended.

"I saw that," Vinnie yelled.

"He had video and sound installed so he doesn't miss something," Connie said.

"Yeah, it's secondhand," Lula said. "It came out of the adult video store that closed. I wouldn't touch it without rubber gloves."

Vinnie's door opened, and Vinnie stuck his head out. "Andy Bender is a drunk, for crissake. He wakes up in the morning, falls into a can of beer, and never climbs out. He should have been a gift. Instead, he's making you look like a moron."

"He's one of them crafty drunks," Lula said. "He can even *run* when he's drunk. And he shot at us last time. You're gonna have to pay me more if I'm gonna get shot at."

"You two are pathetic," Vinnie said. "I could catch this guy with one hand tied behind my back. I could catch this guy blindfolded."

"Hunh," Lula said.

Vinnie leaned forward. "You don't believe me? You think I couldn't bring this guy in?"

"Miracles happen," Lula said.

"Oh yeah? You think it would take a miracle? Well, I'll show you a miracle. You two losers be here at nine tonight, and we'll take this guy down."

Vinnie pulled his head back inside his office and slammed the door shut.

"Hope he's got cuffs," Lula said.

I gave Connie the body receipt for Laura Minello and waited while she wrote my check. We all turned and looked when the front door opened.

"Hey, I know you," Lula said to the woman who walked into the office. "You tried to kill me."

It was Maggie Mason. We'd met her on a previous case. Our relationship with Maggie had started out bad, but had ended up good.

"You still mud wrestling at The Snake Pit?" Lula asked.

"The Snake Pit closed down." Maggie did a *shit happens* shrug. "It was time for me to get out anyway. Wrestling was fun for a while, but my dream was always to open a bookstore. When the Pit folded I persuaded one of the owners to go into business with me. That's why I stopped in. We're going to be neighbors. I just signed a lease on the building next door."

I was sitting in front of Vinnie's office, in my wrecked car, wondering what to do next, and my cell phone rang.

"You gotta do something," Grandma Mazur said.

"Mabel was just over, for the fortieth time. She's driving us nuts. First off, she bakes all day, and now she's giving the stuff to us because she hasn't got any more room in her house. She's wall-to-wall bread. And this last time, she started crying. *Crying.* You know how we don't do good with crying here."

"She's worried about Evelyn and Annie. They're the only family she has left."

"Well, find them," Grandma said. "We don't know what to do with all these coffee cakes."

I drove to Key Street and parked across from Evelyn's house. I thought about Annie sleeping in her bedroom upstairs, playing in the small backyard. A little girl with curly red hair and large serious eyes. A kid who was best friends with my niece, the horse. What kind of a kid would buddy up with Mary Alice? Not that Mary Alice isn't a great kid, but let's face it, she's a couple inches off average. Probably Mary Alice and Annie were both on the outside looking in, needing a friend. And they found each other.

Talk to me, I said to the house. *Tell me a secret.*

I was sitting there, waiting for the house to say something, and a car pulled up behind me. It was the big black Lincoln with two men in the front. I didn't have to think too long or hard to figure out it was Abruzzi and Darrow.

The smart thing would be to take off and not look back. Since I had a long history of rarely doing the smart thing, I locked my door, cracked the window on the driver's side, and waited for Abruzzi to come talk to me.

"You've got your door locked," Abruzzi said when he walked over. "Are you afraid of me?"

"If I was afraid of you, I'd have the motor running. Do you come here often?"

"I like to keep an eye on my properties," he said.

"What are you doing here? You aren't planning on breaking in again, are you?"

"Nope. I'm just sightseeing. Strange coincidence that you always show up when I'm here."

"It's not a coincidence," Abruzzi said. "I have informants everywhere. I know everything you do."

"Everything?"

He shrugged. "Many things. For instance, I know you were at the park on Sunday. And then you had an unfortunate accident with your car."

"Some moron thought it would be cute to put spiders in my car."

"Do you like spiders?"

"They're okay. Not as much fun as bunnies, for instance."

"I understand you hit a parked car."

"One of the spiders took me by surprise."

"The element of surprise is important in a battle."

"This isn't a battle. I'm trying to put an old woman's mind at ease by finding a little girl."

"You must think I'm stupid. You're a bounty hunter. A mercenary. You know perfectly well what this is about. You're in this for the money. You know what the stakes are. And you know what I'm trying to recover. What you don't know is who you're dealing with. I'm toying with you now, but at some point the game will get boring for me. If you haven't come over to my side by the time I get bored with the game, I'll come after you with a vengeance, and I'll rip the heart out of your body while it's still beating."

Yikes.

He was dressed in a suit and tie. Very tasteful. Looked expensive. No gravy stains on the tie. He was insane, but at least he dressed well.

"Guess I'll go now," I said. "You probably want to go home and get medicated."

"Nice to know you like bunnies," he said.

I cranked the engine over and took off. Abruzzi stood there, staring after me. I checked my rearview mirror for a tail. Didn't see anyone. I wiggled around a couple streets. Still no tail. I had a bad feeling in my stomach. It felt a lot like horror.

I drove past my parents' house and noticed Uncle Sandor's Buick was parked in the driveway. My sister was using the Buick until she saved enough money to get her own car. But my sister was supposed to be at work. I pulled in behind her and popped into the house. Grandma Mazur, my mom, and Valerie were all at the kitchen table. They had coffee in front of them but no one was drinking.

I opted for a soda and took the fourth chair. "What's up?"

"Your sister got fired from her job at the bank," Grandma Mazur said. "She got into a fight with her boss, and she got herself fired, on the spot."

Valerie fighting with someone? Saint Valerie? The sister with the disposition of vanilla pudding?

When we were kids Valerie always turned her home-work in on time, made her bed before going to school, and was thought to bear an uncanny resemblance to the serene plaster statues of the Virgin Mary found on Burg lawns and in Burg churches. Even Valerie's period came and went with serenity, always arriving on sched-ule to the minute, the flow delicate, the mood swings going from nice to nicer.

I was the sister who got cramps.

"What happened?" I asked. "How could you get into a fight with your boss? You just started that job."

"She was unreasonable," Valerie said. "And mean. I made one tiny mistake, and she was horrible about it, yelling at me in front of everyone. And before I knew it I was yelling back. And then I got fired."

"You *yelled*?"

"I haven't been myself lately."

No shit. Last month she decided she was going to try being a lesbian, and this month she was yelling. What was next? Full head rotation?

"So what was the mistake?"

"I spilled some soup. That's all I did. I spilled a little soup."

"It was one of them Cup-a-Soup things," Grandma said to me. "It had them itty-bitty noodles in it. Valerie dumped the whole thing onto a computer, and it seeped between the cracks and blew out the system. They just about had to shut the bank down."

I didn't want bad things to happen to Val. Still, it was kind of nice to see her screw up after a lifetime of perfection.

"I don't suppose you remember anything new about Evelyn?" I asked Valerie. "Mary Alice said she and Annie were best friends."

"They were school friends," Valerie said. "I don't remember ever seeing Annie."

I looked over at my mother. "Did you know Annie?"

"Evelyn used to bring her around when she was younger, but they stopped visiting a couple years ago when Evelyn started having problems. And Annie never came to the house with Mary Alice. For that matter, I don't think Mary Alice ever talked about Annie."

"Least not so we could understand," Grandma said. "She might of said something in horse talk."

Valerie was looking depressed, pushing a cookie around on the kitchen table with her finger. If *I* was depressed, the cookie would be history. Come to think of it . . .

"Do you want that cookie?" I asked Valerie.

"I bet those little soup noodles looked like worms," Grandma said. "Remember when Stephanie got worms?

The doctor said they came off the lettuce. He said we didn't wash the lettuce good enough."

I'd forgotten about the worms. Not one of my favorite childhood memories. Right up there with the day I vomited spaghetti and meatballs on Anthony Balderri.

I finished my soda, ate Valerie's cookie, and went next door and checked in with Mabel.

"Anything new?" I asked Mabel.

"I got another call from the bail bonds company. They won't just come in here and throw me out, will they?"

"No. It'll have to go through legal channels. And the bond company involved is reputable."

"I haven't heard from Evelyn since she left," Mabel said. "I thought for sure I'd hear from her by now."

I returned to my car, and I tapped a call in to Dotty.

"It's Stephanie Plum," I said. "Is everything okay?"

"That woman you told me about is still sitting in front of my house. I even took the day off because she's creeping me out. I called the police, but they said they couldn't do anything."

"Do you have my card with my pager number?"

"Yes."

"Call me if you need to see Evelyn. I'll help you get past Jeanne Ellen."

I disconnected and did a palms-up in the car, all by myself. What more could I do?

I jumped when my phone rang. It was Dotty calling back. "Okay, I need help. I'm not saying I know where Evelyn is staying. I'm just saying I need to go somewhere, and I can't be followed."

"Understood. I'm about forty minutes away."

"Come in through the back again."

So maybe Jeanne Ellen was doing me a favor. She'd put Dotty into a situation where she needed me. How bizarre is that?

First thing I did was stop by the office and get Lula.

"Let's rock and roll," Lula said. "I'll distract the heck out of Jeanne Ellen. I'm the queen of distraction."

"Great. Just remember, no shooting."

"Maybe a tire," Lula said.

"Not a tire. Nothing. *No shooting.*"

"I hope you realize this puts a big crimp in my distracting."

Lula was wearing the new boots with a lemon yellow spandex miniskirt. I didn't think she'd have a distraction problem.

"This is the plan," I said when we got to South River. "I'm going to park one street over from Dotty, and we'll go in through the back. Then you can keep Jeanne Ellen busy while I take Dotty to Evelyn."

I took the shortest path through the yards and knocked once on Dotty's back door.

Dotty opened the door and stifled a scream. "Holy Jesus," she said. "I wasn't expecting . . . two people."

What she wasn't expecting was a plus-size black woman bulging out of a tiny yellow skirt.

"This is my partner, Lula," I said. "She's good at creating a distraction."

"No kidding." Dotty was dressed in jeans and sneakers. She had a bag of groceries on the kitchen table and a two-year-old under her arm.

"This is my problem," Dotty said. "I have *a friend* who has no food in the house and can't go out to get any. I want to take these groceries to her."

"Is Jeanne Ellen out front?"

"She left about ten minutes ago. She does that. She'll sit there for hours, and then she'll go away for a while, but she always comes back."

"Why don't you take the groceries to *your friend* when Jeanne Ellen leaves?"

"You said not to do that. You said even if I didn't see her she'd follow me."

"Good point. Okay, here's the plan. You and I will cut through the back and take my car. And Lula will drive your car. Lula will make sure we're not followed, and she'll decoy Jeanne Ellen off, if Jeanne Ellen appears."

"No good," Dotty said. "I have to go alone. And I need someone to sit with the kids. My sitter just punked out on me. It's going to have to be that I cut through the yard and use your car, and you take care of the kids. I won't be long."

Lula and I shouted no simultaneously.

"Not a great idea," I said. "We don't baby-sit. We don't actually know anything about kids." I looked over at Lula. "Do you know anything about kids?"

Lula shook her head vigorously. "I don't know nothing about kids. I don't *want* to know nothing about kids, either."

"If I don't get this food to Evelyn she's going to go out and get it herself. If she's recognized, she'll have to move on."

"Evelyn and Annie can't stay hidden forever," I said.

"I know that. I'm trying to straighten things out."

"By talking to Soder?"

The surprise was obvious on her face. "You were watching me, too."

"Soder didn't look happy. What were you arguing about?"

"I can't tell you. And I need to go. Please let me go."

"I want to talk to Evelyn on the phone. I need to know she's okay. If I can talk to her on the phone, I'll let you go. And Lula and I will baby-sit."

"Hold on here," Lula said. "That don't sound like a deal to me. Kids spook me out."

"Okay," Dotty said. "I don't see where it'll harm anything to let you talk to Evelyn."

She went to the living room to dial. There was a brief conversation, Dotty returned, and passed the phone to me.

"Your grandmother is worried," I told Evelyn. "She's worried about you and Annie."

"Tell her we're alright. And please stop looking for us. You're just making things more complicated."

"I'm not the person you have to worry about. Steven's hired a private investigator, and she's good at finding people."

"Dotty told me."

"I'd like to talk to you."

"I can't talk now. I have to get things straightened out first."

"What things?"

"I can't talk about it." And she hung up.

I gave Dotty the keys to my car. "Keep your eyes open for Jeanne Ellen. Check your rearview mirror for a tail."

Dotty grabbed the bag of groceries. "Don't let Scotty drink out of the toilet," she said. And then she took off.

The two-year-old was standing in the middle of the kitchen floor, looking at Lula and me like he'd never seen humans before.

"You think that's Scotty?" Lula asked.

A little girl appeared in the doorway leading to the bedrooms. "Scotty is a dog," she said. "My brother's name is Oliver. Who are you?"

"We're the baby-sitters," Lula said.

Chapter
EIGHT

"Where's Bonnie?" the little girl asked. "Bonnie always baby-sits for Oliver and me."

"Bonnie punked out," Lula said. "So you get us."

"I don't want you to baby-sit for me. You're fat."

"I'm not fat. I'm a *substantial woman.* And you better watch what you say on account of you say things like that in first grade and they'll kick your ass out of school. I bet they don't put up with that kind of talk in first grade."

"I'm going to tell my mother you said *ass.* She won't pay you after she finds out you said *ass.* And she won't ever have you baby-sit again."

"And what's the *bad* news?" Lula asked.

"This is Lula. And I'm Stephanie," I said to the little girl. "What's your name?"

"My name is Amanda, and I'm seven years old. And I don't like *you,* either."

"Bet she's gonna be a treat when she's old enough for PMS," Lula said.

"Your mom shouldn't be long," I said to Amanda. "How about we put the television on?"

"Oliver won't like that," Amanda said.

"Oliver," I said, "do you want to watch television?" Oliver shook his head. "No," he yelled. "No, no, no!" And he started crying. Loud.

"Now you did it," Lula said. "Why's he crying? Man, I can't hear myself think. Somebody get him to stop."

I bent down to Oliver's level. "Hey, big guy," I said. "What's the matter?"

"No, no, no!" he yelled. His face was brick red, scrinched up in anger.

"He keep frowning like that and he's gonna need Botox," Lula said.

I felt around in the diaper area. He didn't seem wet. He didn't have a spoon stuck up his nose. No limbs seemed to be severed. "I don't know what's wrong," I said. "I mostly know about hamsters."

"Well, don't look at me," Lula said. "I don't know nothing about kids. I never even was one. I was born in a crack house. Being a kid wasn't an option in my neighborhood."

"He's hungry," Amanda said. "He's going to cry like that until you feed him."

I found a box of cookies in the cupboard and held one out to Oliver.

"No," he yelled, and he knocked the cookie out of my hand.

A scruffy-looking dog rushed in from the bedroom area and ate the cookie before it hit the floor.

"Oliver doesn't want to eat a cookie," Amanda said.

Lula had her hands over her ears. "I'm gonna go deaf if he don't stop this howling. I'm getting a headache."

I got a bottle of juice out of the refrigerator. "Do you want this?" I asked.

"No!"

I tried ice cream.

"No!"

"How about a leg of lamb?" Lula asked. "I wouldn't mind having some leg of lamb."

He was on the floor now, on his back, kicking his heels against the tile. "No, no, no!"

"This here's a full-blown tantrum," Lula said. "This kid needs a time-out."

"I'm telling my mother you made Oliver cry," Amanda said.

"Hey, give me a break," I said. "I'm trying. You're his sister. Help me out here."

"He wants a grilled cheese sandwich," Amanda said. "It's his favorite food."

"Good thing he didn't want the leg of lamb," Lula said. "We wouldn't know how to cook that."

I found a pan and some butter and cheese, and I started the bread frying in the pan. Oliver was still bellowing at the top of his lungs, and now the dog was yapping, running in circles around him.

The doorbell rang, and I figured with the sort of luck I was having it was probably Jeanne Ellen. I left Lula in charge of the grilled cheese sandwich, and I went to answer the door. I was wrong about it being Jeanne Ellen, but I was right about my luck. It was Steven Soder.

"What the hell?" he said. "What are you doing here?"

"Visiting."

"Where's Dotty? I need to talk to her."

"Hey," Lula called from the kitchen, "I need an opinion on this grilled cheese."

"Who's that?" Soder wanted to know. "That doesn't sound like Dotty. That sounds like the fatso who hit me with her purse."

"We're in the middle of something right now," I said to Soder. "Maybe you could come back later."

He muscled his way past me and stalked into the kitchen. "You!" he shouted at Lula. "I'm going to kill you."

"Not in front of the k-i-d," Lula said. "You don't want to use that kind of violent talk. It stirs up all kinds of latent shit when they get to be teenagers."

"I'm not stupid," Amanda said. "I can spell. And I'm telling my mother you said *shit*."

"Everybody says *shit*," Lula said. She looked to me. "Doesn't everybody say *shit*? What's wrong with *shit*?"

The grilled cheese looked perfect in the fry pan, so I lifted it out with a spatula, slid it onto a plate, and gave it to Oliver. The dog stopped running in circles, snatched the sandwich off the plate, and ate it. And Oliver went back to howling.

"Oliver has to eat at the table," Amanda said.

"There's a lot of stuff to remember in this house," Lula said.

"I want to talk to Dotty," Soder said.

"Dotty isn't here," I yelled over Oliver's screaming. "Talk to me."

"In your dreams," Soder said. "And for crissake, somebody get this kid to shut up."

"The dog ate his sandwich," Lula said. "And it's all your fault on account of you distracted us."

"So do your Aunt Jemima thing and make him another sandwich," Soder said.

Lula's eyes bugged out of her head. "Aunt Jemima? Excuse me? Did you say Aunt Jemima?" She leaned forward so her nose was inches from Soder's, hands on hips, one hand still holding tight to the fry pan. "Listen to me, you punk-ass loser, you don't want to call me no Aunt Jemima or I'm gonna *give* you Aunt Jemima in the face with this fry pan. Only thing stopping me is I don't want to k-i-l-l you in front of the b-r-a-t-s."

I saw Lula's point, but being working-class white I had a totally different perspective on Aunt Jemima. Aunt Jemima conjured nothing but good memories of steaming pancakes dripping with syrup. I loved Aunt Jemima.

"Knock, knock," Jeanne Ellen said at the open door. "Can anyone come to this party?"

Jeanne Ellen was back to being dressed in the black leather outfit.

"Wow," Amanda said, "are you Catwoman?"

"Michelle Pfeiffer was Catwoman," Jeanne Ellen said. She looked down at Oliver. He was on his back again, kicking and screaming. "Stop," Jeanne Ellen said to Oliver.

Oliver blinked twice and stuck his thumb in his mouth.

Jeanne Ellen smiled at me. "Baby-sitting?"

"Yep."

"Nice."

"Your client is being intrusive," I said.

"My apologies," Jeanne Ellen said. "We're leaving now."

Amanda, Oliver, Lula, and I all stood like statues until the front door closed behind Jeanne Ellen and Soder. Then Oliver went back to his screaming.

Lula tried the stop thing but Oliver only screamed louder. So we made him another grilled cheese.

Oliver was finishing his sandwich when Dotty returned.

"How'd it go?" Dotty asked.

Amanda looked at her mother. Then she took a long look at Lula and me. "Fine," Amanda said. "I'm going to watch television now."

"Steven Soder stopped by," I said.

Dotty's face went ashen. "He was here? Soder came here?"

"He said he wanted to talk to you."

Color flamed on her cheekbones. She put a hand to Oliver. A mother's protective gesture. She smoothed the baby-fine hair back from Oliver's forehead. "I hope Oliver wasn't too much trouble."

"Oliver was terrific," I said. "It took us a while to

figure out he wanted a grilled cheese sandwich, but after that he was terrific."

"Sometimes being a single mom gets a little overwhelming," Dotty said. "The responsibility of it. And the alone part. It's okay when everything's going normal, but sometimes you wish there was another adult in the house."

"You're afraid of Soder," I said.

"He's a terrible person."

"You should tell me what's going on. I could help." At least I *hoped* I could help.

"I need to think," Dotty said. "I appreciate your offer, but I need to think."

"I'll stop around tomorrow morning to make sure you're okay," I said. "Maybe we can straighten this out tomorrow."

Lula and I were halfway to Trenton before either of us spoke.

"Life just gets weirder and weirder," Lula finally said.

That pretty much summed it up as far as I was concerned. I suppose I'd made progress. I'd spoken to Evelyn. I knew she was safe for now. And I knew she wasn't all that far away. Dotty had been gone less than an hour.

Soder was bothersome, but I could understand his actions. He was a jerk, but he was also a distraught dad. Most likely Dotty was negotiating some sort of truce between Soder and Evelyn.

What I couldn't understand was Jeanne Ellen. The fact that Jeanne Ellen was still doing surveillance bothered me. The surveillance seemed pointless now that Dotty knew about Jeanne Ellen. So why was Jeanne Ellen sitting across from Dotty's house when we left? It was possible that Jeanne Ellen was exerting pressure in the form of harassment. Make Dotty's life unpleasant and try to get her to cave. There was another possibility that felt pretty far out but had to be considered. Protection. Jeanne Ellen was sitting out there like the Queen's Guard. Maybe Jeanne Ellen was guarding the link to Evelyn and Annie. This led to a bunch of questions I couldn't answer. Such as, *who* was Jeanne Ellen guarding Dotty *from?* Abruzzi?

"You gonna show up at nine?" Lula asked when I pulled to a stop in front of the bonds office.

"I guess so. How about you?"

"Wouldn't miss it for anything."

I stopped at the store on the way home and picked up a few groceries. By the time I reached my apartment it was dinnertime and the building was filled with cooking smells. Minestrone soup simmering behind Mrs. Karwatt's door. Burritos from the other end of the hall.

I approached my door with my key in my hand, and I froze. If Abruzzi could get into my locked car, he could get into my locked apartment. I needed to be careful. I put the key in the lock. I turned the key. I opened the door. I stood in the hall with the door open for a moment, taking in the feel of my apartment. Listening to the silence. Reassured by my heartbeat and the fact that a pack of wild dogs didn't rush out to devour me.

I crossed the threshold, left my front door wide open, and walked through the rooms, carefully opening drawers and closet doors. No surprises, thank God. Still, my stomach felt icky. I was having a hard time pushing Abruzzi's threat out of my head.

"Knock, knock," a voice called from the open doorway.

Kloughn.

"I was in the neighborhood," he said, "so I thought I'd say hello. I have some Chinese food with me, too. I got it for myself, but I got too much. I thought you might want some. But you don't have to eat it if you don't want to. But then if you want to eat it, that would be great. I didn't know if you liked Chinese food. Or if you liked to eat alone. Or . . ."

I grabbed Kloughn and pulled him into my apartment.

"What's this?" Vinnie said when I showed up with Kloughn.

"Albert Kloughn," I told him, "attorney at law."

"And?"

"He brought me supper, so I invited him along."

"He looks like the Pillsbury Doughboy. What'd he bring you to eat, dinner rolls?"

"Chinese," Kloughn said. "It was one of those last-minute things that I just felt like eating Chinese."

"I'm not crazy about taking a lawyer along on a bust," Vinnie said.

"I won't sue you, I swear to God," Kloughn said. "And look, I have a flashlight and defense spray and everything. I'm thinking about getting a gun, but I can't decide if I want a six shooter or a semiautomatic. I'm sort of leaning to the semiautomatic."

"Go with the semiautomatic," Lula said. "It holds more bullets. You can never have too many bullets."

"I want a vest," I said to Vinnie. "Last time I did a takedown with you, you shot everything to smithereens."

"That was an unusual circumstance," Vinnie said.

Yeah, right.

I got Kloughn and myself suited up in Kevlar, and we all packed off in Vinnie's Cadillac.

A half hour later we were parked around the corner from Bender. "Now you're going to see how a professional operates," Vinnie said. "I have a plan, and I expect everyone to do their part, so listen up."

"Oh boy," Lula said. "A plan."

"Stephanie and I will take the front door," Vinnie said. "Lula and the clown will take the back door. We all enter at the same time and subdue the rat bastard."

"That's some plan," Lula said. "I would never have thought of that one."

"K-l-o-u-g-h-n," Albert said.

"All you have to do is listen for me to yell 'bond enforcement,'" Vinnie said. "Then we crash down the doors and rush in with everyone yelling 'freeze . . . bond enforcement.'"

"I'm not doing that," I said. "I'll feel like an idiot. They only do that on television."

"I like it," Lula said. "I always wanted to crash down a door and yell stuff."

"I could be wrong," Kloughn said, "but crashing down doors might be illegal."

Vinnie buckled himself into a nylon webbed gun belt. "It's only illegal if it's the wrong house."

Lula took a Glock out of her purse and shoved it into the waistband of her spandex miniskirt. "I'm ready," she said. "Too bad we don't have a TV crew with us. This yellow skirt would show up real good."

"I'm ready, too," Kloughn said. "I've got a flashlight in case the lights go off."

I didn't want to alarm him, but that's not why bounty hunters carry two-pound Mag lights.

"Has anyone checked to make sure Bender is home?" I asked. "Anyone talk to his wife?"

"We'll listen under the window," Vinnie said. "It looks like someone's watching television in there."

We all tiptoed across the lawn and pressed ourselves against the building and listened under the window.

"Sounds like a movie," Kloughn said. "Sounds like a *dirty* movie."

"Then Bender's gotta be here," Vinnie said. "His wife

isn't going to be sitting around all by herself, watching a porno flick."

Lula and Kloughn went around to the back door, and Vinnie and I went to the front door. Vinnie drew his gun and rapped on the door, which had been patched with a big piece of plywood.

"Open up," Vinnie shouted. "Bond enforcement!" He took a step back and was ready to give the door a kick with his boot when we heard Lula break into the house from the rear, yelling at the top of her lungs.

Before we had a chance to react, the front door burst open and a naked guy rushed out at us, almost knocking me off the stoop. Inside the house there was pandemonium. Men were scrambling to leave, some of them naked, some of them dressed, all of them waving guns, shouting, "Outta my way, muthafucka!"

Lula was in the middle of it. "Hey," she was yelling, "this here's a bond enforcement operation! Everybody stop running!"

Vinnie and I had worked our way into the middle of the room, but we couldn't find Bender. Too many men in too small a space, all trying to get out of the house. No one cared that Vinnie had his gun drawn. I'm not sure anyone noticed in the mayhem.

Vinnie got off a round and a chunk of ceiling fell down. After that, it was quiet because no one was left in the room but Vinnie, Lula, Kloughn, and me.

"What happened?" Lula asked. "What just happened here?"

"I didn't see Bender," Vinnie said. "Is this the right house?"

"Vinnie?" A female voice called from the bedroom. "Vinnie, is that you?"

Vinnie's eyes opened wide. "Candy?"

A naked woman somewhere in age between twenty and fifty bounced out of the bedroom. She had gigantic breasts and her pubic hair cut into the shape of a thunderbolt. She held her arms out to Vinnie. "Long time no see," she said. "What's up?"

A second woman straggled from the bedroom. "Is it really Vinnie?" she asked. "What's he doing here?"

I eased into the bedroom behind the women and looked for Bender. The bedroom was set with lights and a discarded camera. They hadn't been watching a porno . . . they'd been making one.

"Bender isn't in the bedroom or bathroom," I said to Vinnie. "And that's the whole house."

"You looking for Andy?" Candy asked. "He split earlier. He said he had work to do. That's why we borrowed his place. Nice and private. At least until you showed up."

"We thought we was getting busted," the other woman said. "We thought you was the cops."

Kloughn gave each of the women his card. "Albert Kloughn, attorney at law," he said. "If you ever need a lawyer."

An hour later, I pulled into my lot with Kloughn yammering away alongside me. I had Godsmack plugged into my CD player, but I couldn't get the volume loud enough to totally drown out Kloughn.

"Boy, that was something," Kloughn said. "I've never seen a movie star up close before. And especially naked ones. I didn't look too much, did I? I mean, you couldn't help looking, right? Even *you* looked, right?"

Right. But *I* didn't get down on my knees to examine the pubic hair thunderbolt.

I parked and walked Kloughn to his car, making sure he got safely out of the lot. I turned to go into the building and let out a yelp when I bumped into Ranger.

He was standing close, and he was smiling. "Big date?"

"It's been a strange day."

"How strange?"

I told him about Vinnie and the porno movie.

Ranger tipped his head back and laughed out loud. Not something I see very often.

"Is this a social visit?" I asked.

"As social as I get. I'm on my way home from a job."

"Home to the Bat Cave." No one knew where Ranger lived. The address on his driver's license was a vacant lot.

"Yeah. The Bat Cave," Ranger said.

"I'd like to see the Bat Cave sometime."

Our eyes held.

"Maybe someday," he said. "Looks like you could use some bodywork on your car."

I told him about the spiders and about Abruzzi suggesting to me that at some point in time he'd rip my heart out.

"Let me get this straight," Ranger said. "You were driving along after being attacked by a flock of geese, and a spider jumped at you and caused you to smash into a parked car."

"Stop smiling," I said. "It isn't funny. I *hate* spiders."

He slung an arm around my shoulders. "I know you do, babe. And you're worried Abruzzi will make good on his threat."

"Yes."

"You have too many dangerous men in your life."

I looked at him sideways. "Do you have any suggestions on how I can cut the list down?"

"You could kill Abruzzi."

I raised my eyebrows.

"No one would mind," Ranger said. "He's not a popular guy."

"And the other dangerous men in my life?"

"Not life threatening. You might get your heart *broken,* but you won't get it ripped out of your body."

Oh boy. That's supposed to make me feel relaxed?

"Aside from your suggestion of killing Abruzzi, I don't know how to get him to stop," I said to Ranger. "Soder might want his daughter back, but Abruzzi is after something else. And whatever it is that Abruzzi is after, he thinks I'm after it, too." I looked up at my window. I wasn't real crazy about entering my apartment alone. The heart-ripping-out thing still had me feeling spooked. And every now and then I felt nonexistent spiders crawling on me. "So," I said, "as long as you're here, I don't suppose you'd want to come up and have a glass of wine?"

"Are you inviting me for more than wine?"

"Sort of."

"Let me take a guess. You want me to make sure your apartment is secure."

"Yes."

He beeped his car locked, and when we got to the second floor, he took my key and he opened my apartment door. He flipped the lights on and looked around. Rex was running on his wheel.

"Maybe you should teach him to bark," Ranger said.

He prowled through my living room, into my bedroom. He flipped the light on and looked around. He raised the dust ruffle and looked under the bed. "You need to get a mop under there, babe," he said. He moved to the dresser and opened each drawer. Nothing jumped out. He stuck his head into the bathroom. All clear.

"No snakes, no spiders, no bad guys," Ranger said. He reached out, grasped the collar on my denim jacket with both hands, and pulled me to him, his fingers lightly brushing my neck. "You're running up a bill. I assume you'll tell me when you're ready to settle your account."

"Sure. Absolutely. You'll be the first to know." God, I was being such a dork!

Ranger grinned down at me. "You have cuffs, right?"

Ulk. "Actually, no. I'm currently cuffless."

"How are you going to catch the bad guys if you haven't got cuffs?"

"It's a problem."

"I have cuffs," Ranger said, touching his knee to mine.

My heart was up to about two hundred beats per minute. I wasn't exactly a handcuff-me-to-the-bed kind of person. I was more a turn-out-all-the-lights-and-hope-for-the-best kind of person. "I think I'm hyperventilating," I said. "If I pass out just hold a paper bag over my nose and mouth."

"Babe," Ranger said, "it's not the end of the world to sleep with me."

"There are issues."

He raised an eyebrow. "Issues?"

"Well, actually, relationships."

"Are you in a relationship?" Ranger asked.

"No. Are you?"

"My lifestyle doesn't lend itself to relationships."

"Do you know what we need? Wine."

He released my jacket collar and followed me into the kitchen. He lounged against the counter while I took two wineglasses from the cupboard and grabbed the bottle of merlot that I'd just bought. I poured out two glasses, gave one to Ranger, and kept one for myself.

"Cheers," I said. And I chugged the wine.

Ranger took a sip. "Feel better?"

"I'm getting there. I hardly feel like fainting anymore. And most of the nausea is gone." I refilled my glass and carted the bottle into the living room. "So," I said, "would you like to watch television?"

He picked the remote off the coffee table and relaxed into the couch. "Let me know when you're nausea-free."

"I think it was the handcuff thing that pushed me over the edge."

"I'm disappointed. I thought it was the idea of me naked." He searched through the sports and settled on basketball. "Are you okay with basketball? Or would you rather I search for a violent movie?"

"Basketball is good."

Okay, I know I was the one who suggested television, but now that I had Ranger on my couch it felt too weird. He had his dark hair slicked back into a ponytail. He was dressed in SWAT blacks, fully loaded gun belt removed but a nine-millimeter at the small of his back, Navy SEAL watch on his wrist. And he was slouched on my couch, watching basketball.

I noticed my wineglass was empty, and I poured myself a third glass.

"This feels odd," I said. "Do you watch basketball in the Bat Cave?"

"I don't have a lot of free time for television."

"But the Bat Cave *has* a television?"

"Yeah, the Bat Cave has a television."

"Just curious," I said.

He drank some wine, and he watched me. He was different from Morelli. Morelli was a tightly coiled spring. I was always aware of contained energy with Morelli. Ranger was a cat. Quiet. Every muscle relaxed on command. Probably did yoga. Might not be human.

"*Now* what are you thinking?" he asked.

"I was wondering if you were human."

"What are the other choices?"

I knocked back my glass of wine. "I didn't have anything else specifically in mind."

I woke up with a headache and my tongue stuck to the roof of my mouth. I was on my couch, tucked under the quilt from my bed. The television was silent, and Ranger was gone. From what I could remember, I'd seen about five minutes of basketball before falling asleep. I'm a cheap drunk. Two and a half glasses of wine and I'm comatose.

I stood under a hot shower until I was pruney and the throbbing behind my eyes had partially subsided. I got dressed and made tracks to McDonald's. I got a large fries and a Coke at the drive-thru and ate in the parking lot. This is the Stephanie Plum cure for a hangover. My cell phone rang when I was halfway through with the fries.

"Did you hear about the fire?" Grandma asked. "Do you know anything about it?"

"What fire?"

"Steven Soder's bar burned to the ground last night. Technically, I guess it burned this morning, since it was after closing when it caught fire. Lorraine Zupek just called. Her grandson is a firefighter, you know. He told her they had every truck in the city there but there wasn't anything they could do. I guess they're thinking it might have been arson."

"Was anyone hurt?"

"Lorraine didn't say."

I shoved a handful of fries into my mouth and cranked the engine over. I wanted to see the fire scene. I'm not sure why. Ghoulish curiosity, I guess. If Soder had *partners,* then this wasn't entirely unexpected. Partners were known to come into a business sometimes, drain it of all profits, and then destroy it.

It took me twenty minutes to get through town. The street in front of The Foxhole was closed to traffic, so I parked two blocks away and walked. A fire truck was still on the scene, and a couple cop cars were angled into the curb. A photographer from the *Trenton Times* was taking pictures. Crime-scene tape hadn't been stretched, but sightseers were kept at a distance by the police.

The brick face was blackened. Windows were gone.

There were two levels of apartments above the bar. They looked totally destroyed. Sooty water pooled on the street and sidewalk. A hose snaked into the building from the one remaining truck but it wasn't in use.

"Was anyone hurt?" I asked one of the bystanders.

"Doesn't look like it," he said. "It was after-hours for the bar. And the apartments were empty. There were some code violations, so they were being renovated."

"Do they know how the fire got started?"

"Nobody's said."

I didn't recognize any of the cops or firefighters. I didn't see Soder anywhere. I took one last look, and I left. A quick stop at the office was next on my list. Connie should have the more complete background check on Evelyn by now.

"Jeez," Lula said when I walked in, "you don't look so good."

"Hangover," I said. "I ran into Ranger after I dropped Kloughn off, and we had a couple glasses of wine."

Connie and Lula stopped what they were doing and stared at me.

"Well?" Lula said. "You're not going to stop there, are you? What happened?"

"Nothing happened. I was sort of creeped out about the spiders and stuff, so Ranger came in with me to make sure everything was okay. We had a couple glasses of wine. And he left."

"Yeah, but what about the part between the *drinking* and the *leaving?* What happened there?"

"Nothing happened."

"Hold on here," Lula said. "You're telling me you had Ranger in your apartment, the two of you are drinking wine, and nothing happened. No fooling around at all."

"That makes no sense," Connie said. "Anytime the two of you are in this office, he's looking at you like you're lunch. There has to be some explanation. Your grandma was there, right?"

"It was just the two of us. Just Ranger and me."

"Did you put him off? You smack him, or something?" Lula asked.

"It wasn't like that. It was friendly." In an uncomfortably tense sort of way.

"Friendly," Lula said. "Hunh."

"So how do you feel about that?" Connie asked me.

"I don't know," I said. "I guess friendly is good."

"Yeah, except naked and sweaty would be better," Lula said.

We all thought about that for a moment.

Connie fanned herself with a steno pad. "Whew," she said. "Hot flash."

I resisted looking down to see if my nipples were hard. "Did Evelyn's report come in?"

Connie leafed through a stack of folders on her desk and pulled one out. "Just got it this morning."

I took the folder and read down the first page. I turned to the second page."

"Not a lot there," Connie said. "Evelyn stuck pretty close to home. Even as a kid."

I stuffed the folder into my bag and looked up at the video camera. "Is Vinnie here?"

"He hasn't come in yet. Probably got Candy inflating his ego," Lula said.

Chapter
NINE

I read through Evelyn's file one more time when I got to my car. Some of the information seemed invasive, but this is the age of data for anyone interested. I had a credit report and some medical history. Nothing struck me as incredibly helpful.

A rap on my passenger-side window pulled me away from the file. It was Morelli. I unlocked the door, and he slid in next to me.

"Hung over?" he asked, but it was more of a statement than a question.

"How'd you know?"

He poked at the fast-food carton. "McDonald's french fries and Coke for breakfast. Dark circles under your eyes. Hair from hell."

I checked out my hair in the rearview mirror. *Yow.* "I overdid the wine last night."

He took that in. Nothing was said for a long moment. I didn't volunteer more. He didn't ask.

He looked at the file in my hand. "Are you getting any closer to Evelyn?"

"I've made some progress."

"You heard about Soder's bar."

"I just came from there," I said. "It looked bad. Lucky no one was in the building."

"Yeah, except so far we haven't been able to locate Soder. His girlfriend said he never came home."

"Do you think he could have been in the bar when the fire broke out?"

"The guys are in there checking. They had to wait for the building to cool. No sign of him so far. I thought you'd want to know." Morelli had his hand on the door handle. "I'll let you know if we find him."

"Wait a minute. I have a theoretical question. Suppose you were watching television with me. And we were alone in my apartment. And I had a couple glasses of wine, and I sort of passed out. Would you try to make love to me, anyway? Would you do a little *exploring* while I was asleep?"

"What are we watching? Is it the play-offs?"

"You can leave now," I said.

Morelli grinned and got out of the car.

I dialed Dotty's number on my cell phone. I was anxious to tell her the news about the bar and about Soder going missing. The phone rang a bunch of times and the machine picked it up. I left a message for a callback and tried her work number. I got her voice mail at work. Dotty was on vacation, scheduled to return in two weeks.

The voice mail message sent a strange emotion curling through my stomach. I searched for a name for the emotion. Unease was the closest I could come.

In less than an hour, I was parked in front of Dotty's house. No sign of Jeanne Ellen. And no sign of life in Dotty's house. No car in the driveway. No doors or windows opened. Nothing wrong with that, I told myself. The kids would be in school and day care at this time of day. And Dotty was probably out shopping.

I walked to the door and rang the bell. No one answered. I looked in the front window. The house looked at rest. No lights on. No television blaring. No kids running around. The bad feeling crept into my stomach again. Something was wrong. I walked around and looked in the back window. The kitchen was tidy. No signs of breakfast. No bowls in the sink. No cereal boxes left out. I tried the doorknob. Locked. I knocked on the door. No response. That's when it hit me. No dog. The dog should be running around, barking at the door. It was a one-story ranch. I circled the house and looked in every window. No dog.

Okay, so she's walking the dog. Or maybe she took the dog to the vet. I tried Dotty's two closest neighbors. Neither knew what had happened to Dotty and the dog. Both had noticed they were missing this morning. The consensus was that Dotty and her family vacated the house sometime during the night.

No Dotty. No dog. No Jeanne Ellen. I had other names for the thing in my stomach now. Panic. Fear. With a touch of nausea from the hangover.

I went back to my car and sat in front of the house for a while, taking it all in. At some point I looked down at my watch and realized an hour had passed. I suppose I was hoping Dotty would return. And I suppose I knew it wasn't going to happen.

When I was nine years old I persuaded my mom to let me get a parakeet. On the way home from the pet store the door to the cage came open somehow, and the bird flew away. That's what this felt like. It felt like I left the door open.

I put the car in gear and drove back to the Burg. I went straight to Dotty's parents' house. Mrs. Palowski answered my knock, and Dotty's dog came running from the kitchen, yapping the whole way.

I dredged up my biggest and best phony smile for Mrs. Palowski. "Hi," I said, "I'm looking for Dotty."

"You just missed her," Mrs. Palowski said. "She dropped Scotty off early this morning. We're baby-sitting him while Dotty and the children are on vacation."

"I really need to talk to her," I said. "Do you have a phone number where she can be reached?"

"I don't. She said she was going camping with a friend. A cabin in the woods somewhere. She said she'd be in touch, though. I could give her a message."

I gave Mrs. Palowski my card. "Tell Dotty I have very important information for her. And ask her to call me."

"Dotty isn't in any kind of trouble, is she?" Mrs. Palowski asked.

"No. This is information about one of Dotty's friends."

"It's Evelyn, isn't it? I heard Evelyn and Annie were missing. That's such a shame. Evelyn and Dotty used to be such good friends."

"Do they still get together?"

"Not for years, now. Evelyn kept to herself after she married. I think Steven made it difficult for her to have friends."

I thanked Mrs. Palowski for her time and returned to my car. I reread the report on Evelyn. No mention of a secret cabin in the woods.

My phone chirped, and I wasn't sure what I hoped for . . . a date was high on the list. Next might be news about Soder or a friendly call from Evelyn.

Close to last on the list was a call from my mother. "Help," she said.

Then my grandmother got on the phone. "You gotta come over and see this," she said.

"See what?"

"You gotta see for yourself."

My parents' house was less than five minutes away. My mother and grandmother were at the door, waiting for me. They stepped aside and motioned me into the living room. My sister was there, slouched in my father's favorite chair. She was dressed in a rumpled long flannel nightgown and furry bedroom slippers. Yesterday's mascara hadn't been removed but had been smudged by sleep. Her hair was snarled and untamed. Meg Ryan meets Beetlejuice. California girl goes to Transylvania. She had the television remote in her hand, her attention glued to a game show. The floor around her was littered with candy bar wrappers and empty soda cans. She didn't acknowledge our presence. She burped and scratched her boob and changed the channel.

This was my perfect sister. Saint Valerie.

"I see that smile," my mother said to me. "It's not funny. She's been like that ever since she lost her job."

"Yeah, we had to vacuum around her this morning," Grandma said. "I came too close and almost sucked up one of those bunny slippers."

"She's depressed," my mother said.

No shit.

"We thought maybe you could help get her a job," Grandma said. "Something that would get her out of the house, on account of now *we're* getting depressed looking at her. Bad enough we got to look at your father."

"You're always the one with the jobs," I said to my mother. "You always know when they're hiring at the button factory."

"She ran through all my contacts," my mother said. "I'm left with nothing. And unemployment is up. I can't get her a job boxing tampons."

"Maybe you could take her along with you on a bust," Grandma said. "Maybe that'd perk her spirits up."

"No way," I said. "She already tried being a bounty hunter, and she fainted the first time someone held a gun to her head."

My mother made the sign of the cross. "Dear God," she said.

"Well, you gotta do something," Grandma said. "I'm missing all my TV shows. I tried to change the channel, and she growled at me."

"She growled at you?"

"It was scary."

"Hey, Valerie," I said. "Is there a problem?"

No response.

"I got an idea," Grandma said. "Why don't we give her a zap with your stun gun? Then when she's out cold we can get the remote."

I thought about the stun gun in my bag. I wouldn't mind testing it. I wouldn't even mind zapping Valerie. Truth is, I've secretly wanted to zap Valerie for years. I slid a look at my mother and was instantly discouraged.

"Maybe I can get you a job," I said to Valerie. "Would you be willing to work for a lawyer?"

She kept focused on the television. "Is he married?"

"No."

"Gay?"

"I don't think so."

"How old is he?"

"I'm not sure. Sixteen, maybe." I hauled my cell phone out of my bag and called Kloughn.

"Wow, that would be great if your sister would work for me," Kloughn said. "She could have all the time she wants for lunch. And she could do her laundry while she works."

I severed the connection and turned to Valerie. "You have a job."

"Bummer," Valerie said. "I was just starting to get the hang of this depression thing. Do you think this guy will marry me?"

I did some internal eye rolling, wrote Kloughn's name and address on a piece of paper, and gave it to

Valerie. "You can start tomorrow at nine. If he's late, you can wait for him in the Laundromat. You won't have any trouble recognizing him. He's the guy with the two black eyes."

My mother did another sign of the cross.

I swiped a couple slices of baloney and a slice of cheese from the fridge and headed for the door. I wanted to get out of the house before I had to answer any more questions about Albert Kloughn.

The phone rang as I was leaving.

"Hold up," Grandma said to me. "This here's Florence Szuch, and she says she's at the mall, and she says Evelyn Soder is eating lunch in the food court."

I took off running, and Grandma was right behind me.

"I'm going, too," Grandma said. "I got a right, on account of how it was my snitch that called."

We jumped into the car, and I rocketed away. The mall was twenty minutes on a good day. I hoped Evelyn was a slow eater.

"Was she sure it was Evelyn?"

"Yep. Evelyn and Annie, and another woman and her two children."

Dotty and her kids.

"I didn't have time to get my purse," Grandma said. "So I haven't got a gun. I'm going to be real disappointed if there's shooting, and I'm the only one without a gun."

If my mother knew my grandmother was carrying a gun around in her purse she'd have a cow. "First off, *I* haven't got a gun," I said. "And second thing, there won't be any shooting."

I hit Route 1 and put my foot to the floor. This brought me into the flow of traffic. In Jersey we think the speed limit is merely a suggestion. No one in Jersey would actually *do* the speed limit.

"You should be a race car driver," Grandma said. "You'd be good at it. You could drive in them NASCAR races. I'd do it, but probably you need a driver's license, and I don't have one of those."

I saw the sign for the shopping center and took the off-ramp with my fingers crossed. What had started as a courtesy to Mabel had become a crusade. I *really* wanted to talk to Evelyn. Evelyn was critical to ending the crazy war game. And ending the war game was critical to not getting my heart ripped out.

I knew every square inch of the mall, and I parked at the entrance to the food court. I wanted to tell Grandma to wait in the car, but that would have been wasted energy.

"If Evelyn is still there, I need to talk to her alone," I said to Grandma. "You're going to have to stay out of sight."

"Sure," Grandma said. "I can do that."

We entered the mall together and quickly walked to the food court. I watched the people while I walked, looking for Evelyn or Dotty. The mall was moderately full. Not jammed like on weekends. Just enough people to give me cover. My breath caught when I recognized Dotty and her kids. I'd memorized the photo of Evelyn and Annie, and they were there, too.

"Now that I'm here, I wouldn't mind having a big pretzel," Grandma said.

"You get a pretzel, and I'll talk to Evelyn. Just don't leave the food court."

I stepped away from Grandma and the light suddenly dimmed in front of me. I was in the shadow of Martin Paulson. He didn't look much different than he had in the police station parking lot, rolling around on the ground, trussed up in shackles and handcuffs. I imagine fashion choices are limited when you're shaped like Paulson.

"Well, lookey here," Paulson said. "It's Little Miss Asshole."

"Not now," I said, moving around him.

He moved with me, blocking my way. "I have a score to settle with you."

What are the chances? I finally find Evelyn, and I run into Martin Paulson, itching for a fight. "Forget it," I said. "What are you doing here anyway?"

"I work here. I work at the drugstore, and I'm on my lunch break. I was falsely accused, you know."

Yeah, right. "Get out of my way."

"Make me."

I pulled the stun gun out of my bag, rammed it into Paulson's big belly, and hit the button. Nothing happened.

Paulson looked down at the stun gun. "What is that, a toy?"

"It's a stun gun." A worthless piece of crap stun gun.

Paulson took it from me and looked at it. "Cool," he said. He turned it off, and then he turned it on. And then he touched it to my arm. There was a flash of light in my head, and everything went black.

Before the blackness turned back to light, I could hear voices, far away. I struggled to get to the voices and they became louder, more distinct. I managed to get my eyes open, and faces swam into view. I tried to blink away the buzzing, and I took an assessment of the situation. Flat on my back on the floor. Paramedics hovering over me. Oxygen mask over my nose. Blood pressure cuff on my arm. Grandma beyond the paramedics, looking worried. Paulson beyond Grandma, peeking at me over her shoulder. *Paulson*. Now I remember. The son of a bitch knocked me out with my own stun gun!

I jumped up and lunged at Paulson. My legs gave out and I went down to my knees. "Paulson, you pig!" I yelled.

Paulson ducked back and disappeared.

I was trying to get the oxygen mask off, and the paramedics were trying to keep it on. It was the attack of
the geese all over again.

"I thought you were dead," Grandma said.

"Not nearly. I accidentally came into contact with my
stun gun when it was live."

"Now I recognize you," one of the paramedics said
to me. "You're the bounty hunter who burned the funeral home down."

"I burned it down, too," Grandma said. "You should
have been there. It was like fireworks."

I stood and tested my ability to walk. I was a little
creaky, but I didn't fall down. That was a good sign,
right?

Grandma handed me my shoulder bag. "That nice
round man gave me your stun gun. I guess it got
dropped in all the excitement. I put it in your bag,"
she said.

First chance I got I was going to pitch the damn stun
gun into the Delaware River. I looked around, but Evelyn was long gone. "I don't suppose you saw Evelyn or
Annie?" I asked Grandma.

"No. I got myself one of those big soft pretzels, and
I had them dip it in chocolate."

I dropped Grandma off at my parents' house, and I went
home to my apartment. I stood in the hall at the door
for a moment before inserting the key in the lock. I took
a deep breath, unlocked the door, and pushed it open. I
stepped into the small foyer area, and I very softly sang,
who's afraid of the big bad wolf. . . . I peeked into my
kitchen and felt a sense of relief. Everything was okay in
the kitchen. I moved into the living room and stopped
singing. Steven Soder was sitting on my couch. He was
listing slightly to one side, holding the remote in his right
hand, but he wasn't watching television. He was dead,

dead, dead. His eyes were milky and unseeing, his lips were parted, as if he'd been surprised, his skin was ghoulishly bloodless, and he had a bullet hole in the middle of his forehead. He was wearing a baggy sweater and khaki slacks. And he was barefoot.

Criminey, isn't it bad enough I have a dead guy sitting on my couch? Does he have to be freaking barefoot?

I silently backed out of the room, and out of my apartment. I stood in the hall and tried to dial 911 on my cell phone, but my hands were shaking, and I had to try several times before I got it right.

I stayed in the hall until the police arrived. When my apartment was swarming with cops, I crept back into my kitchen, wrapped my arms around Rex's cage, and took Rex out of the apartment into the hall with me.

I was still in the hall, holding the hamster cage, when Morelli arrived. Mrs. Karwatt from next door and Irma Brown from upstairs were with me. Beyond Mr. Wolesky's door I could hear Regis. Not even for a homicide would Mr. Wolesky miss Regis. No matter it was a rerun.

I was sitting on the floor, back to the wall, hamster cage on my lap. Morelli squatted next to me and looked in at Rex. "Is he okay?"

I nodded yes.

"How about you?" Morelli asked. "Are you okay?"

My eyes filled with tears. I wasn't okay.

"He was sitting on the couch," Irma said to Morelli. "Can you imagine? Just sitting there with the remote in his hand." She shook her head. "That couch has death cooties now. I'd cry, too, if my couch had death cooties."

"There's no such thing as death cooties," Mrs. Karwatt said.

Irma looked over at her. "Would *you* sit on that couch, now?"

Mrs. Karwatt pressed her lips together.

"Well?" Irma asked.

"Maybe if it was washed real good."

"You can't wash away death cooties," Irma said. End of discussion. Voice of authority.

Morelli sat next to me, his back to the wall, too. Mrs. Karwatt left. And Irma left. And it was just Morelli and me and Rex.

"So what do you think about death cooties?" Morelli asked me.

"I don't know what the hell death cooties are, but I'm creeped out enough to want to get rid of the couch. And I'm going to boil the remote and dip it in bleach."

"This is bad," Morelli said. "This isn't fun and games anymore. Did Mrs. Karwatt hear or see anything unusual?"

I shook my head no. "Home is supposed to be the safe place," I said to Morelli. "Where do you go when your home doesn't feel safe anymore?"

"I don't know," Morelli said. "I've never had to face that."

It was hours before the body was removed, and the apartment was sealed.

"Now what?" Morelli asked. "You can't stay here tonight."

Our eyes locked, and we were both thinking the same thing. A couple months ago Morelli wouldn't have asked that question. I would have stayed with Morelli. Things were different now. "I'll stay with my parents," I said. "Just overnight, until I figure things out."

Morelli went in and grabbed some clothes for me and shoved the essentials in a gym bag. He loaded Rex and me into his truck and drove us to the Burg.

Valerie and the kids were sleeping in my old bedroom, so I slept on the couch with Rex on the floor beside me.

I have friends who take Xanax to help them sleep. I take macaroni and cheese. And if my mom is making it for me, so much the better.

I had macaroni and cheese at 11:00 and fell into a fitful sleep. I had more macaroni at 2:00 and more at 4:30. A microwave is a wonderful invention.

At 7:30 I woke up to a lot of yelling going on upstairs. My father was causing the usual morning bottleneck in the bathroom.

"I have to brush my teeth," Angie said. "I'm going to be late for school."

"What about me?" Grandma wanted to know. "I'm old. I can't hold it forever." She hammered on the bathroom door. "What are you doing in there anyway?"

Mary Alice was making snorting horse sounds, galloping in place and pawing the floor.

"Stop that galloping," Grandma shouted to Mary Alice. "You're giving me a headache. Go downstairs to the kitchen and get some pancakes."

"Hay!" Mary Alice said. "Horses eat hay. And I already ate. I have to brush my teeth. It's real bad when horses get cavities."

The toilet flushed, and the bathroom door opened. There was a brief scuffle, and the door slammed shut. Valerie and the two girls groaned. Grandma beat them to the bathroom.

An hour later, my father was out to work. The girls were off to school. And Valerie was in a state.

"Is this too flirty?" she asked, standing in front of me in a gauzy little flowered dress and strappy heels. "Would a suit be better?"

I was scanning the paper, looking for mention of Soder. "It doesn't matter," I said. "Wear what you want."

"I need help," Valerie said, arms flapping. "I can't make these decisions all by myself. And what about the shoes? Should I wear these pink heels? Or should I wear the retro Weitzmans?"

I found a dead man sitting on my couch last night. I have couch cooties, and Valerie needs me to make a shoe decision.

"Wear the pink things," I said. "And take extra quarters, if you have any. Kloughn can always use extra quarters."

The phone rang, and Grandma ran to answer it. The calls would start now and would go on all day. The Burg loved a good murder.

"I have a daughter who finds men dead on her couch," my mother said. "Why me? Lois Seltzman's daughter *never* finds dead men on *her* couch."

"Isn't this something," Grandma said. "Three calls already, and it's not even nine. This could be bigger than the time your car got crushed by the garbage truck."

I had Valerie drive me to my apartment building on her way to work. I needed my car, and my car was parked in the lot. Upstairs, my apartment was sealed. Fine by me. I was in no great rush to move back in.

I got into the CR-V and sat there a moment, listening to the quiet. Quiet was in short supply at my parents' house.

Mr. Kleinschmidt passed me on his way to his car. "Nice going, chicky," he said. "We can always count on you to keep things interesting. Did you really find a dead guy on your couch?"

I nodded. "Yes."

"Boy, that must have been something. I wish I could have seen him."

Mr. Kleinschmidt's enthusiasm dragged a smile out of me. "Maybe next time."

"Yeah," Mr. Kleinschmidt said, happily. "Call me

first thing next time." He gave me a wave and went off to his car.

Okay, so here we have a new point of view when it comes to dead people. Dead people can be fun. I thought about it for a couple minutes but had a hard time buying into the concept. The best I could do was an admission that Soder's death made my job easier. Evelyn had no reason to flee with Annie now that Soder was out of the picture. Mabel could stay in her house. Annie could return to school. Evelyn could get her life together.

Unless Eddie Abruzzi was part of the reason Evelyn had to hide. If Evelyn left because she had something Abruzzi wanted, nothing would change.

I looked at the blue-and-white and the crime-scene truck in my parking lot. The bright spot in all this was that unlike snakes in the hall and spiders in my car, this was a major crime and the police would work hard to solve it. And how hard could it be to solve? Someone had dragged a dead man into the foyer, up a flight of stairs, down the hall, and into my apartment . . . during daylight hours.

I dialed Morelli on my cell phone.

"I have some questions," I said. "How did they get Soder into my apartment?"

"You don't want to know."

"I do!"

"I'll meet you for coffee," Morelli said. "There's a new coffee shop across from the hospital."

I got a coffee and a croissant, and I sat across from Morelli. "Tell me," I said.

"Soder was sawed in half."

"What?"

"Someone used a power saw to cut Soder in half. And then they reassembled him on your couch. The baggy sweater was hiding the fact that they duct-taped Soder back together."

My lips went numb, and I could feel the coffee cup sliding from my grasp.

Morelli reached forward and pushed my head down, between my legs. "Breathe," he said.

The bells stopped clanging in my brain, and the dots went away. I sat up and took a sip of coffee. "I'm better now," I said.

Morelli did a sigh. "If only I could believe that."

"Alright, so they cut him in half. Then what?"

"We think they used a couple big duffel bags to bring him in. Hockey bags, maybe. Now that you've gotten over the gruesome part, the rest of the story is actually ingenious. Two guys, dressed in costume, carrying duffel bags and balloons, were seen entering the lobby and using the elevator. There were two tenants in the lobby at the time. They said they assumed someone was getting one of those singing birthday presents. Mr. Kleinschmidt had turned eighty the week before, and someone sent him two strippers."

"What sort of costume were these guys wearing?"

"One was a bear, and the other was a rabbit. No faces showing. About six foot tall, but hard to tell with the costume. We found the balloons in your closet. They took the bags back with them."

"Did anyone see them leave?"

"No one in your building. We're still canvassing the neighborhood. We're checking on costume rentals, too. So far we haven't come up with anything."

"It was Abruzzi. He was the one who left the snakes and the spiders. He was the one who put the cardboard cutout on my fire escape."

"Can you prove it?"

"No."

"That's the problem," Morelli said. "And probably Abruzzi didn't personally dirty his hands."

"There's a connection between Abruzzi and Soder. Abruzzi was the partner who took over the bar, right?"

"Soder lost his bar to Abruzzi because of a card game. Soder was playing some high stakes guys, and he needed money. He borrowed the money from Ziggy Zimmerli. And Zimmerli is owned by Abruzzi. Soder lost big time at the card game, couldn't repay the money he borrowed from Zimmerli, and Abruzzi took the bar."

"So what's the deal with the bar burning down, and Soder getting shot?"

"I'm not sure. Probably the bar and Soder moved from the asset column to the liability column and were liquidated."

"Did you pick up any prints in my apartment?"

"None that didn't belong there. With the exception of Ranger."

"I work with him."

"Yeah," Morelli said. "I know."

"I'm assuming Evelyn isn't a suspect," I said.

"Anyone can hire a rabbit and a bear to chop a guy up," Morelli said. "We aren't ruling anyone out yet."

I picked at my croissant. Morelli had his cop face on, and it didn't give much away. Still, I had a feeling there was more. "Is there something you're not telling me?"

"There was a detail we're not releasing to the press," Morelli said.

"A gruesome detail?"

"Yeah."

"Let me make a guess. Soder's heart was ripped out."

Morelli looked at me for a couple beats. "This guy is about as crazy as they come," he finally said. "I'd like to protect you, but I don't know how. I could chain you to my wrist. Or I could lock you up in a closet in my house. Or you could pack off for an extended vacation.

Unfortunately, I don't think you're going to agree to any of those things."

Actually, I thought all of those options sounded kind of appealing. But Morelli was right, I couldn't agree to any of them.

Chapter
TEN

I took another sip of coffee and looked around the cafe. It had been nicely decorated with new black-and-white tile on the floor and round, wrought-iron soda fountain–style tables and chairs. Morelli and I were the only ones there. It took the Burg a while to warm up to new things.

"Thanks for being so nice to me last night," I said to Morelli.

He slouched back in his seat. "Against my better judgment, I love you."

I paused with the coffee cup midway to my mouth, and my heart did a flip-flop.

"Don't get all excited," Morelli said. "That doesn't mean I want a relationship."

"You could do worse," I said.

"With who? Lizzy Borden?"

"*You're* not perfect, either!"

"I don't find dead guys sitting on my couch."

"Well, I don't have a knife scar slicing through my eyebrow from a barroom brawl."

"That happened years ago."

"So? The dead guy was on my couch *yesterday.* It's been twenty-four hours since anything bad has happened."

Morelli pushed back from the table. "I have to get back to work. Try to stay out of trouble."

And he was gone, off to fight crime. I, on the other hand, had no crime to fight. Bender was my only open case, and I was willing to pretend he didn't exist. I was thinking about a second croissant when Les Sebring called on my cell phone.

"Could you stop by the office?" Sebring asked. "I'd like to talk to you."

I cut across town and got another call just as I was cruising the street in front of Sebring's office, looking for parking.

"He's a nerd," Valerie said. "You didn't tell me he was a nerd."

"Who?"

"Albert Kloughn. And what's with the hovering? Sometimes I can actually feel him breathing down my neck."

"He's insecure. Try thinking of him as a pet."

"A golden retriever."

"More like a giant hamster."

"I was sort of hoping he'd marry me," Valerie said. "I was hoping he'd be taller."

"Valerie, this isn't a date. This is a job. Where is he now?"

"He went next door. There's something wrong with the vending machine that dispenses detergent."

"He's a nice guy. A little annoying, maybe. But he won't fire you for spilling chicken soup. In fact, he'll buy you a replacement lunch. Think about it."

"And I shouldn't have worn these shoes," Valerie said. "I'm dressed all wrong."

I disconnected and found a place to park on the street across from Sebring. I put a quarter in the meter and made sure it registered. I didn't need another parking ticket. I still hadn't paid the last one.

Sebring's secretary walked me upstairs and led me into Sebring's private office. Sebring was waiting for me. And so was Jeanne Ellen Burrows.

I extended my hand to Sebring. "Nice to see you again," I said. I nodded to Jeanne Ellen. She smiled in return.

"I guess you're out of a job," I said to Jeanne Ellen.

"Yes. And I'll be flying to Puerto Rico later today to pick up an FTA for Les. I wanted to tell you about Soder before I left. For what it's worth, Soder claimed Annie was in danger. He never articulated that danger, but he felt Evelyn was incapable of protecting his daughter. I wasn't successful at locating Annie, but I realized Dotty was the conduit . . . the weak link. So I guarded Dotty."

"What about the back door? That was left unguarded."

"I had the house wired," Jeanne Ellen said. "I knew you were in there."

"The house was wired, but you still couldn't find Evelyn?"

"Evelyn's location was never mentioned. You blew the whistle on me before I had a chance to follow Dotty to Evelyn."

"And what about Soder? The scene in the bookstore and at Dotty's house?"

"Soder was a fool. He thought he could bully Dotty into talking."

"Why are you telling me all this?"

Jeanne Ellen shrugged. "Professional courtesy."

I looked beyond her to Sebring. "Do you have an ongoing interest in this?"

"Not unless Soder comes back from the dead."

"What's your opinion? Do you think Annie's in danger?"

"Someone killed her father," Sebring said. "That's not a good sign. Unless, of course, it was Annie's mom who hired the hit. Then everything works out roses."

"Do either of you know how Eddie Abruzzi fits into this puzzle?"

"He owned Soder's bar," Jeanne Ellen said. "And Soder was afraid of him. If Annie actually was in danger, I thought the threat might be tied to Abruzzi. Nothing concrete, just a feeling I had."

"I hear you found Soder sitting on your couch," Sebring said to me. "Do you know what that means?"

"My couch has death cooties?"

Sebring smiled and his teeth almost blinded me. "You can't wash away death cooties," he said. "Once they're on your couch, they're there to stay."

I left the office on that cheery note. I got into my car, and I took a moment to process the new information. What did it mean? It didn't mean much. It reinforced my fear that Evelyn and Annie were running, not just from Soder, but from Abruzzi, as well.

Valerie called again. "If I go out to lunch with Albert, would it be a date?"

"Only if he rips your clothes off."

I hung up and put the car in gear. I was going back to the Burg, and I was going to talk to Dotty's mom. She was the only connection I had to Evelyn. If Dotty's mom said Dotty and Evelyn were peachy fine and coming home, I'd feel like I was off the hook. I'd go to the mall and get a manicure.

Mrs. Palowski opened her front door and gasped at seeing me on her porch. "Oh dear," she said. As if the death couch cooties were contagious.

I sent her a reassuring smile and a little finger wave. "Hi. I hope I'm not imposing."

"Not at all, dear. I heard about Steven Soder. I don't know what to think."

"Me, either," I said. "I don't know why he was put on my couch." I did a grimace. "Go figure. At least he wasn't killed there. They packed him in." Even as I said it, I knew it was lame. Leaving a sawed-in-half corpse on a girl's couch is rarely a random act. "The thing is, Mrs. Palowski, I really do need to talk to Dotty. I was hoping she might have heard about Soder and gotten in touch with you."

"As a matter of fact, she did. She called this morning, and I told her you were asking after her."

"Did she say when she'd be home?"

"She said she might be gone a while. That was all she said."

There goes the manicure.

Mrs. Palowski wrapped her arms tight around herself. "Evelyn dragged Dotty into this, didn't she? It's not like Dotty to take off from work and pull Amanda out of school to go on a camping trip. I think something bad is going on. I heard about Steven Soder, and I went straight to mass. I didn't pray for Soder, either. He can go to hell for all I care." She crossed herself. "I prayed for Dotty," she said.

"Do you have any idea where Dotty might be? If she was trying to help Evelyn, where would she take her?"

"I don't know. I've tried to think, but I can't figure it out. I doubt Evelyn has much money. And Dotty is on a tight budget. So I can't see them flying off to someplace. Dotty said she had to stop at the mall yesterday to get some last-minute camping things, so maybe she really is camping. Sometimes, before the divorce, Dotty and her husband would go to a campground by Washington's Crossing. I can't think of the name, but it was right on the river, and you could rent a little trailer."

I knew the campground. I'd passed it a million times on the way to New Hope.

Okay, now I was cooking. I had a lead. I could check out the campground. Only thing, I didn't want to check it out alone. It was too isolated at this time of year. Too easy for Abruzzi to ambush me. So I took a deep breath and called Ranger.

"Yo," Ranger said.

"I have a lead on Evelyn, and I could use some backup."

Twenty minutes later, I was parked in the Washington's Crossing parking lot, and Ranger pulled in beside me. He was driving a shiny black 4×4 pickup with over-size tires and bug lights on the cab. I locked my car and hoisted myself into his passenger seat. The interior of the truck looked like Ranger regularly communicated with Mars.

"How's your mental health?" he asked. "I heard about Soder."

"I'm rattled."

"I have a cure."

Oh, boy.

He put the truck in gear and headed for the exit. "I know what you're thinking," he said. "And that wasn't where I was going. I was going to suggest work."

"I knew that."

He looked over at me and grinned. "You want me bad."

I did. God help me. "We're going north," I said. "There's a chance that Evelyn and Dotty are at the campground with the little trailers."

"I know the campground."

The road was empty at this time of day. Two lanes winding along the Delaware River and through the

Pennsylvania countryside. Patches of woods and clusters of pretty houses bordered the road. Ranger was silent while he drove. He was paged twice and both times he read the message and didn't respond. Both times he kept the message to himself. Normal behavior for Ranger. Ranger led a secret life.

The pager buzzed a third time. Ranger unclipped it from his belt and looked at the readout. He cleared the screen, reclipped the pager, and continued to watch the road.

"Hello," I said.

He cut his eyes to me.

Ranger and I were oil and water. He was the Man of Mystery, and I was Ms. Curiosity. We both knew this. Ranger tolerated it with mild amusement. I tolerated it with teeth clenched.

I dropped my eyes to his pager. "Jeanne Ellen?" I asked. I couldn't help myself.

"Jeanne Ellen is on her way to Puerto Rico," Ranger said.

Our eyes held for a moment, and he turned his attention back to the road. End of conversation.

"It's a good thing you have a nice ass," I said to him. Because you sure as hell can be *annoying*.

"My ass isn't my best part, babe," Ranger said, smiling at me.

And that truly did end the conversation. I had no follow-up.

Ten minutes later we approached the campground. It sat between the road and the river and could easily go unnoticed. It didn't have a sign. And for all I knew, it didn't have a name. A dirt road slanted down to a couple acres of grass. Small ramshackle cabins and trailers were scattered along the river's edge, each with a picnic table and grill. It had an air of abandonment at this time of year. And it felt slightly disreputable, and intriguing, like a gypsy encampment.

Ranger idled at the entrance, and we scanned the surroundings.

"No cars," Ranger said. He eased the truck down the drive and parked. He reached under the dash, removed a Glock, and we got out of the truck.

We systematically went down the row of cabins and trailers, trying doors, looking in windows, checking the grills for recent use. The lock was broken on the front door to the fourth cabin. Ranger rapped once and opened the door.

The front room had a small kitchen area at one end. Not high-tech. Sink, stove, fridge circa 1950. The floor was covered with scuffed linoleum. There was a full-size couch at the far end of the room, a square wood table, and four chairs. The only other room to the cabin was a bedroom with two sets of bunks. The bunks had mattresses but no sheets or blankets. The bathroom was minuscule. A sink and a toilet. No shower or tub. The toothpaste in the sink looked fresh.

Ranger picked a pink plastic little girl's barrette off the floor. "They've moved on," he said.

We checked the refrigerator. It was empty. We went outside and investigated the remaining cabins and trailers. All the others were locked. We checked the Dumpster and found a single small bag of garbage.

"Do you have any other leads?" Ranger asked me.

"No."

"Let's walk through their houses."

I picked my car up at Washington's Crossing and drove it across the river. I parked in front of my parents' house and got back into Ranger's truck. We went to Dotty's house first. Ranger parked in the driveway, removed the

Glock from under the dash again, and we went to the front door.

Ranger had his hand on the doorknob and his handy-dandy lock-picking tool in his hand. And the door swung open. No lock picking necessary. It would appear we were coming in second in the breaking-and-entering race.

"Stay here," Ranger said. He stepped into the living room and did a quick survey. He walked through the rest of the house with his gun drawn. He returned to the living room and motioned me in.

I closed and locked the door behind me. "Nobody home?"

"No. There are drawers pulled out and papers scattered on the kitchen counter. Either someone's been through the house, or else Dotty left in a hurry."

"I was here after Dotty left. I didn't go into the house, but I looked in the windows and the house seemed neat. Do you think the house could have been burgled?" I knew in my heart it wasn't burglary, but one can hope.

"Don't think the motive was burglary. There's a computer in the kid's room and a diamond engagement ring in the jewelry box in the mother's room. The television is still here. My guess is, we're not the only ones looking for Evelyn and Annie."

"Maybe it was Jeanne Ellen. She had a bug planted here. Maybe she came back to get her bug before she left for Puerto Rico."

"Jeanne Ellen isn't sloppy. She wouldn't leave the front door open, and she wouldn't leave evidence of a break-in."

My voice inadvertently rose an octave. "Maybe she was having a bad day? Cripes, doesn't she ever have a bad day?"

Ranger looked at me and smiled.

"Okay, so I'm getting a little tired of the perfect Jeanne Ellen," I said.

"Jeanne Ellen isn't perfect," Ranger said. "She's just very good." He slung an arm around my shoulders and kissed me below my ear. "Maybe we can find an area where your skills exceed Jeanne Ellen's."

I narrowed my eyes at him. "Did you have something in mind?"

"Nothing I'd want to get into right now." He pulled a pair of disposable gloves out of his pocket. "I want to do a more thorough search. She didn't take a lot with her. Most of their clothes are still here." He moved into the bedroom and turned the computer on. He opened files that looked promising. "Nothing to help us," he finally said, shutting the computer off.

She didn't have caller ID, and there were no messages on her machine. Bills and shopping lists were scattered across the kitchen counter. We rifled through them, knowing it was probably wasted effort. If there had been anything good, the intruder would have taken it.

"Now what?" I asked.

"Now we look at Evelyn's house."

Uh-oh. "There's a problem with Evelyn's house. Abruzzi has someone watching it. Every time I stop by, Abruzzi shows up ten minutes later."

"Why would Abruzzi care that you're in Evelyn's house?"

"Last time I ran into him he said he knew I was in it for the money, that I knew what the stakes were. And that I knew what he was trying to recover. I think Abruzzi's after something, and it's tied to Evelyn somehow. I think it's possible that Abruzzi thinks this *thing* is hidden in the house, and he doesn't want me snooping around."

"Any ideas on what it is that he's trying to recover?"

"None. Not a clue. I've been through the house, and

I didn't find anything unusual. Of course, I wasn't looking for secret hiding places. I was looking for something to direct me to Evelyn."

Ranger closed the front door behind us and made sure it was locked.

The sun was low in the sky when we got to Evelyn's house. Ranger did a drive-by. "Do you know the people on this street?"

"Almost everyone. Some I know better than others. I know the woman next door to Evelyn. Linda Clark lives two houses down. The Rojacks live in the corner house. Betty and Arnold Lando live across the street. The Landos are in a rental, and I don't know the family next to them. If I was looking for a snitch, my money would be on someone in the family next to the Landos. There's an old man who always seems to be home. Sits out on the porch a lot. Looks like he used to break kneecaps for a living, about a hundred years ago."

Ranger parked in front of Carol Nadich's half of the house. Then we walked around the house and entered Evelyn's half through the back door. Ranger didn't have to break a window to get in. Ranger inserted a small slender tool into the lock, and ten seconds later the door was open.

The house seemed just as I remembered. Dishes in the drain. Mail neatly stacked. Drawers closed. None of the signs of search that we'd seen in Dotty's house.

Ranger did his usual walk-through, starting in the kitchen, eventually moving upstairs into Evelyn's room. I was following behind him when I had a sudden flashback. Kloughn telling me about Annie's drawings. Scary drawings, Kloughn had said. Bloody.

I wandered into Annie's room and flipped pages on the pad on her desk. The first page contained a house drawing similar to the one downstairs. After that came a page of scribbles and doodles. And then the childish drawing of a man. He was laying on the ground. The ground was red. Red spurted from the man's body.

"Hey," I called to Ranger. "Come look at this."

Ranger stood beside me and stared at the drawing. He turned the page and found a second drawing with red on the ground. Two men were laying in the red. Another man pointed a gun at them. There were a lot of erasure marks around the gun. I guess guns are hard to draw.

Ranger and I exchanged glances.

"It could just be television," I said.

"It wouldn't hurt to take the pad with us, in case it isn't."

Ranger finished his search of Evelyn's room, moved to Annie's, and then to the bathroom. He stood hands on hips when he'd completed the search of the bathroom.

"If there's something here, it's well hidden," he said. "It would be easier if I knew what we were looking for."

We left the house the same way we came. Abruzzi wasn't waiting for us on the back porch. And Abruzzi wasn't waiting for us by Ranger's truck. I sat next to Ranger and I looked up and down the street. No sign of Abruzzi. I was almost disappointed.

Ranger rolled the engine over, drove to my parents' house, and parked behind my car. The sun had set and the street was dark. Ranger cut his lights and turned to see me better.

"Are you spending the night here again?"

"Yes. My apartment's still sealed. I imagine I'll get it back tomorrow." Then what? An involuntary shiver sent my lower back into spasm. My couch had death cooties.

"I see you're excited about returning," Ranger said.

"I'll figure it out. Thanks for helping me today."

"I feel cheated," Ranger said. "Usually when I'm with you a car explodes or a building burns down."

"Sorry to disappoint."

"Life is a bitch," Ranger said. He reached out and grabbed me by my jacket sleeves, hauled me across the console, and kissed me.

"*Now* you kiss me?" I said. "What was the deal when we were alone in my apartment?"

"You had three glasses of wine, and you fell asleep."

"Oh yeah. Now I remember."

"And you went into a panic attack at the thought of sleeping with me."

I was sprawled across the console, wedged behind the wheel, half sitting on Ranger's lap. His lips brushed against mine when he spoke and his hands were warm against my T-shirt.

"You weren't entirely responsible for the panic," I told him. "It was a sort of disastrous day."

"Babe, you have *a lot* of disastrous days."

"You sound like Morelli."

"Morelli is a good guy. And he loves you."

"And you?"

Ranger smiled.

I was racked with another spine shiver.

The porch light went on, and Grandma peered out at us from the living room window.

"Saved by the grandma," Ranger said, releasing me. "I'm going to wait for you to get in the house. I don't want anyone kidnapping you on my watch."

I opened the door and I jumped out. And I did a mental grimace because getting kidnapped and/or shot wasn't entirely off the radar screen.

Grandma was waiting for me when I walked through the door. "Who's the guy in the cool truck?"

"Ranger."

"That man is so hot," Grandma said. "If I was twenty years younger . . ."

"If you were twenty years younger you'd still be twenty years too old," my father said.

Valerie was in the kitchen, helping my mother frost cupcakes. I got a glass of milk and a cupcake, and I sat at the table. "How'd work go today?" I asked Valerie.

"I didn't get fired."

"That's great. Before you know it, he'll be proposing marriage."

"Do you think so?"

I slid her a sideways look. "I was joking."

"It could happen," Valerie said, dropping colored sprinkles on the cupcake.

"Valerie, you don't want to marry the first guy who comes along."

"Yes, I do. As long as he has a house with two bathrooms. I swear to God, I don't care if he's Jack the Ripper."

"I'm thinking about getting a computer so I can have cybersex," Grandma said. "Anybody know how that works?"

"You go into a chat room," Valerie said. "And you meet someone. And then you type dirty suggestions to each other."

"That sounds like fun," Grandma said. "How does the *sex* part happen?"

"You sort of have to do the sex part yourself."

"I knew it was too good to be true," Grandma said. "There's always a catch to everything."

It was morning, I was last in line for the bathroom, and I was beginning to appreciate Valerie's point of view. When faced with the choices of forever living with my parents, marrying Jack the Ripper, or going home to the cootie couch, I had to admit Jack the Ripper was looking pretty good. Okay, maybe not Jack the Ripper, but certainly Doug the Dullard could be tolerated.

I was dressed in my usual outfit of jeans and boots and a stretchy shirt. I had my hair brushed out in curls and my mascara on heavy. All my adult life I've hidden behind mascara. And if I'm *really* feeling insecure, I add eyeliner. Today was an eyeliner day. Plus, I painted my toenails. Bring out the heavy artillery, right? Morelli had called earlier and told me the crime scene tape was down. He'd made arrangements for a professional cleaning crew to go through the apartment, using full-strength Clorox wherever needed. He thought they'd be done around noon. For all I cared, they could be done around November.

I was in the kitchen, having a final cup of coffee before starting my day, and Mabel appeared at the back door.

"I just heard from Evelyn," she said. "She called me, and she said everyone was fine. She's staying with a friend, and she said not to worry." She put her hand to her heart. "I feel so much better. And I felt better knowing you were looking for Evelyn. It gave me peace of mind. Thank you."

"Did Evelyn say when she was coming home?"

"No. She said she wouldn't be back for Steven's funeral, though. I guess there are hard feelings."

"Did she say where she was? Did she mention the friend's name?"

"No. She was rushed. It sounded like she was calling from a store or a restaurant. There was a lot of noise in the background."

"If she calls again, tell her I'd like to talk to her."

"There isn't anything wrong, is there? Now that Steven's gone it seems like everything should be okay."

"I'd like to talk to her about her landlord."

"Are you interested in renting a house?"

"I might be." And that was the truth.

The phone rang, and Grandma ran for it. "It's for you," she said, holding the phone out to me. "It's Valerie."

"I need help," Valerie said. "You have to get over here in a hurry." And she hung up.

"Gotta go," I said. "Valerie's got a problem."

"She used to be so smart," Grandma said. "And then she moved to California. Think all that California sun dried her brain up like a raisin."

How bad could the problem be? I thought. More chicken soup in the computer? What would Kloughn care? He had no files to lose because he had no clients.

I pulled into the lot and parked nose first in front of Kloughn's office. I looked into the big plate glass windows but didn't see Valerie. I got out of the car, and Valerie came running from the Laundromat side.

"Over here," she said. "He's in the Laundromat."

"Who?"

"Albert!"

A row of turquoise plastic chairs lined the wall facing the dryers. Two old women sat side-by-side in the chairs, smoking, looking at Valerie. Taking it all in. No one else was in the room.

"Where?" I said. "I don't see him."

Valerie sucked in a sob and pointed to one of the large commercial dryers. "He's in there."

I looked more closely. She was right. Albert Kloughn was in the dryer. He was all scrunched up with his ass to the round porthole glass door, looking like Pooh stuck in the rabbit hole.

"Is he alive?" I asked.

"Yes! Of course he's alive." Valerie crept closer and knocked on the door. "At least, I *think* he's alive."

"What's he doing in there?"

"The lady in the blue sweater thought she lost her

wedding ring in the dryer. She said it was wedged into the back of the drum. So Albert went in to get it. But then somehow the door slammed shut, and we can't get it to open."

"Jeez. Why didn't you call the fire department or the police?"

There was movement in the drum and a lot of muffled noise coming from Kloughn. The noise sounded like *no, no, no.*

"I think he's embarrassed," Valerie said. "I mean, how would it look? Suppose somebody took a picture, and it got in the paper? No one would ever hire him, and I'd be out of a job."

"No one hires him now," I said. I tried the door. I tried pushing buttons. I looked for a safety latch. "I'm scoring a big zero here," I said.

"There's something wrong with that dryer," the lady in the blue sweater said. "It's always getting stuck like that. There's something wrong with the lock. I wrote out a complaint about it last week, but nobody ever does nothing around here. The vending machine with the soap doesn't work, either."

"I really think we need help," I said to Valerie. "I think we should call the police."

There was more frantic movement and more of the *no, no, no.* And then there was something that sounded like a fart coming from inside the dryer.

Valerie and I took a step back.

"I think he's nervous," Valerie said.

Probably there was some sort of door release on the inside, but Kloughn was wedged in and couldn't turn to face the latch.

I fished around in the bottom of my bag and found some change. I dropped a quarter into the slot, turned the heat down to low, and started the dryer tumbling.

Kloughn's mumbling turned to shrieking, and

Kloughn bounced around some, but for the most part he seemed fairly stable. After five minutes the dryer stopped tumbling. You don't get a heck of a lot for a quarter these days.

The door opened easy as anything, and Valerie and I pulled Kloughn out and stood him up. His hair was all fluffy. The kind of fluff you see on a baby robin. He was warm and smelled nice, like fresh ironing. His face was red, and his eyes were glassy.

"I think I farted," he said.

"You know what?" the lady in the blue sweater said. "I found my ring. It wasn't in the dryer after all. I put it in my pocket and forgot."

"That's nice," Kloughn said, his eyes unfocused, a little drool at the corner of his mouth.

Valerie and I had him propped up by his armpits.

"We're going to the office now," I said to Kloughn. "Try walking."

"Everything's still spinning. I'm out of the machine, right? I'm just dizzy, right? I can still hear the motor. I've got the motor in my head." Kloughn moved his legs like Frankenstein's monster. "I can't feel my feet," he said. "My feet fell asleep."

We half dragged, half pushed him back to the office and sat him in a chair.

"That was just like a ride," he said. "Did you see me going around in there? Like a fun house, right? Like an amusement park. I ride all those rides. I'm used to that sort of thing. I sit right up front."

"Really?"

"Well, no. But I think about it."

"Isn't he cute," Valerie said. And she kissed him on top of his fluffy head.

"Gosh," Kloughn said, smiling wide. "Gee."

Chapter

ELEVEN

I declined on an offer of lunch from Kloughn, choosing instead to go to the bonds office.

"Anything new?" I asked Connie. "I'm all out of FTAs."

"What about Bender?"

"I wouldn't want to cut in on Vinnie."

"Vinnie doesn't want him, either," Connie said.

"It isn't that," Vinnie yelled from his inner office. "I've got things to do. Important things."

"Yeah," Lula said, "he's gotta slap his johnson around."

"You better get that guy," Vinnie yelled at me. "I'm not going to be happy if I'm out Bender's bond."

"I think there's something going on with Bender," Lula said. "He's one of them lucky drunks. It's like he's got a direct line to God. God protects the weak and the helpless, you know."

"God isn't protecting Bender," Vinnie yelled. "Bender is still out there because I have a couple of useless boobs on my payroll."

"Okay, fine," I said. "We'll go get Bender."

"We?" Lula asked.

"Yeah, you and me."

"Been there, done that," Lula said. "I'm telling you,

he's under God's protection. And I'm not sticking my nose into God's business."

"I'll buy you lunch."

"I'll get my bag," Lula said.

"One thing," I said to Connie. "I need some cuffs."

"No more cuffs," Vinnie yelled. "What do you think, cuffs grow on trees?"

"I can't bring him in without cuffs."

"Improvise."

"Hey," Lula said, looking out the big plate glass front window, "check out the car that just stopped by Stephanie's car. It's got a big rabbit and a big bear in it. And the bear is driving."

We all stared out the window.

"Uh-oh," Lula said, "did that rabbit just throw something at Stephanie's car?"

There was a loud *barooooom*, the CR-V jumped several feet into the air and burst into flames.

"Guess it was a bomb," Lula said.

Vinnie came running out of his office. "Holy shit," he said. "What was that?" He stopped and gaped at the fireball in front of his office.

"It's just another one of Stephanie's cars got blown up," Lula said. "It got bombed by a big rabbit."

"Don't you hate when that happens," Vinnie said. And he went back into his office.

Lula and Connie and I migrated out to the sidewalk and watched the car burn. A couple blue-and-whites screamed onto the scene, followed by the EMT truck and finally two fire trucks.

Carl Costanza got out of one of the blue-and-whites. "Anyone hurt?"

"No."

"Good," he said, his face creasing into a grin. "Then I can enjoy this. I missed the spiders and the guy on the couch."

Costanza's partner, Big Dog, ambled over. "Way to go, Steph," he said. "We were all wondering when you'd trash another car. Can't hardly remember the last explosion."

Costanza bobbed his head in agreement. "It's been months," he said.

I saw Morelli angle in behind a fire truck. He got out of his truck and walked over.

"Christ," he said, looking at what was fast becoming a charred hunk of scrap metal.

"It was Steph's car," Lula told him. "It was firebombed by a big rabbit."

Morelli set his mouth to grim and glanced over at me. "Is that true?"

"Lula saw it."

"I don't suppose you'd reconsider taking a vacation," Morelli said to me. "Maybe go to Florida for a month or two."

"I'll think about it," I said to Morelli. "As soon as I bring Andy Bender in."

Morelli was still tuned to grim.

"I could bring him in easier if I had a pair of cuffs," I said.

Morelli reached under his sweater and pulled out a pair of cuffs. He handed them to me wordlessly, his expression unchanged.

"Kiss those cuffs good-bye," Lula mumbled behind me.

Generally speaking, a red Trans Am is not a good choice for a surveillance car. Fortunately, with Lula's newly bleached canary yellow hair and my extra-heavy-on-the-mascara eyes we looked like businesswomen who belonged in a red Trans Am, on the street in front of Bender's house.

"Now what?" Lula asked. "You have any ideas?"

I had binoculars trained on Bender's front window. "I think someone's in there, but I can't see enough to identify anyone."

"We could call to see who answers," Lula said. "Except I ran out of money for a cell phone so I haven't got one no more, and your phone burned up in your car."

"I guess we could go knock on the door."

"Yeah, I like that idea. Maybe he'll shoot at us again. I was hoping someone would shoot at me today. That was the first thing I said when I got up: Boy, I hope I get shot at today."

"He only shot at me that one time."

"That makes me feel a lot better," Lula said.

"Well, what's your idea?"

"My idea is we go home. I'm telling you, God don't want us to get this guy. He even sent a rabbit to bomb your car."

"*God* didn't send a rabbit to bomb my car."

"What's your explanation? You think it's every day you see a rabbit driving down the street?"

I shoved the door open and got out of the Trans Am. I had the cuffs in one hand and pepper spray in the other. "I'm in a *bad* mood," I told Lula. "I'm up to here with snakes and spiders and dead guys. And now I don't even have a car. I'm going in, and I'm dragging Bender out. And after I drop his sorry ass off at the police station I'm going to Chevy's, and I'm going to get one of those margaritas they make in the gallon-size glass."

"Hunh," Lula said. "I guess you want me to go with you."

I was already halfway across the yard. "Whatever," I said. "Do whatever the hell you want."

I could hear Lula huffing along behind me. "Don't you pull no attitude with me," she was saying. "Don't you tell me to do whatever the hell I want. I already told you what I want. Did it count for anything? Hell, no."

I got to Bender's front door, and I tried the knob. The door was locked. I knocked loud, three times. There was no answer, so I banged three times with my fist.

"Open the door," I shouted. "Bond enforcement."

The door opened, and Bender's wife looked out at me. "This isn't a good time," she said.

I pushed her aside. "It's never a good time."

"Yes, but you don't understand. Andy is sick."

"You expect us to believe that?" Lula said. "What do we look, stupid?"

Bender lurched into the room. His hair was a wreck and his eyes were half-closed. He was wearing a pajama top and stained khaki work pants.

"I'm dying," he said. "I'm gonna die."

"It's just the flu," his wife said. "You should get back to bed."

Bender held his hands out. "Cuff me. Take me in. They got a doctor that comes around, right?"

I put the cuffs on Bender and looked over at Lula. "Is there a doctor?"

"They got a ward at St. Francis."

"I bet I got anthrax," Bender said. "Or smallpox."

"Whatever it is, it don't smell good," Lula said.

"I got diarrhea. And I'm throwing up," Bender said. "I got a runny nose and a scratchy throat. And I think I got a fever. Feel my head."

"Yeah, right," Lula said. "Looking forward to that opportunity."

He swiped at his nose with his sleeve and left a smear of snot on his pajama top. He hauled his head back and sneezed and sprayed half the room.

"Hey!" Lula yelled. "Cover up! You never heard of a hankie? And what's with that sleeve thing?"

"I'm gonna be sick," Bender said. "I'm gonna puke again."

"Get to the toilet!" his wife yelled. She grabbed a blue plastic bucket off the floor. "Use the bucket."

Bender stuck his head in the bucket and threw up.

"Holy crap," Lula said. "This is the House of Plague. I'm outta here. And you're not putting him in my car, either," she said to me. "You want to take him in, you can call a cab."

Bender pulled his head out of the bucket and held his shackled hands out to me. "Okay, I'm better now. I'm ready to go."

"Wait for me," I said to Lula. "You were right about God."

"It was a drive to get here, but it was worth it," Lula said, licking salt off the rim of her glass. "This is the mother of all margaritas."

"It's therapeutic, too. The alcohol will kill any germs we might have picked up from Bender."

"Fuckin' A," Lula said.

I sipped my drink and looked around. The bar was filled with the after-work crowd. Most of them were my age. And most of them looked happier than me.

"My life sucks," I said to Lula.

"You're just saying that because you had to watch Bender throw up in a bucket."

This was partially true. Bender throwing up in a bucket did nothing to enhance my mood. "I'm thinking about getting a different job," I said. "I want to work where these people work. They all look so happy."

"That's because they got here ahead of us, and they're all snockered."

Or it could be that none of them were being stalked by a maniac.

"I lost another pair of handcuffs," I said to Lula. "I left them on Bender."

Lula tipped her head back and burst out laughing. "And you want to change jobs," she said. "Why would you want to do that when you're so good at this one?"

It was eleven o'clock and most houses on my parents' street were dark. The Burg was early to bed and early to rise.

"Sorry about Bender," Lula said, letting the Trans Am idle at the curb. "Maybe we could tell Vinnie he died. We could say we were all set to bring Bender in, and he died. Bang. Dead as a doorknob."

"Better yet, why don't we just go back and kill him," I said. I opened the door to leave, caught my toe in the floor mat, and fell out of the car, face first. I rolled onto my back and stared up at the stars. "I'm fine," I said to Lula. "Maybe I'll sleep here tonight."

Ranger stepped into my line of sight, grabbed hold of my denim jacket, and pulled me to my feet. "Not a good idea, babe." He looked over at Lula. "You can go now."

The Trans Am laid rubber, and disappeared from view.

"I'm *not* drunk," I said to Ranger. "I only had *one* margarita."

His fingers were still curled into my jacket, but he softened his grip. "I understand you're having rabbit problems."

"Fucking rabbit."

Ranger grinned. "You are definitely drunk."

"I'm *not* drunk. I'm on the verge of being happy." I didn't exactly have the whirlies, but the world wasn't totally in focus, either. I leaned against Ranger for support. "What are you doing here?"

He released my jacket and wrapped his arms around me. "I needed to talk to you."

"You could have called."

"I tried calling. Your phone isn't working."

"Oh yeah. I forgot. It was in the car when the car blew up."

"I did some investigating on Dotty and came up with some names to check out."

"Now?"

"Tomorrow. I'll pick you up at eight."

"I can't get into the bathroom until nine."

"Okay. I'll pick you up at nine-thirty."

"Are you laughing? I can feel you laughing. My life isn't funny!"

"Babe, your life should be a prime-time sitcom."

At precisely 9:30 I stumbled out the door and stood blinking in the sunlight. I'd managed a shower, and I was fully clothed, but that was where it ended. A half hour isn't a lot of time for a girl to get beautiful. Especially when the girl has a hangover. My hair was pulled back into a ponytail, and I had my lipstick in my jeans jacket pocket. When my hand stopped shaking, and my eyeballs stopped being burning globes, I'd try putting lipstick on.

Ranger rolled up in a shiny black Mercedes sedan and waited at the curb. Grandma was standing behind me on the other side of the door.

"I wouldn't mind seeing him naked," she said.

I slid onto the cream-colored leather seat beside Ranger, closed my eyes, and smiled. The car smelled wonderful, like leather and fries. "God bless you," I said. He had fries and a Coke waiting for me on the console.

"Tank and Lester are checking campgrounds in Pennsylvania and New Jersey. They're doing the closest ones first and then moving out. They're looking for either of the cars, and they're talking to people when possible. We have your list of Evelyn's relatives, but I think they're long shots. Evelyn would worry that they'd get in touch with Mabel. The same goes for Dotty's relatives.

"There were four women Dotty was friendly with at work. I have their names and addresses. I think we should start with them."

"It's nice of you to help me with this. We aren't really employed by anyone. This is just an issue about Annie's safety."

"I'm not doing this for Annie's safety. This is about your safety. We need to get Abruzzi locked up. He's playing with you right now. When he stops enjoying the play he's going to get serious. If the police can't tie him to Soder, Annie might be able to tie him to something. Multiple murders, maybe, if the drawings are from life."

"If we bring Annie in, can we keep her safe?"

"I can keep her safe until Abruzzi is sentenced. Keeping you safe is more difficult. As long as Abruzzi is at large, nothing short of locking you in the Bat Cave for the rest of your life will keep you safe."

Hmm. The Bat Cave for the rest of my life. "You said the Bat Cave has television, right?"

Ranger slid a sideways look my way. "Eat your fries."

Barbara Ann Guzman was first on the list. She lived in a tract house in East Brunswick, in a pleasant neighborhood filled with middle-income families. Kathy Snyder, also on the list, lived two doors down. Both houses had attached garages. Neither of the garages had windows.

Ranger parked in front of the Guzman house. "Both women should be at work."

"Are we breaking in?"

"No, we're knocking on the door, hoping we hear kids inside."

We knocked twice, and we didn't hear kids. I squeezed

behind an azalea and peeked in Barbara Ann's front window. Lights off, television off, no little shoes laying discarded on the floor.

We walked two houses down to Kathy Snyder. We rang the bell, and an older woman answered.

"I'm looking for Kathy," I said to the woman.

"She's at work," the woman said. "I'm her mother. Can I help you?"

Ranger passed the woman a stack of photos. "Have you seen any of these people?"

"This is Dotty," the woman said. "And her friend. They spent the night with Barbara Ann. Do you know Barbara Ann?"

"Barbara Ann Guzman," Ranger said.

"Yes. Not last night. They were here the night before. A real full house for Barbara Ann."

"Do you know where they are now?"

She looked at the photo and shook her head. "No. Kathy might know. I just saw them because I was walking. I walk around the block every night for a little exercise, and I saw them drive up."

"Do you remember the car?" Ranger asked.

"It was just a regular car. Blue, I think." She looked from Ranger to me. "Is something wrong?"

"The one woman, Dotty's friend, has had some bad luck, and we're trying to help her straighten things out," I said.

The third woman lived in an apartment building in New Brunswick. We drove through the underground garage, methodically going up and down rows, looking for Dotty's blue Honda or Evelyn's gray Sentra. We scored a goose egg on that, so we parked and took the elevator to the sixth floor. We knocked on Pauline Wood's door and got no answer. We tried neighboring apartments, but no one responded. Ranger knocked one last time on Pauline's door and then let himself in. I stayed outside doing lookout. Five minutes later, Ranger was back in the hall, Pauline's door locked behind him.

"The apartment was clean," he said. "Nothing to indicate Dotty was there. No forwarding address for her displayed in a prominent place."

We left the parking garage and drove through town on our way to Highland Park. New Brunswick is a college town with Rutgers at the one end and Douglass College at the other. I graduated from Douglass without distinction. I was in the top ninety-eight percent of my class and damn glad to be there. I slept in the library and daydreamed my way through history lecture. I failed math twice, never fully grasping probability theory. I mean, first off, who cares if you pick a black ball or a white ball out of the bag? And second, if you're bent over about the color, don't leave it to chance. Look in the damn bag and pick the color you want.

By the time I reached college age, I'd given up all hope of flying like Superman, but I was never able to develop a burning desire for an alternative occupation. When I was a kid I read Donald Duck and Uncle Scrooge comics. Uncle Scrooge was always going off to exotic places in search of gold. After Scrooge got the gold, he'd take it back to his money bin and push his loose change around with a bulldozer. Now this was my idea of a good job. Go on an adventure. Bring back gold. Push it around with a bulldozer. How fun is this? So you can possibly see the reason for my lack of motivation to get grades. I mean, do you really need good grades to drive a bulldozer?

"I went to college here," I said to Ranger. "It's been a bunch of years, but I still feel like a student when I ride through town."

"Were you a good student?"

"I was a terrible student. Somehow the state managed to educate me in spite of myself. Did you go to college?"

"Rutgers, Newark. Joined the army after two years."

When I first met Ranger I would have been surprised by this. Now, nothing surprised me about Ranger.

"The last woman on the list should be at work, but her husband should be at home," Ranger said. "He works food service for the university and goes in at four. The guy's name is Harold Bailey. His wife's name is Louise."

We wound our way through a neighborhood of older homes. They were mostly two-story clapboards with the front porch stretching the width of the house and a single detached garage to the rear. They weren't big, and they weren't small. Many had been badly renovated with fake brick front or add-on front rooms made by enclosing the porch.

We parked and approached the Bailey house. Ranger rang the bell and, just as expected, a man answered the door. Ranger introduced himself and handed the man the photographs.

"We're looking for Evelyn Soder," Ranger said. "We were hoping you might be able to help. Have you seen any of these people in the last couple days?"

"Why are you looking for this Soder woman?"

"Her ex-husband has been killed. Evelyn has been moving around lately, and her grandmother has lost touch with her. She'd like to make sure Evelyn knows about the death."

"She was here with Dotty last night. They came just as I was leaving. They stayed overnight and left in the morning. I didn't see much of them. And I don't know where they were off to today. They were taking the little girls on some sort of field trip. Historical places. That sort of thing. Louise might know more. You could try reaching her at work."

We returned to the car, and Ranger took us out of the neighborhood.

"We're always one step behind," I said.

"That's the way it is with missing children. I've worked a lot of parental abduction cases, and they move around. Usually they go farther from home. And usually they stay in one place longer than a night. But the pattern is the same. By the time information on them comes in, they're usually gone."

"How do you catch them?"

"Persistence and patience. If you stick with it long enough, eventually you win. Sometimes it takes years."

"Omigod, I haven't got years. I'll have to hide in the Bat Cave."

"Once you go into the Bat Cave it's forever, babe."

Eeek.

"Try calling the women," Ranger said. "The work number is in the file."

Barbara Ann and Kathy were cautious. Both admitted that they'd seen Dotty and Evelyn and knew they were also visiting Louise. Both insisted they didn't know where the women were going next. I suspected they were telling the truth. I thought it was possible Evelyn and Dotty were only thinking a day ahead. My best guess was that they'd intended to camp and for some reason that hadn't worked out. Now they were scrambling to stay hidden.

Pauline had been entirely out of the loop.

Louise was the most talkative, probably because she was also the most worried.

"They would only stay the one night," she said. "I know what you're telling me about Evelyn's husband is true, but I know there's more. The kids were exhausted and wanted to go home. Evelyn and Dotty looked exhausted, too. They wouldn't talk about it, but I know they were running away from something. I was thinking it was Evelyn's husband, but I guess that's not it.

Holy Mother of God," she said. "You don't suppose they killed him!"

"No," I said, "he was killed by a rabbit. One more thing, did you see the car they were driving? Were they all in one car?"

"It was Dotty's car. The blue Honda. Apparently, Evelyn had a car but it was stolen when they left it at a campground. She said they went out grocery shopping and when they came back the car and everything they owned was gone. Can you imagine?"

I gave her my home phone number and asked her to call if she thought of anything that might be helpful.

"Dead end," I said to Ranger. "But I know why they vacated the campground." I told him about the stolen car.

"The more likely scenario is that Dotty and Evelyn came back after shopping, saw a strange car parked next to Evelyn's, and they abandoned everything," Ranger said.

"And when they didn't return, Abruzzi cleaned them out."

"It's what I'd do," Ranger said. "Anything to slow them down and make things difficult."

We were driving through Highland Park, approaching the bridge over the Raritan River. We were out of leads again, but at least we'd gotten some information. We didn't know where Evelyn was now, but we knew where she'd been. And we knew she no longer had the Sentra.

Ranger stopped for a light and turned to me. "When was the last time you shot a gun?" he asked.

"A couple days ago. I shot a snake. Is this a trick question?"

"This is a serious question. You should be carrying a gun. And you should feel comfortable shooting it."

"Okay, I promise, next time I go out, I'll take my gun with me."

"You'll put bullets in it?"

I hesitated.

Ranger glanced over at me. "You *will* put bullets in it."

"Sure," I said.

He reached out, opened the glove compartment, and took out a gun. It was a Smith & Wesson .38 five-shot special. It looked a lot like *my* gun.

"I stopped by your apartment this morning and picked this up for you," Ranger said. "I found it in the cookie jar."

"Tough guys always keep their gun in the cookie jar."

"Name one."

"Rockford."

Ranger grinned. "I stand corrected." He took a road that ran along the river, and after a half mile he turned into a parking area that led to a large warehouse-type building.

"What's this?" I asked.

"Shooting gallery. You're going to practice using your gun."

I knew this was necessary, but I hated the noise, and I hated the mechanics of the gun. I didn't like the idea that I was holding a device that essentially created small explosions. I was always sure something would go wrong, and I'd blow my thumb clear off my hand.

Ranger got me outfitted with ear protectors and goggles. He laid out the rounds and set the gun on the shelf in my assigned space. He brought the paper target in to twenty feet. If I was ever going to shoot someone, chances were good they'd be close to me.

"Okay, Tex," he said, "let's see what you've got."

I loaded and fired.

"Good," Ranger said. "Let's try it with your eyes open this time."

He adjusted my grip and my stance. I tried again.

"Better," Ranger said.

I practiced until my arm ached, and I couldn't pull the trigger anymore.

"How do you feel about the gun now?" Ranger asked.

"I feel more comfortable. But I still don't like it."

"You don't have to like it."

It was late afternoon when we left the gallery, and we ran into rush hour traffic going back through town. I have no patience for traffic. If I was driving I'd be cussing and banging my head against the steering wheel. Ranger was unfazed, in his zone. Zen calm. Several times I could swear he stopped breathing.

When we hit gridlock approaching Trenton, Ranger took an exit, cut down a side street, and parked in a small lot set between brick storefront businesses and three-story row houses. The street was narrow and felt dark, even during daylight hours. Storefront windows were dirty with faded displays. Black spray-painted graffiti covered the first-floor fronts of the row houses.

If at that very moment someone staggered out of a row house, blood gushing from bullet holes in multiple places on his body, it wouldn't take me by surprise.

I peered out the windshield and bit into my lower lip. "We aren't going to the Bat Cave, are we?"

"No, babe. We're going to Shorty's for pizza."

A small neon sign hung over the door of the building adjoining the lot. Sure enough, the sign said *Shorty's*. The two small windows in the front of the building had been blacked out with paint. The door was heavy wood and windowless.

I looked over my shoulder at Ranger. "The pizza is good here?" I tried not to let my voice waver, but it sounded squeezed and far away in my head. It was the voice of fear. Maybe fear is too strong a word. After the past week maybe fear should be reserved for life-threatening situations. But then again, maybe fear was appropriate.

"The pizza is good here," Ranger said, and he pushed the door open for me.

The sudden wash of noise and pizza fumes almost knocked me to my knees. It was dark inside Shorty's, and it was packed. Booths lined the walls and tables cluttered the middle of the room. An old-fashioned jukebox blasted out music from a far corner. Mostly there were men in Shorty's. The women who were there looked like they could hold their own. The men were in work boots and jeans. They were old and young, their faces lined from years of sun and cigarettes. They looked like they didn't need gun instruction.

We got a booth in a corner that was dark enough not to be able to see bloodstains or roaches. Ranger looked comfortable, his back to the wall, black shirt blending into the shadows.

The waitress was dressed in a white Shorty's T-shirt and a short black skirt. She had big hooters, a lot of brown curly hair, and more mascara than I'd ever managed, even on my most insecure day. She smiled at Ranger like she knew him better than I did. "What'll it be?" she asked.

"Pizza and beer," Ranger said.

"Do you come here a lot?" I asked him.

"Often enough. We keep a safe house in the neighborhood. Half the people in here are local. Half come from a truck stop on the next block."

The waitress dropped cardboard coasters on the scarred wood table and put a frosted glass of beer on each.

"I thought you didn't drink," I said to Ranger. "You

know, the-body-is-a-temple thing? And now wine at my apartment and beer at Shorty's."

"I don't drink when I'm working. And I don't get drunk. And the body is only a temple four days a week."

"Wow," I said, "you're going to hell in a handbasket, eating pizza and boozing it up three days a week. I thought I noticed a little extra fat around the middle."

Ranger raised an eyebrow. "A little extra fat around the middle. Anything else?"

"Maybe the beginnings of a double chin."

Truth is, Ranger didn't have fat anywhere. Ranger was perfect. And we both knew it.

He drank some beer and studied me. "Don't you think you're taking a chance, baiting me, when I'm the only thing standing between you and the guy at the bar with the snake tattooed on his forehead?"

I looked at the guy with the snake. "He seems like a nice guy." Nice for a homicidal maniac.

Ranger smiled. "He works for me."

Chapter
TWELVE

The sun was setting when we got back to the car.

"That was possibly the best pizza I've ever had," I said to Ranger. "Overall, it was a frightening experience, but the pizza was great."

"Shorty makes it himself."

"Does Shorty work for you, too?"

"Yeah. He caters all my cocktail parties."

More Ranger humor. At least, I was pretty sure it was humor.

Ranger reached Hamilton Avenue and glanced over at me. "Where are you staying tonight?"

"My parents' house."

He turned into the Burg. "I'll have Tank drop a car off for you. You can use it until you replace the CR-V. Or until you destroy it."

"Where do you get all these cars from?"

"You don't actually want to know, do you?"

I took a beat to think about it. "No," I said. "I don't suppose I do. If I knew, you'd have to kill me, right?"

"Something like that."

He stopped in front of my parents' house, and we both looked to the door. My mother and my grandmother were standing there, watching us.

"I'm not sure I feel comfortable about the way your grandma looks at me," Ranger said.

"She wants to see you naked."

"I wish you hadn't told me that, babe."

"Everyone I know wants to see you naked."

"And you?"

"Never crossed my mind." I held my breath when I said it, and I hoped God wouldn't strike me down dead for lying. I hopped out of the car and ran inside.

Grandma Mazur was waiting for me in the foyer. "The darnedest thing happened this afternoon," she said. "I was walking home from the bakery, and a car pulled up alongside me. And there was a rabbit in it. He was driving. And he handed one of them post office mailing envelopes, and he said I should give the envelope to you. It all happened so fast. And as soon as he drove away I remembered that it was a rabbit that set fire to your car. Do you think it could be the same rabbit?"

Ordinarily I would have asked questions. What kind of car and did you get the plate? In this case the questions were useless. The cars were always different. And they were always stolen.

I took the sealed envelope from her, carefully opened it, and looked inside. Photos. Snapshots of me, sleeping on my parents' couch. They were taken last night. Someone had let themselves into the house and stood there, watching me sleep. And then photographed me. All without my knowledge. Whoever it was had picked a good night. I'd slept like the dead thanks to the giant margarita and the sleepless night before.

"What's in the envelope?" Grandma wanted to know.

"Looks like photographs."

"Nothing very interesting," I said. "I think it was a prank rabbit."

My mother looked like she knew better, but she didn't say anything. By the end of the night we'll have a fresh batch of cookies, and she'll have done all the ironing. That's my mother's form of stress management.

I borrowed the Buick, and I drove to Morelli's house. He lived just outside the Burg, in a neighborhood closely resembling the Burg, less than a quarter mile from my parents'. He'd inherited the house from his aunt, and it turned out to be a good fit. Life is surprising. Joe Morelli, the scourge of Trenton High, biker, babe magnet, barroom brawler, now a semi-respectable property owner. Somehow, over the years, Morelli had grown up. No small feat for a male member of that family.

Bob rushed at me when he saw me at the door. His eyes were happy, and he pranced around and wagged his tail. Morelli was more contained.

"What's up?" Morelli said, checking out my T-shirt.

"Something very creepy just happened to me."

"Boy, that's a surprise."

"Creepier than normal."

"Do I need a drink before you tell me this?"

I handed him the photos.

"Nice," he said, "but I've seen you sleep on several occasions."

"These were taken last night without my knowledge. A big rabbit stopped Grandma on the street today and told her to give these to me."

He raised his eyes to look at me. "Are you telling me someone let themselves into your parents' house and took these pictures while you were asleep?"

"Yes." I'd been trying to stay calm, but deep inside I was ruined. The idea that someone, Abruzzi himself, or one of his men, had stood over me and watched me sleep had me completely unnerved. I felt violated and vulnerable.

"This guy has a lot of balls," Morelli said. His voice

was calm enough when he said it, but the line of his mouth tightened, and I knew he was struggling to control his anger. A younger Morelli would have thrown a chair through a window.

"I don't mean to be critical of the Trenton police," I said, "but wouldn't you think someone could catch this goddamn rabbit? He's riding around, handing out photos."

"Were the doors locked last night?"

"Yes."

"What kind of lock?"

"A dead bolt."

"It doesn't take an expert long to open a dead bolt. Can you get your parents to put a security chain on?"

"I can try. I don't want to scare them with these photos. They love their house, and they feel safe there. I don't want to take that away from them."

"Yes, but you're being stalked by a crazy person."

We were standing in the small front hall, and Bob was pressing against me, snuffling into my leg. I looked down, and there was a big wet spot of Bob drool just above my knee. I scratched the top of his head and ruffled his ears. "I need to get out of my parents' house. Take the action away from them."

"You know you can stay here."

"And endanger you?"

"I'm used to being endangered."

This was true. But this was also the basis for almost every argument we had. And it was the primary reason for our breakup. That and my inability to commit. Morelli didn't want a bounty hunter wife. He didn't want the mother of his children regularly dodging bullets. I guess I can't blame him.

"Thanks," I said. "I might take you up on it. I can also ask Ranger to put me in one of his safe houses. Or I can return to my apartment. If I go back to my apartment

I need to have a security system installed. I don't want to come home to any more surprises." Unfortunately, I didn't have the money for a security system. As it was, it didn't matter because I couldn't bring myself to come within fifty feet of the cootie couch.

"What are you going to do tonight?"

"I need to stay in my parents' house and make sure no one breaks in again. Tomorrow I'll move out. I think they'll be safe once I'm gone."

"You're going to stay up all night?"

"Yep. You could come over later if you want, and we could play Monopoly."

Morelli grinned. "Monopoly, hunh? How could I pass that one up? What time does your grandmother go to bed?"

"After the eleven o'clock news."

"I'll be over around twelve."

I fiddled with Bob's ear.

"What?" Morelli asked.

"It's about *us*."

"There's no *us*."

"It feels like there's *some* us."

"This is what I think. I think there's you and me, and sometimes we're together. But there's no *us*."

"That feels a little lonely," I said.

"Don't make this more difficult than it already is," Morelli said.

I packed myself off in the Buick and went in search of a toy store. An hour later, I was done with my shopping, back in the car, heading for home. I stopped for a light on Hamilton, and a split second later, I was rear-ended. Not a big crash. More like a bump. Enough to make the Buick sway, but not enough to push me. My first reaction was my mother's standard reply to anything that was going to make her life more complicated: *Why me?* I doubted there was much damage, but it was going to be a pain in the ass all the same. I yanked the emergency brake on and put the Buick in park. Probably I needed to go out and do the examine-for-dents bullshit. I blew out a sigh and looked in my rearview mirror.

I couldn't see much in the dark, but what I could see wasn't good. I saw ears. Big rabbit ears on the guy in the driver's seat. I swiveled in my seat and squinted out the rear window. The rabbit backed his car up about ten feet and rammed me again. Harder this time. Enough to make the Buick jump forward.

Shit.

I released the brake, put the Buick in gear, and took off, through the red light. The rabbit was close behind. I turned at Chambers Street and ran up and down streets until I slid to a stop in front of Morelli's house. I saw no lights behind me, but that didn't guarantee that the rabbit was gone. He could have cut his lights and parked. I jumped out of the Buick, ran to Morelli's front door, and rang the bell, then I pounded on the door, and then I yelled, "Open up!"

Morelli opened the door, and I jumped inside. "The rabbit is after me," I said.

Morelli stuck his head out and looked up and down the street. "I don't see any rabbits."

"He was in a car. He rear-ended me on Hamilton, and then he chased me here."

"What kind of car?"

"I don't know. I couldn't see in the dark. I could just see his ears sticking up over the wheel." My heart was racing, and I was having a hard time catching my breath. "I'm losing it," I said. "This guy's really pushing my buttons. A rabbit, for crissake! What kind of a mind would think to have me stalked by a rabbit?"

Of course, while I was ranting on about the rabbit and the diabolical mind, I was remembering that it was partially my fault. I was the one who told Abruzzi I liked bunnies.

"We didn't advertise the fact that a rabbit was involved in the Soder murder, so chances of it being a copycat are slim," Morelli said. "If we're going on the assumption that Abruzzi is behind this, then the mind in question is pretty sharp. Abruzzi isn't known for being stupid."

"Just crazy?"

"As crazy as they come. From what I hear, he collects memorabilia and then wears it when he's war gaming. Dresses himself up like Napoleon."

The idea of Abruzzi dressed up like Napoleon got me smiling. He would look ridiculous, second only to the guy in the rabbit suit.

"The rabbit must have been following me from my parents' house," I said to Morelli.

"Where did you go when you left here?"

"I went to buy Monopoly. I got the old-fashioned traditional Monopoly. And I'm going to be the race car."

Morelli took Bob's leash off a hook in the hall and grabbed a jacket. "I'll go back with you, but you have to relinquish the race car to me if Grandma plays. It's the least you can do for me."

At four o'clock I woke up with a start. I was on the couch with Morelli. I'd fallen asleep, sitting up with his arm around me. I'd lost two games of Monopoly, and we'd turned to television. The television was off now, and Morelli was slouched back with his gun on the coffee table next to his cell phone. Lights were off with the exception of the overhead light in the kitchen. Bob was sound asleep on the floor.

"Someone's out there," Morelli said. "I called for a car."

"Is it the rabbit?"

"I don't know. I don't want to go to the window and frighten whoever it is away until backup gets here. They tried the door once, then walked around back and tried that door."

"I don't hear any sirens."

"They won't come with sirens," he whispered. "I got Mickey Lauder. I told him to come in an unmarked car and come in on foot."

There was a muffled crash from the back of the house, and a lot of shouting. Morelli and I ran to the back and flipped the porch light on. Mickey Lauder and two uniforms had two people down on the ground.

"Christ," Morelli said, grinning. "It's your sister and Albert Kloughn."

Mickey Lauder was grinning, too. He'd dated Valerie in high school. "Sorry," he said, hauling her to her feet, "I didn't recognize you at first. You've changed your hair."

"Are you married?" Valerie asked.

"Yeah. Big time. I've got four kids."

"Just curious," Valerie said on a sigh.

Kloughn was still on the ground. "I'm pretty sure she didn't do anything illegal," he said. "She couldn't get in. The doors were locked, and she didn't want to wake anybody. It wouldn't have been breaking and entering, right? You can break into your own house, right? I mean, that's what you have to do if you forget your key, right?"

"I saw you go to bed with the kids," I said to Valerie. "How'd you get out here?"

"The same way you used to sneak out when you were in high school," Morelli said, the grin getting wider. "Out the bathroom window to the back porch roof and then down to the garbage can."

"You must be really hot stuff, Kloughn," Lauder said, still enjoying it. "I could never get her to sneak out for me."

"I don't like to brag or anything," Kloughn said, "but I know what I'm doing."

Grandma came up behind me in her bathrobe. "What's going on?"

"Valerie got busted."

"No kidding?" Grandma said. "Good for her."

Morelli shoved his gun under the waistband of his jeans. "I'm going to get my jacket and have Lauder drop me off at home. You'll be okay now. Grandma can stay up with you. Sorry about Monopoly, but you're a really lousy player."

"I *let* you win because you were doing me a favor."

"Yeah, right."

"I hate to interrupt your breakfast," Grandma said to me, "but there's a great big, scary-looking guy at the door, and he wants to talk to you. He said he's delivering a car."

That would be Tank.

I went to the door, and Tank handed me a set of keys. I looked beyond him, to the curb. Ranger had given me a new black CR-V. Very much like the car that had gotten blown up. I knew from past experience it would be upgraded in every way possible. And probably it had a tracking device stuck in a place I'd never think to look. Ranger liked to keep tabs on his cars and his people. A new black Land Rover with a driver waited behind the CR-V.

"This is for you, too," Tank said, giving me a cell phone. "It's programmed with your number."

And he was gone.

Grandma looked after him. "Was he from the rental car company?"

"Sort of."

I returned to the kitchen and drank my coffee while I checked the answering machine in my apartment. I had two calls from my insurance company. The first told me I would be receiving forms by priority mail. The second told me I was canceled. There were three calls of nothing but breathing. I assumed this was the rabbit. The last message was from Evelyn's neighbor, Carol Nadich.

"Hey, Steph," she said. "I haven't seen Evelyn or Annie, but something funny is going on here. Give me a call when you get a chance."

"I'm going out," I said to my mother and grandmother. "And I'm taking my stuff. I'm going to stay with a friend for a couple days. I'm leaving Rex here."

My mother looked up from cutting soup vegetables. "You aren't moving in with Joe Morelli again, are you?" she asked. "I don't know what to tell people. What do I say?"

"I'm not staying with Morelli. Don't tell people anything. There's nothing to tell. If you need to talk to me, you can reach me on my cell phone." I stopped at the door. "Morelli says you should have a security chain put on the doors. He said they're not safe this way."

"What would happen?" my mother said. "We have nothing to steal. This is a respectable neighborhood. Nothing ever happens here."

I carted my bag out to the car, tossed it onto the backseat, and climbed behind the wheel. Better to talk to Carol in person. It took less than two minutes to get to her house. I parked and did a survey of the street. Everything looked normal. I knocked once, and she answered her door.

"Quiet street," I said. "Where is everybody?"

"Soccer games. Every dad and every kid on this street goes to soccer on Saturday."

"So what's weird?"

"Do you know the Pagarellis?"

I shook my head, no.

"They live next door to Betty Lando. Moved in about six months ago. Old Mr. Pagarelli sits out on the porch all the time. He's a widower, living with his son and daughter-in-law. And the daughter-in-law won't let the old guy smoke in the house, so he's always out on the porch. Anyway, Betty said she was talking to him the other day, and he was bragging about how he was working for Eddie Abruzzi. He told Betty that Abruzzi pays him to watch my house. Is that creepy, or what? I mean, what's it to him that Evelyn took off? I don't see what the problem is as long as she makes her rent payment."

"Anything else?"

"Evelyn's car is parked in the driveway. It showed up this morning."

That took some of the wind out of my sails. Stephanie Plum, master detective. I'd driven past Evelyn's car and never noticed. "Did you hear it drive up? Did you see anyone?"

"Nope. Lenny discovered it. He went out for the paper, and he noticed Evelyn's car was here."

"Do you ever hear anyone next door?"

"Only you."

I did a grimace.

"In the beginning there were lots of people looking for Evelyn," Carol said. "Soder and his friends. And Abruzzi. Soder would just walk into the house. I guess he had a key. Abruzzi, too."

I looked over at Evelyn's front door. "You don't suppose Evelyn's in there now?"

"I knocked on the door, and I looked in the back window, and I didn't see anyone."

I moved from Carol's porch to Evelyn's porch, and Carol tagged along behind me. I knocked on the door, hard. I put my ear to the front window. I shrugged my shoulders.

"Nothing going on in there," Carol said. "Right?"

We walked to the back of the house and looked in the kitchen window. As far as I could tell, nothing had been touched. I tried the knob. Still locked. Too bad the window was repaired, I would have liked to get inside. I did another shrug.

Carol and I walked over to the car. We stood four feet away.

"I didn't look in the car," Carol said.

"We should do that," I told her.

"You first," she said.

I sucked in some air and took two giant steps forward. I looked in the car and blew out a sigh of relief. No dead people. No body parts. No rabbits. Although, now that I was closer, the car didn't smell all that terrific.

"Maybe we should call the police," I said.

There have been times in my life when curiosity has pushed aside common sense. This wasn't one of them. The car was sitting in the driveway, unlocked, with the keys dangling in the ignition. It would have been easy for me to pop the trunk and peek inside, but I had no desire to do this. I was pretty sure I knew the reason for the odor. Finding Soder on my couch had been traumatic enough. I didn't want to be the one to find Evelyn or Annie in the trunk of Evelyn's car.

Carol and I sat huddled together on her porch while we waited for the blue-and-white. Neither of us was willing to articulate our thoughts. It was too awful to speculate aloud.

I stood when the police arrived, but I didn't leave the porch. There were two patrol cars. Costanza was in one of them.

"You're looking white," Costanza said to me. "Do you feel okay?"

I nodded my head. I was afraid to trust my voice.

Big Dog was at the trunk. He had it open, and he was standing hands on hips. "You gotta see this," he said to Costanza.

Costanza walked over and stood next to Big Dog. "Cripes."

Carol and I were holding hands for support. "Tell me," I said to Costanza.

"You sure you want to know?"

I nodded my head yes.

"It's a dead guy in a bear suit."

The world stood still for a moment. "It's not Evelyn or Annie?"

"No. I'm telling you, it's a dead guy in a bear suit. Come look for yourself."

"I'll take your word for it."

"Your grandma's gonna be real disappointed if you don't look at this. Not every day you see a dead guy in a bear suit."

The EMTs rolled in and a couple unmarked cars followed close behind. Costanza stretched some tape around the crime scene.

Morelli parked across the street and strolled over. He looked in the trunk, and then he looked at me. "It's a dead guy in a bear suit."

"That's what they tell me."

"Your grandma's never going to forgive you if you don't take a look at this."

"Do I really want to look at it?"

Morelli studied the body in the trunk. "No, probably not." He walked over to me. "Who owns the car?"

"Evelyn, but nobody's seen her. Carol said the car showed up this morning. Did you draw this case?"

"Nope," Morelli said. "This is Benny's. I'm just sight-seeing. Bob and I were on our way to the park when I heard the call go out."

I could see Bob watching us from the truck. He had his nose pressed to the window, and he was panting.

"I'm okay," I said to Morelli. "I'll call you when I'm done here."

"You have a phone?"

"It came with the CR-V."

Morelli looked at the car. "Rental?"

"Sort of."

"Shit, Stephanie, you didn't get that car from Ranger, did you? No, wait a minute." He held his hands up. "I don't want to know." He looked sideways at me. "Did you ever ask him where he gets all these cars?"

"He said he'd tell me, but then he'd have to kill me."

"Did you ever stop to think he might not be kidding?" He got into his truck, buckled himself in, and cranked the engine over.

"Who's Bob?" Carol asked.

"Bob's the one who's sitting in the truck, panting."

"I'd be panting, too, if I was in Morelli's truck," Carol said.

Benny came over with his pad in his hand. He was in his early forties and probably thinking about retirement in the next couple years. Probably a case like this made retirement even more appealing. I didn't know Benny personally, but I'd heard Morelli talk about him from time to time. From what I heard, he was a good steady cop.

"I need to ask you some questions," Benny said.

I was getting to know these questions by heart.

I sat on the porch with my back to the car. I didn't want to see them haul the guy out of the trunk. Benny sat across from me. I could look beyond Benny and see old Mr. Pagarelli watching us. I wondered if Abruzzi was watching, too.

"You know what?" I said to Benny. "This is getting old."

He looked apologetic. "I'm almost done."

"Not you. This. The bear, the rabbit, the couch, everything."

"Have you ever thought about getting a different job?"

"Every minute of every day." But then, sometimes the job had its moments. "I have to go," I said. "Things to do."

Benny closed his little cop notebook. "Be careful."

That's exactly what I wasn't going to do. I hopped into the CR-V and eased around the emergency vehicles blocking the road. It wasn't quite noon. Lula should still be in the office. I needed to talk to Abruzzi, and I was too chicken to do it all by myself.

I parked at the curb and barreled through the office door. "I want to talk to Eddie Abruzzi," I said to Connie. "Do you have any idea where I might find him?"

"He has an office downtown. I don't know if he'll be there on a Saturday."

"I know where you can find him," Vinnie yelled from his inner sanctum. "He'll be at the track. He goes to the track every Saturday, rain or shine, as long as the horses are running."

"Monmouth?" I asked.

"Yeah, Monmouth. He'll be on the rail."

I looked over at Lula. "Do you feel like going to the track?"

"Hell, yeah. I feel lucky. I might do some betting. My horoscope said I was gonna make good decisions today. Only thing, *you* want to be careful. *Your* horoscope sucked."

This didn't surprise me.

"I see you're driving a new car already," Lula said. "Rental?"

I pressed my lips together.

Lula and Connie exchanged knowing glances.

"Girl, you're gonna *pay* for that car," Lula said. "And I want to know all the details. You better take notes."

"I want measurements," Connie said.

It was a nice day and the traffic was steady. We were going in the general direction of the shore, and lucky for us, it wasn't July because in July the road would be a parking lot.

"Your horoscope didn't say anything about making good decisions," Lula said. "So I think I'm the one who should be deciding things today. And I'm deciding we should play the ponies and stay far away from Abruzzi. What do you want to talk to him about anyway? What are you going to say to the man?"

"I don't have it totally worked out, but it'll be along the lines of 'fuck off.'"

"Uh-oh," Lula said. "That don't sound like a good decision to me."

"Benito Ramirez fed off fear. I have a feeling Abruzzi is like that, too. I want him to know it's not working." And I want to know what he's after. I want to know why Evelyn and Annie are important to him.

"Benito Ramirez didn't only feed off fear," Lula said. "That was just the first part. That was foreplay. Ramirez liked to hurt people. And he'd hurt you until you were dead . . . or wished you were dead."

I thought about that for the forty minutes it took me to get to the track. The awful part is that I knew it to be true. I knew firsthand. I was the one who discovered Lula after Ramirez was done with her. Finding Steven Soder was a walk in the park compared to finding Lula.

"This is my idea of work," Lula said when I pulled into the lot. "Not everybody's got a good job like us. Sure, we get shot at once in a while, but look here, we're not stuck in some crummy office building today."

"Today is Saturday," I said. "Most people aren't working at all."

"Well, yeah," Lula said. "But we could do this on a Wednesday if we wanted."

My cell phone chirped.

"Put ten dollars to win on Roger Dodger in the fifth," Ranger said. And he disconnected.

"Well?" Lula asked.

"Ranger. He wants me to bet ten dollars on Roger Dodger in the fifth."

"Did you tell him we were going to the track?"

"No."

"How's he do that?" Lula asked. "How's he know where we are? I'm telling you, he's not human. He's from space or something."

We looked around to see if we were being followed. I hadn't thought to look for a tail on the way down. "Probably he has the car monitored," I said. "Like OnStar, but his system reports to the Bat Cave."

We followed a tidal wave of people through the gate, into the belly of the grandstand. The first race had just been run and the smell of nervous sweat was already permeating the ticket area. The air was thick with collective angst and hope and the frenzied energy that boils at a track.

Lula's eyes were rolling in her head, not sure where to go first, hearing the conflicting call of nachos, beer, and the five-dollar window.

"We need a racing sheet," she said. "How much time do we got? I don't want to miss this race. There's a horse named Decision Maker. That's a sign from God. First my horoscope and then this. I was meant to come here today and bet on this horse. Outta my way. You're getting in my way."

I stood in the middle of the floor and waited for Lula to place her bet. All around me people were talking

horses and jockeys, living in the moment, enjoying
the diversion. I, on the other hand, wasn't allowed the
diversion. I couldn't get my mind off Abruzzi. I was
being stalked. My emotions were being manipulated.
My security was threatened. And I was angry. I was up
to here with it. Lula was absolutely right about Benito
Ramirez and his sadistic cruelty. And she was probably right that talking to Abruzzi was a bad idea. But
I was going to do it anyway. I couldn't help myself. Of
course, I had to find him first. And that wasn't going to
be as easy as I originally thought. I'd forgotten how big
the area was at the rail, how many people congregated
there.

The bell sounded to close the windows, and Lula
rushed over to me. "I got it. I just got it in time. We got
to hurry up and get seats. I don't want to miss this. I just
know this horse is going to win. He's a long shot, too.
We're going out to dinner tonight. I'm treating."

We found seats in the grandstand and watched the
horses come in. If I'd had my own CR-V there would
have been minibinoculars in the glove compartment.
Unfortunately, the minibinoculars were now a melted
glob of glass and slag, probably compressed to the thick-
ness of a dime.

I systematically worked my way through the crowd
at the rail, trying to find Abruzzi. The horses took off,
and the crowd surged forward, shouting, waving pro-
grams. It was impossible to see anything other than a
blur of color. Lula was screaming and jumping up and
down next to me.

"Go, you motherfucker," she was yelling. "Go, go, go,
you dumb sonovabitch!"

I wasn't sure what to wish for. I wanted her to win,
but I was afraid if she won, she'd be impossible with the
horoscope stuff.

The horses streaked across the finish line, and Lula

was still jumping. "Yes," she was screaming. "Yes, yes, yes!"

I looked over at her. "You won, right?"

"You bet your ass I won. I won big. Twenty to one. I must have been the only genius in this whole freaking place who bet on that four-legged wonder. I'm going to get my money. Are you coming with me?"

"No. I'm going to wait here. I want to look for Abruzzi now that the crowd is thinning."

Chapter

THIRTEEN

Part of the problem was that I was seeing everyone at the rail from the back. Difficult enough to recognize someone you know intimately this way. Almost impossible to recognize someone you've only seen briefly on two occasions.

Lula plunked down into the seat next to me. "You're not going to believe this," she said. "I just looked into the eyes of the devil." She had her ticket clutched tight in her hand, and she made the sign of the cross. "Holy mother of God. Look here. I'm crossing myself. What's with that? I'm Baptist. Baptist don't do this cross shit."

"Eyes of the devil?" I asked.

"Abruzzi. I ran right into Abruzzi. I was coming from collecting my money, and I just placed my bet, and I bumped right into him like it was destiny. He looked down at me, and I looked into those eyes, and I almost messed my pants. It's like all my blood turns cold when I look into those eyes."

"Did he say anything?"

"No. He smiled at me. It was awful. It was that smile that's just a slash in his face and doesn't go to his eyes. And then calm as anything, he turned around and walked away."

"Was he alone? What was he wearing?"

"He was with that Darrow guy again. I think Darrow must be muscle. And I don't know what he was wearing. It's like my brain gets paralyzed when I get five feet from Abruzzi. I just get sucked into those creepy eyes." Lula gave a shiver. "Yeesh," she said.

At least I knew Abruzzi was here. And I knew he was with Darrow. I started working my way through the rail crowd again. I was beginning to recognize people. They tended to go away to bet, but then they gravitated back to their favorite spot on the rail.

They were Jersey people, the younger guys dressed in T-shirts and khakis and jeans, the older guys wearing Sansabelt polyester slacks and three-button knit golf shirts. Their faces were animated. Jersey doesn't hold much back. And their bodies were padded with a good protective layer of deep-fried fish and sausage sandwich fat.

From the corner of my eye I saw Lula make the sign of the cross again.

Lula caught me looking at her. "It's a comfort," Lula said. "I think the Catholics might have hit on something here."

The third race started, and Lula rocketed out of her seat. "Go, Ladies' Choice," she screamed. "Ladies' Choice! Ladies' Choice!"

Ladies' Choice won by a nose, and Lula looked stunned. "I won again," she said. "There's something wrong here. I never win."

"Why did you pick Ladies' Choice?"

"It was the obvious one. I'm a lady. And I had to make a choice."

"You think you're a lady?"

"Fuckin' A," Lula said.

This time, I followed her out of the grandstand to the window. She was moving carefully, looking around, trying to avoid another meeting with Abruzzi. I was looking around for the opposite reason.

Lula stopped and went rigid. "There he is," she said. "Over there at the fifty-dollar window."

I saw him, too. He was third in line. Darrow was behind him. I could feel every muscle in my body go into contraction. It was like I was squinting from my eyeballs clear down to my sphincter.

I marched over and got right up into Abruzzi's face. "Hey," I said, "remember me?"

"Of course," Abruzzi said. "I have your picture in a frame on my desk. Do you know you sleep with your mouth open? It's actually very sensuous."

I went still, hoping not to show emotion. Truth is, he knocked the air out of my lungs. And he sent a stab of revulsion into me that sickened my stomach. I'd expected he'd say something about the photos. I hadn't expected this. "I guess you need to pull these idiot pranks to compensate for the fact that you're not having any success at locating Evelyn," I said. "She's got something you want and you can't get your hands on it, can you?"

Now it was Abruzzi's turn to go still. For a single terrifying moment I thought he was going to hit me. Then his composure returned, and the blood rushed back into his face. "You're a stupid little bitch," he said.

"Yep," I said. "And I'm your worst nightmare." Okay, it was sort of a hokey movie line, but I've *always* wanted to say it. "And I'm not impressed with the rabbit thing. It was clever the first time when you carted Soder into my apartment, but it's getting tired."

"You said you liked bunnies," Abruzzi said. "Don't you like them anymore?"

"Get a life," I said. "Find yourself a new hobby."

And I turned on my heel and stalked off.

Lula was waiting at the mouth of the tunnel that led to our seats. "What'd you say to him?"

"I told him to let it ride on Peaches' Dream in the fourth."

"The hell you did," Lula said. "Not often you see a man turn white like that."

By the time I got to my seat my knees were knocking together, and my hands were shaking so bad I was having a hard time hanging onto my program.

"Jeez," Lula said, "you aren't having a heart attack or anything, are you?"

"I'm okay," I said. "It's the excitement of the horse racing."

"Yeah, I figured that was it."

A hysterical giggle escaped from my mouth. "It's not like Abruzzi scares me."

"Sure, I know that," Lula said. "Nothing scares you. You're a big badass bounty hunter."

"Damn right," I said. And then I concentrated on not hyperventilating.

"We should do this more often," Lula said, getting out of my car, unlocking the Trans Am.

She was parked on the street in front of the office. The office was closed, but the new bookstore in the house next door was open. Lights were on, and I could see Maggie Mason unpacking boxes in the window.

"I had a setback in the last race," Lula said, "but aside from that I had a very good day. I just let it ride. Next time we could go to Freehold, and then we don't have to worry about running into *you know who*."

Lula drove off, but I stayed. I was like Evelyn now. On the run. No place safe to settle. For lack of something better, I went to the movies. Halfway through the movie I got up and left. I got into my car, and I went home. I parked in the lot, and I didn't allow myself to hesitate behind the wheel. I got out of the CR-V, beeped it locked, and walked straight to the back door that led to the lobby. I took the elevator to the second floor, marched down the hall, and unlocked the door to my apartment. I took a deep breath and stepped inside. It was very quiet. And dark.

I flipped the lights on . . . every single light I owned. I walked room to room, avoiding the cootie couch. I went back to the kitchen, removed six cookies from the bag of frozen chocolate chip cookies, and put them on a cookie sheet. I popped them into the oven and stood there, waiting. Five minutes later, the house smelled like homemade cookies. Bolstered by cookie fumes, I marched into the living room and looked at the couch. The couch looked fine. No stains. No dead body imprint.

You see, Stephanie, I said to myself. The couch is okay. No reason to be creeped out by the couch.

Hah! An invisible Irma whispered in my ear. Everyone knows you can't *see* death cooties. Take my word for it, that couch has the biggest, fattest death cooties that ever existed. That couch has the mother of all death cooties.

I tried to sit on the couch but I couldn't bring myself to do it. Soder and the couch were fixed together in my mind. Sitting on the couch was like sitting on Soder's dead, sawed-in-half lap. The apartment was too small for both me *and* the couch. One of us was going to have to go.

"Sorry," I said to the couch. "Nothing personal, but you're history." I put my weight behind one end, and I pushed the couch across the living room, into the small entrance foyer in front of the kitchen, out the front door, and into the hall. I positioned it against the wall between my apartment and Mrs. Karwatt's apartment. Then I ran back into my apartment, closed my door, and did a sigh. I knew there were no such things as death cooties. Unfortunately, that's an intellectual fact. And death cooties are an emotional reality.

I took the cookies out of the oven, put them on a plate, and carted them off to the living room. I zapped the television on and found a movie. Irma hadn't said anything about death cooties on the remote, so I assumed death cooties didn't stick to electronic devices. I pulled a dining room chair over to the television, ate two of the cookies, and watched the movie.

Halfway through the movie, the doorbell rang. It was Ranger. Dressed in his usual black. Full utility belt, looking like Rambo. Hair tied back. He stood there in silence when I opened the door. The corners of his mouth tipped slightly into the promise of a smile.

"Babe, your couch is in the hall."

"It has death cooties."

"I knew there'd be a good explanation."

I shook my head at him. "You're such a show-off." Not only had he placed me at the track, his horse had paid off five to one.

"Even superheroes need to have fun once in a while," he said, looking me over, brushing past me, walking into the living room. "It smells like you're marking your territory with chocolate chip cookies."

"I needed something to chase away the demons."

"Any problems?"

"Nope." Not since I pushed the couch into the hall. "So what's up?" I said. "You look like you're dressed for work."

"I had to secure a building earlier this evening." I'd once been with him when his team secured a building. It involved throwing a drug dealer out a third-story window.

He took a cookie off the plate on the floor. "Frozen?"

"Not anymore."

"How'd it go at the track?"

"I ran into Eddie Abruzzi."

"And?"

"We had words. I didn't find out as much as I'd hoped, but I'm convinced Evelyn has something he wants."

"I know what it is," Ranger said, eating his cookie. I stared at him openmouthed. "What is it?"

He smiled. "How bad do you want to know?"

"Are we playing?"

He slowly shook his head no. "This isn't play." He backed me against the wall, and he leaned into me. His leg slid between mine, his lips brushed lightly across my lips. "How bad do you want to know, Steph?" he asked again.

"Tell me."

"It'll get added to the debt."

Like I was going to worry about that now? I was in way over my credit limit weeks ago! "Are you going to tell me, or what?"

"Remember I told you Abruzzi is a war gamer? Well, he does more than game. He collects memorabilia. Old guns, army uniforms, military medals. And he doesn't just collect them. He wears them. Mostly when he games. Sometimes when he's with women, I'm told. Sometimes when he's settling a bad debt. Word on the street is that Abruzzi is missing a medal.

Supposedly the medal belonged to Napoleon. The story being told is that Abruzzi tried to buy the medal, but the guy who owned it wouldn't sell it, so Abruzzi killed him and took the medal. Abruzzi kept the medal on his desk at his house. He wore it when he gamed. Believed it made him invincible."

"And this is what Evelyn has? The medal?"

"That's what I hear."

"How did she get it?"

"I don't know."

He moved against me and desire skittered through

my stomach and burned low in my belly. He was hard *everywhere*. His thigh, his gun . . . *everything* was hard.

He lowered his head and kissed my neck. He touched his tongue to the place he just kissed. And then he kissed it again. His hand slid under my T-shirt, his palm heating my skin, his fingers at the base of my breast.

"Pay-up time," he said. "I'm collecting on the debt."

I almost collapsed onto the floor.

He took my hand and tugged me toward the bedroom. "The movie," I said. "The best part of the movie is coming up." In all honesty, I couldn't remember a single thing about the movie. Not the name or anyone in it.

He was standing close, his face inches from mine, his hand at the back of my neck. "We're going to do this, babe," he said. "It's going to be good." And then he kissed me. The kiss deepened, became more demanding, more intimate.

I had my hands splayed over his chest, and I felt the toned muscle under my hands, felt his heart beating. So he has a heart, I thought. That's a good sign. He must be at least *part* human.

He broke from the kiss and pushed me into the bedroom. He kicked his boots off, dropped his gun belt, and he stripped. The light was low, but it was enough to see that what Ranger promised in SWAT clothes was kept when the clothes were shed. He was all firm muscle and smooth dark skin. His body was in perfect proportion. His eyes were intense and focused.

He peeled my clothes off and wrangled me onto the bed. And then suddenly he was inside me. He once told me that time spent with him would ruin me for all other men. When he said it, I thought it was an outrageous threat. I no longer thought it outrageous.

We lay together for a while when we were done.

Finally he ran his hand the length of my body. "It's time," he said.

"*Now* what?"

"You didn't think the debt would be paid that easily, did you?"

"Uh-oh, is this the part with the handcuffs?"

"I don't need handcuffs to enslave a woman," Ranger said, kissing my shoulder.

He kissed me lightly on my lips and then dipped his head to kiss my chin, my neck, my collarbone. He moved lower, kissing the swell of my breast and my nipple. He kissed my navel and then my belly, and then he put his mouth to my . . . *omigod!*

He was still in my bed the next morning. He was pressed next to me, his arm holding me close. I woke to the sound of the alarm on his watch. He shut the alarm off and rolled away to check the pager that had been placed on the nightstand, next to his gun.

"I have to go, babe," he said. And he was dressed. And he was gone.

Oh shit. What did I do? I just did *it* with the Wizard. Holy crap! Okay, calm down. Let's examine this more sanely. What just happened here? We did *it*. And he left. The leaving seemed a smidgen abrupt, but then it was Ranger. What did I expect? And he hadn't been abrupt last night. He'd been . . . amazing. I sighed and heaved myself out of bed. I showered and dressed and went into the kitchen to say good morning to Rex. Only there was no Rex. Rex was living with my parents.

The house felt empty without Rex, so I packed myself off to my parents'. It was Sunday and there was the added incentive of doughnuts. My mother and grandmother always bought doughnuts on their way home from church.

The horse kid was galloping through the house in her Sunday School dress. She stopped galloping when she saw me and her face grew thoughtful. "Have you found Annie yet?"

"No," I said. "But I talked to her mom on the phone."

"Next time you talk to her mom you should tell her Annie's missing stuff at school. Tell her I got put in the Black Stallion reading group."

"You're telling another whopper," Grandma said. "You're in the Blue Bird reading group."

"I don't want to be a blue bird," Mary Alice said. "Blue birds are poopy. I want to be a black stallion." And she galloped away.

"I love that kid," I said to Grandma.

"Yep," Grandma said. "She reminds me a lot of you when you were that age. Good imagination. It comes from my side of the family. Except it skipped a generation with your mother. Your mother and Valerie and Angie are blue birds through and through."

I helped myself to a doughnut and poured out a cup of coffee.

"You look different," Grandma said to me. "I can't put my finger on it. And you've been smiling ever since you walked in."

Damn Ranger. I noticed the smile when I brushed my teeth. It wouldn't go away! "Amazing what a good night's sleep can do for you," I said to Grandma.

"I wouldn't mind having a smile like that," Grandma said.

Valerie came to the table, looking morose. "I don't know what to do about Albert," she said.

"Not got a two-bathroom house?"

"He lives with his mother, and he has less money than I do."

No surprises there. "Good men are hard to find," I

said. "And when you find them, there's always something wrong with them."

Valerie looked in the doughnut bag. "It's empty. Where's my doughnut?"

"Stephanie ate it," Grandma said.

"I only had one!"

"Oh," Grandma said, "then maybe it was me. I had three."

"We need more doughnuts," Valerie said. "I have to have a doughnut."

I grabbed my bag and hiked it onto my shoulder. "I'll get more. I could use another one, too."

"I'll go with you," Grandma said. "I want to ride in your shiny black car. I don't suppose you'd let me drive?"

My mother was at the stove. "Don't you *dare* let her drive. I'm holding you responsible. If she drives and gets in an accident, you're going to be the one visiting her in the nursing home."

We went to Tasty Pastry on Hamilton. I worked there when I was in high school. Gave away my virginity there, too. Behind the eclair case, after-hours, with Morelli. I'm not sure how it happened. One minute I was selling him a cannoli and next thing I knew I was on the floor with my pants down. Morelli's always been good at talking the pants off women.

I parked in the small lot on the side of Tasty Pastry. The after-church rush was over, and the lot was empty. There were seven parking slots that went nose in to the redbrick wall of the bakery, and I parked square in the middle slot.

Grandma and I went into the bakery and picked out another dozen doughnuts. Probably overkill, but better to have too many than to be doughnut deprived.

We came out of the bakery, and we were approaching Ranger's CR-V when a green Ford Explorer careened into the lot and came to a screeching halt next to us. The driver had a rubber Clinton mask over his face, and the passenger seat was occupied by the rabbit.

My heart went *ka-thunk* in my chest, and I got a rush of adrenaline. "Run," I said, shoving Grandma, plunging my hand into my bag to find my gun. "Run back to the bakery."

The guy in the rubber mask and the guy in the rabbit suit were out of the car before it stopped rolling. They rushed at Grandma and me with guns drawn and herded us between the two cars. The rubber mask guy was of average height and build. He was wearing jeans and running shoes and a Nike jacket. The rabbit was wearing the big rabbit head and street clothes.

"Against the car, and hands where I can see them," the mask guy said.

"Who are you supposed to be?" Grandma asked. "You look like Bill Clinton."

"Yeah, I'm Bill Clinton," the guy said. "Get against the car."

"I never understood that part about the cigar," Grandma said.

"Get against the car!"

I backed against the car and my mind was racing. Cars were moving on the street in front of us, but we were hidden from sight. If I screamed I doubted I'd be heard by anyone, unless someone walked by on the sidewalk.

The rabbit got up close to me. *"Thaaa id ya raa raa da haaar id ra raa."*

"What?"

"Haaar id ra raa."

"We can't figure out what you're saying, on account of you're wearing that big stupid rabbit head," Grandma said.

"Raa raa," the rabbit said. *"Raa raa!"*

Grandma and I looked over at Clinton.

Clinton shook his head in disgust. "I don't know what he's saying. What the hell's *raa raa?*" he asked the rabbit.

"*Haaar id ra raa.*"

"Christ," Clinton said. "Nobody can understand you. Haven't you ever tried to talk in that thing before?"

The rabbit gave Clinton a shove. "*Ra raa,* you fraaa-kin' *aar* ho."

Clinton flipped the rabbit the bird.

"*Jaaaark,*" the rabbit said. And then he unzipped his pants and pulled out his wanger. He waggled his wanger at Clinton. And then he waggled it at Grandma and me.

"I remember them as being bigger than that," Grandma said.

The rabbit yanked and pulled at himself and managed to get half a hard-on.

"*Rogga. Ga rogga,*" the rabbit said.

"I think he's trying to tell you this is a preview," Clinton said. "Something to look forward to."

The rabbit was still working it. He'd found his rhythm, and he was really whacking away.

"Maybe you should help him out," Clinton said to me. "Go ahead. Touch it."

My lip curled back. "What are you nuts? I'm not touching it!"

"I'll touch it," Grandma said.

"*Kraaa,*" the rabbit said. And his wanger wilted a little.

A car turned off the street, into the lot, and Clinton gave the rabbit a shot in the arm. "Let's roll."

They backed up, still holding us at gunpoint. Both men jumped into the Explorer and took off.

"Maybe we should have got some cannoli," Grandma said. "I got a sudden taste for cannoli."

I loaded Grandma into the CR-V and drove her back to the house.

"We saw that rabbit again," Grandma told my mother. "The one who gave me the pictures. I think he must live by the bakery. This time he showed us his ding-a-ling."

My mother was justifiably horrified.

"Was he wearing a wedding band?" Valerie asked.

"I didn't notice," Grandma said. "I wasn't looking at his hand."

"You were held at gunpoint and sexually assaulted," I said to Grandma. "Weren't you frightened? Aren't you upset?"

"They weren't real guns," Grandma said. "And we were in the parking lot to the bakery. Who would be serious about something like that in a bakery parking lot?"

"They were real guns," I said.

"Are you sure?"

"*Yes.*"

"Maybe I'll sit down," Grandma said. "I thought that rabbit was just one of those exhibitionists. Remember Sammy the Squirrel? He was always dropping his drawers in people's backyards. Sometimes we'd give him a sandwich after."

The Burg has had its share of exhibitionists, some mentally challenged, some drunk beyond reason, some just out for a good time. For the most part, the attitude is eye-rolling tolerance. Once in a while someone drops his drawers in the wrong backyard and ends up with an ass filled with buckshot.

I called Morelli and told him about the rabbit. "He was with Clinton," I said. "And they weren't getting along all that great."

"You should file a report."

"There's only one body part I'd ever recognize on this guy, and I don't think you've got it in the mug books."

"Are you carrying a gun?"

"Yes. I didn't have time to get to it."

"Put it on your hip. It's illegal to carry concealed anyway. And it wouldn't be a bad idea to actually put a couple bullets in it."

"I *have* bullets in it." Ranger put them in. "Have they identified the guy in the trunk yet?"

"Thomas Turkello. Also known as Thomas Turkey. Muscle for hire out of Philadelphia. My guess is he was expendable, and better to snuff him than take a chance on him talking. The rabbit is probably inner circle."

"Anything else?"

"What would you want?"

"Abruzzi's fingerprint on a murder weapon."

"Sorry."

I was reluctant to disconnect, but I didn't have anything else to say. The truth is, I had a hollow feeling in my stomach that I hated to put a name to. I was mortally afraid it was loneliness. Ranger was fire and magic, but he wasn't real. Morelli was everything I wanted in a man, but he wanted me to be something I wasn't.

I hung up and retreated to the living room. If you sat in front of the television in my parents' house, you weren't expected to talk. Even if asked a direct question, the viewer had the discretion of feigning hearing loss. Those were the rules.

Grandma and I were side by side on the sofa, watching the Weather Channel. Hard to tell which of us was more shell-shocked.

"I guess it's a good thing I didn't touch it," Grandma said. "Although, I gotta admit, I *was* kind of curious. It wasn't real pretty, but it was big toward the end there. Have you ever seen one that big?"

The perfect time to invoke the television no-answer privilege.

After a couple minutes of weather I went back to

the kitchen and had my second doughnut. I collected my things and I headed out. "I'm going," I said to Grandma. "All's well that ends well, right?"

Grandma didn't answer. Grandma was zoned out to the Weather Channel. There was a high pressure area moving across the Great Lakes.

I went back to my apartment. This time I had my gun in my hand before I got out of the car. I crossed the lot and entered the building. I paused when I got to my door. This was always the tricky part. Once I was in the apartment I felt fairly secure. I had a security chain and a bolt besides the deadlock. Only Ranger could get in unannounced. Either he walked through the door ghost style, or else he vaporized himself like a vampire and slid under the jamb. I guess there might be a mortal possibility, but I didn't know what it was.

I unlocked my door and searched through my apartment like the movie version of a CIA operative, skulking from room to room, gun drawn, crouched position, ready to fire. I was crashing open doors and jumping around. Good thing no one was there to see me because I knew I looked like an idiot. The good part was, I didn't find any rabbits with their tools hanging out. Compared to rape by the rabbit, spiders and snakes seemed like small change.

Ranger called ten minutes after I got into my apartment.

"Are you going to be home for a while?" he asked. "I want to send someone over to set up a security system."

So the man of mystery reads minds, too.

"My man's name is Hector," Ranger said. "He's on his way."

Hector was slim and Hispanic, dressed in black. He had a gang slogan tattooed onto his neck and a single tear tattooed under his eye. He was in his early twenties, and he only spoke Spanish.

Hector had my door open and was making a final adjustment when Ranger arrived. Ranger gave a barely audible greeting to Hector in Spanish and glanced at the sensor that had just been installed in my doorjamb.

Then Ranger looked at me, giving away nothing of his thoughts. Our eyes held for a few long moments, and Ranger turned back to Hector. My Spanish is limited to burrito and taco, so I couldn't understand the exchange between Ranger and Hector. Hector was talking and gesturing, and Ranger was listening and questioning. Hector gave Ranger a small gizmo, picked up his tool chest, and left.

Ranger crooked his finger at me, giving me the *come here* sign. "This is your remote. It's a keypad, small enough to hook to your car key. You have a four-digit code to open and close your door. If the door has been violated the remote will tell you. You're not attached to a watchdog. There's no alarm. This is designed to give you easy access and to tell you if someone's broken into your apartment, so you have no more surprises. You have a steel fire door, and Hector's installed a floor bolt. If you lock yourself in, you should be safe. There's not much I can do about your windows. The fire escape is a problem. It's less of a problem if you keep your gun on your nightstand."

I looked down at the remote. "Does this go on the tab?"

"There's no tab. And there's no price for what we give each other. Not ever. Not financial. Not emotional. I have to get back to work."

He stepped away to leave, and I grabbed him by the front of his shirt. "Not so fast. This isn't television. This is my life. I want to know more about this no-emotional-price thing?"

"It's the way it has to be."

"And what's this job you have to get back to?"

"I'm running a surveillance operation for a government agency. We're independent contractors. You aren't going to grill me on details, are you?"

I released his shirt and blew out a sigh. "I can't do this. This isn't going to work."

"I know," Ranger said. "You need to repair your relationship with Morelli."

"We needed a time-out."

"I'm being a good guy right now because it suits my purposes, but I'm an opportunist, and I'm attracted to you. And I'll be back in your bed if the Morelli time-out goes on for too long. I could make you forget Morelli if I put my mind to it. That wouldn't be good for either of us."

"Yeesh."

Ranger smiled. "Lock your door." And he was gone.

I locked my door, and I set the floor bolt. Ranger had successfully taken my mind off the masturbating rabbit. Now if I could just get my mind to stop thinking about Ranger. I knew everything Ranger said was true, with the possible exception of forgetting Morelli. It wasn't easy to forget Morelli. I'd put a lot of effort into it over the years, but had never been successful.

My phone rang, and someone made kissy sounds to me. I hung up, and it rang again. More kissy sounds. When it rang a third time I pulled the plug.

A half hour later, someone was at my door. "I know you're in there," Vinnie yelled. "I saw the CR-V in the parking lot."

I unlocked the floor bolt, the door bolt, the security chain, and the dead bolt.

"Jesus Christ," Vinnie said when I finally opened the door. "You'd think there was something valuable in this rat trap."

"*I'm* valuable."

"Not as a bounty hunter, you aren't. Where's Bender?

I've got two days to produce Bender, or I pay the money to the court."

"You're here to tell me that?"

"Yeah. I figured you needed some reminding. I've got my mother-in-law at my house today, driving me nuts. I thought this would be a good time to get Bender. I tried to call you, but your phone isn't working."

What the hell, I didn't have anything else to do. I was sitting here trapped in my apartment with my phone disconnected.

I left Vinnie to wait in the entrance hall, and I went in search of my gun belt. I returned with the black nylon web holster strapped to my leg and my .38 loaded and ready for quick draw.

"Whoa," Vinnie said, clearly impressed. "You're finally serious."

Right. Serious about not getting porked by a rabbit. We cruised out of the lot with me driving and Vinnie working the radio. I turned toward the center of town, keeping one eye on the road ahead and one eye on the rearview mirror. A green SUV came up behind me. He cut over a double line and passed me. The guy in the Clinton mask was behind the wheel, and the big ugly rabbit was riding shotgun. The rabbit turned and popped up through the sun roof and looked back at me. His ears were whipping around in the wind, and he was holding his head on with both hands.

"It's the rabbit," I yelled. "Shoot him! Take my gun and shoot him!"

"What are you, nuts?" Vinnie said. "I can't shoot an unarmed rabbit."

I was struggling, trying to get my gun out of the holster, trying to drive at the same time.

"*I'm* going to shoot him then. I don't care if I get sent to jail. It'll be worth it. I'm going to shoot him in his stupid rabbit head." I wrenched the gun out of the holster, but I didn't want to shoot through Ranger's windshield. "Take the wheel," I yelled to Vinnie. I opened the window, leaned out, and got off a shot.

The rabbit instantly retreated into the car. The SUV accelerated and turned left, onto a side street. I waited for traffic to pass, and then I turned left, also. I saw them ahead of me. They were turning and turning until we went full circle, and we were back on State. The SUV pulled up at a convenience store, and the two men took off on foot, around the brick building. I slid to a stop beside the Explorer. Vinnie and I jumped from the CR-V and ran after the men. We chased them for a couple blocks, they cut through a yard, and they disappeared.

Vinnie was bent at the waist, sucking air. "Why are we chasing a rabbit?"

"It's the rabbit who firebombed my CR-V."

"Oh yeah. Now I remember. I should have asked sooner. I would have stayed in the car. Jesus, I can't believe you got off a shot hanging out the window. Who do you think you are, the Terminator? Christ, your mother would have my nuts if she knew you did that. What were you thinking?"

"I got excited."

"You weren't excited. You were berserk!"

Chapter
FOURTEEN

We were in a neighborhood of large old houses. Some of them had been renovated. And some were waiting for renovation. Some had been turned into apartment buildings. Most of the houses were on good-size lots and sat back from the road. The rabbit and his partner had disappeared around the side of one of the apartment houses. Vinnie and I prowled around the house, standing still from time to time, listening, hoping the rabbit would give himself away. We checked between cars parked in the driveway, and we looked behind shrubs.

"I don't see them," Vinnie said. "I think they're gone. Either they slipped past us and doubled back to their car, or else they're holed up in this house."

We both looked at the house.

"Do you want to search the house?" Vinnie asked.

It was a big Victorian. I'd been in houses like this before, and they were filled with closets and hallways and closed doors. Good houses for hiding. Bad houses for searching. Especially for a chickenshit like me. Now that I was out in the air, sanity was returning. And the longer I was out walking around, the less I wanted to find the rabbit.

"I think I'll pass on the house."

"Good call," Vinnie said. "Easy to get your head

blown off in a house like this. Of course, that wouldn't figure into the equation for you, because you're so freaking nuts. You've gotta stop watching those old Al Capone movies."

"You should talk. What about the time you shot up Pinwheel Soba's house? You just about destroyed it."

Vinnie's face creased into a smile. "I got lost in the moment."

We walked back to the car with guns still drawn, staying alert to sounds and movement. Half a block from the convenience store, we saw smoke billowing from the other side of the brick building. The smoke was black and acrid, smelling like burning rubber. The sort of smoke you get when a car catches fire.

Sirens were wailing in the distance, and I had another one of those parakeet-flying-away feelings. Dread in the pit of my stomach. It was followed by a rush of calm that signaled the arrival of denial. It couldn't possibly be happening. Not another car. Not *Ranger's* car. It had to be *someone else's* car. I started making deals with God. Let it be the Explorer, I suggested to God, and I'll be a better person. I'll go to church. I'll eat more vegetables. I'll stop abusing the shower massage.

We turned the corner and, sure enough, Ranger's car was burning. Okay, that's it, I told God. All deals are *off*.

"Holy crap," Vinnie said. "That's your car. That's the second CR-V you've burned up this week. This might set a new record for you."

The clerk was standing outside, watching the spectacle. "I saw the whole thing," he said. "It was a big rabbit. He rushed into the store and got a can of barbecue starter fuel. And then he poured it in the black car and lit a match to it. Then he drove away in the green SUV."

I holstered my gun, and I sat on the cement apron in front of the store. Bad enough the car was totaled, my bag had been in it. My credit cards, my driver's license, my lip gloss, my defense spray, and my new cell phone were all gone. And I'd left the keys in the ignition. And the keypad to my security system was hooked onto the key ring.

Vinnie sat next to me. "I always have a good time when I go out with you," Vinnie said. "We should do this more often."

"Do you have your cell phone on you?"

Morelli was the first number I dialed, but Morelli wasn't home. I hung my head. Ranger was next on the list.

"Yo," Ranger said when he answered.

"Small problem."

"No kidding. Your car just went off the screen."

"It sort of burned up."

Silence.

"And you know that keypad you gave me? It was in the car."

"Babe."

Vinnie and I were still sitting on the curb when Ranger arrived. Ranger was dressed in jeans and a black T-shirt and boots, and he looked almost normal. He glanced at the smoldering car, then he looked at me and shook his head. The head shake was actually more the *suggestion* of a head shake. I didn't want to try to guess the thought that prompted the head shake. I didn't imagine it would be good. He spoke to one of the cops and gave him a card. Then he collected Vinnie and me and brought us back to my apartment building. Vinnie got into his Caddie and took off.

Ranger smiled and gestured to the gun on my hip. "Looking good, babe. Did you shoot anyone today?"

"I tried."

He gave a soft laugh, crooked his arm around my neck, and kissed me just above my ear.

Hector was waiting for us in the hall. Hector looked

like he should be wearing an orange jumpsuit and leg irons. But hey, what do I know? Probably Hector is a real nice guy. Probably he doesn't know that a teardrop under the eye signifies a gang kill. And even if he *does* know, it's only *one* teardrop, so it's not like he's a *serial* killer, right?

Hector gave Ranger a new keypad, and he said something in Spanish. Ranger said something back, they did one of those complicated handshakes, and Hector left.

Ranger beeped my door open and went in with me. "Hector's already been through. He said the apartment is clean." He put the keypad on the kitchen counter. "The new keypad is programmed exactly like the last."

"Sorry about the car."

"It was just a matter of time, babe. I'll write it off as entertainment." He glanced at the readout on his pager. "I have to go. Make sure you engage the floor bolt when I leave."

I kicked the bolt into place, and I paced around in my kitchen. Pacing is supposed to be calming, but the more I paced, the more annoyed I became. I needed a car for tomorrow, and I wasn't going to take another car from Ranger. I didn't like being entertainment. Not automotive entertainment. Not sexual entertainment.

Ah hah! a voice inside me said. Now we're getting somewhere. This pacing you're doing isn't about the car. This is about the sex. You're all bummed out because you got boinked by a man who wanted nothing more than physical sex. *Do you know what you are?* the voice asked. *You're a hypocrite.*

So? I said to the voice. And? What's your point?

I thrashed through my cupboards and refrigerator looking for a Tastykake. I knew there were none left, but I looked anyway. Another exercise in futility. My specialty.

Okay. Fine. I'll go out and buy some. I grabbed the keypad Ranger left for me, and I stomped out of the apartment. I slammed the door shut, punched in the code, and realized I was standing out there with nothing but a keypad. No car keys. Unnecessary, of course, because I didn't have a car. Also, I was without money and credit cards. Large sigh. I needed to go back inside and rethink this.

I punched in the code and tried the door. The door wouldn't open. I put the code in again. Nothing. I didn't have a key. All I had was the damn stupid keypad. No reason to panic. I had to be doing something wrong. I went through it again. It wasn't that complicated. Punch in the numbers and the door unlocks. Maybe I was remembering the numbers wrong. I tried a couple other combinations. No luck.

Piece of shit technology. I hate technology. Technology *sucks*.

Okay, take it easy, I told myself. You don't want a repeat performance of the car window shoot-out. You don't want to go gonzo over a silly keypad. I took a couple deep breaths, and I fed the numbers into the keypad one more time. I grabbed the doorknob and pulled and twisted, but the door wouldn't open.

"Goddamn!" I threw the keypad down on the floor and jumped up and down. *"Damn, damn, damn!"* I kicked the keypad all the way to the far end of the hall. I ran down the hall, unholstered my gun, and shot the keypad. *BAM!* The keypad jumped, and I shot it again.

An Asian woman opened the door across the hall. She looked out at me, gave a gasp, pulled back inside, and closed and locked her door.

"Sorry," I called out to her, through the door. "I got carried away."

I retrieved the mangled keypad and skulked back to my half of the hall.

My next door neighbor, Mrs. Karwatt, was in her doorway. "Are you having a problem, dear?" she asked.

"I'm locked out of my apartment." Fortunately, Mrs. Karwatt kept a key.

Mrs. Karwatt gave me the spare key, I inserted it in the lock, and the door wouldn't open. I followed Mrs. Karwatt into her house, and I used her phone to call Ranger.

"The frigging door won't open," I said.

"I'll send Hector."

"No! I can't understand Hector. I can't talk to him." And he scares the bejeezus out of me.

Twenty minutes later, I was sitting in the hall with my back to the wall, and Ranger and Hector showed up.

"What's wrong?" Ranger asked.

"The door won't open."

"Probably just a programming glitch. Do you have the keypad?"

I dropped the keypad into his hand.

Ranger and Hector looked down at the keypad. They looked up at each other, exchanged raised eyebrows, and smiled.

"I think I see the problem," Ranger said. "Someone's shot the shit out of this keypad." He turned it over in his hand. "At least you were able to hit it. Nice to know the target practice paid off."

"I'm good at close range."

It took Hector twenty seconds to open my door and ten minutes to remove the sensors.

"Let me know if you want the system put back in," Ranger said.

"I appreciate the thought, but I'd rather walk blindfolded into an apartment filled with alligators."

"Do you want to try your luck with another car? We could raise the stakes. I could give you a Porsche."

"Tempting, but no. I'm expecting an insurance check tomorrow. As soon as I get it, I'll have Lula drive me to a dealer."

Ranger and Hector took off, and I locked myself into my apartment. I'd worked out a lot of aggression shooting the keypad, and I felt much more mellow now. My heart was only skipping a beat once in a while, and the eye twitch was hardly noticeable. I ate the last lump of frozen cookie dough. It wasn't a Tastykake, but it was pretty good, all the same. I zapped the television on and found a hockey game.

"Uh-oh," Lula said the next morning. "Was that a taxi that brought you to the office? What happened to Ranger's car?"

"It burned up."

"Say what?"

"And my bag was in it. I need to go shopping for a new handbag."

"I'm the woman for the job," Lula said. "What time is it? Are the stores open yet?"

It was ten o'clock, Monday morning. The stores were open. I'd reported my melted credit cards. I was ready to roll.

"Hold on," Connie said. "What about the filing?"

"The filing's just about all done," Lula said. She took a stack of files and shoved them into a drawer. "Anyway, we aren't gonna be long. Stephanie always gets the same boring bag. She goes straight to the Coach counter and gets one of them big-ass black leather shoulder bags, and that's the end of that."

"Turns out that my driver's license burned up, too," I said. "I was hoping you might also give me a ride to the DMV."

Connie did a big eye roll. "Go."

It was noon when we got to Quaker Bridge Mall. I bought my shoulder bag, and then Lula and I tested out some perfume. We were on the upper level, walking toward the escalators on our way to leave for the lot, and a familiar shape loomed in front of me.

"You!" Martin Paulson said. "What is it with you? I can't get away from you."

"Don't start with me," I said. "I'm not happy with you."

"Gee, that's too bad. I almost really care. What are you doing here today? Looking for somebody new to brutalize?"

"I didn't brutalize you."

"You knocked me down."

"You *fell* down. Twice."

"I told you I have a bad sense of balance."

"Look, just get out of my way. I'm not going to stand here and argue with you."

"Yeah, you heard her," Lula said. "Get out of her way."

Paulson turned to better see Lula, and apparently he was caught off guard by what he saw, because he lost his balance and fell backward, down the escalator. There were a couple people in front of him, and he knocked them over like bowling pins. They all landed in a heap on the floor.

Lula and I scrambled down the escalator to the pile of bodies.

Paulson seemed to be the only one who was hurt. "My leg's broken," he said. "I bet you anything my leg's broken. I keep telling you, I have a problem with equilibrium. Nobody ever listens to me."

"There's probably a good reason why no one listens to you," Lula said. "You look like a big bag of wind, if you ask me."

"It's all your fault," Paulson said. "You scared the hell out of me. They should get the fashion police out after you. And what's with the yellow hair? You look like Harpo Marx."

"Hunh," Lula said. "I'm outta here. I'm not standing here getting insulted. I got to get back to work anyway."

We were in the car at the exit to the parking lot, and Lula stopped short. "Hold on. Do I have my shopping bags in the backseat?"

I turned and looked. "No."

"Damn! I must have dropped them when that sack of monkey doodie pushed me."

"No problem. Pull up to the door, and I'll run in and get them."

Lula drove to the entrance, and I retraced our steps, back to the middle of the mall. I had to walk past Paulson to get to the escalator. The EMTs had him on a stretcher and were getting ready to wheel him out. I took the escalator to the second level and found the shopping bags laying on the floor by the bench, right where Lula had left them.

Thirty minutes later, we were back at the office, and Lula had her bags spread out on the couch. "Uhoh," she said. "We got one too many bags. You see this here big brown bag? It's not mine."

"It was on the floor with the other bags," I said.

"Oh boy," Lula said. "Are you thinking what I'm thinking? I don't even want to look in that bag. I got a bad feeling about that bag."

"You were right about the bad feeling," I said, looking into the bag. "There are a pair of pants in here that could only belong to Paulson. Plus a couple shirts. Oh crap, there's a box all wrapped up in happy birthday kid's wrapping paper."

"My suggestion is you throw that bag in the Dumpster, and you go wash your hands," Lula said.

"I can't do that. The guy just broke his leg. And there's a kid's birthday present in here."

"No big deal," Lula said. "He can go onto the Internet and steal some more stuff and get another present."

"This is my fault," I said. "I took Paulson's bag. I need to get it back to him."

There are several hospitals in the Trenton area. If Paulson was taken to St. Francis, I could walk up the street and give him his bag before he was discharged. And there was a good chance Paulson was at St. Francis because it was the closest hospital to his home.

I called the switchboard and had them check with ER. I was told Paulson was indeed in ER, and they expected him to be there a while longer.

I wasn't looking forward to seeing Paulson, but it was a nice spring day, and it felt good to be outside. I decided I'd walk to the hospital, and then I'd walk to my parents' and mooch dinner and say hello to Rex. I had my new bag over my shoulder, and I was feeling confident because my gun was in my bag. Plus new lip gloss. Am I a professional, or what?

I swung along Hamilton for a couple blocks and then cut off just before the hospital's main entrance and took the side street to the emergency entrance. I found the nurse in charge and asked her to give the bag to Paulson.

So now I was off the hook, the bag was no longer my responsibility. I'd gone the extra mile to get it back to Paulson, and I left the hospital feeling all elated with my own goodness.

My parents lived behind the hospital, in the heart of the Burg. I walked past the parking garage and paused at the intersection. It was midafternoon, and there were few cars on the roads. Schools were still in session. Restaurants were empty.

A lone car rolled down the street and paused at the stop sign. A car was parked at the curb to my left. I heard a foot scrape against gravel. I turned my head at the sound. And the rabbit popped up from behind the parked car. He was fully suited this time.

"Boo!" he said.

I gave an involuntary shriek. He'd caught me by surprise. I shoved my hand into my bag in search of my gun, but a second person was suddenly in front of me, grabbing at my shoulder strap. It was the guy in the Clinton mask. If I could have gotten to my gun, I would gladly have shot them. And if it had been a single man, I might have been able to get to my gun. As it was, I was overpowered.

I went down kicking and screaming and clawing with both men on top of me. The streets were deserted, but I was making a lot of noise and there were houses nearby. If I yelled loud enough and long enough I knew I'd be heard. The car in the intersection wheeled around and rolled to a stop inches away from us.

The rabbit opened the back door and tried to drag me into the car. I was spread-eagle in the car door opening, hanging on with my fingernails, screaming my head off. The Clinton mask guy tried to grab my legs, and when he came in close I kicked out and caught him under the chin with my CAT. The guy staggered backward and keeled over. *Crash!* Flat on his back on the sidewalk.

The driver was out of the car now. He was wearing a Richard Nixon mask, and I was pretty sure I recognized the build. I was pretty sure it was Darrow. I wriggled away from the rabbit. Hard to hold onto things when you're wearing a rabbit suit with rabbit paws. I tripped on the curb and went down on one knee. I scrambled up and took off, running for all I was worth. The rabbit ran after me.

There was a car in the intersection, and I streaked past it yelling. My voice felt hoarse, and I was probably croaking more than yelling. The knee was torn out of my jeans, my arm was scratched and bleeding, and my hair was in my face, wild and tangled from rolling on the ground with the rabbit. I barely glanced at the car, noting only that it was silver. I could hear the rabbit behind me. My lungs were burning, and I knew I couldn't outrun him. I was too scared to think ahead. I was blindly running down the street.

I heard the screech of wheels and a car motor getting gunned. Darrow, I thought. Coming to get me. I turned to look, and I saw it wasn't Darrow behind me. It was the silver car that had been in the intersection. It was a Buick LeSabre. And my mother was at the wheel. She ran flat-out into the rabbit. The rabbit did a flip off the car in an explosion of fake fur and landed in a crumpled heap at the side of the road. The Darrow-driven car slid to a stop beside the rabbit. Darrow and the other rubber mask guy got out, scooped the rabbit up, dumped him into the backseat, and took off.

My mother was stopped a few feet from me. I limped to the car, she popped the lock, and I got in.

"Holy Mary, mother of God," my mother said. "You were being chased by Richard Nixon, Bill Clinton, and a rabbit."

"Yeah," I said. "Good thing you came along when you did."

"I ran over the rabbit," she wailed. "I probably killed him."

"He was a bad rabbit. He deserved to die."

"He looked like the Easter bunny. I killed the Easter bunny," she sobbed.

I pulled a tissue out of my mother's purse and handed it to her. Then I looked through the purse more thoroughly. "You have any Valium in here? Any Klonapin or Ativan?"

My mother blew her nose and put the car in gear. "Do you have any idea what it's like for a mother to drive down the street and see her daughter being chased by a rabbit? I don't know why you can't have a normal job. Like your sister."

I rolled my eyes. My sister again. Saint Valerie.

"And she's dating a nice man," my mother said. "I think he has honorable intentions. And he's a lawyer. He'll make a good living someday." My mother drove back to the intersection, so I could retrieve my shoulder bag. "And what about you," she wanted to know. "Who are you dating?"

"Don't ask," I said. I wasn't dating anyone. I was fornicating with Batman.

"I'm not sure what I should do next," my mother said. "Do you think I should report this to the police? What would I say to them? I mean, how would it sound? I was on my way to Giovichinni's for lunch meat when I saw a rabbit chasing my daughter down the street, so I ran over him, but now he's gone."

"Remember when I was a kid, and we were all going to the movies, and Daddy hit the dog on Roebling? We got out and looked for the dog, but we couldn't find him. He just ran off somewhere."

"I felt terrible about that."

"Yeah, but we went to the movies anyway. Maybe we should just go get the lunch meat."

"It *was* a *rabbit*," my mother said. "And he had no business being in the road."

"Exactly."

We drove to Giovichinni's in silence and parked in front of the store. We both got out and looked at the front of the Buick. There was some rabbit fur stuck to the grille, but aside from that the LeSabre looked okay.

While my mother was talking to the butcher, I stole off and called Morelli on the outside pay phone. "This is a little awkward," I said, "but my mother just ran over the rabbit."

"Ran over?"

"As in *roadkill*. We're not sure what to do about it."

"Where are you?"

"Giovichinni's, buying lunch meat."

"And the rabbit?"

"Gone. He was with two other guys. They scooped him up off the road and drove away with him."

There was a long silence on the phone. "I'm fucking speechless," Morelli finally said.

An hour later, I heard Morelli's truck pull up in front of my parents' house. He was in jeans and boots and a cotton crew with the sleeves pushed up. The crew was loose enough to hide the gun that was always at his waist.

I'd showered and fixed my hair, but I didn't have fresh clothes to change into, so I was still in the torn, blood-stained jeans and dirt-smudged T-shirt. I had a ragged cut on my knee, a large scrape on my arm, and another on my cheek. I met Morelli on the porch and closed the door behind me. I didn't want Grandma Mazur joining us.

Morelli gave me the long, slow lookover. "I could kiss that cut on your knee and make it all better."

A skill acquired from years of playing doctor.

We sat side by side on the step, and I told him about the rabbit at the bakery and the attempted abduction at the intersection. "And I'm almost sure Darrow was driving," I said.

"Do you want me to have him brought in?"

"No. I couldn't positively ID him."

Morelli's face broke into a smile. "Your mother really ran the rabbit over?"

"She saw him chasing me. And she ran him over. Threw him about ten feet into the air."

"She likes you."

I nodded yes. And my eyes filled.

A car drove by. Two men.

"That could be them," I said. "Two of Abruzzi's guys. I try to be vigilant, but the cars are always different. And

I only know Abruzzi and Darrow. The others have always had their faces covered. I have no good way of knowing when I'm being stalked. And it's worse at night when all I can see are lights coming and going."

"We're working overtime, trying to find Evelyn, canvassing the neighborhoods for witnesses, but so far there hasn't been a break. Abruzzi's got himself well protected."

"Do you need to talk to my mom about the rabbit thing?"

"Were there any witnesses?"

"Only the two guys in the car."

"We don't usually write up accidents involving rabbits. This *was* a *rabbit,* right?"

Morelli declined dinner. I couldn't blame him. Valerie had Kloughn home with her, and the table was standing room only.

"Isn't he the cute one," Grandma whispered to me in the kitchen. "Just like the Pillsbury Doughboy."

After dinner I got my dad to drive me home.

"What do you think of this clown?" he asked on the way. "He seems to be sweet on Valerie. Do you think there's any chance this could turn into something?"

"He didn't get up and leave when Grandma asked him if he was a virgin. I thought that was a good sign."

"Yeah, he hung in there. He must really be desperate if he's willing to get involved with this family. Has anyone told him the horse kid belongs to Valerie?"

I figured there wasn't a problem with Mary Alice. Kloughn probably had empathy for a kid who was different. What Kloughn might not understand was Valerie in the fluffy pink slippers. Probably we should make sure he never sees the slippers.

It was almost nine when my dad dropped me off. The parking lot was filled and lights were on in all the apartment windows. The seniors were settled in for the night, victims of failing night vision and television addiction. By nine o'clock they were happy campers, having self-medicated with tumblers of booze and *Diagnosis Murder*. At 10:00 they'd pop a little white pill and hurl themselves into hours of sleep apnea.

I approached my front door and decided I'd been hasty in rejecting Ranger's security system. It would be nice to know if someone was waiting for me inside. I had my gun shoved into the waistband of my jeans. And I had a plan outlined in my head. My plan was to open the door, take the gun in hand, flip all the lights on, and do another embarrassing imitation of a television cop.

The kitchen was easy to cover. Nothing there. The living room and dining room were next. Again, easy to take in. The bathroom was more tense. I had the shower curtain to contend with. I needed to remember not to close the shower curtain. I ripped the shower curtain open and let out a whoosh of air. No one dead in my tub.

At first glance, my bedroom was fine. Unfortunately, I knew from past experience that the bedroom was filled with hiding places for all sorts of nasty things, like snakes. I looked under the bed and in all my drawers. I opened my closet door and let out another whoosh of air. Nobody here. I'd gone through the entire apartment and not found anyone, dead or alive. I could lock myself in and feel perfectly safe.

I was leaving the bedroom when it hit me. A visual memory of something odd. Something out of place. I returned to my closet and opened the door. And there it was, hanging with the rest of my clothes, smashed between my suede jacket and a denim shirt. The rabbit suit.

I snapped on rubber gloves, removed the rabbit suit from my closet, and deposited it in the elevator. I didn't want another full-scale crime-scene investigation assault on my apartment. I used the pay phone in the lobby to put in an anonymous call to the police about the suit in the elevator. And then I returned to my apartment and slid *Ghostbusters* into the DVD player.

Halfway through *Ghostbusters* I got a call from Morelli. "You wouldn't happen to know anything about the rabbit suit in your elevator, would you?"

"Who me?"

"Off the record, out of morbid curiosity, where did you find it?"

"It was hanging in my closet."

"Christ."

"Do you suppose this means the rabbit no longer needs the suit?" I asked.

I dialed Ranger first thing the next morning. "About that security system," I said.

"Are you still having visitors?"

"I found a rabbit suit in my closet last night."

"Anybody in it?"

"Nope. Just the suit."

"I'll send Hector."

"Hector scares the hell out of me."

"Yeah, me, too," Ranger said. "But he hasn't killed anybody in over a year now. And he's gay. You're probably safe."

Chapter

FIFTEEN

The next call was from Morelli. "I just got into work, and I heard an interesting piece of information," Morelli said to me. "Do you know Leo Klug?"

"No."

"He's a butcher at Sal Carto's Meat Market. Your mother probably gets her kielbasa there. Leo is about my height but heavier. He has a scar running the length of his face. Black hair."

"Okay. I know who you mean. I was in there a couple weeks ago, picking up some sausage, and he waited on me."

"It's pretty well known here that Klug has done some contract butchering."

"You're not talking about cows."

"Cows are the day job," Morelli said.

"I have a feeling I'm not going to like the direction of this conversation."

"Lately, Klug has been hanging out with a couple guys who work for Abruzzi. And this morning, Klug turned up dead, the victim of a hit-and-run."

"Omigod."

"He was found on the side of the road half a block from the butcher shop."

"Any idea who hit him?"

"No, but statistics are high for a drunk driver."

We pondered that for a moment.

"Probably your mother should run the LeSabre through a car wash," Morelli said.

"Holy crap. My mother killed Leo Klug."

"I didn't hear that," Morelli said.

I got off the phone and made some coffee. I scrambled an egg and popped a piece of bread into the toaster. Stephanie Plum, domestic goddess. I sneaked out into the hall, swiped Mr. Wolesky's paper, and read it with my breakfast.

I was returning the paper when Ranger and Hector stepped out of the elevator.

"I know where she is," Ranger said. "I just got a call. Let's roll."

I cut my eyes to Hector.

"Don't worry about Hector," Ranger said.

I grabbed my bag and a jacket and ran to keep up with Ranger. He was driving the bug-eyed truck again. I hauled myself up to seat level and buckled in.

"Where is she?"

"Newark Airport. Jeanne Ellen was returning with her FTA, and she saw Dotty and Evelyn and the kids in the waiting area one gate over. I had Tank check on their flight. It was scheduled to take off at ten but it's been delayed an hour. We should be able to get there in time."

"Where were they going?"

"Miami."

Traffic was heavy through Trenton. It eased up for a while and then got heavy again on the Turnpike. Fortunately, the flow on the Turnpike was steady. Good Jersey traffic. The kind that gets your adrenaline going. Bumper to bumper at eighty miles an hour.

I looked at my watch when we took the airport exit. It was almost 10:00. A few minutes later, Ranger swung into the Delta passenger drop-off and stopped at the curb. "It's getting tight," he said. "You go ahead while I park. If you have a gun on you, you have to leave it in the truck."

I gave him my gun and took off. I checked the departures monitor when I entered the terminal. The flight was now on time. Still leaving from the same gate. I cracked my knuckles while I stood in line at the security check. I was so close to Evelyn and Annie. It would be a killer headache if I missed them here.

I passed through security and followed the signs to the gate. I was moving down the corridor, and I was looking at everyone. I scanned ahead, and I saw Evelyn and Dotty and the kids, two gates away. They were sitting, waiting. Nothing unusual about them. A couple moms and their kids, going to Florida.

I quietly approached them and sat in the empty seat next to Evelyn. "We need to talk," I said.

They seemed only mildly surprised. As if nothing could surprise them much anymore. They both looked tired. Their clothes looked slept in. The kids were amusing each other, being loud and obnoxious. The sort of kids you see all the time in airports. Strung out.

"I meant to call you," Evelyn said. "I would have called when we got to Miami. You should tell Grammy I'm okay."

"I want to know why you're running. And if you don't tell me I'm going to make problems for you. I'm going to stop you from leaving."

"*No*." Evelyn said. "Please don't do that. It's important that we catch this plane."

The first boarding announcement went out.

"The Trenton police are looking for you," I said. "You're wanted for questioning for two murders. I can call security and have you brought back to Trenton."

Evelyn's face went white. "He'll kill me."

"Abruzzi?"

She nodded.

"Maybe you should tell her," Dotty said. "We haven't got much time."

"When Steven lost the bar to Abruzzi, Abruzzi came over to the house with his men and he *did* something to me."

I felt myself instinctively suck in some air. "I'm sorry," I said.

"It was his way of making us afraid. He's like a cat with a mouse. He likes to play before he kills. And he likes to dominate women."

"You should have gone to the police."

"He would have killed me before I got to testify. Or worse, he might have done something to Annie. The legal system moves too slow with a man like Abruzzi."

"Why is he after you now?" Ranger had already told me the answer, but I wanted to hear it from Evelyn.

"Abruzzi is a war nut. He plays war games. And he collects medals and things. And he had one medal that he kept on his desk. I guess it was his favorite medal because it belonged to Napoleon.

"Anyway, when Steven and I got divorced the court gave Steven visitation rights. He got Annie every Saturday. A couple weeks ago Abruzzi had a birthday party at his house for his daughter, and he demanded that Steven bring Annie."

"Was Annie friends with Abruzzi's daughter?"

"No. It was just Abruzzi's way of asserting his power. He's always doing things like that. He calls the people around him his *troops*. And they have to treat him like the Godfather or Napoleon or some big general. So he gave this party for his daughter and the troops were all supposed to attend with their kids.

"Steven was considered one of the troops. He lost the bar to Abruzzi, and it was like Abruzzi owned him after that. Steven didn't like losing the bar, but I think he liked belonging to Abruzzi's family. Made him feel like a big shot to be associated with someone everyone was afraid of."

Until he got sawed in half.

"Anyway, while the party was going on, Annie wandered into Abruzzi's office, spotted the medal on Abruzzi's desk, and took it back to the party to show the rest of the children. No one paid much attention and, somehow, the medal got stuffed into Annie's pocket. And she brought it home."

There was a second boarding call and from the corner of my eye I could see Ranger standing at a distance, watching.

"Keep going," I said. "There's still time."

"As soon as I saw the medal I knew what it was."

"Your ticket out?"

"*Yes*. As long as I was in Trenton, Abruzzi would own Annie and me. And I had no money to leave. No job skills. And worse, there was the divorce agreement. But the medal was worth a lot of money. Abruzzi used to brag about it all the time.

"So I packed up and left. I was out of the house an hour after the medal walked in. I went to Dotty for help because I didn't know where else to go. Until I sold the medal I didn't have any money."

"Unfortunately, it takes time to sell a medal like that," Dotty said. "And it had to be done quietly."

A tear slid down Evelyn's cheek. "I made a mess of it for Dotty. Now she's dragged into it and can't get out."

Dotty was keeping watch over the pack of kids. "It'll work out okay," she said. But she didn't look like she believed it.

"What about the pictures Annie drew in her pad?" I asked. "They were pictures of people getting shot. I thought maybe she witnessed a murder."

"If you look more closely you'll see the men are wearing medals. She drew the pictures while I was packing. Everyone who came into contact with Abruzzi, even children, knew about war and killing and medals. It was an obsession."

I suddenly felt very defeated. There was nothing here for me. No witness to a murder. No one who could help remove Abruzzi from my life.

"We have a buyer waiting for us in Miami," Dotty said. "I sold my car to get these tickets."

"Can you trust this buyer?"

"He seems to be okay. And I have a friend meeting us at the airport. He's a pretty sharp guy, and he's going to oversee the transaction. I think the transaction is pretty simple. We hand over the medal. Some expert examines it. And Evelyn gets a suitcase filled with money."

"Then what?"

"We'll probably have to stay hidden. Start a new life somewhere. If Abruzzi gets caught or killed, we can come home."

I had no reason to detain them. I thought they'd made some bad choices, but who was I to judge? "Good luck," I said. "Keep in touch. And call Mabel. She worries about you."

Evelyn jumped up and hugged me. Dotty gathered the kids together, and they all toddled off to Miami.

Ranger came over and slung an arm around me. "They told you a sob story, didn't they?"

"Yep."

He smiled and kissed me on the top of my head. "You really should think about getting into a different line of work. Grooming kitty cats, maybe. Or floral design."

"It was very convincing."

"Did the little girl witness a murder?"

"No. She stole a medal that was worth a suitcase full of money."

Ranger raised his eyebrows and grinned. "Good for her. I like to see enterprise in kids."

"I haven't got a murder witness. And the bear and the rabbit are dead. I think I'm fucked."

"Maybe after lunch," he said. "My treat."

"You mean *lunch* is your treat?"

"That, too. I know a place here in Newark that makes Shorty's look like a sissy joint."

Oh boy.

"And by the way, I checked your thirty-eight when you left it in the truck. You only have two bullets in it. I have this sinking feeling that the gun will go back to the cookie jar when you empty the cylinder."

I smiled at Ranger. I can be mysterious, too.

Ranger paged Hector when we were on our way home, and Hector was in front of my apartment, waiting for us when we stepped out of the elevator. He handed the new keypad to Ranger, and he smiled at me and made a gun with his fist and forefinger. *"Bang,"* he said.

"Pretty good," I said to Ranger. "Hector's learning English."

Ranger flipped me the keypad, and he left with Hector.

I let myself into my apartment, and I stood in my kitchen. Now what? Now I had to hang out and wonder when Abruzzi would come for me. What form would it take? And how awful would it be? Awful beyond my imaginings, probably.

If I was my mother I'd be ironing. My mother ironed under stress. Stay far away from my mother when she is ironing. If I was Mabel I'd be baking. What about Grandma Mazur? That was an easy one. The Weather Channel. So what do I do? I eat Tastykakes.

Okay, there's my problem. I haven't got any Tastykakes. I'd had a burger with Ranger, but I'd skipped dessert.

And now I needed a Tastykake. Without a Tastykake I was left to sit here and worry about Abruzzi. Unfortunately, I had no way of taking myself out to Tastykake Land because I didn't have a car. I was still waiting for the stupid insurance check to arrive.

Hey, hold the phone. I could *walk* to the convenience store. Four blocks. Not the sort of thing a Jersey girl ordinarily did, but what the hell. I had my gun back in my bag with two bullets ready and waiting. That was a confidence builder. I would have shoved it under the waistband of my jeans like Ranger and Joe, but there wasn't room. Probably I should restrict myself to just *one* Tastykake.

I locked up and took the stairs to the first floor. I didn't live in a fancy building. It was kept clean, and it was adequately maintained. It had been built without frills. And for that matter, without quality. Still, it was enduring. It had a back door and a front door and both doors opened to a small foyer. The stairs and the elevator also opened to the foyer. Mailboxes banked one wall. The floor was tiled. Management had added a potted palm and two wingback chairs in an attempt to compensate for the lack of a swimming pool.

Abruzzi was sitting in one of the wingback chairs. His suit was impeccable. His shirt was a brilliant white. His face was expressionless. He motioned to the wingback next to him. "Sit down," he said, "I thought we should have a conversation."

Darrow was motionless at the door.

I sat in the chair, and I took the gun out of my bag, and I aimed it at Abruzzi. "What would you like to talk about?"

"Is that gun supposed to frighten me?"

"It's a precaution."

"Not good military strategy for a meeting of surrender."

"Which one of us is supposed to be surrendering?"

"You, of course," he said. "You're soon to be taken as a prisoner of war."

"News flash. You need serious psychiatric help."

"I've lost troops because of you."

"The rabbit?"

"He was a valued member of my command."

"The bear?"

Abruzzi gave a distracted wave of his hand. "The bear was hired help. He was sacrificed for your benefit and my protection. He had an unfortunate habit of gossiping to people outside my family."

"Okay, how about Soder. Was he troops?"

"Soder failed me. Soder had no character. He was a coward. He couldn't control his own wife and daughter. He was a useless liability. Just like his bar. The insurance on the bar was worth more than the bar itself."

"I'm not sure what part I play in all this."

"You're the enemy. You chose to be on Evelyn's side in this game. As I'm sure you know, Evelyn has something I want. I'll give you a last chance to survive. You can help me get back what's rightfully mine."

"I don't know what you're talking about."

Abruzzi looked down at my gun. "Two bullets?"

"That's all I need." Oh man, I couldn't believe I just said that. I hoped Abruzzi left first because I probably just wet the chair.

"It's war, then?" Abruzzi asked. "You should reconsider. You won't like what's going to happen to you. No more fun and games."

I didn't say anything.

Abruzzi stood and walked out the door. Darrow followed.

I sat in the chair for a while with the gun in my hand, waiting for my heart rate to drop back to normal. I stood up and checked the chair seat. Then I checked *my* seat. Both dry. It was a miracle.

Walking four blocks for a Tastykake had lost some of its appeal. Maybe it would be better to set my affairs in order. Aside from establishing a legal guardian for Rex, the only open end in my life was Andy Bender. I went upstairs to my apartment, and I called the office.

"I'm going after Bender," I said to Lula. "Do you want to ride shotgun?"

"No way, Jose. You'd have to put me in a full contamination suit before I'd go anywhere near that place. Even then, I wouldn't go. I'm telling you, God's got something going on there. He's got plans."

I hung up with Lula, and I called Kloughn.

"I'm going after Bender," I said to him. "Do you want to ride along?"

"Oh darn. I can't. I'd like to. You know how much I'd like to do that. But I can't. I just got a big case. A car crash, right in front of the Laundromat. Well, okay, it wasn't exactly in *front* of the Laundromat. I had to run a few blocks to get to it in time. But I think there's going to be some good injury."

Maybe this is for the best, I told myself. Maybe at this point in time I'm better off doing the job alone. Maybe I would have been better off alone *always*. Unfortunately, I still don't have handcuffs. And what's worse, I don't have a car. What I have is a gun with two bullets.

So I chose the only alternative left to me. I called a cab.

"Wait here for me," I told the driver. "I won't be long."

He cut his eyes to me, and then he looked out at the projects. "Good thing I know your father, or I wouldn't sit here idling my engine. This isn't exactly an upscale neighborhood."

I had my gun in the black nylon webbed holster,

strapped to my leg. I left my bag in the cab. I walked to the door and knocked.

Bender's wife answered.

"I'm looking for Andy," I told her.

"You're kidding, right?"

"I'm serious."

"He's dead. I thought you would have heard."

For a moment my mind went blank. My second reaction was disbelief. She was lying. Then I looked beyond her and realized the apartment was clean, and there was no sign of Andy Bender. "I didn't hear," I said. "What happened?"

"Remember how he had the flu?"

I nodded.

"Well, it killed him. Turned out he had one of those superbugs. After you left, he got a neighbor to take him to the hospital, but it went into his lungs and that was that. It was an act of God."

All the hair stood up on my arm. "I'm sorry."

"Yeah, right," she said. And she closed the door.

I walked back to the cab and slunk into the backseat.

"You're awful white," the driver said. "Are you okay?"

"Something bizarre just happened, but I'm fine. I'm getting used to bizarre things."

"Now what?"

"Take me to Vinnie's."

I burst into the bonds office. "You're not going to believe this," I said to Lula. "Andy Bender is dead."

"Get *out*. Are you shitting me?"

The door to Vinnie's inner office whipped open. "Were there witnesses? Cripes, you didn't shoot him in the back, did you? My insurance company *hates* that."

"I didn't shoot him at all. He died from the flu. I was just at his apartment. His wife told me he was dead. From the flu."

Lula did the sign of the cross. "I'm glad I learned about this cross thing," she said.

Ranger was at Connie's desk. He had a file in his hand, and he was smiling. "Did you just get out of a cab?"

"Maybe."

The smile widened. "You went after an FTA in a cab."

I rested my hand on my gun and blew out a sigh. "Don't give me a hard time. I'm not having a great day, and as you know, I've got two bullets left. I might end up using them on one of us."

"Do you need a ride home?"

"Yes."

"I'm your man," Ranger said.

Connie and Lula fanned themselves behind his back.

I climbed into the truck and looked around.

Ranger cut his eyes to me. "Are you looking for someone?"

"Abruzzi. He threatened me again."

"Do you see him?"

"No."

It's not a long drive from the office to my apartment building. A couple miles. Progress is slowed by lights and occasionally traffic, depending on the time of day. I would have liked the drive to be longer today. I felt safe from Abruzzi when I was with Ranger.

Ranger turned into my lot and parked. "There's a man in the SUV by the Dumpster," Ranger said. "Do you know him?"

"No. He doesn't live in the building."

"Let's talk to him."

Ranger and I got out of the truck, walked to the SUV, and Ranger rapped on the driver's side window. The driver rolled the window down. "Yeah?"

"Waiting for someone?"

"What's it to you?"

Ranger reached in, grabbed the guy by the front of his jacket, and pulled him halfway through the window.

"I'd like you to take a message to Eddie Abruzzi," Ranger said. "Can you do that for me?"

The driver nodded.

Ranger released the driver and stepped back. "Tell Abruzzi he's lost the war, and he should move on."

We both had guns drawn, and we kept them steady on the SUV until it was out of sight.

Ranger looked up at my window. "We're going to stand here for a minute to give the rest of the team time to get out of your apartment. I don't want to have to shoot anybody. I'm on a tight schedule today. I don't want to get hung up filling out police forms."

We waited five minutes and then went into the building and took the stairs. The second-floor hall was empty. The keypad reported that security had been breached on my apartment. Ranger went in first and walked through. The apartment was empty.

The phone rang just as Ranger was leaving. It was Eddie Abruzzi and he wasted no time with me. He asked for Ranger.

Ranger put him on the speakerphone.

"Stay out of this," Abruzzi said. "This is a private matter between the girl and me."

"Wrong. As of this moment, you're out of her life."

"So you're choosing sides?"

"Yeah, I'm choosing sides."

"You leave me no choice then," Abruzzi said. "I suggest you look out the window, into the parking lot." And he disconnected.

Ranger and I walked to the window and looked out. The SUV was back. It pulled up to Ranger's truck with the bug-eyed lights, the guy in the passenger side lobbed a package into the truck bed, and the truck was instantly engulfed in flames.

We stood there for a few minutes, watching the spectacle, listening to the sirens get closer.

"I liked that truck," Ranger said.

By the time Morelli arrived it was after six and the remains of the truck were being hauled onto a flatbed. Ranger was finishing up police paperwork. He looked over at Morelli and gave him a nod of acknowledgment.

Morelli stood very close to me. "Do you want to tell me about this?" he asked.

"Off the record?"

"Off the record."

"We had a tip that Evelyn was at Newark Airport. We drove to Newark and caught her before she boarded. After hearing her story I decided she needed to get on the plane, so I let her go. I had no reason to detain her anyway. I just wanted to know what this was about. When we got back, Abruzzi's men were waiting. There were some words, and they torched the truck."

"I need to talk to Ranger," Morelli said. "You're not going anywhere, are you?"

"If I could borrow your truck I'd get a pizza. I'm starved."

Morelli gave me his keys and a twenty. "Get two. I'll call it in to Pino's for you."

I pulled out of the lot and headed for the Burg. I turned at the hospital, and I checked my rearview mirror. I was being careful now. I was trying not to let my fear surface but it was boiling inside me. I kept telling myself it was only a matter of time before the police got something on Abruzzi. He was too flagrant. He was too wrapped up in his own craziness, playing the game. There were too many people involved. He'd killed the bear and Soder to keep them quiet, but there were others. He couldn't kill everyone.

I didn't see anyone turn with me, but that was no guarantee. If more than one car is used it's sometimes hard to spot a tail. Just to be safe, I had my gun out when I parked in the lot. I had just a short distance to go. Once I was inside I'd be okay. There were always a couple cops in Pino's. I swung down from the truck and started for the door to the bar. I took two steps and a green van appeared from nowhere. It glided to a stop, the window rolled down, and Valerie looked out at me, her mouth duct-taped shut, her eyes wild with fear. There were three other men in the van, including the driver. Two of them wore full rubber masks: Nixon and Clinton again. Plus there was a guy in a paper bag with two eyes torn out. I guess the budget only covered two rubber masks. The Bag held a gun to Valerie's head.

I didn't know what to do. I was frozen. Mentally and physically paralyzed.

"Drop the gun," the Bag said. "And slowly walk to the van, or I swear to God, I'll kill your sister."

The gun fell out of my hand. "Let her go."

"After you get in."

I reluctantly moved forward, and Nixon shoved me into the backseat. He duct-taped my mouth and wrapped tape around my hands. The van roared off, out of the Burg, across the river into Pennsylvania.

After ten minutes we were on a dirt road. Houses were small and sporadic, stuck into patches of woods. The van slowed and then stopped on the shoulder. The Bag opened the door and shoved Valerie out. I saw her hit the ground and roll, off the shoulder, into the brush at the side of the road. The Bag pulled the door shut and the van took off.

Minutes later the van turned into a driveway and stopped. We all got out and went into a small clapboard bungalow. It was pleasantly decorated. Not expensive stuff, but comfortable and clean. I was directed to a kitchen chair and told to sit. A short while after I took my place, a second car crunched on the dirt and gravel outside. The bungalow door opened, and Abruzzi walked in. He was the only man not in a mask.

He took a chair opposite me. We were close enough that our knees touched, and I could feel the heat from his body. He reached out and ripped the tape from my mouth.

"Where is she?" he asked me. "Where is Evelyn?"

"I don't know."

He hit me with an openhanded slap to the face that caught me off guard and knocked me off my chair. I was in shock when I hit the floor, too stunned to cry, too frightened to protest. I tasted blood, and I blinked tears away.

The guy in the Clinton mask hauled me up by my armpits and set me back on the chair.

"I'm going to ask you again," Abruzzi said. "I'm going to keep asking you until you tell me. Each time you don't answer I'm going to give you pain. Do you like pain?"

"I don't know where she is. You give me too much credit. I'm not that good at finding people."

"Ah, but you're friends with Evelyn, aren't you? Her grandmother lives next door to your parents. You've known Evelyn all your life. I think you know where she is. And I think you know why I want to find her." Abruzzi got up and went to the stove. He turned the gas on, got a poker from the fireplace, and held it into the flame. He tested the poker with a drop of water. The water sizzled and evaporated. "What first?" Abruzzi said. "Should we poke out an eye? Should we do something sexual?"

If I told Abruzzi Evelyn was in Miami, he'd go down

there and find her. Probably he'd kill her and Annie. And probably he'd kill me, too, no matter what I said.

"Evelyn is on her way across the country," I said. "She's driving."

"That's the wrong answer," Abruzzi said. "I know she boarded a plane for Miami. Unfortunately, Miami is a big place. I need to know where she's staying in Miami."

The Bag held my hands on the tabletop, the guy in the Nixon mask cut my sleeve away, then held my head, and Abruzzi held the hot poker to my bare arm. Someone screamed. I guess it was me. And then I fainted. When I came around I was on the floor. My arm felt like fire, and the room smelled like pot roast cooking.

The Bag dragged me to my feet and set me on the chair again. The most horrifying part to all this was that I honestly didn't know where Evelyn was staying. No matter how much they tortured me, I couldn't tell them. They'd have to torture me until I was dead.

"Okay," Abruzzi said. "One more time. Where is Evelyn?"

There was the sound of a motor revving outside, and Abruzzi paused to listen. The guy in the Nixon mask went to the window, and suddenly lights blazed through the curtains, and the green van crashed through the picture window in the front of the house. There was a lot of dust and confusion. I was on my feet, not sure where to go, when I realized Valerie was driving the van. I wrenched the side door open, threw myself inside, and yelled at her to *go*. She put the van into reverse, backed out of the house at about forty miles per hour, and careened out of the driveway.

Valerie still had her mouth and hands duct-taped together, but it wasn't slowing her down. She barreled down the dirt road, hit the highway, and skidded onto the bridge approach. My fear now was that she'd dump us into the river if she didn't slow down. There were chunks of wallboard stuck to the windshield wipers, the windshield was cracked, and the front of the van was smashed.

I ripped the tape off Valerie's mouth, and she let out a howl. Her eyes were still wild, and her nose was running. Her clothes were torn and dirt-smudged. I yelled at her to ease off the gas, and she started to cry.

"Jesus Christ," she said between sobs. "What the hell kind of a life do you lead? This isn't real. This is fucking television."

"Wow, Val, you said *fuck*."

"Damn fucking right. I'm fucking freaked out. I can't believe I found you. I just started walking. I thought I was walking back to Trenton, but I got turned around somehow. And then I saw the van. And I looked in the window and saw them burning you. And they'd left the keys hanging in the ignition. And . . . and I'm going to throw up." She screeched to a stop at the side of the road, opened the door, and heaved.

I took over the driving after that. I couldn't take Valerie home in her present condition. My mother would have a plotz. I was afraid to go to my apartment. I didn't have a phone, so I couldn't get in touch with Ranger. That left Morelli. I turned into the Burg on the way to Morelli's house, and on a long shot, went a block out of my way and drove past Pino's.

Morelli's truck was still there, plus Ranger's Mercedes and the black Range Rover. Morelli, Ranger, Tank, and Hector were in the lot. I pulled the van in next to Morelli's truck, and Valerie and I tumbled out.

"He's in Pennsylvania," I said. "In a house on a dirt road. He would have killed me, but Valerie drove the van into the house and somehow we got out."

"It was fucking awful," Valerie said, teeth chattering. "I was so fucking scared." She looked down at her wrists, still wrapped in duct tape. "My wrists are taped together," she said, as if it was the first she noticed.

Hector produced a knife and slit the tape, first on me and then on Valerie.

"How do you want to do this?" Morelli asked Ranger.

"Take Steph and Valerie home," Ranger said.

Ranger looked at me, and our eyes held for a moment. Then Morelli slid an arm around me and eased me up, into his truck. Tank boosted Val up next to me.

Morelli took us to his house. He made a phone call and some clean clothes appeared. His sister's, I imagine. I was too tired to ask. We cleaned Val up and took her home to my parents. We made a fast stop at the hospital emergency room to have my burn bandaged, and then we went back to Morelli's house.

"Stick a fork in me," I said to Morelli, "I'm done."

Morelli closed and locked his front door and turned the lights off. "Maybe you should consider taking a less dangerous job, like human cannonball or crash test dummy."

"You were worried about me."

"Yeah," Morelli said, gathering me into him. "I was worried about you." He held me close and rested his cheek on my head.

"I haven't got any jammies with me," I said to Morelli.

His lips skimmed my ear. "Cupcake, you're not going to need any."

I woke up in Morelli's bed with my arm burning like mad and my upper lip swollen. Morelli had me tucked in next to him. And Bob was on the other side of me. The alarm was buzzing on the clock beside the bed. Morelli reached out and knocked the clock off the nightstand.

"Gonna be one of those days," he said.

He rolled out of bed and a half hour later he was

dressed and in the kitchen. He was wearing running shoes and jeans and a T-shirt. He stood at the counter while he had coffee and toast. "Costanza called while you were in the bathroom," he said, sipping his coffee, watching me over the rim of his mug. "One of the patrols found Eddie Abruzzi about an hour ago. He was in his car, in the farmer's market parking lot. Looks like he killed himself."

I stared at Morelli blank-faced. Not able to believe what I just heard.

"He left a note," Morelli said. "It said he was depressed over some business deals."

There was a long silence between us.

"It wasn't a suicide, was it?" I phrased it as a question, when it was actually a statement.

"I'm a cop," Morelli said. "If I thought it was anything other than a suicide I'd have to look into it."

Ranger killed Abruzzi. I knew it as sure as I was standing there. Morelli knew it, too.

"Wow," I said softly.

Morelli looked at me. "Are you okay?"

I nodded yes.

He drank the last of his coffee, and he put the mug in the sink. He pulled me in tight against him and he kissed me.

I said *wow* again. More feeling this time. Morelli really knew how to kiss.

He took his gun from the kitchen counter and holstered it at his waist. "I'll take the Ducati today and leave you the truck. And when I get off work we should talk."

"Oh boy. More talk. That never gets us anywhere."

"Okay, maybe we shouldn't talk. Maybe we should just have sweaty sex."

Finally, a sport I could enjoy.

TO THE NINES

This book was spectacularly edited by SuperJen!

Thanks to Denise Margo Moy for suggesting the title for this book.

ONE

My name is Stephanie Plum and I was born and raised
in the Chambersburg section of Trenton, where the top
male activities are scarfing pastries and pork rinds and
growing love handles. The pastry and pork rind scarfing I've seen firsthand. The love handle growing happens over time. Thank God for small favors.

The first guy I saw up close and personal was Joe Morelli. Morelli put an end to my virgin status and showed
me a body that was masculine perfection . . . smooth
and muscular and sexy. Back then Morelli thought a
long-term commitment was twenty minutes. I was one
of thousands who got to admire Morelli's best parts as
he pulled his pants up and headed for the door.

Morelli's been in and out of my life since then. He's
currently *in* and he's improved with age, butt included.

So the sight of a naked ass isn't exactly new to me,
but the one I was presently watching took the cake.
Punky Balog had an ass like Winnie the Pooh . . . big
and fat and furry. Sad to say, that was where the simi-
larity ended because, unlike Pooh Bear, there was nothing endearing or cuddly about Punky Balog.

I knew about Punky's ass because I was in my
new sunshine yellow Ford Escape, sitting across from
Punky's dilapidated row house, and Punky had his huge

Pooh butt plastered against his second-story window. My sometime partner, Lula, was riding shotgun for me and Lula and I were staring up at the butt in open-mouthed horror.

Punky slid his butt side to side on the pane and Lula and I gave a collective, upper-lip-curled-back *eeyeuuw!*

"Think he knows we're out here," Lula said. "Think maybe he's trying to tell us something."

Lula and I work for my bail bonds agent cousin, Vincent Plum. Vinnie's office is on Hamilton Avenue, his big plate-glass front window looking into the Burg. He's not the world's best bonds agent. And he's not the worst. Truth is, he'd probably be a better bondsman if he wasn't saddled with Lula and me. I do fugitive apprehension for Vinnie and I have a lot more luck than skill. Lula mostly does filing. Lula hasn't got luck or skill. The thing Lula has going for her is the ability to tolerate Vinnie. Lula's a plus-size black woman in a size-seven white world and Lula's had a lot of practice at pulling attitude.

Punky turned and gave us a wave with his johnson.

"That's just so sad," Lula said. "What do men think of? If you had a lumpy little wanger like that, would you go waving it in public?"

Punky was dancing now, jumping around, wanger flopping, doodles bouncing.

"Holy crap," Lula said. "He's gonna rupture something."

"It's gotta be uncomfortable."

"I'm glad we forgot the binoculars. I wouldn't want to see this up close."

I didn't even want to see it from a distance.

"When I was a ho I used to keep myself from getting grossed out by pretending men's privates were Muppets," Lula said. "This guy looks like an anteater Muppet. See the little tuft of hair on the anteater head and then there's the thing the anteater snuffs up ants with . . . except ol' Punky here's gotta get real close to the ants on account of his snuffer isn't real big. Punky's got a pinky."

Lula was a ho in a previous life. One night while plying her trade she had a near-death experience and decided to change everything but her wardrobe. Not even a near-death experience could get Lula out of spandex. She was currently wearing a skintight hot pink miniskirt and a tiger-print top that made her boobs look like big round overinflated balloons. It was early June and midmorning and the Jersey air wasn't cooking yet, so Lula had a yellow angora sweater over the tiger top.

"Hold on," Lula said. "I think his snuffer is growing."

This produced another *eeyeuuw* from us.

"Maybe I should shoot him," Lula said.

"No shooting!" I felt the need to discourage Lula from hauling out her Glock, but truth was, it seemed like it'd be a public service to take a potshot at Punky.

"How bad do we want this guy?" Lula asked.

"If I don't bring him in, I don't get paid. If I don't get paid, I don't have rent money. If I don't have rent money, I get kicked out of my apartment and have to move in with my parents."

"So we want him real bad."

"*Real* bad."

"And he's wanted for what?"

"Grand theft auto."

"At least it's not armed robbery. I'm gonna be hoping the only weapon he's got, he's holding in his hand right now . . . on account of it don't look like much of a threat to me."

"I guess we should go do it."

"I'm ready to rock 'n' roll," Lula said. "I'm ready to kick some Punky butt. I'm ready to do the job."

I turned the key in the ignition. "I'm going to drop you at the corner so you can cut through the back and take the back door. Make sure you have your walkie-talkie on so I can let you know when I'm coming in."

"Roger, that."

"And no shooting, no breaking doors down, no Dirty Harry imitations."

"You can count on me."

Three minutes later, Lula reported she was in place. I parked the Escape two houses down, walked to Punky's front door, and rang the bell. No one responded so I rang a second time. I gave the door a solid rap with my fist and shouted, "Bond enforcement! Open the door!"

I heard shouting carrying over from the backyard, a door crashing open and slamming shut, and then more muffled shouting. I called Lula on the talkie, but got no response. A moment later the front door opened to the house next to me and Lula stomped out.

"Hey, so excuse me," she yelled at the woman behind her. "So I got the wrong door. It could happen, you know. We're under a lot of pressure when we're making these dangerous apprehensions."

The woman glared at Lula and slammed and locked her door shut.

"Must have miscounted houses," Lula said to me. "I sort of let myself in through the wrong door."

"You weren't supposed to open *any* door."

"Yeah, but I heard someone moving around inside. Guess that's 'cause it was the neighbor lady's house, hunh? So what's going on? How come you're not in yet?"

"He hasn't opened the door."

Lula took a step back and looked up. "That's because he's still mooning you."

I followed Lula's line of sight. She was right. Punky had his ass to the window again.

"Hey," Lula yelled up. "Get your fat ass off the

window and get down here! We're trying to do some bond enforcement!"

An old man and an old woman came out of the house across the street and settled themselves on their front stoop to watch.

"Are you going to shoot him?" the old man wanted to know.

"I don't hardly ever get allowed to shoot anybody," Lula told him.

"That's darn disappointing," the man said. "How about kicking the door down?"

Lula gave the man one of her hand-on-hip *get real* looks. "Kick the door down? Do I look like I could kick a door down in these shoes? These are Via Spigas. You don't go around kicking down doors in Via Spigas. These are classy shoes. I paid a shitload of money for these shoes and I'm not sticking them through some cheap-ass door."

Everyone looked at me. I was wearing jeans, a T-shirt topped by a black jeans jacket, and CAT boots. CAT boots could definitely kick down a door, but they'd have to be on someone else's foot because door kicking was a skill I lacked.

"You girls need to watch more television," the old man said. "You need to be more like those Charlie's Angels. Nothing stopped them girls. They could kick doors down in all kinds of shoes."

"Anyways, you don't need to kick the door in," the old woman said. "Punky never locks it."

I tried the door and, sure enough, it was unlocked.

"Sort of takes the fun out of it," Lula said, looking past the door into Punky's house.

This is the part where if we were Charlie's Angels we'd get into crouched positions, holding our guns in two hands in front of us, and we'd hunt down Punky. This didn't work for us because I left my gun home, in the cookie jar on my kitchen counter, and Lula'd fall over if she tried to do the crouch thing in her Via Spigas.

"Hey Punky," I yelled up the stairs, "put some clothes on and come down here. I need to talk to you."

"No way."

"If you don't get down here, I'm going to send Lula up to get you."

Lula's eyes got wide and she mouthed, *Me? Why me?*

"Come up here and get me," Punky said. "I have a surprise for you."

Lula pulled a Glock out of her handbag and gave it over to me. "You should take this on account of *you're* gonna be the one going up the stairs first and you might need it. You know how I hate surprises."

"I don't want the gun. I don't like guns."

"Take the gun."

"I don't want the gun," I told her.

"*Take* the *gun!*"

Yeesh. "Okay, okay. Give me the stupid gun."

I got to the top of the stairs and I peeked around the corner, down the hall.

"Here I come, ready or not," Punky sang out. And then he jumped from behind a bedroom door and stood spread eagle in full view. "Ta-dahhhh."

He was buck naked and slick as a greased pig. Lula and I swallowed hard and we both took a step backward.

"What have you got all over you?" I asked.

"Vaseline. Head to toe and extra heavy in the cracks and crevices." He was smiling ear to ear. "You want to take me in, you have to wrestle with me."

"How about we just shoot you?" Lula said.

"You can't shoot me. I'm not armed."

"Here's the plan," I said to Lula. "We cuff him and put him in leg irons and then we wrap him in a blanket so he doesn't get my car greasy."

"I'm not touching him," Lula said. "Not only is he an ugly naked motherfucker, but he's a dry cleaning bill waiting to happen. I'm not ruining this top. I'll never find another top like this. It's genuine fake tiger. And Lord knows what he'd do to rabbit."

I reached for him with the cuffs. "Give me your hand."

"Make me," he said, waggling his butt. "Come get me, sweetie pie."

Lula looked over at me. "You *sure* you don't want me to shoot him?"

I took my jacket off and snatched at his wrist, but I couldn't hold tight. After three attempts I had Vaseline up to my elbow, and Punky was skipping around going, ". . . Nah, nah, nah. Kiss my can, you can't catch me, I'm the Vaseline man."

"This guy's in the red zone on the Breathalyzer," Lula said. "Think he might also be missing a few marbles in his greased-up jug head."

"I'm crazy like a fox," Punky said. "If you can't catch hold of me, you can't take me in. If you can't take me in, I don't go to jail."

"If I don't take you in, I don't pay my rent and I get kicked out of my apartment," I told Punky, lunging for him, swearing when he slid away from me.

"This here's embarrassing," Lula said. "I can't believe you're trying to grab this funky fat man."

"It's my job. And you could help! Take the damn top off if you don't want it to get ruined."

"Yeah, take your top off, momma. I've got plenty of extra Vaseline for you," Punky sang out.

Punky turned away from me, I gave him a good hard kick to the back of his knee, and he crashed to the floor. I threw myself on top of him and yelled to Lula to cuff him. She managed to get both cuffs on and my cell phone chirped.

It was my Grandma Mazur on the phone. When my Grandpa Mazur cashed in his two-dollar chips and moved on to the High Rollers' Suite in the sky, my Grandma Mazur moved in with my parents.

"Your mother's locked herself in the bathroom and she won't come out," Grandma said. "She's been in there for an hour and a half. It's the menopause. Your mother was always so sensible until the menopause hit."

"She's probably taking a bath."

"That's what I thought at first, but she's never in there this long. I went up and yelled and banged on the door just now and there's no answer. For all I know, she's dead. She could have had a heart attack and drowned in the tub."

"*Omigod.*"

"Anyways, I thought you could get over here and unlock the door like you did last time when your sister locked herself in the bathroom."

At Christmastime my sister Valerie locked herself in the bathroom with a pregnancy test kit. The test kit kept turning up positive, and if I was Valerie I would have wanted to spend the rest of my life locked in the bathroom, too.

"I wasn't the one who unlocked the door," I told Grandma. "I was the one who climbed onto the roof over the back stoop and went in through the window."

"Well, whatever you did, you better get over here and do it again. Your father's off somewhere and your sister's out. I'd shoot the lock off, but last time I tried to do that the bullet ricocheted off the doorknob and took out a table lamp."

"Are you sure this is an emergency? I'm sort of in the middle of something."

"Hard to tell what's an emergency in this house anymore."

My parents lived in a small three-bedroom, one-

bathroom house that was bursting at the seams with
my mom and dad, my grandma, my recently divorced,
very pregnant sister, and her two kids. Emergencies
tended to blend with the normal.

"Hang tight," I told Grandma. "I'm not far away. I'll
be there in a couple minutes."

Lula looked down at Punky. "What are we gonna do
with him?"

"We're going to take him with us."

"The hell you are," Punky said. "I'm not getting up.
I'm not going anywhere."

"I don't have time to mess with this," I said to Lula.
"You stay here and baby-sit and I'll send Vinnie over to
do the pickup."

"You're in trouble now," Lula said to Punky. "I bet
Vinnie likes greased-up fat men. People tell me Vinnie
used to be romantically involved with a duck. I bet he's
gonna think you're just fine."

I hustled down the stairs and out the front door to
the Escape. I called Vinnie on the way to my parents'
house and gave him the word on Punky.

"What are you, nuts?" Vinnie yelled at me. "I'm not
gonna go out to pick up some greased-up naked guy.
I write bonds. I don't do pickups. Read my lips . . .
you're the pickup person."

"Fine. Then *you* go to my parents' house and get my
mother out of the bathroom."

"All right, all right, I'll do your pickup, but it's come
to a sad state of affairs when I'm the normal member
of this family."

I couldn't argue with that one.

Grandma Mazur was waiting for me when I pulled
to the curb. "She's still in there," Grandma said. "She
won't talk to me or nothing."

I ran up the stairs and tried the door. Locked. I
knocked. No answer. I yelled to my mother. Still no

response. Damn. I ran down the stairs out to the garage and got a step ladder. I put the ladder up to the back stoop and climbed onto the small shingled roof that attached to the back of the house and gave me access to the bathroom window. I looked inside.

My mom was in the tub with earphones on, eyes closed, knees sticking out of the water like two smooth pink islands. I rapped on the window, and my mom opened her eyes and gave a shriek. She grabbed for the towel and continued to scream for a good sixty seconds. Finally she blinked, snapped her mouth shut, pointed straight-armed to the bathroom door, and mouthed the word *go*.

I scuttled off the roof, down the ladder, and slunk back to the house and up the stairs, followed by Grandma Mazur.

My mother was at the bathroom door, wrapped in a towel, waiting. "What the hell were you doing?" she yelled. "You scared the crap out of me. Dammit. Can't I even relax in the tub?"

Grandma Mazur and I were speechless, standing rooted to the spot, our mouths open, our eyes wide. My mom never cursed. My mom was the practical, calming influence on the family. My mom went to church. My mom *never* said *crap*.

"It's the change," Grandma said.

"It is *not* the change," my mother shouted. "I am *not* menopausal. I just want a half hour alone. Is that too much to ask? A crappy half hour!"

"You were in there for an hour and a half," Grandma said. "I thought you might have had a heart attack. You wouldn't answer me."

"I was listening to music. I didn't hear you. I had the headset on."

"I can see that now," Grandma said. "Maybe I should try that sometime."

My mother leaned forward and took a closer look at my shirt. "What on earth do you have all over you? It's in your hair and on your shirt and you have big grease stains on your jeans. It looks like . . . Vaseline."

"I was in the middle of a capture when Grandma called."

My mother did an eye roll. "I don't want to know the details. Not ever. And you should be sure to pretreat when you get home or you're never going to get that stuff out."

Ten minutes later I was pushing through the front door to Vinnie's office. Connie Rosolli, Vinnie's office manager and guard dog, was behind her desk, newspaper in hand. Connie was a couple years older than me, an inch or two shorter, and had me by three cup sizes. She was wearing a blood red V-neck sweater that showed a lot of cleavage. Her nails and her lips matched the sweater.

There were two women occupying the chairs in front of Connie's desk. Both women were dark-skinned and wearing traditional Indian dress. The older woman was a size up from Lula. Lula is packed solid, like a giant bratwurst. The woman sitting across from Connie was loose flab with rolls of fat cascading between the halter top and the long skirt of her sari. Her black hair was tied in a knot low on her neck and shot through with gray. The younger woman was slim and I guessed slightly younger than me. Late twenties, maybe. They both were perched on the edges of their seats, hands tightly clasped in their laps.

"We've got trouble," Connie said to me. "There's an article in the paper today about Vinnie."

"It's not another duck incident, is it?" I asked.

"It's about the visa bond Vinnie wrote for Samuel Singh. Singh is here on a three-month work visa and

Vinnie wrote a bond insuring Singh would leave when his visa was up. A visa bond is a new thing, so the paper's making a big deal about it."

Connie handed me the paper and I looked at the photo accompanying the feature. Two slim, shifty-looking men with slicked-back black hair, smiling. Singh was from India, his complexion darker, his frame smaller than Vinnie's. Both men looked like they regularly conned old ladies out of their life savings. Two Indian women stood in the background, behind Vinnie and Singh. The women in the photo were the women sitting in front of Connie.

"This is Mrs. Apusenja and her daughter Nonnie," Connie said. "Mrs. Apusenja rented a room to Samuel Singh."

Mrs. Apusenja and her daughter were staring at me, not sure what to do or say about the globs of goo in my hair and gunked into my clothes.

"And this is Stephanie Plum," Connie told the Apusenjas. "She's one of our bond enforcement agents. She's not usually this . . . greasy." Connie squinted at me. "What the hell have you got all over you?"

"Vaseline. Balog was covered with it. I had to wrestle him down."

"This looks sexual to me," Mrs. Apusenja said. "I am a moral woman. I do not want to become involved with this." She clapped her hands to her head. "Look at me. I have my ears covered. I am not hearing this filth."

"There's no filth," I shouted at her. "There was this guy I had to bring in and he was covered in Vaseline . . ."

"Lalalalalalala," Mrs. Apusenja sang.

Connie and I rolled our eyes.

Nonnie pulled her mother's hand away from her head. "Listen to these people," she said to her mother. "We need them to help us."

Mrs. Apusenja stopped singing and crossed her arms over her chest.

"Mrs. Apusenja is here because Singh's disappeared," Connie said.

"This is true," Mrs. Apusenja said. "We are very worried. He was an exemplary young man."

I skimmed the article. Samuel Singh's bond was up in a week. If Vinnie couldn't produce Singh in a week's time, he was going to look like an idiot.

"We think something terrible happened to him," Nonnie said. "He just disappeared. *Poof.*"

The mother nodded in agreement. "Samuel has been staying with us while working in this country. My family is very close to Samuel Singh's family in India. It's a very good family. Nonnie and Samuel were to be married, in fact. She was to travel to India with Samuel to meet his mother and father. We have a ticket for the plane."

"How long has Samuel been gone?" Connie asked.

"Five days," Nonnie said. "He left for work and he never returned. We asked his employer and they said Samuel didn't show up that day. We came here because we hoped Mr. Plum would be able to help us find Samuel."

"Have you checked Samuel's room to see if anything is missing?" I asked. "Clothes? Passport?"

"Everything seems to be there."

"Have you reported his disappearance to the police?"

"We have not. Do you think we should do that?"

"*No*," Connie said, voice just a tad too shrill, hitting Vinnie's cell phone number on her speed dial.

"We've got a situation here," Connie said to Vinnie. "Mrs. Apusenja is in the office. Samuel Singh has gone missing."

At two in the morning when the weather is ideal and the lights are all perfectly timed, it takes twenty minutes

to drive from the police station to the bail bonds office.
Today, at two in the afternoon, under an overcast sky,
Vinnie made the run in twelve minutes.

Ranger, Vinnie's top gun, had ambled in a couple
minutes earlier at Vinnie's request. He was dressed in
his usual black. His dark brown hair was pulled back
from his face and tied into a short ponytail at the nape
of his neck. His jacket looked suspiciously like Kevlar and I knew from experience it hid a gun. Ranger
was always armed. And Ranger was always dangerous. His age was somewhere between twenty-five and
thirty-five and his skin was the color of a mocha latte.
The story goes that Ranger had been Special Forces
before signing on with Vinnie to do bond enforcement.
He had a lot of muscle and a skill level somewhere between Batman and Rambo.

A while ago Ranger and I spent the night together.
We were in an uneasy alliance now, working as a
team when necessary, avoiding contact or conversation that would lead to a repeat sexual encounter. At
least *I* was avoiding a repeat encounter. Ranger was
his usual silent mysterious self, his thoughts unknown,
his attitude provocative.

He'd looked me over before taking a chair. "Vaseline?" he asked.

"I am thinking it must be something sexual," Mrs.
Apusenja said. "No one has told me otherwise. I am
thinking this one must be a slut."

"I am *not* a slut," I said. "I had to capture a guy who
was all greased up and some of the gunk rubbed off on
me."

The back door burst open and Vinnie came in like
gangbusters, followed by Lula.

"Talk to me," Vinnie said to Connie.

"Not much to tell. You remember Mrs. Apusenja and
her daughter Nonnie. Samuel Singh rented a room in the

Apusenja house and they were at the photo session last week. They haven't seen him in five days."

"Christ," Vinnie said. "National print coverage on this. A week to go. And this sonovabitch goes missing. Why didn't he just come over to my house and feed me rat poison? It would have been an easier death."

"We think there might be foul play involved," Nonnie said.

Vinnie made a halfhearted effort to squash a grimace. "Yeah, right. Give me a refresher course on Samuel Singh. What was his normal routine?" Vinnie had the file in his hand, flipping pages, mumbling as he read. "It says here he worked at TriBro Tech. He was in the quality control department."

"During the week Samuel would be at work from seven-thirty to five. Every night he would stay home and watch television or spend time on his computer. Even on weekends he would spend most of his time on the computer," Nonnie said.

"There is a word to call him," Mrs. Apusenja said. "I can never remember."

"Geek," Nonnie said, not looking all that happy about it.

"Yes! That's it. He was a computer geek."

"Did he have friends? Relatives in the area?" Vinnie asked.

"There were people at his workplace that he spoke of but he didn't spend time with them socially."

"Did he have enemies? Debts?"

Nonnie shook her head no. "He never spoke of debts or enemies."

"Drugs?" Vinnie asked.

"No. And he would drink alcohol only on special occasions."

"How about criminal activity? Was he involved with anyone shady?"

"Certainly not."

Ranger was impassive in his corner, watching the women. Nonnie was leaning forward in her chair, uncomfortable with the situation. Mama Apusenja had her lips pressed tight together, her head tipped slightly, not favorably impressed with what she was seeing.

"Anything else?" Vinnie asked.

Nonnie fidgeted in her seat. Her eyes dropped to the purse in her lap. "My little dog," Nonnie finally said. "My little dog is missing." She opened her purse and extracted a photo. "His name is Boo because he is so white. Like a ghost. He disappeared when Samuel vanished. He was in the backyard, which is fenced, and he disappeared."

We all looked at the photo of Nonnie and Boo. Boo was a small cocker spaniel and poodle mix with black button eyes in a fluffy white face. Boo was a cockapoo.

I felt something tug inside me for the dog. The black button eyes reminded me of my hamster, Rex. I remembered the times when I'd been worried about Rex, and I felt the same sharp stab of concern for the little dog.

"Do you get along okay with your neighbors?" Vinnie asked. "Have you asked any of them if they've seen the dog?"

"No one has seen Boo."

"We must leave now," Mrs. Apusenja said, glancing at her watch. "Nonnie needs to get back to work."

Vinnie saw them to the door and watched them cross the street to their car. "There they go," Vinnie said. "Hell's message bearers." He shook his head. "I was having such a good day. Everyone was saying how good I looked in the picture. Everyone was congratulating me because I was doing something about visa enforcement. Okay, so I took a few comments when I dragged a naked, greased-up fat guy into the station, but I could handle that." He gave his head another shake. "*This* I can't handle. This has to get fixed. I can't afford to lose this guy. Either we find this guy, dead or alive, or we're all unemployed. If I can't enforce this visa bond after all the publicity, I'm going to have to change my name, move to Scottsdale, Arizona, and sell used cars." Vinnie focused on Ranger. "You can find him, right?"

The corners of Ranger's mouth tipped up a fraction of an inch. This was the Ranger equivalent of a smile.

"I'm gonna take that as a yes," Vinnie said.

"I'll need help," Ranger told him. "And we'll need to work out the fee."

"Fine. Whatever. You can have Stephanie."

Ranger cut his eyes to me and the smile widened ever so slightly—the sort of smile you see on a man when he's presented with an unexpected piece of pie.

TWO

Connie handed a stack of papers over to Ranger. "Here's everything we have," she said. "A copy of the bond agreement, photo, background information. I'll check the hospitals and the morgue, and I'll run a full investigative report. I should have some of it tomorrow."

This was the information age. Sign up with a service, tap a few keys on the computer, and within seconds facts start pouring in . . . all the names on the family tree, employment records, credit history, a chronology of home addresses. If you pay enough and search hard enough it's possible to access medical secrets and marital infidelities.

Ranger read through the Singh file and then looked at me. "Are you available?"

Connie fanned herself and Lula bit into her lower lip.

I blew out a sigh. This apprehension was going to create problems. My involvement with Trenton cop Joe Morelli was on the fast track again. Joe and I had a long, strange history and we probably loved each other. Neither of us felt marriage was the answer right now. It was one of the few things we agreed on. Morelli hated my job and I wasn't crazy about his grandmother. And Morelli and I had clashing views on

Ranger's acceptability as a partner. We both agreed
Ranger was dangerous and a shade off normal. Morelli wanted me to stay *far* away from Ranger. I thought
six to ten inches was sufficient.

"What's the plan?" I asked Ranger.

"I'll take the neighborhood. You talk to Singh's employer, TriBro Tech. TriBro should be cooperative.
They put the money up for the visa bond."

I snapped him a salute. "Okeydokey," I said. "Don't
forget about the dog."

The almost smile returned to Ranger's mouth. "No
stone unturned," he said.

"Hey," I said, "dogs are people, too."

The truth was, I didn't give a hoot about Samuel
Singh. I know that's not a great attitude, but I was
stuck with it. And I certainly didn't care about Mrs.
Apusenja. Mrs. Apusenja was a bridge troll. Nonnie
and the dog seemed like they needed help. And the
dog pushed a button on me that triggered a rush of
protective feelings. Go figure that. I really wanted to
find the dog.

Ranger took off and I headed for home to degrease
before questioning Singh's boss. I live in a three-story
brick apartment building that houses the newly wed and
the nearly dead . . . and me. The building lacks a lot
of amenities, but the price is right and I can get pizza
delivered. I parked in the lot, took the stairs to the second floor, and was surprised to find my apartment door
unlocked. I stuck my head in and yelled, "Anybody
home?"

"Yeah, it's me," Morelli yelled back from the bedroom. "I'm missing a set of keys. I thought maybe I left
them here last night."

"I put them in the cookie jar for safekeeping."

Morelli walked into the kitchen, lifted the lid

on the cookie jar, and removed his keys. Morelli looked like a real badass . . . lean and hard in a black T-shirt, washed-out jeans that fit him great across the butt, and new running shoes. He wore his gun at his hip, out of sight under a lightweight jacket. His hair was dark and his eyes were dark and he looked like he frequently traveled through places where men's hearts were dark.

"I'm not surprised to find the thirty-eight in here," he said. "But what's with the box of condoms?"

"They're for an emergency. Like the gun."

He pocketed the keys and looked me over. "You get into a fight with the guy who owns the lube gun at Midas?"

"Punky Balog. He thought if he was greased up and naked I wouldn't take him in."

"Hah," Morelli said. "Greased up and naked is your specialty. Are you done for the day?"

"No. I came home to get cleaned. Did you see the article about Vinnie and the visa bond?"

"Yeah."

"Samuel Singh, the bondee, is missing."

Morelli grinned. "That's fun."

No one wanted to see Vinnie selling used cars in Scottsdale, but we all enjoyed watching him sweat. Vinnie sat on a rotting branch of my family tree. Only a couple roaches from my Aunt Tootie's kitchen sat lower than Vinnie. He was a pervert, a con man, and a paranoid grouch. And in spite of all that (or maybe because of it) he was liked. He was Jersey. How can you not like Jersey?

"As soon as I change my clothes I'm going out to talk to Singh's boss," I told Morelli.

"I'm surprised Vinnie didn't give this to Ranger."

Our eyes locked for a long moment while I searched for a reply, thinking a fib might be the way to go.

"Shit, Stephanie," Morelli finally said, hands on hips, hard set to his mouth. "Don't tell me you're working with Ranger again."

Morelli and I were legitimately separated when I slept with Ranger. When Morelli and I got back together, he never asked and I never told. Still, the suspicion was there and the association rankled. And beyond the suspicion, there was a very real concern that Ranger sometimes operated a tad too far left of the law. "It's my job," I told Morelli.

"The guy's nuts. He doesn't have an address. The address on his driver's license is an empty lot. And I think he kills people."

"I'm pretty sure he only kills bad guys."

"That makes me feel a lot better."

I didn't actually know if Ranger killed people. Truth is, no one knows much about Ranger. The only thing I know for sure is that he's a primo bounty hunter. And he's the sort of lover who could make a woman forget she values commitment.

"I have to take a shower," I told Morelli.

"Need help?"

"No! I want to talk to Singh's employer, TriBro Tech. It's on the other side of Route One and I want to get there before the workday ends."

"I think I'm getting turned on by the Vaseline," Morelli said.

Everything turns Morelli on. "Go to work! Catch a drug dealer or something."

"I'll hold the thought for tonight," Morelli said. "Maybe you should come home and take a nap after Tri Bro." And he left.

Twenty minutes later, I was out the door. My clean hair was pulled into a ponytail. I was wearing sandals, a short black skirt, and a white sweater with a low scoop neck. I had pepper spray in my purse, just in case.

I couldn't match Connie in the cleavage department, but thanks to Victoria's Secret I was making the most of what I had.

TriBro was located in a light industrial park just east of the city. I cut across town, picked up Route 1, and counted off two exits. I took the off-ramp directly into the complex, located B Street, and parked in TriBro's lot. The structure in front of me was single story, cinderblock construction, brick front, sign to the right of the front door. TriBro Tech.

The reception area was utilitarian. Industrial-grade charcoal carpet, commercial-grade dark wood furniture, overhead fluorescent lighting. Large fake potted plant by the door. Very orderly. Very clean. The woman behind the desk was professionally friendly. I introduced myself and asked to speak to Singh's superior.

A man appeared in an open doorway behind the woman. "I'm Andrew Cone," he said. "Perhaps I can help you."

He was mid-forties, average height, slim build, seriously thinning brown hair, amiable brown eyes. He wore a blue dress shirt, one button open at the throat, sleeves neatly rolled. Khaki slacks. He ushered me into his office and directed me to a chair across from his desk. His office was tastefully decorated. He had a *World's Best Dad* coffee mug on his desk and framed photos in his bookcase. The photos were of two little boys and a blond woman. They were at the beach. They were dressed for a party. They were hugging a small spotted dog.

"I'm looking for Samuel Singh," I told Andrew Cone, passing him a business card.

He smiled at me with slightly raised eyebrows. "Bond enforcement? What's a nice girl like you doing in a tough job like that?"

"Paying the rent, mostly."

"And Singh skipped out on you?"

"Not yet. He has another week left on his visa. This is routine monitoring."

Cone wagged his finger at me. "That's a fib. Singh's landlord and her daughter were here earlier. They haven't seen Singh in five days. And neither have we. Singh didn't show up for work last Wednesday and we haven't seen or heard from him since. I read the article in today's paper. Unfortunate timing."

"Do you have any idea where he might be?"

"No, but I don't think it's any place good. He didn't pick up his paycheck on Friday. Usually, only the dead and the deported don't show up for their paycheck."

"Did he have a locker here? Any friends I might talk to?"

"No locker. I've asked around, but I didn't come up with much. The general opinion is that Singh's likeable enough, but a loner."

I looked around the office. No clues as to the nature of TriBro's business. "So what sort of business is this? And what did Singh do for you?"

"TriBro makes very specific parts for slot machines. My father and his two brothers started the business in fifty-two, and now it's owned by me and my two brothers, Bart and Clyde. My mother had hopes for a large family and thought it would simplify things to name her children alphabetically. I have two sisters. Diane and Evelyn."

"Your parents stopped at five?"

"They divorced after five. I think it was the stress of living in a house with one bathroom and five kids."

I felt myself smiling. I liked Andrew Cone. He was a pleasant guy and he had a sense of humor. "And Singh?"

"Singh was a techie, working in quality control. We

hired him to temporarily fill in for a woman who was out on maternity leave."

"Do you think his disappearance could be work related?"

"Are you asking if the Mob rubbed him out?"

"That would be part of the question."

"We're actually a pretty boring little cog in the casino wheel," Cone said. "I don't think the Mob would be interested in Singh's contribution to gambling."

"Terrorist connection?"

Cone grinned and tipped back in his chair. "Not likely. From what I hear, Singh was addicted to American television and junk food and would give his life to protect the country that spawned the Egg McMuffin."

"Did you know him personally?"

"Only as boss to employee. This is a small company. Bart and Clyde and I know everyone who works here, but we don't necessarily socialize with the people on the line."

Raised voices carried in to us.

"My brothers," Andrew said. "No volume control."

A slightly younger, balder version of Andrew stuck his head in the doorway. "We got a problem." He looked my way. "And you would be who?"

I gave him my card.

"Bond enforcement?"

A third face appeared in the doorway. This face was round and cherubic with eyes peering out from behind wire-rimmed glasses. The face came with a chubby body dressed in homeboy jeans, a Buzz Lightyear sweatshirt that had been washed almost to oblivion and beyond, and ratty sneakers.

"You're a bounty hunter, right?" the baby-faced guy said. "Do you have a gun?"

"No gun."

"They always have guns on television."

"I left my gun home."

"I bet you don't need one. I bet you're real sneaky. You just sneak up to someone and *bam,* you've got him in handcuffs, right?"

"Right."

"Are you going to handcuff someone here?"

"Not today."

"My brothers," Andrew said, gesturing to the two men. "Bart and Clyde Cone."

Bart was wearing a black dress shirt, black slacks, and black loafers. Black Bart.

"If you're here about Samuel Singh, we have nothing to say on the matter," Bart said. "He was very briefly in our employ."

"Did you know him personally?"

"I did not. And I'm afraid I have to speak to my brother privately. We have a problem on the line."

Clyde leaned close to me. Friendly. "There's always a problem on the line," he said, smiling, not caring much. "Shit's always breaking. Gizmos and stuff like that." His eyes got wide. "How about a taser? Have you ever used a taser?"

Bart pressed his lips together and threw Clyde a dark look.

The look rolled off Clyde. "I never met a bounty hunter before," Clyde said, his breath steaming his glasses.

I'd hoped for more information from TriBro. The name of a friend or enemy would have been helpful. Some knowledge of travel plans would have been nice. What I got was a vague idea of the nature of Singh's job and a dinner invitation from Clyde Cone, who I suspected was only interested in my stun gun.

I declined the dinner invitation and I rolled out of the lot. Ranger was working the Apusenjas' neighborhood. I didn't want to step on Ranger's toes, but I worried that Boo the cockapoo wasn't a priority for him. It was getting to be late afternoon. I could cut across town and do a quick drive around, looking for Boo, and then I'd be in a good position to mooch dinner from my mom.

I called Morelli and told him the plan. "You can mooch dinner, too," I said.

"Last time I ate dinner at your parents' house your sister threw up three times and your grandmother fell asleep in her mashed potatoes."

"And?"

"And I'd like to mooch dinner, but I have to work late. I swear to God, I really do have to work late."

Nonnie and Mama Apusenja lived a quarter mile from my parents' house, in a neighborhood that was very similar to the Burg. Houses were narrow, two stories, set on narrow lots. The Apusenja house was a two-toned clapboard, painted a bilious green on the top and chocolate brown on the bottom. A ten-year-old burgundy Ford Escort was parked curbside. The small backyard was fenced. I couldn't see all the yard, but what I *could* see didn't contain a dog. I cruised four blocks without a Boo sighting. Also, no Ranger sighting. I turned a corner and my cell phone chirped.

"Yo," Ranger said.

"Yo yourself," I told him. "Do you have Singh in leg irons?"

"Singh is nowhere to be found."

"And the dog?"

A couple beats of silence. "What's with you and the dog?"

"I don't know. I just have these *dog* feelings."

"Not a good sign, babe. Next thing you'll be adopting

cats. And then one day you'll get all choked up when you walk down the baby food aisle in the supermarket. And you know what happens after that . . ."

"What?"

"You'll be punching holes in Morelli's condoms."

I would like to think the scenario was funny, but I was afraid it might be true. "I visited with the people at TriBro," I told Ranger. "I didn't come away with anything useful."

I caught a familiar reflection in my rearview mirror. Ranger in his truck. How he always managed to find me was part of the mystery.

Ranger flashed his lights to make sure I saw him. "Let's talk to the Apusenjas," he said.

We drove around the block to Sully Street, parked behind the burgundy Escort, and walked to the door together.

Mama Apusenja answered. She was still in the sari and her fat rolls made me think of the Michelin tire guy.

"Well," she said to me, with a head wag. "I see you've cleaned yourself up. You must be a terrible burden to your mother. I am feeling so sorry for her not to have a proper daughter."

I narrowed my eyes and opened my mouth to speak and Ranger leaned into me and rested a hand on my shoulder. Probably he thought I was going to do something rash, like call Mrs. Apusenja a fat cow. And in fact he was right. *Fat cow* was on the tip of my tongue.

"I thought it might be helpful to see Singh's room," Ranger said to Mrs. Apusenja.

"Will you be bringing *this one* in with you?"

Ranger's grip on me tightened. "*This one's* name is Stephanie," Ranger said pleasantly. "And yes, she'll be coming with me."

"I suppose it will be all right," Mrs. Apusenja said grudgingly. "I will expect you to be careful. I keep a very nice house." She stepped back from the door and motioned us into the living room. "This is the formal parlor," she said proudly. "And beyond that is the dining room. And then the kitchen."

Ranger and I stood speechless for a moment, taking it all in. The house was filled to the bursting with overstuffed furniture, end tables, lamps, trinkets, dried flowers, faded photos, stacks of magazines and bowls of fake fruit. And elephants. There were ceramic elephants, elaborate elephant couch pillows, elephant clocks, foot stools, and planters. Elephants aside, there was no dominant style or color. It was a garage sale waiting to happen.

I watched Ranger scan the room and I suspected he was doing a mental grimace. It would be easy to miss a note in the mess. For that matter, it would be easy to miss Singh. He could be slouched in a chair somewhere and never be noticed.

Mrs. Apusenja led the way upstairs, across the short hallway to a small bedroom. She was wearing pink rubber flip-flops that slapped against her heels and hit the floor at an angle so her heel was always half off the shoe. Her toenails were massive, painted a virulent shimmering purple. I was directly behind her and from my angle her ass looked to be about three feet across.

"This is Samuel's room," she said, gesturing to the open door. "It's so sad that it's empty. He was such a nice young man. So polite. Very respectful." She said this cutting a look back at me, sending the message that she knew I had none of those wonderful qualities.

Ranger and I stepped inside the room and I was hit with a wave of claustrophobia. The double bed was neatly made, covered with a green, yellow, and purple-flowered quilted bedspread that shouted *yikes*. The curtains matched the bedspread and hung over seasick green sheers. The walls were plastered with outdated calendars and thumbtacked posters, subjects ranging from Winnie the Pooh to Springsteen, the Starship *Enterprise,* and Albert Einstein. There was a nightstand beside the bed and a small desk and rickety chair wedged between the bed and the wall.

"You see, it's such a nice room," Mrs. Apusenja said. "He was lucky to have this room. We have a room in the basement that we also rent out on occasion, but we gave Samuel this room because I knew he would be a suitor for Nonnie."

Ranger rifled through the nightstand and desk drawers. "Was Samuel unhappy about anything?"

"No. He was very happy. Why would he be unhappy? He had everything. We even allowed him kitchen privileges."

"Have you notified his family of his disappearance?"

"I have. I thought perhaps he was suddenly called home, but they have heard nothing from him."

Ranger moved on to the desk. He opened the middle drawer and extracted Singh's passport. "New York is his only entry."

"This was his first time away from home," Mrs. Apusenja said. "He was a good boy. He was not one of those good-for-nothing wanderers. He came here to make money for his family in India."

Ranger returned the passport to the drawer and continued his search. He abandoned the desk and went to the closet. "What's missing from the room?" Ranger asked Mrs. Apusenja. "What did Singh take with him?"

"So far as I know, just the clothes he was wearing. And his backpack, of course."

Ranger turned to look at her. "Do you know what he carried in his backpack?"

"His computer. He was never without his computer.

It was a laptop. It always went to work with him. Samuel was very smart. That's how he got such a good job. He said he got his job over the Internet."

"Do you know his email address?" I asked.

"No. I don't know anything about that. We don't own a computer. We have no need for such a thing."

"How did Samuel get to work?" Ranger asked.

"He drove himself."

"Has his car been found?"

"No. He just drove away in the car and that was the last we saw of him and the car. It was a gray Nissan Sentra . . . an older model."

Ranger did a quick search of the bathroom and Nonnie's room and we all moved downstairs to search the kitchen.

We were still in the kitchen when Nonnie came home.

"Have you found Boo?" Nonnie asked.

"Not yet," I said. "Sorry."

"It's difficult to concentrate on my work with him missing like this," Nonnie said.

"Nonnie is a manicurist at Classy Nails in the mall," Mrs. Apusenja said. "She is one of their most popular girls."

"I never skimp on the top coat," Nonnie said. "That's the secret to a superior manicure."

It was a few minutes after six when Ranger and I left the Apusenjas'. There was still time to make dinner at my parents' house, but I was losing enthusiasm for the experience. I was thinking I'd had enough chaos for one day. I was thinking maybe what I wanted to do was get take-out pizza and go home and watch a bad movie.

Ranger lounged against my car, arms crossed over his chest. "What do you think?"

"Nonnie never asked about Singh. She only asked about Boo."

"Not exactly the distraught fiancée," Ranger said.

"If we believe everything we hear, we've got a nice geeky guy who got himself engaged and disappeared along with the dog."

"The dog could be a coincidence."

"I don't think so. My Spidey Sense tells me the disappearances are related."

Ranger grinned at me. "Your Spidey Sense tell you anything else?"

"Is that a mocking grin?"

"It's the grin of a man who loves you, babe."

My heart skipped around a little and I got warm in places only Morelli should be warming. "Love?"

"There's all kinds of love," Ranger said. "This kind doesn't come with a ring attached."

"Nice, but you avoided answering my question about the mocking grin."

He gave my ponytail a playful tug.

"I'm going back to TriBro tomorrow," I said. "I'll make a pest of myself. Find out about the Internet job search. Talk to co-workers. If it's anything other than a random murder, I should be able to get a lead."

I decided against the family dinner and instead I stopped at Pino's on the way home. I slid the Pino's pizza box onto my kitchen counter, kicked my shoes off, and got a beer out of the fridge. I punched the message button on my machine and listened to my messages while I ate.

"Stephanie? It's your mother. Hello? Are you there?" Disconnect.

Second message. "Bad news. I'm gonna punk out on lunch tomorrow. The kids are sick." It was my best friend, Mary Lou. Mary Lou and I grew up together. We went to school together and we were married within months of each other. Mary Lou's marriage stuck and she had a pack of kids. My marriage lasted about twenty minutes and ended in a screaming divorce.

The third message was from Vinnie. "What are you doing at home listening to this dumb machine? Why aren't you out looking for Singh? I'm dying here, for crissake. Do something!"

And my mother again. "I didn't want anything the first time. You don't have to call me back."

I erased the messages and dropped a tiny piece of pizza into Rex's cage. Rex is my hamster roommate. He lives in a glass aquarium in my kitchen and sleeps in a Campbell's tomato soup can. Rex rushed out of his soup can, shoved the pizza into his cheek pouch, and scurried back to the can. Quality pet time.

I carted the pizza box, the beer, and my purse into the living room, flopped onto the couch, powered up the television, and found a *Seinfeld* rerun. A couple months ago I entered the computer age and bought myself an Apple iBook. I keep the iBook on my coffee table so I can check my mail and watch television at the same time. Am I a multitasker, or what?

I opened the iBook and signed on. I deleted the junk mail advertising Viagra, mortgage rates, and porn sites. A single message was left. It was from Andrew Cone. *If I can be of any further help, don't hesitate to call.*

The phone jarred me awake at 7:00 A.M.

"Something just came across my desk that I thought you might want to see," Morelli said. "I'm at the station and I have a few things to do and then I'll come over."

I dragged myself out of bed and into the bathroom. I did the shower thing and the hair thing and a half-assed job at the makeup thing. I got dressed in my usual uniform of T-shirt and jeans and felt ready to face the day. I made coffee and treated myself to a strawberry Pop-Tart, feeling righteous because I'd resisted the S'mores

Pop-Tart. Best to have fruit for breakfast, right? I gave a corner of the Pop-Tart to Rex and sipped my coffee.

I was pouring myself a second cup of coffee when Morelli arrived. He backed me against a wall, made certain there were no spaces between us, and he kissed me. His pager buzzed and he did some inventive cussing.

"Trouble?" I asked.

He looked at the display. "The usual crap." He stepped back and pulled a folded piece of paper out of his jacket pocket. "I knew there was some sort of mess associated with TriBro, so I ran a search for you. It turned up this newspaper article from two years ago."

I took the paper from Morelli and read the headline. "Bart Cone Charged in Paressi Slaying." The article went on to say that hikers had stumbled over the body of Lillian Paressi just hours after Paressi had been killed with a single shot to the head at close range. The murder had occurred in a wooded area just north of Washington's Crossing State Park. Cone had been spotted leaving the scene and police claimed to have physical evidence linking Cone to the murder.

"What happened?" I asked Morelli.

"He was released. The witness who reported Cone fleeing from the scene recanted part of his story. And the physical evidence tested out negative. Cone had been carrying a twenty-two when the police picked him up for questioning. Paressi had been shot with a twenty-two, but ballistics ruled out Cone's gun as the murder weapon. And there wasn't a DNA match-up. Paressi had been sexually assaulted after her death and the DNA didn't match to Cone.

"As I remember, the guys assigned to the case still thought Cone killed Paressi. They just couldn't get anything to stick on him. And the case has never been solved."

"Was there a motive?"

"No motive. They were never able to develop a connection between Paressi and Cone."

"Bart Cone isn't exactly Mr. Nice Guy, but it's hard to see him as a killer."

"Killers come in all sizes," Morelli said.

THREE

Morelli walked me to my car, gave me a dismissive kiss on the forehead, and told me to be careful. He was driving a Piece Of Shit cop car that was parked next to my Ford. It was a Crown Vic that probably had originally been dark blue, but had now faded to a color that defied description. Paint was scraped off the right rear, and part of the back bumper was ripped away. A Kojak light was rolling around on the floor in the back.

"Nice car," I said to Morelli.

"Yeah, I had a hard choice to make between this and the Ferrari." He angled into the Vic, cranked it over, and rolled out of the lot.

It was early morning, but already the day was heating up. I could hear the drone of traffic, not far off on Hamilton. The sky was murky above me and I felt the rasp of ozone in the back of my throat. As the day wore on cars, chemical plants, and backyard barbecues would make their contribution to the stew that cooked over Jersey. Fancy-pants wimps in L.A. rated their pollution and curtailed activity. In Jersey we just call it *air* and get on with life. If you're born in Jersey, you know how to rise to a challenge. Bring on the Mob. Bring on bad air. Bring on taxes and obesity, diabetes, heart

JANET EVANOVICH

disease, and macaroni at every meal. Nothing defeats us in Jersey.

First thing on my activities list was a drive around the Apusenja neighborhood, keeping my eyes peeled for Boo and Singh. Sometimes missing persons turned up surprisingly close to home. They moved in with neighbors, hid out in garages, and sometimes turned up dead in a Dumpster.

Neither Boo nor Singh showed up after fifteen minutes of searching, so I headed across town to Route 1 and TriBro.

I still didn't have a clear idea of TriBro's product. Parts for slot machines. What did that mean? Gears? Handles? Bells and whistles? Not that it mattered. What mattered was squeezing a lead out of someone.

Black Bart hadn't been impressed with my charm or cleavage. I didn't think I'd get a lot of help from him. Clyde was eager, but not real bright. Andrew seemed like my best shot. I took the turnoff to TriBro and called Andrew on my cell phone.

"Guess what?" I said. "I'm in the neighborhood. Can I take a couple more minutes of your time?"

"Absolutely."

Absolutely was a good answer. Very positive. No sign of annoyance. No lecherous side remark. Professional. Andrew was definitely the brother of choice.

I parked in the lot, entered the lobby, and was immediately directed to Andrew's office. More good luck. No Bart or Clyde to slow me down. I took a chair across from Andrew and thanked him for seeing me.

"TriBro has an interest in finding Singh," he said. "We signed for the visa bond. If Singh skips, TriBro pays the bill."

"Do you have other employees on work visas?"

"Not now, but we have in the past. And I have to tell you, Singh isn't the first to disappear."

I felt my eyebrows raise.

"It's nothing suspicious," Andrew said. "In fact, I find it understandable. If I was in a similar position I might disappear, too. These men come to work for three months and are seduced by the potential for success. Everything is within their reach . . . rental movies, burgers, designer jeans, a new car, microwave popcorn, and frozen waffles. I have some sympathy for their flight, but at the same time TriBro can't keep absorbing bond losses. If this sort of thing continues we'll have to stop using visa workers. And that would be a shame, because they make very good temporary employees."

"Singh must have had some friends on the job. I'd like to talk to them."

Andrew Cone sat through a couple beats of silence, his eyes holding mine, his thoughts private, his expression guarded. "Why don't we put you undercover?" he finally said. "I can give you Singh's job for a day. We haven't filled it yet."

"I'm not even sure what you make here."

"We make little things. Machine-tooled gears and locks. Singh's job primarily consisted of measuring minutia. Each part we supply must be perfect. The first day onboard you wouldn't be expected to know much." He reached for his phone and his mouth tipped into a small smile. "Let's see how good you are at bluffing."

Ten minutes later I was a genuine bogus TriBro employee, following after Andrew, learning about TriBro Tech. The gears and locks that composed the bulk of TriBro's product were made at workstations housed in a large warehouse-type facility adjoining the reception area and offices. The far end of the warehouse was divided off into a long room where the quality control work was done. Windows looked into the interior. In the entire facility there were no windows looking out. The quality control area consisted of a series of cubbies with built-in tables, shelves, and cabinets. The tables held an odd assortment of weights, measures, machine torture devices, and chemicals. A single worker occupied each of the tables. There were seven people in the quality control area. And there was one unoccupied table. Singh's table.

Andrew introduced me to the area supervisor, Ann Klimmer, and returned to his office. Ann took me table by table and introduced me to the rest of the team. The women were in their thirties and forties. There were two men. One of the men was Asian. Singh would have gravitated to the asian, I thought. But the women would warm to me faster.

After the introductions and an overview lecture on the operation, I was partnered with Jane Locarelli. Jane looked like she'd just rolled off an embalming table. She was late forties, rail thin, and drained of color. Even her hair was faded. She spoke in a monotone, never making eye contact, her words slightly slurred as if the effort of speech was too much to manage.

"I've worked here for thirty-one years," she said. "I started working for the senior Cones. Right out of high school."

No wonder she looked like a walking cadaver. Thirty-one years under fluorescent lights, measuring and torturing little metal doohickeys. Jeez.

Jane hitched herself up onto a stool and selected a small gear from a huge barrel of small gears. "We do two kinds of testing here. We do random testing of new product." She sent me an apologetic grimace. "I'm afraid that's a little tedious." She displayed the gear she held in her hand. "And we test parts which have failed and been returned. That sort of testing is much more interesting. Unfortunately, today we're testing new product."

Jane carefully measured each part of the gear and examined it under a microscope for flaws. When she was done, she reached into the barrel and selected another gear. I had to bite back a groan. Two gears down. Three thousand gears to go.

"I heard Singh didn't show up for work one day," I said, going for casual curious. "Was he unhappy with the job?"

"Not sure," Jane said, concentrating on the new gear. "He wasn't very talkative." After extensive measuring, she decided the gear was okay and went on to a third.

"Would you like to try one?" she asked.

"Sure."

She handed the gear over and showed me how to measure.

"Looks good to me," I said after doing the measuring thing.

"No," she said, "it's off on one side. See the little burr on the edge of the one cog?" Jane took the gear from me, filed the side, and measured again. "Maybe you should just watch a while longer," she said.

I watched Jane do four more gears and my eyes glazed over and some drool oozed from between my lips. I quietly slid from my stool and moved to the next cubicle.

Dolly Freedman was also testing new gears. Dolly would drink some coffee and measure. Then she'd drink more coffee and perform another test. She was as thin and as pale as Jane, but not as lifeless. She was cranked on coffee. "This is such a bullshit job," Dolly said to me. She looked around. "Anyone watching?" she asked. Then she took a handful of gears and dumped them into the perfect gear bucket. "They looked good to me," she said. Then she drank more coffee.

"I'm going to be doing Samuel Singh's job," I told her.

"Do you know what happened to him? I heard he just didn't show up for work one day."

"Yeah, that's what I heard, too. No one's said much about him. He was real quiet. Carried his computer around and spent all his breaks on the computer."

"Playing computer games?"

"No. He was always plugged into a phone line. Surfing. Doing email. Real secretive about it, too. If someone came over to him he'd close up the computer. Probably was on some porno site. He looked like the type."

"Slimy?"

"Male. I keep protection in my desk for those types." She opened her top desk drawer to show me her canister of pepper spray.

I continued to move around the room, saving Edgar, the Asian guy, for last. Several of the women thought Singh looked unhappy. Alice Louise thought he might be secretly gay. No one could fault his work habits. He arrived on time and he did his barrel. No one knew he was engaged. No one had any idea where he lived or what he did in his spare time, other than surf the Net. Everyone had seen the newspaper article and thought Vinnie looked like a weasel.

I called Ranger at noon.

"Yo," Ranger said.

"Just checking in."

"How are the folks at TriBro?"

"Not giving me a lot, but it's still early."

"Go get 'em, babe." And he disconnected.

I drifted over to Edgar's table midafternoon. Edgar was dropping acid on a small metal bar with threads at either end. One drop at a time. Drip, wait, and measure. Drip, wait, and measure. Drip, wait, and measure. There had to be a thousand bars waiting to be tortured.

Nothing was happening. This job made watching grass grow look exciting.

"We're testing a new alloy," Edgar said.

"This seems more interesting than the gear measuring."

"Only for the first two million bars. After that, it's pretty routine."

"Why do you keep this job?"

"Benefits."

"Health insurance?"

"Gambling. If the product fails, one of us goes to Vegas as a tech rep. And the products fail all the time."

"What's a tech rep?"

"A technical representative. You know, a repairman."

"Did Singh ever go to Vegas?"

"Once."

"And you?"

"On an average, once a month. Failure is usually stress related. And that's my area of expertise."

"Did Singh like Vegas?"

"Why are you so interested in Singh?" Edgar asked.

"I'm taking over his job."

"If you were taking over his job you'd be sitting at his desk doing measurements. Instead, you're floating around, talking to everyone. I think you're looking for Singh."

A point for Edgar. "Okay, suppose I am looking for Singh. Would you know where to find him?"

"No, but I'd know where to start looking. The day before he disappeared he was in the lunch room calling all the McDonald's places, asking if a guy named Howie worked there. It was pretty strange. He was all excited. And it was the first time I'd ever seen him make a call."

I looked through the window, into the manufacturing

area, and I caught Bart Cone's eye. He was examining a machine, standing with three other men. He glanced up and saw me talking to Edgar.

"That's not a happy face," Edgar said, his attention shifting to Bart.

"Does he ever have a happy face?"

"Yeah, I saw him smile once when he ran over a toad in the parking lot."

Bart made a *wait here* gesture to the men at the machine and marched across the work floor to the test area. He wrenched the door open and asked me to follow him out to the offices. I took my purse since it was the end of the day and there wasn't much chance I'd be returning.

Bart was once again dressed in black. His expression was menacing. I followed him into an office that smelled like metal shavings and was a cluttered mess of stacked catalogues and spare parts collected in tattered cardboard boxes. His desk was large, the top heaped with loose papers, disposable coffee cups, more spare parts, a multiline phone, and a workstation computer.

"What the hell were you doing in there?" Bart asked, looking like a guy who might have murdered Lillian Paressi. "I thought I made it clear that we had nothing to tell you about Singh."

"Your brother feels otherwise. He suggested I work undercover for a day."

Bart snatched at his phone and punched a key on speed dial. "What's the deal with Ms. Plum?" he asked. "I found her in the test area." His expression darkened at Andrew's answer. He gave a terse reply, returned the handset to the cradle, and glared at me. "I don't care what my brother told you, I'm going to give you good advice and God help you if you don't follow it. Stay out of my factory."

"Sure," I said. "Okeydokey." And I left. I might be a little slow sometimes, but I'm not *totally* stupid. I know a genuinely scary dude when I see one. And Bart was a genuinely scary dude.

My cell phone rang as I was pulling out of the lot.

"Stephanie? It's your mother."

As if I wouldn't recognize her voice.

"We're having a nice chicken for dinner tonight."

My unmarried sister was nine months pregnant, living with my parents, and had turned into the hormone queen. I'd have to endure Valerie's mood swings to get to the chicken dinner. Valerie's boyfriend, Albert Kloughn, would most likely be there, too. Kloughn was also Valerie's boss and the father of her unborn baby. Kloughn was a struggling lawyer, and he was practically living at the house, trying to get Valerie to marry him. Not to mention Valerie's two little girls by a previous marriage who were nice kids, but added to the bedlam potential.

"Mashed potatoes with gravy," my mother said, sensing my hesitation, sweetening the offer.

"Gee, I sort of have things to do," I said.

"Pineapple upside-down cake for dessert," my mother said, pulling out the big gun. "Extra whipped cream." And she knew she had me. I'd never in my life turned down pineapple upside-down cake.

I looked at my watch. "I'm about twenty minutes away. I'll be a couple minutes late. Start without me."

Everyone was at the table when I arrived.

My sister, Valerie, was pushed back about a foot and a half to accommodate her beach ball belly. A couple weeks ago she'd started using the belly like a shelf, balancing her plate on it, tucking her napkin into the neck of her shirt, catching spilled food on her huge swollen breasts. She'd gained seventy pounds with the baby and she was all big boobs and double chins and ham hock arms. Unheard of for Valerie, who previous to her divorce had been the perfect daughter, resembling the serene and slim Virgin Mary in every way, with the possible exception of virginity and hair style. The hair was Meg Ryan.

Albert Kloughn was at her side, his face round and pink, his scalp gleaming under his thinning sandy hair. He was watching Valerie with unabashed awe and affection. Kloughn wasn't a subtle guy. He hadn't any idea how to hide an emotion. Probably he wasn't great in a courtroom, but he was always fun at the dinner table. And he was surprisingly endearing in an oddball way.

Valerie's two girls from her first and only marriage, Angie and Mary Alice, were on the edges of their seats, hoping for a fun disaster . . . like Grandma Mazur setting the tablecloth on fire or Albert Kloughn spilling hot coffee into his lap.

Grandma Mazur was happily sipping her second glass of wine. My mom was at the head of the table, all business, daring anyone to find fault with the chicken. And my dad shoveled food into his mouth and acknowledged me with a grunt.

"I read in the paper where aliens from a different galaxy are buying up all the good real estate in Albany," Grandma said.

"They'll get hit hard with taxes," Kloughn told her. "They'd be better to buy real estate in Florida or Texas."

My father never raised his head, but his eyes slid first to Kloughn and then to my grandmother. He muttered something that was too low to carry. I suspected it was in the area of *good grief.*

My father is retired from the post office and now he drives a cab part-time. When my grandmother came to live with my parents, my mother stopped storing the rat poison in the garage. Not that my father would actually take to poisoning my grandmother, but why tempt fate? Better to store the rat poison at cousin Betty's house.

"If I was an alien I'd rather live in Florida anyway," Grandma said. "Florida has Disney World. What's Albany got?"

Valerie looked like she was ready to drop the baby on the dining room floor. "Get me a gun," Valerie said. "If I don't go into labor soon I'm going to shoot myself. And pass the gravy. Pass it *now*."

My mother jumped to her feet and handed the gravy boat to Valerie. "Sometimes the contractions are hardly noticeable in the beginning," my mother said. "Do you think you could be having hardly noticeable contractions?"

Valerie's attention was fully focused on the gravy. She poured gravy on everything . . . vegetables, applesauce, chicken, dressing, and a heap of rolls. "I love gravy," she said, spooning the overflow into her mouth, eating the gravy like soup. "I *dream* about gravy."

"It's a little high in saturated fats," Kloughn said.

Valerie glanced sideways at Kloughn. "You're not going to lecture me on my diet, are you?"

Kloughn sat up straight in his seat, his eyes wide and birdlike. "Me? No, honest, I wouldn't do anything like that. I like fat women. Just the other day I was thinking how fat women were soft. Nothing I like better than big, soft, squishy pillows of fat."

He was nodding his balding head, trying hard, running down dark roads of panic.

"Look at me. I'm nice and fat, too. I'm like the Doughboy. Go ahead, poke my stomach. I'm just like the Doughboy," Kloughn said.

"Omigod," my sister wailed. "You think I'm fat."

She went into open-mouthed sobbing and the plate slid from her stomach and crashed onto the floor.

Kloughn bent to retrieve the plate and farted. "That wasn't me," he said.

"Maybe it was me," Grandma said. "Sometimes they sneak out. Did I fart?" she asked everyone.

My eyes inadvertently went to the kitchen door.

"Don't even *think* about it," my mother said. "We're all in this together. Anyone sneaks out the back way, they answer to me."

When the table was cleared and the dishes were done, I made my move to leave.

"I need to talk to you," my mother said, following me out of the house to stand curbside, where we had privacy.

The bottom of the sun had sunk into the Krienski's asbestos shingle roof, a sure sign that the day was ending. Kids ran in packs, burning off the last of their energy. Parents and grandparents sat on small front porches. The air was dead still, heavy with the promise of a hot tomorrow. Inside my parents' house, my father and grandmother sat glued to the television. The muffled rise and fall of a sitcom laugh track escaped the house and joined the mix of street noise.

"I'm worried about your sister," my mother said. "What's to become of her? A baby due in two weeks and no husband. She should marry Albert. You have to talk to her."

"No way! One minute she's all smiley face and crying because she loves me so much and then next thing I know she's grumpy. I want the old Valerie back. The one with no personality. And besides, I'm not exactly an expert at marriage. Look at me . . . I can't even figure out my *own* life."

"I'm not asking a lot. I just want you to talk to her. Get her to understand that she's having a baby."

"Mom, she knows she's having a baby. She's as big as a Volkswagen. She's already done it twice before."

"Yes, but both times she did it in California. It's not the same. And she had a husband then. And a house."

Okay, now we're getting somewhere. "This is about the house, right?"

"I feel like the old lady who lived in a shoe. Remember the rhyme? She had so many children she didn't know what to do? One more person in this house and we're going to have to sleep in shifts. Your father's talking about renting a Porta Potti for the backyard. And it's not just the house. This is the Burg. Women don't go off and have babies without husbands here. Every time I go to the grocery, I meet someone who wants to know when Valerie is getting married."

I thought this was a good deal. It used to be that people wanted to know when *I* was getting married.

"She's in the kitchen eating the rest of the cake," my mother said. "She's probably got it topped with gravy. You could go in and talk to her. Tell her Albert Kloughn is a good man."

"Valerie doesn't want to hear this from me."

"What's it going to take?" my mother wanted to know. "German chocolate torte?"

The German chocolate torte took hours to make. My mother hated to make the German chocolate torte.

"German chocolate torte and a leg of lamb. That's my best offer," she said.

"Boy, you're really serious."

My mother grabbed me by the front of my shirt. "I'm desperate! I'm on the window ledge on the fortieth floor and I'm looking down."

I did an eye roll and a sigh and I trudged back into the house, into the kitchen. Sure enough, Valerie was at the small kitchen table, snarfing down cake.

"Mom wants me to talk to you," I said.

"Not now. I'm busy. I'm eating for two, you know."

Two elephants. "Mom thinks you should marry Kloughn."

Valerie forked off a huge piece and shoved it into her mouth. "Kloughn's boring. Would you marry Kloughn?"

"No, but then, I won't even marry Morelli."

"I want to marry Ranger. Ranger is hot."

I couldn't deny it. Ranger was hot. "I don't think Ranger's the marrying type," I said. "And there would be a lot of things to consider. For instance, I think once in a while he might kill people."

"Yeah, but not random, right?"

"Probably not random."

Valerie was scraping at the leftover smudges of whipped cream. "So that would be okay. Nobody's perfect."

"Okay, then," I said. "Good talk. I'll pass this on to Mom."

"It isn't as if I'm antimarriage," Valerie said, eyeing the grease and drippings left in the roasting pan.

I backed out of the kitchen and ran into my mom.

"Well?" she asked.

"Valerie's thinking about it. And the good news is . . . she's not antimarriage."

Streetlights were on when I cruised into my parking lot. A dog barked in a nearby neighborhood of single-family homes, and I thought of Boo. Mrs. Apusenja told Ranger and me that she'd tacked lost dog signs up at local businesses and at street corners. The signs had a photo of the dog and offered a small reward, but there'd been no takers.

Tomorrow I'd track down Howie. It was my Spidey Sense again. I had a feeling Howie was important. Singh had been trying to call him. It had to mean something, right?

I let myself into my apartment and said howdy to Rex. I checked my phone messages. Three in all.

The first was from Joe. "Hey, cupcake." That was it. That was the whole message.

The second was from Ranger. "Yo." Ranger made Joe look like a chatterbox.

The third was a hang-up.

I ambled into the living room, slouched onto the couch, and grabbed for the remote. A splash of color caught my eye from across the room. The color was coming from a vase of red roses and white carnations, sitting on an end table. The flowers hadn't been there this morning. A white envelope was propped against the vase.

My first thought was that someone had broken into my apartment. Ranger and Morelli did this on a regular basis, but they'd never left me flowers, and I was pretty certain they hadn't left them this time, either. I did a quick backtrack to the kitchen with my heart beating way too hard and too fast in my chest. I took my gun out of the brown bear cookie jar and started creeping through my apartment. There were only two rooms left unseen. Bedroom and bath. I looked into the bathroom. No creepy deranged killers lurking behind the shower curtain. None on the toilet. The bedroom was also monster free.

I shoved the gun under the waistband of my jeans and returned to the flowers. There was a message printed on the outside of the white envelope. *Tag. You're it.* I had no idea what this meant. I opened the envelope and removed three photos. It took a moment for the images to register. I clapped a hand to my mouth when I figured it out. They were pictures of a gunshot victim. A woman. Shot between the eyes. The photos were close-ups that were too tight in to reveal the woman's identity. One photo showed part of an eyebrow and an open sightless eye. The other two recorded the destruction to the back of her head, the exit point.

I dropped the photos, ran to the phone, and dialed Joe.

"Someone broke into my apartment," I said. "And they left me flowers and some ph-ph-photos. Should I call the police?"

"Honey, I am the police."

"So I'm covered. Okay, just checking."

"Do you want me to come over?"

"Yes. Drive fast."

FOUR

Morelli stood hands on hips, staring at the flowers on the table and the photos still spread out on the floor. "It's like you have a sign on your door welcoming nuts and stalkers to walk in. Everyone breaks into your apartment. I've never seen anything like it. You have three top-of-the-line locks on your door and it doesn't deter anyone." He glanced over at me. "Your door was locked, right?"

"Yes. It was locked." Yeesh. "Do you think this is serious?"

Morelli looked at me like I was speaking a foreign language. "Someone broke into your apartment and left you gunshot pictures. Don't *you* think it's serious?"

"I'm completely freaked out, but I was really hoping you'd tell me I was overreacting. I was going for the outside chance that you'd think this was someone's idea of a joke."

"I hate this," Morelli said. "Why can't I have a girlfriend who has normal problems . . . like breaking a fingernail or missing a period or falling in love with a lesbian?"

"Now what?" I asked.

"Now I call this in and get a couple guys out here

to collect evidence and maybe look for prints. Do you have any idea what this is about?"

"No idea at all. Not a clue. Nothing."

The phone rang and I went to the kitchen to answer it.

"I definitely think it might work between Ranger and me," Valerie said. "You're pals with him. You could fix me up."

"Valerie, you're nine months pregnant. This isn't a good time for a fix-up."

"You think I should wait until after I deliver?"

"I think you should wait until never."

Valerie did a big sigh and disconnected.

Ranger on a fix-up date. Can you see this?

"You're smiling," Morelli said.

"Valerie wants to get fixed up with Ranger."

Now Morelli was smiling. "I like it. Wear body armor when you tell Ranger." Morelli opened the refrigerator, took out a piece of leftover pizza, and ate it cold. "I think it would be smart to get you out of this apartment. I don't know what this is about, but I'm not comfortable ignoring it."

"And I would go where?"

"You'd go home with me, cupcake. And there'd be benefits."

"Such as?"

"I'd warm up your pizza."

Morelli lived in a two-story row house he inherited from his Aunt Rose. It was about a half mile from my parents' house with an almost identical floor plan. Rooms were stacked one behind the other . . . living room, dining room, kitchen. There were three bedrooms and a bath upstairs. Morelli had added a half bath downstairs. He was slowly claiming the house as his own. The wood floors were all newly sanded and varnished, but Aunt

Rose's filmy old-fashioned curtains remained. I liked the mix and in an odd way would be sorry to see the house turn over entirely to Joe. There was something comforting about the curtains enduring beyond Aunt Rose. A tombstone is okay, but curtains are so much more personal.

We stood on the small front porch and Morelli cautioned me as he unlocked his door. "Brace yourself," he said. "Bob hasn't seen you in a couple days. I don't want you knocked on your ass in front of the neighbors."

Bob was a big scruffy red-haired dog that Morelli and I shared. Technically I suppose it was Morelli's dog. Bob had originally come to live with me, but in the end had chosen Morelli. One of those guy things, I guess.

Morelli opened the door and Bob bounded out, catching me at chest level. What Bob lacked in manners he made up for in enthusiasm. I hugged him to me and gave him some big loud kisses. Bob endured this for a beat and then turned tail and hurled himself back inside, galloping from one end of the house to the other with ears flapping and tongue flopping.

A half hour later I was all settled in with my car parked at the curb behind Morelli's truck, my clothes in the guest room closet, and Rex's hamster cage sitting on Morelli's kitchen counter.

"I bet you're tired," Morelli said, flipping the lights off in the kitchen. "I bet you can't wait to get into bed."

I gave him a sideways look.

He slung an arm around my shoulders and steered me in the direction of the stairs. "I bet you're so tired you don't even want to bother getting into pajamas. In fact, you might need some help getting out of all these clothes."

"And you're volunteering for the job?"

He kissed me at the nape of my neck. "Am I a good guy, or what?"

I woke up in a tangle of sheets and nothing else. Sunlight was streaming through Morelli's bedroom window and I could hear the shower running in the bathroom. Bob was at the foot of the bed, watching me with big brown Bob eyes, probably trying to decide if I was food. Depending on Bob's mood, food could be most anything . . . a chair, dirt, shoes, a cardboard box, a box of prunes, a table leg, a leg of lamb. Some foods sat better with Bob than others. You didn't want to be too close after he ate a box of prunes.

I pulled on a pair of jeans and a T-shirt and trudged downstairs, hair uncombed, following the smell of coffee brewing. A note on the counter told me Bob had been fed and walked. Morelli was better at this cohabitation stuff than I was. Morelli was invigorated by sex. An orgasm for Morelli was like taking a vitamin pill. The more orgasms he had, the sharper he got. I'm the opposite. For me, an orgasm is like a shot of Valium. A night with Morelli and the next morning I'm a big contented cow.

I was coffee mug in hand, debating the merits of toast versus cereal, when Morelli's doorbell rang. I scuffed to the door with Bob close on my heels and I opened the door to Morelli's mother and grandmother.

The Morelli men are all charming and handsome. And with the exception of Joe, they're all worthless drunks and womanizers. They die in barroom fights, kill themselves in car crashes, and explode their livers. The Morelli women hold the family together, ruling with an iron hand, spotting a fib a mile away. Joe's mother was a revered and respected pillar of the community. Joe's Grandma Bella sent a chill down the spine and into the heart of all who crossed her path.

"Ah-hah!" Grandma Bella said. "I knew it. I knew they were living together in sin. I had a vision. It came to me last night."

Two doors down Mrs. Friolli stuck her head out her front door so she didn't miss anything. I was guessing Grandma Bella's vision came to her last night after Mrs. Friolli called her.

"How nice to see you," I said to the women. "What a nice surprise." I turned and shrieked up the stairs. *"Joe! Get down here!"*

It was always a shock to stand next to Mrs. Morelli and realize she was only five foot, four inches in her chunky two-inch-heeled shoes. She was a dominant and fearful force in a room. Her snapping black eyes could spot a speck of dust at twenty paces. She was a fierce guardian of her family and sat at the head of the table of the large Morelli tribe. She'd been widowed a lot of years and had never shown any interest in trying marriage a second time. Once around with a Morelli man was more than enough for most women.

Grandma Bella was half a head shorter than Joe's mom, but no less fearsome. She kept her white hair pulled into a bun, tied at the nape of her narrow chicken neck. She wore somber black dresses and sensible shoes. And some people believed she had the ability to cast a spell. Grown men scurried for cover when she turned her pale old woman's eye on them or pointed her boney finger in their direction.

"This is a temporary arrangement," I told Mrs. Morelli and Bella. "I had to leave my apartment for a couple days and Joe was nice enough to let me stay here."

"Hah!" Bella said, "I know your type. You take advantage of my grandson's good nature and the next thing you know, you've seduced him and you're pregnant. I know these things. I see them in my visions."

Jeez. I hoped these visions weren't too graphic. I

didn't like the idea of being naked and woman-on-top in Bella's home movies.

"It's not like that," I said. "I'm not going to get pregnant."

I felt Joe move in behind me.

"What's up?" Joe asked his mother and grandmother.

"I had a vision," Bella said. "I knew she was here."

"Lucky me," Joe said. And he ruffled my hair.

"I see babies," Bella said. "Mark my words, this one is pregnant."

"That would be nice," Joe said, "but I don't think so. You're getting your visions confused. Stephanie's sister is pregnant. Right kitchen, wrong pot."

My breath stuck in my chest. Did he say it would be nice if I was pregnant?

When Joe left for work I ran a computer check on McDonald's franchises in the area. I started dialing the numbers that turned up, asking for Howie, and I got a hit on the third McDonald's. Yes, I was told, a guy named Howie worked there. He would be in at ten.

It was early so I packed off in my happy yellow car and I checked in at the office before cutting across town to look for Howie.

"Anything happening?" I asked Connie.

"Vinnie's at the pokey, writing bail. Lula hasn't come in yet."

"Yes she has," Lula said, bustling through the door, big tote bag on her shoulder, take-out coffee in one hand, brown grocery bag in the other. "I had to stop at the store on account of I need special food. There's a new man in my life and I've decided I'm too much woman for him, so I'm losing some weight. I'm gonna turn myself into a supermodel. I'm gonna lose about a hundred pounds.

"It'll be easy because I joined FatBusters last night.

I got everything I need to lose weight now. I got a notebook to write in every time I eat something. And I got a FatBusters book that tells me how to do it all. Every single food's got a number assigned to it. All you gotta do is add up those numbers and make sure you don't go over your limit. Like my limit is twenty-nine."

Lula set the bag on the floor, plopped herself down on the couch, and took out a small notepad. "Okay, here I go," she said. "This here's my first entry in my notebook. This here's the beginning of a new way of life."

Connie and I exchanged glances.

"Oh boy," Connie said.

"I know I've tried diets in the past and they haven't worked out, but this is different," Lula said. "This one's realistic. That's what they say in the pamphlet. It's not like that last diet where all I could eat was bananas." She paged through her FatBusters book. "Let's see how I'm doing. No points for coffee."

"Wait a minute," I said. "You never get plain coffee. I bet that's a caramel mochaccino you're drinking. I bet that's at least four points."

Lula narrowed her eyes at me. "It says here coffee's got no points and that's what I'm writing. I'm not getting involved with all that detail bullshit."

"You have anything else for breakfast?" Connie asked.

"I had a egg. Let's see what an egg's gonna cost me. Two points."

I looked over her shoulder at the book. "Did you cook that egg yourself? Or did you get it on one of those fast-food breakfast sandwiches with sausage and cheese?"

"It was on a sausage and cheese sandwich. But I didn't eat it all."

"How much didn't you eat?"

Lula flapped her arms. "Okay, I ate it all."

"That's got to be at least ten points."

"Hunh," Lula said. "Well, I still got a lot of points left for the rest of the day. I got nineteen points left."

"What's in the grocery bag?"

"Vegetables. You don't get any points for vegetables, so you can eat as much as you want."

"I didn't know you were a big vegetable eater," Connie said.

"I like beans when you put them in a pan with some bacon. And I like broccoli . . . except it's got to have cheese sauce on it."

"Bacon and cheese sauce might up your points," Connie said.

"Yeah, I'm gonna have to wean myself off the bacon and cheese sauce if I want to get to supermodel weight."

"I'm heading out to look for a guy named Howie. Supposedly he and Singh were buddies," I said to Connie. "Anything new come in that I should know about?"

"We got a new skip this morning, but Vinnie doesn't want anyone working on anything other than Singh. Vinnie's in a state over this Singh thing."

"Maybe I should go look for Howie with you," Lula said. "If I stay here I'll file all day and filing makes me hungry. I don't know if I got enough vegetables for a full day of filing."

"Bad idea. Howie works at a fast-food place. You have no willpower when it comes to that stuff."

"No problemo. I'm a changed woman. And anyway, I got my fill of fast food for the day. I had a good fast-food breakfast."

A half hour later, Lula and I parked in the McDonald's lot. Lula had gone through a bunch of celery and was half-way into a bag of carrots.

"This isn't doing much for me," she said, "but I guess you gotta sacrifice if you want to be a supermodel."

"Maybe you should wait in the car."

"Hell no, I'm not missing out on the questioning. This could be an important lead. This Howie guy and Singh are supposed to be friends, right?"

"I don't know if they're friends. I just know Singh tried to find Howie the day before he disappeared."

"Let's do it."

As soon as I was through the door to the restaurant I spotted Howie. He was working a register and he looked to be in his early twenties. He was dark-skinned and slim. Pakistani, maybe. I knew he was Howie because he was wearing a name tag. Howie P.

"Yes?" he asked, smiling. "What will it be?"

I slid a card across to him and introduced myself. "I'm looking for Samuel Singh," I said. "I understand you're friends."

He went immobile for a moment while he held my card. He appeared to be studying it, but I had a suspicion his mind wasn't keeping up with his eyes.

"You are mistaken. I do not know Samuel Singh," he finally said, "but what would you like to order?"

"Actually, I'd just like to talk to you. Perhaps on your next break?"

"That would be my lunchtime at one o'clock. But you must order now. It is a rule."

There was a big guy standing behind me. He was wearing a sleeveless T-shirt, scruffy cutoffs, and mud-clogged grungy boots.

"Cripes, lady," he said. "You think we got all day? Give him your order. I gotta get back to work."

Lula turned and looked at him and he moved to another register. "Hunh," Lula said.

"I *must* take your order," Howie said.

"Fine. Great. I'll have a cheeseburger, a large fries, a Coke, and an apple pie."

"Maybe some chicken nuggets," Lula said.

"No nuggets," I told Howie. "What about Samuel Singh?"

"First, you must pay me for your food."

I shoved a twenty at him. "Do you know where Singh is?"

"I do not. I am telling you I do not know him. Would you like extra ketchup packets with this cheeseburger? I have extra ketchup packets to give at my discretion."

"Yeah, extra ketchup would be great."

"If it was me, I would have gotten some chicken nuggets," Lula said. "Always good to have nuggets."

"You're not eating this, remember?"

"Well, maybe I could have had a nugget."

I took my bag of food. "You have my card. Call me if you think of anything," I said to Howie. "I'll try to stop back at one."

Howie nodded and smiled. "Yes. Thank you. Have a good day. Thank you for eating at McDonald's."

"He was nice and polite," Lula said when we got back to the car, "but he didn't give us a lot." She looked at the bag of food. "Boy, that smells good. I can smell the fries. Wonder how many points it would cost me to eat a French fry?"

"No one can eat just one French fry."

"I bet supermodels eat just one French fry."

I didn't like the way Lula was looking at the bag. Her eyes were too wide and sort of bugged out of her head. "I'm going to throw this food away," I said. "I got it so I could talk to Howie. We don't really need this food."

"It's a sin to throw food away," Lula said. "There's children starving in Africa. They'd be happy to get this food. God's gonna come get you if you throw that food away."

"First off, we're not in Africa, so I can't give this food to any of those starving kids. Second, neither of us needs this food. So God's just going to have to understand."

"I think you might be blaspheming God."

"I'm *not* blaspheming God." But just in case, I did a mental genuflect and asked for forgiveness. Guilt and fear remain long after blind belief.

"Give me that food bag," Lula said. "I'm going to save your immortal soul."

"No! Remember the supermodel. Have some carrots."

"I hate those fucking carrots. Give me that bag!"

"Stop it," I said. "You're getting scary."

"I need that burger. I'm outta control."

No shit. I was afraid if I didn't get rid of the bag Lula would squash me like a bug. I eyed the distance between me and the trash receptacle and I was pretty sure I could outsprint Lula, so I took off at a run.

"Hey!" she yelled. "You come back here." And then she pounded after me.

I reached the trash and shoved the bag in. Lula knocked me out of the way, took the top off the trash receptacle, and retrieved the bag of food.

"This here's good as new," she said, testing a couple French fries. She closed her eyes. "Oh man, they just made these fresh. And they got a lot of salt. I love it when they got a lot of salt."

I took a couple fries from the box. She was right. They were great fries. We finished the fries, Lula broke the cheeseburger in half, and we ate the cheeseburger. Then we each ate half of the apple pie.

"Would have been nice to have some nuggets," Lula said.

"You're a nut."

"It's not my fault. That was a bogus diet. I can't go around eating plain-ass vegetables all day. I'll get weak and die."

"Wouldn't want that to happen."

"Hell no," Lula said.

We went back to the car and I called Ranger. "Having any luck?" I asked him.

"I found someone who saw Singh with the dog the day after it disappeared. It looks like Singh ran as opposed to getting himself whacked. And you were right, he took the dog with him."

"Any idea why he might want to disappear?"

"The future mother-in-law would do it for me."

"Anything else?"

"No. Have you got something?"

"I have a guy who says he doesn't know Singh, but I don't believe him." And I have horrific photos of a dead woman. Best to wait until I'm alone with Ranger to tell him about the horrific photos. Lula isn't always great at keeping a secret and Morelli asked me not to share the details.

"Later," Ranger said.

I called Connie next. "I need an address for a guy named Howie P. He works at the McDonald's on Lincoln Avenue. See if you can get his address out of the manager."

Five minutes later Connie got back to me with the address.

"This is the deal," I said to Lula. "We're going to check out Howie's apartment. We are *not* going to break in. You accidentally smash a window or bust down a door, and I swear I'll never take you on a case with me again."

"Hunh," Lula said. "When did I ever bust down a door?"

"Two days ago. And it was the *wrong* door."

"I didn't bust that door. I just tapped it open."

Howie lived in a hard times neighborhood a short distance from his job. He rented two rooms in a house that was originally designed to contain one family and now was home to seven. Paint peeled off the clapboard siding, and window ledges rotted in the sun. The small yard was hard-packed dirt, the perimeter marked by chain-link fencing. A fringe of weed clung to life at the base of the fence.

Lúla and I stood in the dark, musty foyer and ran through the names on the mailboxes. Howie was 3B. Sonji Kluchari was 3A.

"Hey, I know her," Lula said. "Back when I was a ho. She worked the corner across from me. If she's living in three A you can bet there's eight other people in there with her. She's a scabby ol' crackhead, doing whatever she has to so she can get her next fix."

"How old is she?"

"She's my age," Lula said. "And I'm not saying how old I am, but it's twenty-something."

We climbed the stairs to the second-floor landing, which was illuminated by a bare twenty-watt bulb hanging from a ceiling cord, and then we went to the third floor, which clearly had been the attic. The third-floor landing was small and dark and smelled like rot. There were two doors. Someone had scrawled 3A and 3B on the doors with black magic marker.

We knocked on 3B. No answer. I tried the door. Locked.

"Hunh," Lula said. "Looks flimsy. Too bad you got all these rules about breaking things. I bet I could lean on this door and it'd fall down."

That was a good possibility. Lula wasn't a small woman.

I turned and knocked on 3A. I knocked louder the second time and the door opened and Sonji peered out at us. She was bloodless white with red-rimmed eyes and yellow straw hair. She was rail thin and I would have put her age closer to fifty than twenty. Not easy being a crackhead ho.

Sonji stared at Lula, recognition struggling through the dope haze.

"Girl," Lula said. "You look like shit."

"Oh yeah," Sonji said, flat-voiced, dull-eyed. "Now I remember. Lula. How you doin', you big ugly ho?"

"I'm not a ho anymore," Lula said. "I'm working for a bail bondsman and we're looking for a scrawny little Indian guy. His name's Samuel Singh and he might know Howie."

"Howie?"

"The guy across the hall from you."

I showed Sonji a photo of Singh.

"I don't know," she said. "These guys all look the same to me."

"Anybody living over there besides Howie?" I asked her.

"Not that I know. From what I can tell, Howie's not exactly Mr. Social. Maybe Singh came over once . . . or somebody who looked like him. Don't think anybody but Howie's living there. But hell, what do I know?"

I gave Sonji my card and a twenty. "Give me a call if you see Singh."

Sonji disappeared behind her closed door and Lula and I trudged down the stairs. We went outside, walked around the building to the backyard, and looked up at Howie's single window.

"Could be me living here," Lula said. "I still got some pain from what that maniac Ramirez did to me, but turned out it was a favor. He stopped me from being a ho. When I got out of the hospital I knew I had to change my life. God works in strange ways."

Benito Ramirez was an insane boxer who loved inflicting pain. He'd beaten Lula to within an inch of her life and tied her to my fire escape. I found her, bloody and battered. Ramirez wanted the beating to serve as a lesson for Lula and for me.

I thought getting brutalized like that was a pretty harsh wake-up call.

"So what do you think?" Lula asked. "You think Singh could be hiding out up there?"

It was possible. But it was a long shot. There were a million reasons why Singh could have been looking for Howie. And for that matter, I wasn't even sure I had the right guy. There were a lot of McDonald's around. Singh could have been calling McDonald's in Hong Kong for all I knew.

I'd been keeping watch for the gray Sentra, but it hadn't surfaced. It could be in a nearby garage. Or it could be in Mexico. A rusted fire escape precariously clung to the back of the building. The ladder had been dropped and hung just a few inches from the ground. "I could go up the fire escape," I said. "Then I could look in the window."

"Now *you're* the nut. That thing's falling apart. No way I'm going up that rusted-out piece of junk."

I grabbed a rail and pulled. The rail held tight. "It's in better shape than it looks," I said. "It'll hold me."

"Maybe. But it sure as hell won't hold *me*."

Only one of us needed to go anyway. I'd be up and down in a couple minutes. And I'd be able to see if there was any indication of Singh or the dog. "You need to stay on the ground and do lookout anyway," I told Lula.

FIVE

Nothing ventured, nothing gained. I went hand over hand up the ladder and pulled myself onto the first level. I climbed the second ladder, steadied myself on the third-floor platform, and looked into Howie's window. Howie lived directly under the roof. There were rafters where the ceiling should be and the floor was chipped linoleum. Howie had a sofa that was lumpy and faded, but looked comfy in a dilapidated sort of way. He had a small television and a card table and two metal folding chairs. That was the extent of his furniture. A sink hung on a far wall. A half refrigerator had been placed beside the sink. There were two wood shelves over the refrigerator. Howie had stacked two plates, two bowls, and two mugs on one of the shelves. The other shelf held condiments, a couple boxes of cereal, a jar of peanut butter, and a bag of chips.

When you come right down to it, this is really all anyone needs, isn't it? A television and a bag of chips.

I could see the front door and a doorway leading to another room, but the second room wasn't visible. The bedroom, obviously. I tried the window, but it was either locked or painted shut.

"Coming down," I said to Lula. "No dog biscuits on the kitchen shelf." I put my foot on the ladder and it disintegrated in a shower of rust flakes and chunks of broken metal. The chunks of metal crashed onto the second-floor platform and the whole thing pulled away from the building, and with more of a sigh than a screech the entire bottom half of the fire escape landed on the ground in front of Lula.

"Hunh," Lula said.

I looked down at Lula. Too far to jump. The only way off the platform was through Howie's apartment.

"Are you coming down soon?" Lula asked. "I'm getting hungry."

"I don't want to break his window."

"You got any other choices?"

I dialed Ranger on my cell phone.

"I'm sort of stuck," I told Ranger.

Ten minutes later, Ranger opened Howie's apartment door, crossed the room, unlocked and raised the window, and looked out at the mangled mess of metal on the ground. He raised his eyes to mine and the almost smile twitched at the corners of his mouth. "Good job, Destructo."

"It wasn't my fault."

He dragged me through the window, into the apartment. "It never is."

"I wanted to see if there were any signs that Singh or the dog had been here. I don't have much to tie Howie to Singh, but once I get past Howie I have *nothing*."

Ranger closed and locked the window. "I don't see any boxes of dog biscuits."

"Poor little Boo." The instant I said it I knew it was a mistake. I clapped my hand over my mouth and looked at Ranger.

"I could help you with these maternal urges," Ranger said.

"Get me pregnant?"

"I was going to suggest a visit to the animal shelter."

He grabbed me by the front of my shirt and pulled me close. "But I could get you pregnant if that's what you really want."

"Nice of you to want to help," I said, "but I think I'll pass on both offers."

"Good decision." He released my shirt. "Let's take a look at the rest of the apartment."

We moved from the living room to the bedroom and found more clutter, but no evidence of Singh or Boo. Howie had placed a double mattress on the floor and covered it with an inexpensive quilt. There were two cardboard boxes filled with neatly folded pants and shirts and underwear. The poor man's dresser. No closet in the room. A bare bulb hung from the ceiling. It was the only light source. A laptop computer with a cracked screen was on the floor near the only outlet.

I looked around. "No bathroom."

"There's a common bathroom on the second floor."

Yikes. Howie shares a bathroom with the scabby ho and her crackhead friends. I tried to remember if he used gloves when he handled my food.

"Spartan," I said to Ranger.

"Adequate," Ranger said. He looked down at the mattress. "I don't think Howie's been sharing his apartment with anyone lately."

I was feeling a little panicky about being alone in a room with a mattress and Ranger, so I scooted out of the room and out of Howie's apartment. Ranger followed and closed and locked Howie's door. We descended the stairs in silence.

Ranger was smiling when we got to the front foyer. Not the half smile, either. This was a full-on smile.

I narrowed my eyes at the smile. "What?"

"It's always fun to see you get worried about a mattress."

Lula hustled over. "So what's going on?" she asked.

"You find anything up there? Any dog hairs in the bedroom?"

"Nothing. It was clean," I told her.

Lula turned her attention to Ranger. "I didn't hear you breaking any doors down."

"It wasn't necessary to break the door down."

"How'd you do it then? You use a pick? You use some electronic gizmo? I wish I could open doors like you."

"I'd tell you, but then I'd have to kill you," Ranger said.

It was an old line, but it was worrisome when Ranger said it.

"Hunh," Lula said.

"Tell me about Boo and Singh," I said to Ranger. "Who saw them. Where were they?"

"A kid working the drive-through window at Cluck in a Bucket saw him. He remembered Singh and the dog because the dog was barking and jumping around. He said Singh got a bucket of chicken and two strawberry shakes and the dog ate two pieces of chicken before Singh got the window rolled up to drive off."

"Guess he was hungry."

"Speaking of hungry," Lula said. "We haven't had lunch yet."

"We just had a cheeseburger," I told her.

"We shared it. That don't count. If you share, it's a snack."

"I want to go back to talk to Howie at one o'clock. Can you wait until then?"

"I guess. What are we going to do in the meantime?"

"I want to wander around the neighborhood. Maybe snoop in a few garages."

Lula looked up and down the street. "You're going to snoop in *this* neighborhood? You got a gun on you?"

Ranger reached behind him, under his shirt, and pulled out a .38. He pulled my T-shirt out of my jeans and he shoved the .38 under my waistband and draped my shirt over the gun. The gun was warm with his body heat, and his fingers had been even warmer sliding across my belly.

"Thanks," I said, trying to keep my voice from cracking.

He curled his hand around my neck and kissed me lightly on the lips. "Be careful." And he was gone. Off to make the world a better place in his shiny new black Porsche.

"He had his hand in your pants and he kissed you," Lula said. "I'm wetting myself."

"It wasn't like that. He gave me a gun."

"Girl, he gave you more than a gun. I tell you, he ever put his hand in *my* pants I'll stop breathing and faint dead away. He is so hot." Lula did some fanning motions with her hand. "I'm getting flashes. I think I'm sweating. Look at me. Am I sweating?"

"It's ninety degrees out," I said. "Everyone's sweating."

"It's not ninety," Lula said. "I just saw the temperature on the bank building. It's only seventy-eight."

"Feels like ninety."

"Ain't that the truth," Lula said.

An alley ran behind the houses. Cars were parked in the alley and garages opened to the alley. Lula and I walked to the end of the block and then cut down the alley, peering into filthy garage windows, cracking garage doors to look inside. Most of the garages were used for storage. A few were empty. None contained a gray Nissan. We walked three more blocks and three more alleys. No dog. No car. No Singh.

It was 1:15 when I parked in the McDonald's lot. Lula went inside to order and I walked to the outdoor seating area where Howie was eating lunch.

Howie was hunched over his tray, concentrating on his burger, attempting invisibility.

"Hey," I said, sitting across from him. "Nice day."

He nodded his head without making eye contact. "Yes."

"Tell me about Samuel."

"There is nothing to tell you," he said.

"He called you at work last week."

"You are mistaken." He had his fists balled and his head down. He gestured for emphasis and knocked his empty soda cup over. We both reached for the cup. Howie caught it first and set it straight. "You must stop bothering me now," he said. "Please."

"Samuel is missing," I said to Howie. "I'm trying to find him."

For the first time, Howie picked his head up and looked at me. "Missing?"

"He disappeared the day after he called you."

For a fleeting moment Howie looked relieved. "I know nothing," he repeated, dropping his eyes again.

"What's the deal?" I asked Howie. "Did you owe him money? Did you go out with his girlfriend?"

"No. None of those things. I truly do not know him." Howie's eyes darted from one side of the lot to the other. "I must go inside now. I do not like associating with the customers. Americans are a crazy people. Only the games are good. The American games are righteous."

I looked around. I didn't see any crazy people . . . but then, I'm from Jersey. I'm used to crazy.

"Why do you think Americans are crazy?"

"They are very demanding. Not enough fries in the box. The fries are not hot enough. The sandwich is wrapped wrong. I cannot control these things. I do not wrap the sandwiches. And they are very loud when they tell you about the wrappings. All day people are shouting at me. 'Go faster. Go faster. Give me this. Give me that.' Wanting an Egg McMuffin at eleven o'clock when it is a rule you cannot have an Egg McMuffin past ten-thirty."

"I hate that rule."

Howie gathered his wrappers onto his tray. "And another thing. Americans ask too many questions. How many grams of fat are in a cheeseburger? Are the onions real? What do I know? The onions come in a bag. Do I look like the onion man to you?"

He stood at his seat and took his tray in two hands. "You should leave me alone now. I am done talking to you. If you continue to stalk me, I will report you to the authorities."

"I'm not stalking you. This isn't stalking. This is asking a couple questions."

There was a momentary lull in the ambient traffic noise. I heard something go *pop pop*. Howie's eyes got wide, his mouth opened, the tray slid from his hands and crashed to the concrete patio. Howie's knees buckled and he collapsed without uttering a word.

A woman screamed behind me and I was on my feet, thinking, He's been shot, help him, take cover, do something! My mind was racing, but my body wasn't responding. I was paralyzed by the unfathomable horror of the moment, staring down at Howie's unblinking eyes, mesmerized by the small hole in the middle of his forehead, by the pool of blood that widened under him. Just a moment ago I was talking to him and now he was dead. It didn't seem possible.

People were scrambling and shouting around me. I didn't see anyone with a gun. No one in the lot had a gun in his hand. I didn't see anyone armed on the road or in the building. Howie seemed to be the only victim.

Lula ran to me with a big bag of food in one hand and a large chocolate shake in her other hand. "Holy

crap," she said, eyes bugged out, looking down at Howie.
"Holy moly. Holy Jesus and Joseph. Holy cow."

I eased away from the body, not wanting to crowd
Howie, needing some distance from the shooting. I
wanted to make time stand still, to back up ten minutes
and change the course of events. I wanted to blink and
have Howie still be alive.

Sirens screamed on the highway behind us and Lula
furiously sucked on the shake. "I can't get anything up
this freakin' straw," she shrieked. "Why do they give
you a straw if you can't suck anything up it? Why don't
they give you a goddamn spoon? Why do they make
these things so freakin' thick anyways? Shakes aren't
supposed to be solid. This here's like trying to suck up
a fish sandwich.

"And don't think I'm hysterical, either," Lula said. "I
don't get hysterical. You ever see me hysterical before?
This here's *transference*. I read about it in a magazine.
It's when you get upset about one thing only you're
really upset about something else. And it's different
from hysterical. And even if I was hysterical, which
I'm not, I'd have a perfect right. This guy got shot dead
in front of you. If you'd have moved an inch to the left
you probably would have lost an ear. And he's dead.
Look at him. He's dead! I *hate* dead."

I grimaced at Lula. "Good thing you're not hysterical."

"You bet your sweet ass," Lula said.

A Trenton PD blue and white angled to a stop, lights
flashing. Seconds later, another blue and white pulled
in. Carl Costanza was riding shotgun in the second car.
He rolled his eyes when he saw me and reached for
the radio. Calling Joe, I thought. His partner, Big Dog,
ambled over.

"Holy crap," Big Dog said when he saw Howie. "Holy

moly." He looked over at me and winced. "Did you shoot him?"

"No!"

"I got to get out of here," Lula said. "Cops and dead people give me diarrhea. Anybody wants to talk to me, they can send me a letter. I didn't see anything anyway. I was getting extra sauce for my chicken nuggets. I don't suppose you'd want to give me your car keys?" she asked me. "I'm starting to feel transference coming on again. I need a doughnut. Calm me down."

Costanza was pushing people around, laying out crime scene tape. An EMS truck arrived, followed by a plainclothes cop car and Morelli's POS.

Morelli jogged over to me. "Are you okay?"

"Pretty much. I'm a little rattled."

"No bullet holes?"

"Not in me. Howie wasn't so lucky."

Morelli looked down at Howie. "You didn't shoot him, did you? Tell me you didn't shoot him."

"I didn't shoot him. I never even carry a gun!"

Morelli dropped his eyes to my waist. "Looks to me like you're carrying one now."

Shit. I'd forgotten about the gun.

"Well, I *almost never* carry a gun," I said, doing my best to smooth out the bulge in my T-shirt. I looked around to see if anyone else noticed. "Maybe I should lose the gun," I said to Morelli. "There might be a problem."

"Besides carrying concealed without a permit?"

"It might not be registered."

"Let me guess. Ranger gave you the gun." Morelli stared down at his feet and shook his head. He muttered something indiscernible, possibly in Italian. I opened my mouth to speak and he held a hand up. "Don't say anything," he said. "I'm working hard here. Notice I'm not ranting over the fact that not only are you partners with Ranger, but you were stupid enough to take a gun from him."

I waited patiently. When Morelli mutters in Italian it's a good idea to give him some room.

"Okay," he said, "this is what we're going to do. We're going to walk over to my car. You're going to get in, take the gun out of your goddamn pants, and slide the gun under the front seat. Then you're going to tell me what happened."

An hour later, I was still sitting in the car, waiting for Morelli to leave the scene, when my cell phone rang.

It was my mother. "I heard you shot someone," she said. "You've got to stop shooting people. Elaine Minardi's daughter never shoots anyone. Lucille Rice's daughter never shoots anyone. Why do I have to be the one to have a daughter who shoots people?"

"I didn't shoot anyone."

"Then you can come to dinner."

"Sure."

"That was too easy," my mother said. "Something's wrong. Omigod, you really did shoot someone, didn't you?"

"I didn't shoot anyone," I yelled at her. And I disconnected.

Morelli opened the driver's side door and angled himself behind the wheel. "Your mother?"

I sagged in the seat. "This is turning into a really long day. I told my mother I'd show up for dinner."

"Let's go over this one more time," Morelli said.

"One of Singh's co-workers told me Singh tried to make a phone call to Howie the day before he disappeared. I questioned Howie just now and he denied knowing Singh. I'm pretty sure he was lying. And when I told him Singh was missing I could swear he looked relieved. He ended the interview by telling me Americans are crazy. He stood to go inside and *pop pop* . . . he was dead."

"Only two shots."

"That's all I heard."

"Anything else?"

"Off the record?"

"Oh boy," Joe said. "I hate when a conversation with you starts like that."

"I happened to accidentally wander into Howie's apartment this morning."

"I don't want to hear this," Morelli said. "They're going to go to Howie's apartment and dust for prints and you're going to be all over the place."

I chewed on my lower lip. Unfortunate timing. Who knew Howie would get killed?

Morelli raised eyebrows in question. "So?"

"The apartment is clean," I told him. "No sign that Singh's been there. No diary detailing secret activities. No hastily scribbled notes that someone wanted him dead. No evidence of drugs. No weapons."

"It could have been a random shooting," Morelli said. "This isn't a great neighborhood."

"He was in the wrong place at the wrong time."

"Yeah."

Not for a single second did either of us believe that to be true. Deep inside I knew Howie's death was tied to Singh and to me. That he was killed in my presence wasn't a good thing.

Morelli's eyes softened and he ran a fingertip along my jaw line. "Are you sure you're okay?"

"Yeah. I'm okay." And I was . . . sort of. My hands had stopped shaking and the pain in my chest was subsiding. But I knew that somewhere hiding in my head were sad thoughts of Howie. The sadness would creep forward and I would cram it back into crevices thick with brain gunk. I'm a firm believer in the value of denial. Anger, passion, and fear spill out of me in real time. Sadness I save until the edge dulls. Someday three months from now I'll stroll down the cereal aisle of a supermarket and burst into tears for Howie, a man I didn't even know, for crissake. I'll stand in front of the cereal boxes and blow my nose and blink the tears out of my eyes so no one realizes I'm an emotional idiot. I mean, what about Howie's life? What was it like? Then I'll think about Howie's death and I'll go hollow inside. And then I'll go to the freezer section and get a tub of coffee-flavored Häagen-Dazs ice cream and eat it all.

Morelli turned the engine over and chugged out of the lot. "I'll take you back to the office so you can get your car. I have paperwork to do at the station. If I'm not home by five-thirty, go to dinner without me. I'll catch up with you as soon as I can."

Lula and Connie weren't looking happy when I got to the office.

"We only have a couple days left before everyone finds out Singh's skipped," Connie said. "Vinnie's freaking. He's locked in his office with a bottle of gin and the real estate section from the Scottsdale paper."

"I don't need this cranky shit he's pulling, either," Lula said. "I had a bad day. I didn't lose any weight and the guy we wanted to talk to got dead. And every time I think about poor ol' Howie I get hungry on account of I'm a comfort eater. I relieve my stress with comfort food."

"You've eaten everything but the desk," Connie said. "It'd be cheaper to get you addicted to drugs."

Vinnie stuck his head out his office door. "You get one crappy lead and he gets himself killed," Vinnie yelled at me. "What's with that?" And he pulled his head back into his office and slammed the door shut.

"See, that's what I mean," Lula said. "Makes me want some macaroni and cheese."

Vinnie stuck his head out of his office again. "Sorry," he said. "I didn't mean to say that. I meant to say . . . uh, I'm glad you're not hurt."

We all went silent, thinking about how awful it actually had been. And how it could have been worse.

"The world's a crazy place," Lula finally said.

I needed to get out and do something to take my mind off Howie. My car keys were lying on Connie's desk. I pocketed the keys and gave my shoulder bag a hitch up. "I'm heading out to talk to the Apusenjas. Nonnie should be getting home from work soon."

"I'll go with you," Lula said. "I'm not letting you go out alone."

Nonnie was home when I arrived. She answered the door on my second knock and peered out at me, first surprised, then cautiously happy. "Did you find him?" she asked. "Did you find Boo?"

"I haven't found him, but I have something I'd like to run by you. Did Samuel ever mention a man named Howie?"

"No. I've never heard him speak of Howie."

"Samuel was on the computer all the time. Did you ever get a chance to see what he was doing? Did he get mail? Do you think he might have gotten email from Howie?"

"I saw a mail from work one time. Samuel was at the kitchen table. He sometimes preferred to sit there because his room was small. I came to the kitchen for a glass of tea and I passed behind him. He was typing a letter to someone named Susan. The letter was nothing, really. It only said *thank you for the help*. Samuel said it was work related. That is the only time I have seen any of his computer mails."

"Did he ever get mail from the post office?"

"He received a few letters from his parents in India. My mother would know more of that. She collects the mail. Would you like to talk to my mother?"

"No!"

"Who is that?" Mrs. Apusenja called from the hall.

Lula and I put our heads down and took a deep breath.

"It is two women from the bonds agency," Nonnie said.

Mrs. Apusenja rumbled to the door and elbowed Nonnie aside. "What do you want? Have you found Samuel?"

"I had a couple questions to ask Nonnie," I said.

"Where is the man named Ranger?" Mrs. Apusenja said. "I can tell you are just his worthless assistant. And who is this fat woman with you?"

"Hunh," Lula said. "There was a time when I would have kicked your nasty ass for calling me fat, but I'm on a diet to be a supermodel and I'm above all that now."

"Such language," Mrs. Apusenja said. "Just as I would expect from sluts."

"Hey, watch who you're calling a slut," Lula said. "You're starting to get on my nerves."

"Get off my porch," Mrs. Apusenja said. And she shoved Lula.

"Hunh," Lula said. And she gave Mrs. Apusenja a shot to the shoulder that rocked her back on her heels.

"Disrespectful whore," Mrs. Apusenja said to Lula. And she slapped her.

This was where I took two steps back.

Lula grabbed Mrs. Apusenja by the hair and the two of them stumbled off the porch to the small front yard. There was a lot of bitch slapping and name calling and hair pulling. Nonnie was shouting for them to stop and I had my stun gun in my hand just in case it looked like Lula was going to lose.

An old lady tottered out of the house next door and turned her garden hose on Lula and Mrs. Apusenja. Lula and Mrs. Apusenja broke apart sputtering. Mrs. Apusenja turned tail and scuttled into her house, her soaked sari leaving a trail of water behind her that looked like slug slime.

The old lady shut the water off at the spigot on her front porch. "That was fun," she said. And she disappeared into her house.

Lula squished to the car and climbed in. "I could have taken her if I'd had more time," she said.

I dropped Lula off at the office and drove on autopilot to Hamilton and eased into the stream of traffic. Hamilton is full of lights and small businesses. It's a road that leads to everything and everywhere and at this time of the day it was clogged with cars going nowhere. I turned from Hamilton, cut through a couple side streets, and swung into my apartment building lot. I parked and looked up at my building and realized I'd driven myself to the wrong place. I wasn't living here these days. I was living with Morelli. I thunked my head on the steering wheel. "Stupid, stupid, stupid."

I was on the third thunk when the passenger side door swung open and Ranger took the seat next to me. "You should be careful," Ranger said. "You'll shake something loose in there."

"I didn't see you in the lot when I pulled in," I said. "Were you waiting for me to come home?"

"I followed you, babe. I picked you up a block from the office. You should check your mirrors once in a while. Could have been a bad guy on your tail."

"And you're a good guy?"

Ranger smiled. "Are you parked here for any special reason? I thought you moved in with Morelli."

"Navigation error. My mind wasn't on my driving."

"Do you want to tell me about it?"

"The shooting?"

"Yeah," Ranger said. "And anything else I should know about."

I told him about the shooting and then I told him about the flowers and the photos.

"I could keep you safer than Morelli," Ranger said.

I believed him. But I would also be more restricted. Ranger would lock me up in a safe house and keep a guard with me 24-7. Ranger had a small army of guys working for him who made Marine commandos look like a bunch of sissies.

"I'm okay for now. Is there any word on the street about Bart Cone? Like does he rape and murder women?"

"The street doesn't talk about Bart Cone. The street doesn't even *know* Bart Cone. The Cone brothers run a tight factory and pay their bills on time. I had Tank ask around. The only interesting thing he turned up was the murder inquiry. Two months after the police dropped Bart as a suspect, Bart's wife left him. He's the nuts-and-bolts guy at the factory. Has an engineering degree from MIT. Smart. Serious. Private. The direct opposite of Clyde, who spends most of his day reading comic books and gets together several times a week with his friends to play Magic."

"Magic?"

"It's one of those role-playing card games."

"Like Dungeons and Dragons?"

"Similar. Andrew is the people person. Manages the human resources side of the business. He's been married for ten years. Has two kids, ages seven and nine." Ranger's pager went off and he checked the readout. "Do you have any candidates for the flowers and photos?"

"I've made my share of enemies since I've had this job. No one stands out. Bart Cone crossed my mind. The business with the murder is hard to ignore even though the charge didn't stick. And the break-in occurred right after I was at the factory. Sort of a strange set of coincidences. If he's the nuts-and-bolts guy maybe he knows how to open locks."

"Don't go walking in the woods with him," Ranger said. And he was gone.

SIX

I opened the front door to Morelli's house and Bob exploded out at me. He knocked me to one side, took the concrete and brick stairs in a single bound, and ran up the street. He stopped and turned and ran back full speed. He got to Morelli's property line, applied the brakes, hunched, and pooped.

Lesson number one when cohabitating with a man and a dog: Never be the first to arrive home.

I went to the backyard, got the snow shovel from the shed, and used the shovel to flip the poop into the street. Then I sat on the stoop and waited for a car to run over the poop. Two cars drove by, but both of them avoided the poop. I gave a sigh of resignation, went into the kitchen, got a plastic baggie, scooped the poop up off the street, and threw it into the garbage. Sometimes you just can't catch a break.

Bob looked like he still had lots of energy, so I snapped the leash on him and we took off. The sun was warm on my back and Joe's neighborhood felt comfortable. I knew a lot of the people who lived here. It was an older population consisting of parents and grandparents of kids who went to school with me. From time to time a house would turn over to the new generation and a stroller or baby swing would appear on the porch.

Sometimes I'd look at the strollers and my biological clock would tick so loud in my head and my heart it would blur my vision, but more often than not there were days like today when I came home to a load of fresh poop and babies didn't seem all that alluring.

Bob and I went for a nice long walk and we were on our way home. Two people, Mrs. Herrel and Mrs. Gudge, popped out of their houses to ask if it was true that I shot someone today. Word travels fast in the Burg and its surrounding neighborhoods. Story accuracy isn't always a top priority.

I crossed the street and saw a car pull to the curb in front of Joe's house half a block away. There were two women in the car. Joe's mother and grandmother. Damn. I'd rather face Howie's killer. I had a moment of indecision, wondering if I was spotted, if it was too late to sneak off. Joe's mother got out of the car, our eyes caught, and my fate was sealed.

By the time Bob and I got to Joe's house, Grandma Bella was out of the car and on the sidewalk beside Joe's mother.

"I had a vision," Grandma Bella said.

"I didn't shoot anyone," I told her.

"You were dead in my vision," Grandma Bella said. "Cold as stone. The blood drained from your lifeless body. I saw you go into the ground."

My jaw went slack and the world lost focus for a moment.

"Don't pay attention to her," Joe's mother said. "She has these visions all the time." Mrs. Morelli gave me a loaf of bread in its white paper bakery bag. "I came over to give Joe this bread. It's fresh baked from Italian People's. Joe likes it in the morning with his coffee."

"I saw you in the box," Grandma Bella said. "I saw them close the lid and put you in the ground."

Bella was doing a bang-up job of creeping me out.

This wasn't a good time to tell me I was going to die. I was working hard not to get overwhelmed by the shooting, the photos, and flowers.

"Stop that," Joe's mother said to Bella. "You're scaring her."

"Mark my words," Bella said, shaking her finger at me.

The two women got back into the car and drove off. I took Bob and the bread into the house. I gave Bob fresh water and a bowl filled with dog crunchies. I sliced the end off the bread and ate it with strawberry jam.

A tear slid out of my eye and rolled down my cheek. I didn't want to give in to the tear, so I wiped it away and looked in at Rex. Rex was sleeping, of course. "Hey!" I said real loud into the cage. Still no movement. I dropped a chunk of the bread and jam a couple inches away from the soup can. The soup can vibrated a little and Rex backed out. He stood blinking in the light for a moment, whiskers whirring, nose twitching. He scurried over to the bread, ate all the jam, shoved the remaining bread into his cheek pouch, and scuttled back into his soup can.

I checked the phone machine. No messages. I opened my iBook, went online, and my screen filled with more of the penis enlargement, hot chicks with horses, get out of debt ads.

"We can send a man to the moon, but we can't find a way to stop junk mail!" I yelled at the computer.

I calmed myself and deleted the garbage. I was left with one piece of mail. No subject in the subject line. The body of the letter was short: *Did you like my flowers? Were you impressed with my marksmanship this afternoon?*

My stomach went hot and sick and my vision got cobwebby. I put my head between my legs until the ringing stopped in my ears and I was able to breathe again.

This was from Howie's killer. He knew my email

address. Not that my email address was a secret. It was printed on my business cards. Still, the message was chilling and eerily invasive. It tied the flowers and the photos to the shooting. It was a message from a madman.

I typed back to him. *Who are you?*

Seconds later, my message was returned as undeliverable.

I saved the email to show to Morelli and I shut down.

"My day is in the toilet," I told Bob. "I'm taking a shower. Don't let any maniacs in the house." I stood up as tall as I could and I made sure my voice was steady. The bravado was partly for Bob and partly for me. Sometimes if I acted brave, I almost became a little brave. And just in case Bob fell asleep on the job, I went to the closet in Morelli's room, helped myself to his spare gun, and took it into the bathroom with me.

Grandma Mazur was waiting at the door when I pulled up. "What do you think of my new hair?" she asked.

It was punk-rock-star red and stuck out in little spikes. "I think it's fun," I told Grandma.

"It brings out the color of my eyes."

"And it's flattering to your skin tone." Definitely drags attention away from the liver spots.

"It's a wig," she said. "I got it at the mall today. Me and Mabel Burlew went shopping. I just got home. I missed all the excitement when everybody thought you shot someone again."

Albert Kloughn came in behind me. "What about shooting someone? Do you need a lawyer? I'd give you a real good rate. Business has been a little slow. I don't know why. It's not like I'm not a good lawyer. I went to school and everything."

"I don't need a lawyer," I told him.

"Too bad. I could use a high-profile case. That's what

really helps your practice to take off. You gotta win something big."

"What do you think of my hair?" Grandma asked Kloughn.

"It's nice," he said. "I like it. It's real natural looking."

"It's a wig," Grandma said. "I got it at the mall."

"Maybe that's what I should get," Kloughn said. "Maybe I'd get more cases if I had more hair. A lot of people don't like bald men. Not that I'm bald, but it's starting to get thin." He smoothed his hand over his few remaining strands of hair. "You probably didn't notice that it was thin, but I can tell when the light hits it just right."

"You should try that chemical stuff you pour on your head," Grandma said. "My friend Lois Grizen uses it and she grew some hair. Only problem was she used it at night and it rubbed off on her pillow and got on her face and now she has to shave twice a day."

My father looked up from his paper. "I always wondered what was wrong with her. I saw her in the deli last week and she looked like Wolfman. I thought she had a sex change."

"I have everything on the table," my mother said. "Come now before it gets cold. The bread will go stale."

Valerie was already at the table with her plate filled. My mother had put out an antipasto platter, fresh bread from People's, and a pan of sausage-and-cheese lasagna. Nine-year-old Angie, the perfect child and an exact replica of Valerie at that age, sat hands folded, patiently waiting for food to be passed. Her seven-year-old sister, Mary Alice, thundered down the stairs and galloped into the room. Mary Alice has for some time now been convinced she's a horse. Outwardly she has all the characteristics of a little girl, but I'm beginning to wonder if there's more to the horse thing than meets the eye.

"Blackie tinkled in my bedroom," Mary Alice said.

"And I had to clean it up. That's why I'm late. Blackie couldn't help it. He's just a baby horse and he doesn't know any better."

"Blackie's a new horse, isn't he?" Grandma asked.

"Yep. He came to play with me just today," Mary Alice said.

"It was nice of you to clean it up," Grandma said.

"Next time you should put his nose in it," Kloughn said. "I heard that works sometimes."

Valerie impatiently looked around the table. She folded her hands and bowed her head. "Thank God for this food," Valerie said. And she dug in.

We all crossed ourselves, mumbled *Thank God,* and started passing dishes.

There was a rap on the front door, the door opened, and Joe strolled in. "Is there room for me?" he asked.

My mother beamed. "Of course," she said. "There's always room for you. I set an extra plate just in case you could make it."

There was a time when my mother warned me about Joe. *Stay away from the Morelli boys,* my mother would say. *They can't be trusted. They're all sex fiends. And no Morelli man will ever amount to anything.* A while back my mother had decided Joe was the exception to the rule and that somehow, in spite of genetic disadvantage, he'd actually managed to grow up. He was financially and professionally stable. And he could be trusted. Okay, so he was still a sex fiend, but at least he was a monogamous sex fiend. And most important, my mother had come to think that Joe was her best, and possibly *only,* shot at getting me off the streets and respectably married.

Grandma shoveled a wedge of lasagna onto her plate. "I've got to get the facts straight on the shooting," she said. "Mitchell Farber just got laid out and Mabel and me are going to his viewing at Stiva's funeral parlor right after dinner, and people are gonna be on me like white on rice."

"There's not much to tell," I said. "Lula and I stopped for lunch and the man eating across from me was shot. No one knows why, but it's not a great neighborhood. It was probably just one of those things."

"One of those things!" my mother said. "Accidentally dinging your car door with a shopping cart is one of those things. Having someone shot right in front of you is *not* one of those things. Why were you in such a bad neighborhood? Can't you find a decent place to have lunch? What were you thinking?"

"I bet there's more to it than that," Grandma said. "I bet you were after a bad guy. Were you packin' heat?"

"No. I wasn't armed. I was just having lunch."

"You aren't giving me a lot to work with here," Grandma said.

Kloughn turned to Morelli. "Were you there?"

"Yep."

"Boy, it must be something to be a cop. You get to do all kinds of cool stuff. And you're always in the middle of everything. Right there where the action is."

Joe forked off a piece of lasagna.

"So what do you think about Stephanie being there? I mean, she was sitting right across from this guy, right? How far away? Two feet? Three feet?"

Morelli sent me a sideways glance and then looked back at Kloughn. "Three feet."

"And you're not freaked? If it was me, I'd be freaked. But hey, I guess that's the way it is with cops and bounty hunters. Always in the middle of the shooting."

"I'm never in the middle of the shooting," Joe said. "I'm plainclothes. I investigate. The only time my life is in danger is when I'm with Stephanie."

"How about last week?" Grandma asked. "I heard from Loretta Beeber that you were almost killed in some big shoot-out. Loretta said you had to jump out of Terry Gilman's second-story bedroom window."

I swiveled in my seat and faced Joe and he froze with his fork halfway to his mouth. There'd been rumors about Joe and Terry Gilman all through high school. Not that a rumor linking Morelli to a woman was unusual. But Gilman was different. She was a cool blonde with ties to the Mob and an ongoing relationship with Morelli. Morelli swore the relationship was professional and I believed him. That isn't to say that I liked it. It bore a disturbing parallel to my relationship with Ranger. And I knew that as hard as I tried to ignore the chemistry between Ranger and me, it still simmered below the surface.

I narrowed my eyes just a tiny bit and leaned forward, invading Morelli's space. "You jumped out of Terry Gilman's window?"

"I told you."

"You didn't tell me. I would have remembered."

"It was the day you wanted to go out for pizza and I said I had to work."

"And?"

"And that was it. I told you I had to work. Can we discuss this later?"

"I wouldn't put up with that," Valerie said, working the lasagna around in her mouth, grabbing a meat-and-cheese roll-up from the antipasto tray. "I ever get married again, I want full disclosure. I don't want any of this 'I have to work, honey' baloney. I want all the answers up front, in detail. You don't keep your eyes open and next thing your husband's in the coat closet with the baby-sitter."

Unfortunately, Valerie was speaking from firsthand experience.

"I've never jumped out of a window," Kloughn said. "I thought people just did that in the movies. You're the first person I've ever met who jumped out of a window," he said to Morelli. "And a bedroom window, too. Did you have your clothes on?"

"Yeah," Morelli said. "I had my clothes on."

"How about your shoes? Did you have your shoes on?"

"*Yes*. I had my shoes on."

I almost felt sorry for Morelli. He was making a major effort not to lose his temper. A younger Morelli would have broken a chair over Kloughn's head.

"I heard Terry didn't hardly have anything on," Grandma said. "Loretta's sister lives right across from Terry Gilman and she said she saw the whole thing and Terry was wearing a flimsy little nightie. Loretta's sister said even from across the street you could see right through the nightie and she thinks Terry got a boob job because Terry's boobs were perfect. Loretta's sister said there was a big to-do with the police showing up on account of all the shooting."

I tried to control my eyebrows from jumping halfway up my forehead. "Nightie? Shooting?"

"Loretta's sister was the one who *called* the police," Joe said. "And there wasn't a lot of shooting. A gun accidentally discharged."

"And the nightie?"

The anger disappeared and Morelli tried unsuccessfully to stifle a smile. "It wasn't exactly a nightie. She was wearing one of those camisole tops and a thong."

"No kidding!" Kloughn said. "And you could see through it, right? I bet you could see through it."

"That does it," I said, standing at my seat, throwing my napkin onto the table. "I'm out of here." I stomped out of the dining room into the foyer and stopped with my hand on the door. "What did you make for dessert?" I yelled to my mother.

"Chocolate cake."

I wheeled around and flounced off to the kitchen. I cut a good-size wedge from the cake, wrapped it in aluminum foil, and swept out of the house. Okay, so I was acting like an idiot. At least I was an idiot with cake.

I took to the road and drove off, spewing indignation and self-righteous fury. I was still fuming when I reached Joe's house. I sat there for a couple beats, considering my predicament. My clothes and my hamster were in the house. Not to mention my safety and great sex. Problem was, there was all this . . . emotion. I know emotion covers a lot of ground, but I couldn't hang a better name on my feelings. *Wounded* might be in the ballpark. I was stung that Morelli couldn't keep from smiling when he thought back to Gilman in her thong and camisole. Gilman and her perfect boobs. *Unh.* Mental head slap.

I opened the aluminum foil and ate the chocolate cake with my fingers. When in doubt, eat some cake. Halfway through the cake I started to feel better. Okay, I said to myself, now that we have some calm, let's take a look at what happened here.

To begin with, I was a big fat hypocrite. I was all bent out of shape over Morelli and Gilman when I had the exact same situation going on between Ranger and me. These are working relationships, I told myself. Get over it. Grow up. Have some trust here.

Okay, so now I've yelled at myself. Anything else going on? Jealousy? Jealousy didn't feel like a fit. Insecurity? Bingo. Insecurity was a match. I didn't have a *lot* of insecurity. Just enough insecurity to surface at times of mental health breakdown. And I was definitely having a mental health breakdown. The denial thing wasn't working for me.

I put the car in gear and drove to my apartment building. I wouldn't stay long, I decided. I'd just go in and retrieve a few things . . . like my dignity, maybe.

I parked in the lot, shoved the door open, and swung from behind the wheel. I beeped the car locked with the remote and headed for the back door to my building. I was halfway across the lot when I heard a sound behind me. *Phunf.* I felt something sting my right shoulder blade and heat swept through my upper body. The world went gray, then black. I put my hand out to steady myself and felt myself slide away.

I was swimming in suffocating blackness, unable to surface. Voices only partially penetrated. Words were garbled. I ordered myself to open my eyes. Open them. *Open them!*

Suddenly there was daylight. The images were blurred, but the voices snapped into focus. The voices were calling my name.

"Stephanie?"

I blinked a couple times, clearing my vision, recognizing Morelli. My first words were, "What the fuck?"

"How do you feel?" Morelli asked.

"Like I've been hit by a truck."

A guy I didn't know was bending over me, opposite Joe. A paramedic. I had a blood pressure cuff on and the paramedic was listening.

"She's looking better," he said.

I was on the ground in the parking lot and Joe and the paramedic brought me up to sitting. An EMS truck idled not far off. There was a lot of equipment beside me. Oxygen, stretcher, medical emergency kit. A couple Trenton cops stood hands on hips. A small crowd was gathered behind the cops.

"We should take her to St. Francis to have her checked by a doctor," the medic said. "They might want to keep her overnight."

"What happened?" I asked Morelli.

"Someone shot you in the back with a tranquilizer

dart. The impact was partially absorbed by your jacket, but you got enough tranq to knock you out."

"Am I okay?"

"Yeah," Morelli said. "I think you're okay. More than I can say for me. I just had three heart attacks."

"I don't want to go to St. Francis. I want to go home . . . wherever that is."

The medic looked over at Morelli. "Your call."

"I'll take responsibility," Morelli said. "Help me get her to her feet."

I walked around for a couple minutes on shaky legs. I was feeling really crappy, but I didn't want to broadcast it. I didn't want to overnight in the hospital. They take your clothes away and hide them and make you sleep in one of those cotton gowns that your ass hangs out of. "Jeez," I said. "What was I shot with, an elephant gun?"

Morelli had the dart in a plastic evidence bag in his pocket. He held the bag out for me to see. "Looks to me to be more large dog size."

"Oh great. I was shot with a dog dart. That doesn't even make good bar conversation."

Morelli eased me into his truck. "We'll leave your car here. I don't think we want to put you behind the wheel yet."

I wasn't going to argue. I was developing a monster headache.

There was a single red rose on the dash. A square white card in a plastic evidence bag had been placed beside the rose.

Morelli gestured at the rose. "That was left on your windshield." He reached across and took the card and turned it so I could read the message. *You should be more careful. If you make it too easy, the fun will be gone.*

"This is creepy," I said. "This is definitely psycho."

"It started right after you became involved with Singh," Morelli said.

"Do you think it's Bart Cone?"

"He'd be on the list, but I'm not convinced he's the one. I can't see him leaving roses. Bart Cone doesn't strike me as a man who has a flair for the dramatic."

I wanted it to be Bart Cone. He was an easy mark. I had a fantasy scenario going in my head. Stephanie and Lula break into Bart's home, find the tranquilizer gun stashed beside the gun that killed Howie, and call the police. The police immediately arrest Bart. And Stephanie lives happily ever after. Needless to say, the fantasy scenario didn't include Stephanie doing time for illegal entry. "This has moved way beyond my comfort zone," I said to Morelli. "If I wasn't shot full of tranquilizer you'd be seeing some first-rate hysteria."

Morelli left-turned out of the lot. "What were you doing here, anyway?"

"I was returning to my apartment because you liked looking at Gilman in her thong."

"Shit," Morelli said. "You're such a *girl*."

I closed my eyes and rested my head on the seat back. "You're lucky I'm drugged."

"Did you notice anything unusual when you parked? A strange car? A paranoid schizophrenic lurking in the shadows?"

"Nothing. I wasn't looking. I was making the most of my indignation."

By the time we reached Morelli's house the sun was low in the sky and the night insects were singing. I looked down the street, more from comfort than fear. Hard to believe anything bad could happen on Morelli's street. Mrs. Brodsky was sitting on her porch and Aunt Rose's second-story curtains, filmy behind the glass, floated like a protective charm. Morelli's neighborhood felt benign. Of course, none of that stopped Morelli from doing his cop thing. He'd been checking his tail all the way over, making sure we weren't followed. He parked and helped me out of the truck, hustling me into the house, partially shielding me with his body.

"I appreciate the effort," I said, sinking onto his couch. "But I hate when you put yourself in danger to protect me."

Bob climbed up next to me, leaving no room for Morelli. Bob had a piece of dog biscuit stuck to his head.

"How does he always get food stuck to him?" I asked Morelli.

"I don't know," Morelli said. "It's a Bob mystery. I think stuff falls out of his mouth and he rolls in it, but I'm not sure."

"About Gilman . . ." I said.

"I can't talk about Gilman. It's police business."

"This isn't one of those James Bond things where you sleep with Gilman to get information out of her, is it?"

Morelli slouched into a chair and clicked the television on. "No. This is one of those Trenton cop things where we threaten and bribe Gilman to get information out of her." He found a ball game, adjusted the sound, and turned to me. "So are you sleeping with me tonight?"

"Yes. But I have a headache." I closed my eyes and tried to relax. "Omigosh!" I said, my eyes popping open. "I forgot to tell you. I have an email from Howie's killer and it links the killing and the flowers."

Morelli was long gone by the time I dragged myself out of bed. I shuffled into the bathroom, took a shower, dressed in jeans and T-shirt, and found my way to the kitchen. I got coffee brewing and put a couple slices of bread in the toaster while I drank my orange juice and checked my email. I suspected there would be a message from the killer. I wasn't disappointed. *Now the hunter is the hunted,* the email read. *How does it feel? Does it excite you? Are you prepared to die?*

Bob was sitting beside me, waiting for bread crumbs to fall out of my mouth.

"I'm not excited," I told Bob. "I'm scared." The words echoed in the kitchen and made my breath catch in my chest. I didn't like the way the words sounded and decided not to say them out loud again. I decided to give denial another chance. Some thoughts are best kept silent. That's not to say I was going to ignore being scared. I was going to try very, very hard to be very, very careful.

I signed off and called Morelli and told him about the latest email. Then I called Lula and asked her to pick me up. I wanted to go back to TriBro and my car was still parked in my apartment building lot. I needed a ride. And I needed a partner. I wasn't going to stay inside, hiding in a closet, but in all honesty I didn't want to go out alone.

Ten minutes later, Lula rolled to a stop in front of Morelli's house. Lula drove a big ol' red Firebird that had a sound system that could shake the fillings loose in your teeth. The front door to Joe's house was closed and locked and I was in the kitchen in the back of the house . . . and I knew Lula had arrived because Shady's bass was giving me heart arrhythmia.

"You don't look so good," Lula said when I got into the car. "You got big bags under your eyes. And your eyes are all bloodshot. You must have really had a good time last night to look this bad this morning."

"I was shot with a tranquilizer dart last night and I had a killer hangover from it until about four this morning."

"Get out! What were you doing getting shot with a tranquilizer dart?"

"I wasn't doing anything. I was walking from my car to my apartment building and someone shot me in the back."

"Get out! Did you find out who did it?"

"No. The police are investigating."

"I bet it was Joyce Barnhardt. Joyce would do something like that, trying to even the score for all the times we zapped her with the stun gun and you let Bob poop on her front lawn."

Joyce Barnhardt. I'd forgotten about Joyce Barnhardt. She'd be a prime contender, too, except for the Howie shooting. Joyce wasn't a killer.

I went to school with Joyce and she'd made my life a misery. Joyce publicized secrets. When she didn't have a secret she fabricated stories and started rumors. I wasn't the only one singled out, but I was a favorite target. A while back, Vinnie hired Joyce to do some apprehension work and once again Joyce and I crossed paths.

"I don't think it's Joyce," I told Lula. "I think the tranq incident is related to the Howie shooting."

"Get out!"

If Lula said *get out* one more time I was going to choke her until her tongue turned blue and fell out of her head.

"And you're probably in danger when you hang with me," I told Lula. "I'd understand if you wanted to bail."

"Are you shitting me? Danger's my middle name."

SEVEN

We were out of Joe's neighborhood and moving across town. Lula had Eminem cranked up. He was rapping about trailer park girls and how they go round the outside, and I was wondering what the heck that meant. I'm a white girl from Trenton. I don't know these things. I need a rap cheat sheet.

I was checking the rearview mirror now. I didn't want a second dart between the shoulder blades. It was time to be vigilant. I had no indication that the creep who was stalking me knew I was living with Joe. And I was riding in Lula's car. So maybe today would be uneventful.

We hit Route 1 and I noticed there was a cooler on the backseat. "Are you still on the diet?" I asked. "Is the cooler filled with vegetables?"

"Hell no. That was a bogus dict. You could waste away and die on that diet. I'm on a new diet. This here's the all-protein diet that I'm on. I'm going to be a supermodel in no time on this diet. All I have to do is stay away from the carbs. Carbohydrates are the enemy. I can eat all the meat and eggs and cheese I want, but I can't eat any bread or starch or any of that shit. Like, I can have a burger but I can't eat the roll. And I can only eat the cheese and grease on the pizza. Can't eat the crust."

"How about doughnuts?"

"Doughnuts are gonna be a problem. Don't think there's anything I can eat on a doughnut."

"So what's in the cooler?"

"Meat. I got ribs and rotisserie chicken and a pound of crispy bacon. I can eat meat until I grow a tail and moo. This is the *best* diet. I can eat things on this diet that I haven't been able to eat in years."

"Like what?"

"Like bacon."

"You always eat bacon."

"Yeah, but I feel guilty. It's the guilt that puts the weight on."

Lula turned into the industrial park and wound around some until she came to TriBro.

"Now what?" she asked. "You want me to go on in with you? Or you want me to stay here and guard the chicken?"

"*Guard* the chicken?"

"Okay, so I'm gonna *eat* the chicken. That's the good part of this diet. You eat all the time. You could shove pork roast and leg of lamb down your throat all day long and it's okay. Long as you don't have biscuits with it. I had a steak for breakfast. A whole steak. And then I had a couple eggs. Is that a diet, or what?"

"Sounds a little screwy."

"That's what I thought at first, but I bought a book that explains it all and now I can see where it makes sense."

"Keep your eyes open while you're *guarding* the chicken. I shouldn't be more than a half hour. Call me on my cell if you see anyone suspicious in the lot."

"You mean like someone setting up a dart gun?"

"Yeah. That would be worth a phone call."

I'd gotten in touch with Andrew first thing this morning, before leaving the house. I told him I needed some information and he said he'd be happy to help. Andrew, the people person. Hopefully I could get to him without crossing paths with Bart. I hated to admit it, but I was afraid of Bart.

I did a brisk walk across the lot to the building entrance and hurried through the large glass door. The woman at the desk smiled and waved me through to Andrew's office. I thanked her on a *whoosh* of expelled air. I'd just had two bad parking lot experiences and many of my body functions, like breathing, now stopped when I set foot on parking lot pavement.

Andrew stood and smiled when I entered his office. "You didn't say much on the phone. How's the Singh search going?"

"We're making progress. I'm looking for a woman named Susan. I was hoping you could check through your employee list and pull out the Susans."

"Susan is a pretty common name. What's the connection to Singh?"

"It's vague. She's just a name that turned up and I thought I should check it through."

Andrew turned to his computer, typed in a series of commands, and the screen filled with the employee database. Then it executed a search for all Susans.

"We employ eight Susans," he finally said. "When I set the age at forty or below, I'm left with five Susans. I'll give you a printout and you can talk to them if you want. All are married. None work in Singh's department, but he would have had a chance to mingle with the general population during breaks and at lunch. We're a relatively small company. Everyone knows everyone else."

Clyde appeared in the open doorway. He was wearing a faded Star Trek T-shirt and new black jeans that were pooled around his ankles. Scruffy sneakers peaked out from under the jeans. He had a can of Dr Pepper in one hand and a bag of Cheez Doodles in the other. He had a Betty Boop tattoo on his chunky left arm.

"Hey, Stephanie Plum," Clyde said. "I was taking a break and I heard you were here. What's up? Anything exciting going on? Did you find Samuel Singh?"

"I haven't found Singh, but I'm working on it." My eyes strayed to Betty Boop.

Clyde grinned and looked down at Betty. "It's a fake. I got it last night. I'm too chicken to get a real one."

"Stephanie has a list of people she'd like to talk to," Andrew said. "Do you have time to take her around?"

"You bet. Sure I do. Is this part of the investigation? How do you want me to act? Should I be casual?"

"Yeah," I said. "You should be casual."

Clyde reminded me a lot of Bob with the unruly hair and goofy enthusiasm.

"These are all Susans," Clyde said, looking at the list. "That's a lead, right? Some woman named Susan knows where Singh is hiding. Or maybe some woman named Susan bumped Singh off! Am I close? Am I getting warm?"

"It's nothing that dramatic," I told Clyde. "It was just a name that popped up as a possible friend."

"I know all these women," Clyde said, leading me out of Andrew's office. "I can tell you all about them. The first Susan is real nice. She has two kids and a beagle. And the beagle's always at the vet. I think her whole paycheck goes to the vet. The dog eats everything. One time he was real sick and they x-rayed him and found out he had a stomach full of loose change. Her husband works here, too. He's in shipping. They live in Ewing. They just bought a house there. I haven't seen the house, but I think it's one of those little tract houses."

Clyde was right about the first Susan. She was very nice. But she only knew Singh from a distance. And the same was true for the other four Susans. And I believed them all. None of the Susans seemed like girlfriend material. None of them looked like sharpshooters or killers. They all looked like they might send roses and carnations.

"Those are all the Susans," Clyde said. "None of them worked out, huh? Do you have any other leads? Any clues we could work on next?"

"Nope. That's it for now."

"How about lunch?"

"Gee, sorry. I have a friend waiting for me in the parking lot." Thank God.

"I'm a pretty interesting guy, you know," he said. "I have a lot going on." His eyes got round. "You haven't seen my office yet. You *have* to see my office."

I glanced at my watch. "It's getting late . . ."

"My office is right here." He galloped down the hall and opened the door to his office. "Look at this."

I followed him and stepped into his office. One wall was floor-to-ceiling shelves and the shelves were filled with action figures. Star Trek, professional wrestlers, GI Joe characters, Star Wars, Spawn, about two hundred Simpsons figures.

"Is this an awesome collection, or what?" he asked.

"It's fun."

"And I collect comic books, too. Mostly action comics. I have a whole stack of original Spider-Man McFarlanes. Man, I wish I could draw like him."

I looked around the room. Large old wooden partner's desk with desk chair, computer with oversize LCD monitor, trash basket filled with squashed Dr Pepper cans, framed poster of Barbarella behind the desk, single chair in front of the desk, dog-eared comics piled high on the chair seat. None of the catalogues and product samples I saw in Bart's office.

"So," I said, "what's your part in the business?"

Clyde giggled. "I don't have one. Nobody trusts me to do anything. Now, on the surface that might seem a little insulting, but if you examine it more closely you see that I have a good deal. I collect a paycheck for staying out of the way! How good is that?"

"Does it get boring? Do you have to sit here all day?"

"Yeah, I guess sometimes it's a little boring. But everyone's nice to me and I get to do all the things I like. I can play with my action figures and read comics and play games on the computer. It isn't like I'm mentally retarded . . . it's just that I screw up a lot. The truth is, I'm not real interested in making thingamabobs."

"What would you like to do?"

He shrugged. "I don't know. I guess I'd like to be Spider-Man."

Too bad Clyde wasn't older. He'd be perfect for Grandma Mazur.

Lula was sound asleep with the driver's seat tipped back when I returned to the car. I jumped in and locked my door and nudged Lula.

"Hey," I said. "You're supposed to be on lookout."

Lula sat up and stretched. "There wasn't anything to see. And I got sleepy after eating all that chicken. I ate the whole thing. I even ate the skin. I love skin. And you know how all other diets tell you not to eat the skin? Well, guess what? I'm doing the skin diet now, girlfriend."

"That's great. Let's get out of here."

"Something happen in there to make you in such a rush to take off?"

"Just feeling antsy."

"Fine by me. Where we going next?"

I didn't know. I was out of leads. Out of ideas. Out of courage. "Let's go back to the office."

Lula and I saw the black truck simultaneously. It was parked in front of Vinnie's office. It was a new Dodge Ram. It didn't have a speck of dust on it. It had bug lights on the cab, oversize tires, and a license plate that was probably made in someone's basement. Ranger drove a variety of cars. All of them were black. All were new. All were expensive. And all were of dubious origin. The Ram was his favorite.

"Be still my beating heart," Lula said. "Does my hair look okay? Am I starting to drool?"

I wasn't nearly so excited. I suspected he was waiting for me. And I worried that it wasn't going to be a good conversation.

I followed Lula into the office. Connie was at her desk, head down, furiously shuffling papers. Vinnie's door was closed. Ranger was slouched in a chair, elbows on the arms, fingers steepled in front of him, his eyes dark and intense, watching us.

I smiled at Ranger. "Yo," I said.

He smiled back but he didn't yo.

"We're just checking in," I said to Connie, leaning on the front of her desk. "Do you have anything for me?"

"I have skips piling up on my desk," Connie said, "but Vinnie doesn't want anyone even *looking* at them until Singh is found."

"No calls? No messages?"

Ranger unfolded himself and crossed the room, standing close behind me, sucking me into his force field. "We need to talk."

A flash of heat rippled through my stomach. Ranger always evoked a mixture of emotion. Usually that mixture was attraction followed by a mental eye roll.

"Sure," I said.

"Now. Outside."

Lula scurried behind the file cabinets and Connie bent into the nonsense paper shuffling. No one wanted to get caught in the line of fire when Ranger was in a mood. I followed Ranger out the door to the sidewalk and stood blinking in the sun.

"Get into the truck," Ranger said. "I feel like driving."

"I don't think so."

The line of his mouth tightened.

"Where are we going?" I asked.

"Do you want a full itinerary?"

"I don't want to get locked up in a safe house."

"I'd love to lock you up in a safe house, babe, but that wasn't my plan for the day."

"Promise? Cross your heart and hope to die?"

There was a slight narrowing of his eyes. Ranger wasn't feeling playful. "I guess you have to decide if it's more dangerous to be in the truck with me or to stand out here as a potential target for the sniper."

I stared at Ranger for a beat.

"Well?" he asked.

"I'm thinking."

"Christ," Ranger said, "get in the damn truck."

I climbed into the truck and Ranger drove two blocks down Hamilton and turned into the Burg. He wound through the Burg and parked on Roebling in front of Marsilio's restaurant.

"I thought you wanted to drive," I said.

"That was the original plan, but you smell like rotisserie chicken and it's making me hungry."

"It's from Lula. She's on this diet where she eats meat all day."

Bobby V. met us at the door and gave us a table in the back room. The Burg is famous for its restaurants. They're stuck all over the place in the neighborhood, between houses, next to Betty's bridal shop and Rosalie's beauty parlor. Most are small. All are family affairs. And the food is always great. I'm not sure where Bobby V. fits in the scheme of things at Marsilio's, but he's always on hand to direct traffic and shmooze. He's a snappy dresser, he's got a handful of rings and a full head of wavy silver hair, and he looks

like hc wouldn't have much trouble breaking someone's nose. If you're in bad with Bobby V. don't even
bother showing up, because you won't get a table.

Ranger sat back in his chair, took a moment to scan
the menu, and ordered. I didn't need the menu. I always
got the fettuccini Alfredo with sausage. And then because I didn't want to die, I got some red wine to help
unclog my arteries.

"Okay," Ranger said when we were alone. "Talk
to me."

I filled him in on the shooting, the dart, the email.
"And what really has me freaked is that Joe's grandma
saw me dead in one of her visions," I said, an involuntary shiver ripping through me.

Ranger was motionless. Face impassive.

"Every lead I get ends up in the toilet," I told him.

"Well, you must be doing something right. Someone
wants to kill you. That's always a good sign."

I guess that was one way of looking at it. "Problem
is, I'm not ready to die."

Ranger looked at the food in front of me. Noodles and
sausage in cheese and cream sauce. "Babe," he said.

Ranger's plate held a chicken breast and grilled
vegetables. He was hot, but he didn't know much about
eating.

"Where are you now?" Ranger wanted to know. "Do
you have any more leads to follow?"

"No leads. I'm out of ideas."

"Any gut instincts?"

"I don't think Singh's dead. I think he's hiding. And
I think the freak who's stalking me is directly or indirectly associated with TriBro."

"If you had to take a guess, could you pull a name
out of a hat?"

"Bart Cone is the obvious."

Ranger made a phone call and asked for the file

on Bart Cone. In my mind I imagined the call going into the nerve center of the Bat Cave. No one knows the source of Ranger's cars, clients, or cash. He operates a number of businesses which are security related. And he employs a bunch of men who have skills not normally found outside a prison population. His right-hand man is named Tank and the name says it all.

Tank walked into the restaurant twenty minutes later with a manila envelope. He smiled and nodded a hello to me. He helped himself to a slice of Italian bread. And he left.

Ranger and I read through the material, finding few surprises. Bart was divorced and living alone in a townhouse north of the city. He had no recorded debts. He paid his credit cards and his mortgage on time. He drove a two-year-old black BMW sedan. The packet included several newspaper clippings on the murder trial and a profile on the murdered woman.

Lillian Paressi was twenty-six years old at the time of her death. She had brown hair and blue eyes and from the photo in the paper she looked to be of average build. She was pretty in a girl-next-door way, with curly shoulder-length hair and a nice smile. She was unmarried, living alone in an apartment on Market just two blocks from the Blue Bird luncheonette, where she'd worked as a waitress.

In a very general sort of way I suppose she resembled me. Not a good thought to have when investigating an unsolved murder that had serial killer potential. But then, half the women in the Burg fit that same description, so probably there was no reason for me to be alarmed.

Ranger reached over and tucked a brown curl behind my ear. "She looks a little like you, babe," Ranger said. "You want to be careful."

Super.

Ranger looked at my pasta dish. I'd eaten everything but one noodle. A smile twitched at the corner of his mouth.

"I don't want to get fat," I told him.

"And that noodle would do it?"

I narrowed my eyes. "What's your point?"

"Do you have room for dessert?"

I sighed. I always had room for dessert.

"You're going to have dessert at the Blue Bird luncheonette," Ranger said. "I bet they have good pie. And while you're eating the pie you can talk to the waitress. Maybe she knew Paressi."

Halfway across town I rechecked the reflection in my side mirror for the fourth time. "I'm pretty sure we're being followed by a black SUV," I said.

"Tank."

"Tank's following us?"

"Tank's following you."

Ordinarily I'd be annoyed at the invasion of privacy, but right now I was thinking privacy was overrated and it wasn't a bad idea to have a bodyguard.

The Blue Bird sat cheek to jowl with several small businesses on Second Avenue. This wasn't the most prosperous part of town, but it wasn't the worst, either. Most of the businesses were family owned and operated. The yellow brick storefronts were free of graffiti and bullet holes. Rents were reasonable and encouraged low-profit businesses: a shoe repair shop, a small hardware store, a vintage clothing store, a used book store. And the Blue Bird luncheonette.

The Blue Bird was approximately the size of a double-wide railroad car. There was a short counter with eight stools, a pastry display case and cash register. Booths stretched along the far wall. The linoleum was black-and-white checkerboard and the walls were bluebird blue.

We took a booth and looked at the menu. There was the usual fare of burgers and tuna melts and pie. I ordered lemon meringue and Ranger ordered coffee, black.

"Excuse me?" I said, palms down on the Formica tabletop. "Coffee? I thought we came here for pie."

"I don't eat the kind of pie they serve here."

I felt a flash of heat go through my stomach. I knew firsthand the kind of pie Ranger liked.

The waitress stood with pencil poised over her pad. She was late fifties with bleached blond hair piled high on her head, heavily mascaraed eyes, perfectly arched crayoned-on eyebrows, and iridescent white lipstick. She had big boobs barely contained in a white T-shirt, her hips were slim in a black spandex miniskirt, and she was wearing black orthopedic shoes.

"Honey, we got *all* kinds of pie," she said to Ranger.

Ranger cut his eyes to her and she took a step backward. "But then, maybe not," she said.

"I'm not usually in this neighborhood," I told the waitress, "but my little sister knew a girl who used to work here. And she always said the food was real good. Maybe you knew my sister's friend. Lillian Paressi."

"Oh, honey, I sure did. She was a sweetheart. Didn't have an enemy. Everyone loved Lillian. That was a terrible thing that happened to her. She was killed on her day off. I couldn't believe it when I heard. And they never caught the guy who did it. They had a suspect for a while, but it didn't turn out. I tell you, if I knew who killed Lillian he'd never come to trial."

"Actually, I lied about my sister," I said. "We're investigating Lillian's murder. There've been some new developments."

"I figured," the waitress said. "You get to be a good judge of people with a job like this and Rambo's got 'fed' written all over him. A local cop would have ordered pie."

Ranger looked at me and winked and I almost fell off my seat. It was the first time he'd ever winked at me. Somehow Ranger and winking didn't go together.

"Did Lillian have a boyfriend?" I asked.

"Nothing serious. She was going out with this one guy, but they broke up. She hadn't seen him for a couple months. His name was Bailey Scrugs. You don't forget a name like Bailey Scrugs. The cops talked to him early on. So far as I know she wasn't dating anyone when she was killed. She was real depressed after breaking up with Scrugs and she spent a lot of time on her computer. Chat rooms and stuff.

"Do you want to know what I think? I think it was one of them random killings. Some nut saw her out walking in the woods. The world's full of nuts."

"I know this all happened a while ago," I said. "But try to think back. Was Lillian ever worried? Scared? Upset? Anything unusual happen to her?" Like was she ever shot with a tranquilizer dart?

"The police asked me all those same questions. At the time I couldn't think of anything to tell them. But there was something that popped into my head months later. I couldn't decide if I should go tell someone. It was sort of an odd thing and all that time had passed, so I ended up keeping it to myself."

"What was it?" I asked.

"This is probably stupid, but a couple days before she was killed someone left a red rose and a white carnation on her car. Stuck them under her windshield wiper with a card. And the card said *Have a nice day*. Lillian was kind of upset about it. She brought them in here and threw them away. I guess that's why it bothered me when I remembered. She didn't say anything more about them, like who they were from or anything. Do you think the flowers might have been important?"

"Hard to say," Ranger told her.

"You should talk to her neighbor," the waitress said to us. "Carl. I don't remember his last name. They were real good friends. Nothing romantic. Just good friends."

I ate my pie and Ranger drank his coffee. Neither of us said anything until we were out of the cafe and into his truck.

"Shit," I said. "Shit, shit, shit, shit, shit."

"I have a house in Maine," Ranger said. "It's nice there at this time of year."

It was a tempting offer. "Is there an outlet mall nearby? Is it close to a Cheesecake Factory? A Chili's?"

"Babe, it's a safe house. It's on a lake in the woods."

Oh boy. Bears, black flies, rabid raccoons, and spiders. "Thanks for the offer, but I think I'll pass. Just tell Tank to stick close to me."

Ranger put the truck in gear, turned at the corner, drove two blocks down Market, and parked in front of an old Victorian clapboard house. The front door was unlocked and led to a small foyer. There were six mailboxes lined up on the wall. Beyond the mailboxes, a hand-carved mahogany railing followed a broad staircase to the second and third floors. The carpet was threadbare and the wall covering was faded and had begun to peel at the corners, but the foyer and staircase were clean. An air freshener had been plugged into a baseboard outlet and spewed lemony freshness that mingled with the natural mustiness of the house.

We ran through the names on the mailboxes and found Carl Rosen. Apartment 2B. We both knew chances weren't good that he'd be in, but we took the stairs and knocked on his door. No answer. We knocked on the door across the hall. No answer there, either.

We could get Carl Rosen's work address easy enough,

but most people were reluctant to talk in their work environment. Better to wait a couple hours and catch him at home.

"Now what?" I asked Ranger.

"I want to go through Bart Cone's house. It'll be easier to do alone, so I'm taking you back to the office. You should be safe there. I'll pick you up at five and we'll try Rosen again."

EIGHT

Mrs. Apusenja was sitting in the office when Ranger dropped me off. She was on the couch, arms crossed over her chest, lips pressed tightly together.

She jumped up when I walked in and pointed her finger at me. "You!" Mrs. Apusenja said. "What do you do all day? Do you look for Samuel Singh? Do you look for poor little Boo? Where are they? Why haven't you found them?"

Connie rolled her eyes.

"Hunh," Lula said from behind a file cabinet.

"I've only been looking for a couple days . . ." I said.

"This is the fourth day. Do you know what I think? I think you don't know what you're doing. I want someone new on the case. I *demand* someone new."

We all looked at the door to Vinnie's inner office. It was closed and locked. There was silence behind the door.

Connie got up and rapped on the door. No response. "*Hey,*" Connie yelled. "Mrs. Apusenja wants to talk to you. Open the door!"

The door still didn't open.

Connie returned to her desk, got a key from the middle drawer, and went back and opened Vinnie's door. "Guess you didn't hear me," Connie said, standing hand on hip, looking in at Vinnie. "Mrs. Apusenja wants to talk to you."

Vinnie came to the door and smiled an oily smile out at Mrs. Apusenja. "Nice to see you again," he said. "Do you have some new information for us?"

"I have this for you. The new information is that I will go to the papers if you do not find Samuel Singh. I will ruin you. How does it look for my Nonnie? People will talk. And he owes me two weeks' rent. Who will pay that?"

"Of course we'll find him," Vinnie said. "I've got my best man looking for Singh. And Stephanie's helping him."

"You are a boil on the backside of your profession," Mrs. Apusenja said. And she left.

"How many years have I been in this business? A lot of years, right?" Vinnie asked. "And I'm good at it. I'm good at writing bond. I do a service for the community. Does the honest law-abiding taxpayer have to pay my salary? No. Does the city of Trenton have to hire cops to go find their scofflaws? No. All because of me. I go get the scumbags at no cost to the general population. I risk my neck!"

Connie and Lula and I raised our eyebrows.

"Well, okay, I risk *Stephanie's* neck," Vinnie said. "But it's all in the family, right?"

"Yeesh," Lula said.

"I should have let Sebring write the damn visa bond," Vinnie said. "What was I thinking?"

Les Sebring was Vinnie's competitor. There were several bail bonds offices in the Trenton area, but Sebring's agency was the largest.

"So what are you doing standing here?" Vinnie asked, flapping his arms. "Go find him, for crissake." Vinnie looked around and sniffed the air. "What's that smell? It smells like roast leg of lamb."

"It was my afternoon snack," Lula said. "I got it delivered from the Greek deli. I'm on the all-you-can-eat meat diet. I didn't eat the whole leg, though. I don't want to go overboard."

"Yeah," Connie said. "She only ate half a leg."

Vinnie stepped back into his office and closed and locked the door.

"Sounds like we should go find this guy," Lula said.

I'd like nothing better than to find Samuel Singh, but I didn't know how. And worse, I was having a hard time focusing on the hunt. I couldn't get Lillian Paressi out of my head. I kept seeing her marching into the Blue Bird, angrily clutching the flowers. Red rose, white carnation. The note was innocuous. Nothing to get angry over. So the flowers had to be part of a continuing harassment. And surely she talked to someone about it. I was hoping Carl Rosen was that someone.

"Earth to Stephanie," Lula said. "You got any ideas?"

"No."

"Me, either," Lula said. "I think this diet's clogging things up inside me. This isn't a creative thinker's diet. You need Cheez Doodles to do that shit. And birthday cake. The kind with the lard icing and the big pink and yellow icing roses."

Connie and I looked at Lula.

"Not that I'm gonna eat anything like that ever again," Lula said. "I was just saying that's why I haven't got any good ideas."

Since we were all out of how-to-find-Singh ideas, I asked Lula if she'd give me a ride so I could move my car to Joe's house.

"Hell yeah," Lula said. "I could use some air. It's too nice to be inside on a day like today. And besides, it smells like leg of lamb in here. This office needs some ventilation."

We were half a block down Hamilton when Lula

looked in her rearview mirror. "I think we're being followed. That black SUV pulled out right after us and
now he's sitting on our bumper."

"It's Tank. Ranger thinks I need a baby-sitter."

Lula took another look. "He's fine. He's not as hot
as Ranger. But he's fine all the same. I wouldn't mind
having my way with him."

"I thought you had a new boyfriend?"

"Don't mean I can't think someone else is fine. I'm
just going steady, girl. I'm not *dead*."

In a couple minutes we were at my apartment building and Lula parked in the lot, beside the Escape.

"I think you should go up to your apartment just to
check it out and shit," Lula said. "I could go with you
and I bet King Kong over there'll go, too. And I'd get a
chance to see him up close."

"Sure," I said. "I should probably see if everything's
okay, anyway."

We all got out of our cars and walked to the back
door. Tank is about six foot six and is built like . . . a
tank. He hasn't an ounce of fat on him. He wears his
hair in a Marine buzz cut. He was dressed in desert
cammies.

We climbed the stairs and walked down the hall.
Tank took the key from me and opened the door. He
was the first to step through. He looked around and he
motioned us in.

It was cool and quiet inside. No flowers. No photos.
No killers. I gathered together some clean shirts and underwear and we left.

"I'd forgotten about Tank following me," I said to
Lula. "He can chauffeur me around if you want to get
back to the office."

"What are you, crazy? If I go back there I'll have to
file. And Vinnie's there. Vinnie creeps me out these
days. All he does is mope around, worrying about

Samuel Singh. It's unnatural. Vinnie's usually out having a nooner with a goat. I hate having him just hang around the office."

Tank smiled at the part about the nooner, but he didn't say anything. He got into his shiny black SUV. Lula got into her red Firebird. And I got into my yellow Escape. And we all motored off to Joe's house.

Lula parked behind me and immediately got out of her car. "Are you going in?" she asked. "I hope you're going in because I've never been in Morelli's house. I'm dying to see the inside. What's the decor? Modern? Traditional? Colonial?"

"Mostly Pizza Hut with a splash of Aunt Rose."

I opened the door and Bob rushed out at us, nose twitching, eyes wild. He looked from Tank to Lula to me and then his head swung back to Lula and he gave a loud *woof.*

"What the . . ." Lula said.

Bob gave another *woof,* chomped down on Lula's purse, ripped it out of her hand, and took off out the door down the street.

"Hey," Lula yelled. "Come back with that! That's my purse." She looked to Tank. "Do something. I paid good money for that purse."

Tank whistled, but Bob paid no attention. Bob was at the end of the block, tearing the purse to shreds. We jogged down to Bob and found him gnawing on a pork chop.

"That was my snack," Lula said. "It was barbecue. I was looking forward to that pork chop."

I took Bob by the collar and dragged him back to Morelli's house.

"I'm on a diet," Lula explained to Tank. "The fat just melts away on this diet, but you've gotta eat lots of pork chops."

I locked Bob in the house and Lula and I drove back to the office with Tank following.

"That was sort of embarrassing," Lula said. "It's hard to explain a pork chop in your purse."

"Sorry it all got destroyed."

"Yeah, I really wanted that pork chop. I don't care so much about the bag. I bought the bag from Ray Smiley, out of the back of his Pontiac. It was one of those things that accidentally fell off a truck." Lula's eyes got bigger. "Hey, we should make a stopover at the mall. I could get a new purse and then just for the hell of it we could go into Victoria's Secret and see if Tank follows us in. That's how you tell what a man's really made of. It's one thing for a man to be big and brave and kill a spider. Any man could do that. Trailin' after a woman when she's shopping for thongs and push-up bras is a whole other category of man. And then if you want to see how far you can go with it, you ask him to carry one of those little pink bags they give you."

I've never been shopping with Ranger so I can't say how he'd do with the Victoria's Secret test. Morelli flunked hands down. Morelli takes off for soft-serve ice cream when I head for Victoria's Secret.

"No time," I told Lula. "Ranger's picking me up at five o'clock." And Ranger doesn't like to be kept waiting.

At precisely five, I saw Ranger's truck ease to a stop in front of the bonds office. I grabbed my bag and my jacket and I went out to meet him. The instant I got in beside Ranger I saw Tank peel away and take off.

"I thought he was supposed to be guarding my body," I said to Ranger.

Ranger looked at me with dark eyes. "It's my turn to guard your body, babe."

Oh boy.

Ever since I could remember I've loved adventure stories and heroes. I guess that's true for all kids. And maybe all adults, too. My best friend Mary Lou Molnar and I would choose up roles when we were kids. I'd be Snake Eyes from *GI Joe* or Inspector Gadget or Han Solo. I'd run through the neighbors' yards, shouting, *Thundercats, ho!* And Mary Lou would follow after me, living her own fantasy as Smurfette or Wendy Darling or Marcia Brady. Mary Lou always had a good sense of gender and of her own abilities. Mary Lou's fantasies were close to the reality of her life. I, on the other hand, have never been able to merge the reality with the fantasy. In my mind, I'm still Snake Eyes. In truth, I'm closer to Lucy Ricardo. I don't have a lot of the skills I should have as a crime fighter. I'm not good with guns and I've never found the time to take self-defense. The only black belt in my closet is a narrow snakeskin with a gold buckle.

"Tell me about Bart Cone," I said to Ranger. "Was his house filled with florist bills? Photos of murdered women? Body parts in the freezer?"

"None of the above. He has the minimum furniture. A bed, a chair, a table, a desk. No computer on the desk. No television. He had two books at bedside. *Into Thin Air.* And a nuts and bolts catalogue. It didn't look to me like he'd cracked the spine on *Into Thin Air.*"

"Sounds like his wife had a good divorce lawyer."

"Cone had minimum food in the refrigerator. His medicine chest was filled with antidepressants and sleeping pills."

"Do you think he's crazy?"

"I think he has no life. I think he's the job."

"Like us."

Ranger looked over at me. "You have a life. You shop for shoes. You eat Butterscotch Krimpets. You have a hamster, half ownership of a dog, thirty percent of a cop. And you have a scary family."

"You think I only have thirty percent of Morelli?"

"I think you have as much as he can give anyone right now."

"How about you?" I asked. "How much can you give?"

Ranger kept his eyes on the road. "You ask a lot of questions."

"So I've been told."

It was close to 5:30 when we reached the apartment house on Market. Ranger pulled into the driveway and parked in a small lot to the rear of the house. We took the back entrance and went directly to the second floor. We knocked on Carl Rosen's door. No one answered. Ranger crossed the hall and knocked on 2A. A woman in her fifties opened the door and peered out.

"We're looking for Carl Rosen," Ranger said. "I don't suppose you've seen him."

"No," the woman said. "I haven't seen him, but he's usually home by now. Sorry."

The woman slipped back into her apartment. Her door closed and three locks tumbled into place. Ranger paced away from the door, called Tank, and asked him to run a basic information check on Rosen. Three minutes later the information came back. Carl Rosen worked at the hospital. He drove a '94 blue Honda Civic. He was unmarried. Tank also had previous addresses and jobs and a list of relatives. Ranger disconnected and knocked one more time on Rosen's door. When no one answered, Ranger slid a slim tool into the lock and opened the door. He left me outside to do lookout and he disappeared into the apartment.

Ten minutes later, Ranger walked out of the apartment and locked the door behind him. "I can't remember the last time I broke into so many places and found so little," Ranger said. "Not even a computer. Just the power cord plugged into the wall. Either Rosen takes his laptop with him to work or else someone's gone through his apartment in front of us."

"Now what?"

"Now we wait."

I called Morelli and told him I'd be late. I was thinking an hour maybe, but we were still waiting at nine o'clock. We were sitting on the floor outside Rosen's apartment, backs to the wall, legs outstretched.

"My ass is asleep," I said to Ranger.

"And you'd like me to do something about it?" Ranger asked.

"Just making conversation."

"There are a lot of reasons why Rosen might not be home yet, but I have a bad feeling in my gut that this isn't going to turn out good," Ranger said.

"How much longer do you want to sit here?"

"Let's give him until ten."

"Okay," Morelli said, "tell me again. You were doing *what* with Ranger?"

"We wanted to talk to Carl Rosen, but he never came home." I told Morelli about the waitress at the Blue Bird and how she remembered about the flowers.

"Christ," Morelli said. "That never came out in any of the investigation. I've read through the file. Carl Rosen was questioned, along with everyone else in that apartment building, but no one ever said anything about flowers."

"I guess they didn't think it related."

"Tomorrow morning I'll talk to Ollie. He was the principal on the case."

Oh great. Blubber-butt Ollie. The Bain of my exis-

tence. The guy who once tried to arrest me for imper-
sonating a bounty hunter.

It was late. And I was tired. I'd done nothing for
hours and it had sapped my energy. Spending time with
Ranger was an odd experience. I was always aware of
the sexual pull, magnified by the silence that surrounded
him. The attraction had changed since we'd had the one
night together. We knew the power of it now. We set
boundaries after that night. His were different from
mine. My boundaries were physical and Ranger's were
emotional. I still knew almost nothing about him. And
I suspected it would always be that way.

I had one task left before going to bed. I needed to
check my email. Not a pleasant experience anymore. I
knew there'd be a message from the killer. I had a terrible feeling of dread that it would be about Carl Rosen.

I tapped my code into AOL and waited for my mail
to appear. A chill slid along my spine when I saw the
subject line *tally ho*.

Dear prey, the email began, *so sorry you couldn't
get to talk to Carl, but that might have ruined the hunt.
Alas, it's necessary to eliminate participants. After all,
this is a survival game, isn't it?*

Morelli was reading over my shoulder. "Doesn't
sound good for Carl."

"This guy thinks he's playing a game."

"Have you run across any paranoid schizophrenics
lately? Any completely wacko nut cases?"

"My path is littered with them. Have you guys had
any luck tracking the emails?"

"No. Hiding the origin of an email requires some so-
phistication, but it's possible. The Mercer County Pros-
ecutor's Office is working with us. We'll see what we
can do with this new one. I'm going to confiscate your
computer for a while."

"Were you able to locate the flower source?"

"They didn't come from any of the local florists. This guy probably picked them up at a supermarket. We have notices up in all the supermarket lunchrooms for checkers to watch for red roses and white carnations going out. We've dusted your apartment for prints, but nothing worthwhile came up."

"This is very creepy."

"Yeah," Morelli said. "Let's go to bed and I'll take your mind off your problems."

I woke up the next morning thinking maybe I only had thirty percent of Morelli, but it was a damn good thirty percent.

My schedule for fighting crime began considerably later in the day than Morelli's, so by the time I wandered into the kitchen Morelli was already at work. I got coffee brewing and dropped a frozen waffle into the toaster. The morning paper was on the table. I did a fast scan, but saw nothing about a body found floating in the Delaware.

I took a mug of coffee and padded out to the living room, opened the door, and looked up and down the street for Tank. No Tank in sight. That didn't mean he wasn't there.

I called Ranger and told him about the latest email. "I don't suppose you've seen Carl Rosen this morning?" I asked.

"No. His car hasn't surfaced. And he didn't show up for work."

"Is Tank out there? I didn't see him."

"He saw *you*. He said you were frightening."

"I haven't taken a shower yet. My hair might be a little unruly."

"Takes a lot to scare Tank," Ranger said. And he was gone.

I took a shower and I did the full-on hair thing. Hot rollers, gel, the works. I tweezed my eyebrows, painted my toenails, and spent an hour applying makeup. I shrugged into a swirly flowered skirt and finished it all off with a stretchy little white knit top. I was Jersey Girl right down to the strappy sandals with the four-inch heels. Not only did I have to do some image correction for Tank, but I'd be damned if I was going to die needing a pedicure.

I clacked out of the house carrying my big leather shoulder bag and took off for the office in the Escape. I looked great, but I couldn't run for a damn in the shoes so I had sneakers in my shoulder bag . . . just in case I had to chase down a bad guy.

I turned onto Hamilton and Andrew Cone called.

"I have something for you," he said. "This is really good. Can you stop around?"

Andrew sounded excited. Maybe this was my lucky day. Hot dog.

Connie was at her desk when I swung in. "Uh-oh," she said, "big hair and full face paint, high heels, and a Barbie shirt. What's going on?"

"It's too complicated to explain." And I wasn't sure I understood, anyway. "Where's Lula?"

"She's up the street. She's still on the diet. Went through all her meat in a half hour and had to walk up to the coffee shop for some bacon."

"Lula *walked* to the coffee shop? That's two blocks away. Lula never walks anywhere."

"She parked in back and got blocked in by someone. I guess she figured it was faster to walk."

"She must have really needed the bacon."

"She was on a mission."

I moseyed over to the door, looked up the street, and spotted Lula at the end of the block. She was walking fast in her Via Spiga heels, holding a white food bag

against her chest. Two dogs, a beagle and a golden retriever, trotted close behind Lula. A third dog crossed
the street and joined the pack. Every couple steps Lula
would turn and yell something at the dogs. When the
beagle jumped for the bag when Lula was half a block
away, Lula let out a shriek and started running.

"Stop running," I yelled at her. "You're making it
worse. They think it's a game."

They were snapping at her heels now and barking.

"Do something," Lula yelled. "Shoot them!"

"Drop the bag! They want the bacon."

"No way I'm giving up my bacon."

Lula was running knees high, arms pumping. She
was wearing the Via Spigas and a short black spandex
skirt that was hiked up to her waist, showing Hamilton Avenue what a big woman looks like in a red satin
thong.

"Open the door!" Lula shouted. "I can make it. I'm
almost there. Just hold the damn door open!"

Lula tossed the dogs a slice of bacon from the bag,
the dogs dove after the bacon, and Lula rushed past me
into the office. I slammed the door shut and we all stood
looking at the dogs milling around outside.

Lula tugged her skirt down. "Tank's out there, isn't
he?"

"Yep."

"I explained pretty good about the pork chop, but I'm
at a loss here."

"It speaks for itself," I said to Lula.

Grease stains were starting to show through the bag.
"I love this diet," Lula said. "I love pork chops. And I
love ribs. And I love bacon. I love bacon most of all."

Lula was eating bacon like it was popcorn, chomp-
ing on it out of the bag, rolling her eyes in gastronomic
ecstasy.

"How much bacon do you have there?" Connie wanted to know.

"Three pounds minus the one strip I gave up to the dogs."

"Sounds like a lot of bacon," Connie said.

"I'm pushing the boundaries of science here," Lula said. "I'm gonna be a supermodel with a smile on my face on account of I'm gonna be full of bacon."

"I need to go to TriBro," I said. "I'm looking for someone to ride shotgun."

"That would be me," Lula said.

Lula and Tank waited in the lot while I went in to talk to Andrew Cone.

"This is really good," Cone said. "I had to tell you this in person. First thing this morning I found an email from one of the people I do business with in Vegas. Bill Weber. He said Samuel Singh filled out a job application and Weber was emailing to check references. I got so excited, I called the guy. Got him out of bed. Forgot about the time change."

"Singh's in Vegas? And he was dumb enough to list you as a reference?"

Cone bobbed his head up and down, smiling wide. "Yes."

"I bet he even gave a street address."

"He did." Cone slid a piece of paper my way with all the information neatly printed out. "I told Weber about the visa bond and he's going to string Singh along until you get there. You're going to go get him, right?"

"Right."

Lula was looking kind of sick when I got back to the car.

"How much of that bacon did you eat?" I asked her.

"I ate it all. It didn't seem like so much while I was

eating it, but it doesn't feel like it fits in my stomach now."

I called Ranger and told him about Singh. "He's in Vegas, waiting for you to go get him," I said.

"I'm having a small legal problem with Nevada on a weapons violation," Ranger said. "You're going to have to make the capture. Take Tank. I don't want you to go alone."

Good grief.

NINE

Lula was up straight in her seat. "What's this about Vegas?"

"Samuel Singh is in Vegas and Ranger can't make the capture. So either I go or Vinnie farms the capture out to a Vegas agency."

"Don't even suggest farming it out. All my life I've wanted to go to Vegas. I hear there's a shopping center that's just like being in Venice with canals and boats and everything. And there's all those casinos and fancy hotels. There's the Strip. *The Strip!* I could get to see the Strip." Lula stopped and blinked. "You were gonna take me, right?"

"Ranger wants me to go with Tank."

"Tank? Are you shittin' me?" Lula pulled back, eyes bugged out with the injustice of it all. "Hunh. I get to go along on all the chicken-shit stuff. Sit in the car while you go into TriBro. And I'm the one goes to the back door when you go to the front door on a bust. I *always* get the back door. Do I complain? Hell no. I guess I know where I stand here."

I narrowed my eyes at her. "Are you done?"

"No way. I'm not done. And I'm feeling anxious now. I need a burger or something."

"You just ate three pounds of bacon!"

"Yeah, but the dogs ate one of those strips."

I drove out of the lot and headed for the office. "Okay, fine. I'll take you to Vegas if you can clear it with Connie."

"I knew it," Lula said. "I knew you wouldn't go without me. We're a team, right? We're like those two cops in the *Lethal Weapon* movies. We're like Mel Gibson and Danny Glover."

More like Thelma and Louise, driving off a cliff.

The office was quiet when we walked in. No Mrs. Apusenja. No Vinnie. Only Connie, sitting at her desk, reading the latest Nora Roberts.

"I found Singh," I told her. "He's in Vegas."

"Vegas! I *love* Vegas," Connie said.

"You see? Everybody's been to Vegas but me," Lula said. "It's not fair. I lead a deprived life. Bad enough I grew up underprivileged and all and now I'm the only one not been to Vegas."

"Let me go get my violin," Connie said.

"What do you want to do about this now that I've found him?" I asked Connie. "Can we forcibly bring him back? Has he violated his bond agreement?"

"The bond agreement states that he can't leave the tristate area without permission. So the answer is yes, you can forcibly bring him back. I'll page Vinnie to double-check, but I'm sure he'll want Singh brought back here."

"Ranger can't go to Vegas to make the capture," I told Connie.

Connie nodded. "He's got an outstanding weapons violation. Stepped on a few toes last time he was in Nevada. His lawyer's working on it."

"So that leaves me, I guess," I said. "And Lula."

"I get the picture," Connie said.

"And Tank," I added. "Ranger said I should take Tank."

"Anyone else?" Connie asked, turning to the computer. "You want a permit for a parade?"

"Boy, this here's going to be fun," Lula said. "And what with this new diet, I'll probably be real thin by the time I get there."

"It's only a five-hour flight," I told her.

"Yeah, but this diet works fast."

"Okay, here we go," Connie said. "I've got us on a flight out of Newark at four o'clock. We have a plane change in Chicago and we arrive in Vegas at nine. It's not a direct flight, but it's the best I can do."

"Us?"

"You don't think I'm going to send you and Lula to Vegas without me, do you? I'm feeling lucky. I'm going straight to the craps table. I'm not going to page Vinnie, either. I'm going to leave him a note."

We didn't have a lot of time if we were going to catch a four o'clock flight. "Here's the plan," I said. "It doesn't make sense to take more than one car. I'll tell Tank he's driving and he can pick all of us up. Everyone go home and pack and be ready to go in an hour. And remember, there's tight security now. No guns, no knives, no pepper spray, no nail files."

"What? How am I supposed to travel without a nail file?" Lula wanted to know.

"You have to put it in your suitcase and check your suitcase."

"What if I break a nail getting onto the plane and I got to file it down?"

"You'll have to gnaw it down with your teeth. I'll get you in an hour."

Tank was parked in front of the bonds office and he was being surveillant. I went out to him and gave him the game plan. He said his assignment was to stick to me and he didn't need to pack.

"Not even a toothbrush?" I asked. "Not even an extra pair of tighty whiteys?"

Tank almost smiled.

Okay then. I ran to my car and took off for my apartment. I hit the ground running when I got to my building. I took the stairs two at a time, barefoot with my shoes in my hands. Tank was ahead of me in the hall. He opened my apartment door and stepped inside. Four eight-by-ten glossies were spread across the floor. We bent to look at them without touching anything. They were photos of a man with half his head blown away. Like the first set of photos, they were enlarged to hide the victim's identity. My first thought, of course, was of Carl Rosen.

"Do you recognize him?" Tank asked.

"No."

Tank closed the front door and gave me a gun. "Stay here while I check the rest of the apartment." Moments later he was back. "No one here. No more photos that I can see. I didn't go through your drawers."

"Okay," I said, "here's what we do. We leave these photos exactly where they are. We try not to disturb any prints that might have been left. I pack as fast as possible and we get the hell out. When we're ready to board I'll call Morelli. If I call him now I'll have to stay for questioning and we'll never make the plane."

"Works for me," Tank said.

Ten minutes later I was out of the apartment, a change of clothes and essential makeup in a tote bag slung over my shoulder. We left my car in the lot and took Tank's SUV.

Connie lived in the Burg, so she was next on the pickup list. We beeped once when we pulled to the curb and Connie hustled out to us. Connie's house was a narrow single-family, similar to my parents' duplex, but half of Connie's house had been chopped away. Vito

Grecci used to live in the adjoining half house. Vito was a Mob bagman who came in with a light bag one time too many. Next day Vito's house mysteriously caught fire and Vito turned up in the Camden landfill. Fortunately for Connie, the fire didn't go beyond the brick firewall between the two adjoining houses. Connie bought Vito's fire-gutted half at a bank auction, tore the trashed house down, and never rebuilt. Connie liked having the empty lot. She put a big free-standing pool with a wraparound cedar deck in the newly created side yard. And she set up a shrine to the Virgin for sparing her house.

Lula lived on the other side of Hamilton, down by the train station. There wasn't a lot of money in the neighborhood, but year after year it held its own. Lula rented a tiny two-room apartment on the second floor of a small house. The house was gray clapboard with touches of Victorian trim. Last year the owner painted the trim pink. In a weird way it seemed just right for Lula.

Lula was on the curb waiting when we drove down her street. She had two huge suitcases with her, a big leather purse hung on her shoulder, and she was holding a large canvas tote.

Tank smiled. "I bet they're all filled with pork chops."

"We're only staying overnight," I told Lula when she climbed into the backseat next to Connie.

"I know that, but I like to be prepared. And I couldn't decide what to wear. I got a whole suitcase filled with shoes. You can't go to Vegas without a change of shoes. How many shoes did you bring?" Lula asked me.

"The shoes I'm wearing and sneakers."

"How about you?" she asked Connie.

"Four pairs of shoes," Connie said.

"Dog," Lula said to Tank. "How many shoes you got?"

Tank looked at Lula in the rearview mirror and didn't say anything.

Lula turned and checked out the luggage in the back of the SUV. "I don't even see any Tank suitcases," Lula said. "Where's your suitcases?"

"Tank hasn't got any suitcases," I said. "Tank's traveling light."

"Where's he keep his extra tighty whiteys?" Lula wanted to know.

Tank cut another look at Lula. "I don't wear tighty whiteys," he said.

"You *devil!*" Lula yelled. "I bet you go commando."

Lula and Connie fanned themselves in the backseat. Tank kept his eyes on the road, but I could see him smiling.

An hour later, we were in the terminal, standing in line. Seventy-three people in front of us. An airline employee was going person to person, suggesting electronic ticket holders use the automatic ticketing machines. We looked over at the machines with flocks of people gathered around them.

"I don't know," Lula said. "Those people trying to use those machines look pissed off. Don't look to me like they're having a whole lot of luck getting tickets out of those machines. Looks to me like after they waste some time they give up and get back in line over here."

We sent Connie over to investigate and we stayed in line. After a couple minutes Connie came back. "I think they're just decoys," Connie said. "I never saw anybody have any luck getting a ticket out of them."

"I bet I know," Lula said. "You go over there and try to get a ticket and you give them your name and address. And then you don't get a ticket, but you get put on some list for junk mail and telephone solicitors. I bet the airlines make money selling those lists. I bet they get extra on account of they're lists of gullible people who'll buy anything. You didn't give them your name and address, did you, Connie?"

"That's ridiculous," Connie said. And because she was snippy when she said it, we all knew she gave the machine her name and address.

Forty-five minutes later, we got to the counter and got ticketed. Lula checked two of her bags. Tank didn't have any bags. I carried my single tote bag with me. Connie had one small suitcase on rollers, which she checked.

"We're on our way now," Lula said. "Boy, this is gonna be fun. Hold on. What are we doing in another line?"

"This is the line to go through the security check," I told her.

"Say what?"

We inched our way along again. I had a low-grade headache from the terminal noise and the tedium and I had a backache from an hour of carrying the tote on my shoulder. Twenty minutes ago I'd dropped the tote onto the floor and now I kicked it along ahead of me. I suspected I was growing pale and in another twenty minutes I'd look like I'd spent fifteen years at TriBro testing nuts and bolts.

I was first in line. Lula stood behind me. Then Connie. Tank was in line behind Connie. We showed our tickets. We flashed our photo IDs. I approached the conveyor belt leading to the scanner. I placed my tote and my purse on the belt.

A security attendant asked me to place my shoes on the belt, as well. I looked down at the strappy sandals I'd put on first thing this morning. Brown leather and not a single part of the shoe thicker than an eighth of an inch with the exception of the slim wood stacked stiletto heel, which was a quarter of an inch. Guess security thought I had a bomb in the shoe. Bombs must frequently be hidden in women's strappy sandals.

I took the shoes off and shuffled barefoot along the filthy floor, through the metal detector. I didn't set the detector off but the security attendant told me I was a random female, so I was pulled aside and asked to stand spread eagle. I supposed they thought I had box cutters hidden under my skintight, slightly see-through white stretchy shirt. I was wanded and released. My shoes were returned to me after careful scrutiny.

An attendant in rubber gloves extracted all the items from my tote. Two pairs of bikini panties, a pair of jeans, two little white T-shirts, white socks, sneakers, a travel box of tampons (just in case), hair spray, roller brush, assorted cosmetics. Forty or fifty people passing by admired the panties and a couple women suggested a different brand of tampon.

The items were returned to my bag and I was told I could continue on my way. Lula was causing a scene behind me. She had to go through the same routine and they found fried chicken in her purse.

"You're not allowed to take unpackaged food past security," the attendant said to Lula.

"What am I supposed to eat?" Lula wanted to know. "I'm on a diet to be a supermodel. I need this fried chicken. Suppose they don't feed me on the plane?"

"There are kiosks by the gate that sell food," Lula was told.

I looked at the fried chicken displayed on the examining table. A leg and a breast. I guess security was on the lookout for chicken leg bombs.

"I don't like this," Lula said, shouldering her bags. "Had to take my shoes off, my jacket off, got felt up under my bra clip. Had to take my belt off. And look at this, I can't button the top snap on my stretch pants and now everybody knows. This here's been a humiliating experience. And on top of it all they took my chicken."

Connie had breezed through without a hitch. "That's the way it is now," Connie said. "You want to be safe, right? This is just a small thing to keep us safe."

"Shut up," Lula said. "I hate people who don't get searched." Her eyes were wild and her lower lip was jutting out. "I'm feeling a lot of anxiety," Lula said. "If this was supposed to make me feel safe it isn't working. All I can think of now is terrorists. I wasn't thinking of terrorists before. I need some ham. Where's the place they sell ham?"

It was announced that our plane was boarding and Tank still hadn't cleared security. I knew he didn't have weapons on him. He'd locked everything in the truck when we parked. They brought a dog in and two armed guards moved closer. Apparently they were picking up traces of explosives on his shoes and clothes. Wow, big surprise there. He had his identification displayed, including a license to carry, but security was having none of it.

He cut his eyes to me and I sent him a blank-faced look back. No way was I going to come to his rescue. I wasn't taking any chances on guilt by association. I was afraid the airport gestapo would haul my ass off to a back room and give me a body cavity search.

I grabbed Lula and pulled her along. Connie followed. We only had a couple minutes until boarding.

"What about Tank?" Lula asked.

"He'll catch up with us." Maybe.

We got to the gate and Lula was wide-eyed, looking everywhere. "I don't see no kiosk with fried chicken," she said. "I just see doughnuts and ice cream and bagels and big pretzels. I can't eat none of that food. Where's the friggin' meat?"

"Maybe we'll get something on the plane," I said.

"We'll be in the air over dinnertime, so maybe we'll get some dinner." Yeah, right. If we were flying first class we might get a bag of peanuts.

We were seated three across, six rows back in coach. Lula was on the aisle. I sat next to her. Tank's seat was empty. Connie sat on the other side of the aisle.

I called Morelli and told him about the photos.

"And here's the thing," I said to Morelli. "I'm sort of on a plane. Singh is in Vegas and I'm going out to apprehend him. So I was thinking maybe you could just let yourself in and, uh, take charge."

Silence.

"Joe?"

"This is the sort of thing Ranger usually takes."

"He has a problem with the state of Nevada."

"Okay, let me rerun this," Morelli said. "You went home to pack and you found more snuff photos. Then you drove to the airport and waited until you were boarded before calling me so it was impossible for me to bring you back to Trenton."

"Yup. That's about it."

The conversation deteriorated pretty quickly after that, so I said good-bye and shut my phone off.

The plane filled and the usual announcements were made. No Tank. I was feeling a little worried without my bodyguard. I had Connie and Lula with me. I liked Connie and Lula, but I suspected they were more liability than asset.

The flight attendants closed the doors and the plane began taxiing. Lula was singing with her headset on and her eyes shut. Connie was talking to the woman next to her.

All right, calm down, I told myself. Probably flying to Vegas was safer than staying in Trenton. Tank would get the next plane and everything would be fine. If I'd stayed with Tank I wouldn't be on the plane. I would have had to call Morelli and he would have insisted I return to Trenton.

Minutes after taking off it was announced that no food or beverages would be served. "What about peanuts?" Lula yelled out. "Don't we even get any freakin' peanuts?" Lula turned to me. "I want to get off this plane. I'm hungry and I'm uncomfortable. And look at the seat in front of me. It's all ripped. How am I supposed to have confidence when they can't even keep their seats sewed up? I bet some terrorist was practicing on that seat."

I put my finger to my eye.

"You getting that nervous eye twitch back?" Lula asked. "It's from this plane, isn't it? I feel nervous, too. I'm just a bundle of nerves."

"It's from *you*," I said. "Put your headset back on and listen to your music."

An hour into the flight Lula was fidgeting again. "I smell coffee," she said. "I bet they're gonna give us coffee. Probably they feel bad about treating us like a bunch of cows and they're gonna hand out coffee." She sniffed the air. "Hey, I smell *real food*. I smell something cooking." She hung over the armrest and looked up the aisle at the front of the plane. "It's not first class," she said. "I can see into first class and they're not getting any food, either."

Now I was smelling it. Definitely coffee. And maybe a tomato sauce and pasta dish. And cookies baking!

"It's like there's ghosts up there," Lula said. "I haven't seen a flight attendant walk down the aisle since we took off. It's like they vanished and their ghosts are cooking. I'm dying here. I'm starving. I'm getting weak."

Connie looked over. "What's going on?"

"I smell coffee," Lula said. "I must be hallucinating from hunger."

"Maybe the flight attendants are making coffee for the pilots," Connie said.

"I don't like the sound of that," Lula said. "That sounds like an emergency. Like the pilots are tired. Just my luck I get on a plane with a pilot who was up all night. I'm going to be really pissed off if he falls asleep and we crash and we all die and it's before I get to Vegas."

Connie went back to her magazine, but Lula was still leaning over the armrest into the aisle. "I can see them!" Lula said. "It's the flight attendants. Someone pulled the curtain aside and I can see the flight attendants eating. They're having coffee and fresh-baked cookies. Can you freaking believe it? They're not even going to offer any to us."

I was starting to think crashing and dying might be the way to go. Compared to another two hours in the air, crashing and dying held some appeal.

Lula's eyes were slitty and her forehead was scrunched up. She reminded me of a bull pawing the ground, nostrils flaring, shaggy head steaming. "I'm not calling them flight attendants anymore," Lula said. "I'm calling them stewardesses. See how they like that."

"Keep it down," Connie said. "Maybe they've been working all day and they didn't get a chance to eat."

"*I've* been working all day," Lula said. "*I* didn't get a chance to eat. You see anybody feeding me? I guess not. Look at me. I'm beside myself. I feel like the Hulk. Like I'm getting all swollen up with frustration."

"Well, take it easy," I said. "You'll burst something."

"You know what this is?" Lula said. "This here's plane rage."

"Plane rage isn't allowed. It got taken off the allowed activities list along with eating. If you make a scene they'll haul you off in leg irons."

"I'm tired of being strapped in here, too," Lula said. "This seat belt's too tight and it's giving me gas."

"Anything else?"

"There's no movie."

When we landed at Chicago I positioned myself between Lula and the flight attendants.

"Keep your head down and walk," I told Lula. "Don't look at them. Don't talk to them. Don't grab any of them by the throat. We need to get on the next plane. Just keep thinking about Vegas."

Our connecting flight was ten gates down. We started walking and almost immediately we hit fast food. Lula hurried over and ordered seven double cheeseburgers. She threw the buns away and ate the rest.

"I'm impressed," I said to Lula. "You're really sticking to this diet." Hard to believe she was going to lose weight on it, but at least she was trying.

An hour later our row was called to board and Lula, Connie, and I got in line. We reached the gate and I was pulled aside to be searched. Random female.

"Step over here," the security attendant said. "And take your shoes off."

I looked down at the sandals. "What could you possibly be looking for in these sandals?" I asked.

"It's standard procedure."

"I've already gone through this at Newark!"

"Sorry. You're going to have to take your shoes off if you want to get on the plane."

"Uh-oh," Lula said to me. "Your face is getting red. Remember about getting to Vegas. Just take the freakin' shoes off."

"It's not like it's personal," Connie said. "You should be happy security precautions are in place."

"Easy for you to say," I told her. "You're not the one

getting picked on. You're not the one getting singled out *for a second time*. Your tampons and panties aren't getting pawed through." I stared down at the shoes. There wasn't any way to hide a weapon in them, but I thought I could do some pretty good damage if I hit the security idiot in the head with one. Spike heel directly into the eyeball, I thought. I visualized the bleeding eyeball falling out of the woman's head and felt much more calm. I stepped out of my sandals and waited peacefully for them to be scrutinized.

When we were seated on the plane Lula turned to me. "You know, sometimes you can be real scary. I don't know what you were thinking back there when you took those shoes off, but all the hair stood up on the back of my neck."

"I had airport rage."

"Fuckin' A," Lula said.

Lula had airport rage when we landed and her luggage wasn't there.

Connie had us booked into the Luxor. It was on the Strip, and because the bail bonds conferences were held there every year we got good rates.

"Look at this," Lula said, head tipped back, taking it all in. "It's a freaking pyramid. It's like being in some big-ass Egyptian tomb. I *love* this. I'm ready to gamble. Outta my way. I'm looking for the slots. Where's the blackjack tables?"

I didn't know where Lula's energy came from. I'd exhausted myself trying to stay calm while mentally maiming airport employees, screaming kids, and security personnel.

"I'm going to bed," I told Lula. "We need to get an early start tomorrow, so don't stay out too late."

"I can't believe I'm hearing this. You're in Vegas and you're going to bed? Unh uh, girlfriend. I don't think so."

"I don't gamble. I'm not good at it."

"You can play slots. There's nothing to slots. You put your money in and you push the button."

"I'm feeling hot for the craps," Connie said. "I'm going to drop my suitcase off in the room and then I'm going to hit the craps tables."

"You see?" Lula said to me. "You don't come with, I'm gonna be all alone on account of Connie's gonna play craps."

Lula had a point. Maybe it wasn't a good idea to have Lula all alone in Vegas. "Okay," I said. "I'll tag along, but I'm not playing. I don't know what I'm doing and I always lose."

"You gotta play once," Lula said. "It wouldn't be right if you came to Vegas and didn't even play one slot. I bet there's even a law that says you gotta play a slot."

Fifteen minutes later, we were checked into our room. We all applied fresh lipstick, and we were ready to roll.

"Look out, Vegas, here I come," Lula said, closing the door behind us.

"I'm wearing my lucky shoes," Connie said, leading the way down the hall. "I can't lose in my lucky shoes."

It was the first time I'd ever walked any distance behind Connie and I was knocked over by the sight in front of me. Connie was a small Italian version of Mae West. Her hips were big and round and her boobs were big and round. And when Connie walked everything was in motion. Connie swung her ass down the hall. Connie was a *broad*. Connie belonged in a gangster movie set in Chicago during Prohibition.

We got to the elevator and the three of us stood waiting for the doors to open, cackling and preening in front of the hall mirror. We stepped into the elevator, went down one floor, and two guys got on. One was about five foot ten, had a big beer belly, and looked to be in his sixties. The other was average build, early forties, and was short enough that his eyes were even with my breasts. They were both dressed in tight white jumpsuits with bell-bottoms and big stand-up collars. The jumpsuits were decorated with sequins and glittered under the elevator lights. They had huge rings on their fingers and shoe-polish-black pompadour hairdos with long sideburns. They were wearing name tags. The big guy was named Gus and the little guy was named Wayne.

"We're Elvis impersonators," the little guy said.

"No shit, Sherlock," Lula said.

"We're part of a convention. There are fourteen hundred Elvis impersonators here at the hotel."

"We just got here," Lula said. "We're going down to play some slots."

"We're going to the show," Gus said. "We hear Tom Jones is singing in the lounge."

Lula's eyes got the size of duck eggs and popped out of her eye sockets. "Tom Jones! Are you shitting me? I *love* Tom Jones."

"You should come with us," Wayne said. "We wouldn't mind having a couple chicks tagging along, right, Gus?"

Lula looked down at little Wayne. "Listen up, Shorty," she said. "I don't do that patronizing, sexist chick shit."

"We gotta say things like that," Wayne told her. "We're Elvis impersonators. We're Vegas, baby."

"Oh yeah, I guess I could see that. Sorry," Lula said.

The elevator hit the casino floor and we all got out and hustled across the casino to the lounge. Me, Connie, Lula, and two over-the-hill Elvis impersonators. We reached the lounge and were stopped by a crush of people waiting to get in.

"Oh man," Lula said. "Look at this crowd. We're not gonna get in."

"They always let Elvis in," the big guy said, and he started bumping people out of the way with his belly.

"Uh, s'cuze me. The King's comin' through," he'd say. And then he'd sort of snarl and curl his lip the way Elvis used to.

We were packed up behind him, moving in his wake. All of us getting excited about seeing Tom Jones, willing to step on a few toes to do it. Gus got us a position close to the stage, off to the side. The room lights were dim and the stage was washed in red light. A band was playing. We ordered drinks and Tom Jones was introduced.

The minute Jones came onstage Lula went ape-shit. Lula didn't care about anything but Tom Jones. "Hey, Tom, honey, look over here," she yelled out. "Look at Lula!"

All around us women were throwing room keys and panties onto the stage. And then from the corner of my eye I caught sight of Lula pitching a giant hot-pink satin thong at Tom Jones. It was the biggest thong I'd ever seen. It was a King Kong thong. It hit Tom Jones square in the face. *Wap!*

"Holy crap," Connie said.

Tom Jones staggered back a step, snagged the thong from off his face, looked at it, and forgot the words to the song he was singing. The band was playing, but Tom Jones was just standing there staring at the thong.

"Maybe I should throw my bra, too," Lula said.

"No!" Connie and I said, worried Tom Jones would go into cardiac arrest at the sight. "Not a good idea. Overkill."

Tom Jones snapped out of his coma, stuffed the thong into his tux pocket, and went back to singing.

"I don't think Tom Jones looks all that good," Connie said to me. "He looks different somehow. Like he's had a face-lift that went wrong."

"And he's sort of fat," I said. "And he can't sing anymore."

"That's blasphemous to say about Tom Jones," Lula said. "You can't go dissin' Tom Jones."

Wayne leaned across Lula. "It's not Tom Jones. I thought you knew that. It's a Tom Jones impersonator. They're having a convention here, too."

"What?" Lula yelled. "I gave my underpants to an impostor?"

"He's pretty good, though," Gus said. "He's got a lot of the moves down pretty good."

"I want my underpants back," Lula shouted to the stage. "I don't go giving away perfectly good underpants to impostors. You got my underpants under false pretenses. And you can't even sing! I bet these two Elvis impersonators could sing better than you."

The guy on the stage stopped singing, shaded his eyes against the lights with his hand, and squinted over at us. "Elvis impersonators? I've got some goddamn Elvis impersonators at my show?"

"Uh oh," Wayne said. "Elvis impersonators and Tom Jones impersonators don't get along."

A low rumble went through the crowd. *Elvis impersonators,* they were grumbling. *The nerve!*

"Get them," someone shouted. "Get the dirty lousy Elvis impersonators."

Someone reached for little Wayne, and Lula stepped in. "Hold on here," she said. "We came with these guys. They're good guys. They got us in here."

"Get the Elvis impersonators and their *bitches,*" someone yelled. "The Elvis impersonators have *bitches!*"

The room was packed, and we were getting jostled and shoved. A Cher impersonator with a beard and mustache reached for Connie. Connie cold-cocked him and he went to the floor like a sack of sand. After that it was bedlam.

Lula took to the stage to wrestle Tom Jones for her underpants, and Connie and I scrambled after Lula to help with the thong retrieval. We were getting pelted with beer nuts and wasabi peas, and I could see casino security at the door, trying to make its way through the crowd. Lula ripped the thong out of Tom Jones's hands and we all ran backstage.

"Which way out?" I asked a greasy-haired guy in the wings.

The greasy-haired guy pointed to a door and we all crashed through it, ran down a hall, through another door, and found ourselves back on the casino floor.

Connie smoothed out her skirt and felt to see if she had any beer nuts stuck in her hair. "That was fun," she said. "I'm going to go play craps now."

"Yeah," Lula said, stuffing her thong into her purse. "I'm hitting the slots. I'm gonna start there."

"Wait a minute," I said to Lula. "Where'd you get the thong?"

"I had it in my purse," Lula said. "I read some-where that you should carry emergency undies when you travel." Lula squinted at my hair. "You got some-thing green slimed in your hair," she said. "It looks like someone got you with one of those fancy drinks."

Great. "I'm going back to the room," I said. "I'm go-ing to wash my hair and go to bed. I've had enough excitement for one day."

"What about the slots?" Lula wanted to know.

"Tomorrow." Maybe.

At seven in the morning Lula and Connie still hadn't re-turned to the room. I pulled on jeans and a Lakewood Blue Claws T-shirt that had the message *Got Crabs?* printed on the front. I covered my hair with a baseball cap and went downstairs to look for Lula. I found her in the cafe eating breakfast with Connie. Lula had about two dozen scrambled eggs and five pounds of sausage links on her plate. Connie had coffee.

Lula looked wired and not much different from everyday Lula. Connie looked like she'd died and come back from the dead. Connie's black hair was completely frazzled, sticking out at odd places. Her mascara had smudged, making the bags under her eyes more pronounced. Most shocking of all . . . she was without lipstick. I'd never seen Connie without lipstick.

I took a seat and I snitched a sausage link from Lula.

"What time is it?" Connie asked.

"Seven-thirty," I told her.

"Day or night?"

"Day."

The cafe was located on the perimeter of the casino floor. That's the way it always is in a casino. Everything opens to the floor. The casino was business as usual, but the attendance was light. The tables were populated mostly by bedraggled men in shirtsleeves. Leftovers from the night. The slots had a more alert crowd. Early risers, getting a jump on the day. I wasn't much of a gambler. But I liked the flash and color of the casino. I liked the neon lights, the bells and whistles, and the *ka-ching* of money being won and lost.

"Las Vegas never closes," Lula said. "Can you believe it? And I haven't been out of the hotel yet, but there's supposed to be an Eiffel Tower out there and the Brooklyn Bridge and all kinds of shit."

"What did you do all night?"

"I started with the slots," Lula said, "but I wasn't having any luck there, so I went over to the blackjack tables. I did pretty good and then I did really bad. And here I am . . . broke. Good thing Vinnie's buying me breakfast."

Connie had her head down on the table. "I lost all my money. I drank too much. And I lost my shoes."

We all looked under the table. Sure enough, Connie didn't have any shoes.

"I left them someplace," Connie said. "I don't know where."

"That's not even the best part," Lula said to me. "Ask Connie about the photograph."

Connie pulled a cardboard framed photo out of her big leather shoulder bag. It was a picture of Connie and a short guy in a powder blue tuxedo. The short guy had sideburns and an Elvis hairdo. Connie was holding a bouquet of flowers. "I think I might have gotten married to an Elvis impersonator," Connie said, dragging herself to her feet. "I'm going to bed. Wake me up when you get Singh and I'll do the paperwork for the locals."

Lula watched Connie stagger away. "I wouldn't hardly recognize her without lipstick," Lula said. "She sat down and I didn't know who she was at first."

"We have to snatch Singh today," I said to Lula. "Are you going to be up for it?"

"Damn straight I'm up for it. I'm just getting started. I'm like that Energizer Rabbit dude. How we gonna get this guy?"

"Singh applied for a job at a small casino downtown. My contact's name is Louis Califonte. He's the casino manager. Cone said I should call Califonte at nine o'clock. I'm hoping we can get Singh to come into the casino. It'll be easier to apprehend him there."

"Get Singh to come in tonight so I can have the day to go shopping. I gotta see the talking statues at Caesars. And we gotta stay to see the fountains at the Bellagio. It wouldn't be right if we left before we saw the fountains."

Shopping would be fun, but there were other things on my mind. Photos of dead people. Carl Rosen missing. Red roses and white carnations. Plus I've never made an out-of-state apprehension and I was counting on Tank's help.

I ate a second sausage and I punched Ranger's number into my phone.

"Have you heard from Tank?" I asked Ranger.

"Tank's here. By the time he got security straight he couldn't get a flight out. The earliest flight we could get him on is today's four o'clock."

"Probably we don't need him. Connie has me on a seven-thirty out of Vegas. I don't expect problems. Connie will get me the paperwork necessary to bring Singh back restrained and she'll make the arrangements with the local police." Now if I just felt half as confident as I sounded, I'd be in good shape. "Unfortunately the hardware's packed in Lula's suitcase. And the airlines lost both her bags."

"I'll have everything you need delivered to your room by noon."

"Did Tank tell you about the photos?"

"Yeah. And I heard from Morelli, too. He's not happy."

"Did Carl Rosen ever show up?"

"You don't want to know about Rosen, babe."

I blew out a sigh and disconnected. Even at seven in the morning, smoke hung in the air on the casino floor. I squinted into the haze and wondered if they were matching the new photos to Rosen. I called Morelli at home. When he didn't pick up I realized it was ten on the East Coast and I tried his cell.

"Yeah," Morelli answered. Halfway through the morning and sounding pissed off.

"Guess who?"

Silence.

I grimaced at Lula.

"He should chill," Lula said, shoveling eggs. "We're working hard here. We got a job to do."

"I heard that," Morelli said. "Tell Lula I've got an outstanding arrest from when she was on the street."

"Tell me about the photos and Carl Rosen."

"They're working on the photos now, but at first glance they look like a match. We found Rosen late last night. Someone dumped him at the corner of Laurel Drive and River Road. He had a white carnation stuffed down his pants and you've seen the photos, so I don't have to describe his head."

"Any suspects?"

"A few. No arrests, if that's what you're asking."

I wasn't looking forward to returning to Trenton. It felt safer in Vegas. Far away from Carl Rosen and the carnation freak. I could easily stay here and sit by the pool and do a little shopping and tell Vinnie the apprehension was more complicated than expected.

"Connie tells me you have a flight out at seven-thirty tonight," Morelli said. "Do you already have Singh in custody?"

"No. If I have problems today, Connie will change the flight."

There was a moment's pause. "Are you expecting problems?"

"I'm *hoping* for problems. If there are problems I might get to stay another day. Maybe another week. It feels safer here than it does in Trenton."

I disconnected and waited while Lula ate the last sausage.

"From the conversation I just heard between you and Ranger, I'm guessing they didn't deliver my bags yet," Lula said. "So I'm going shopping. I gotta get some clothes. All that dumb-ass airline gave me was a toothbrush."

"I thought you gambled all your money away."

"Yeah, but if I shop here in the hotel it goes on our room bill and Vinnie pays. It's only right he pays anyway, on account of this is a business disaster."

I returned to the room and took a shower while Lula

went shopping. We were all packed together to save some money. The room had an Egyptian motif and two queen-size beds. Connie was sound asleep with a pillow over her face. She didn't seem to be bothered by my presence, so I ordered room service coffee and a bakery basket and put a call in to Lou Califonte.

Lou suggested he call Singh and ask him to come in to discuss a job. I was expecting a handcuff delivery sometime this morning, so I asked that Singh be given an early afternoon appointment. Califonte said he'd call back as soon as everything was in place.

I could see the mountains from my room. They were shimmering in the morning heat, smokey blue, lost behind haze. The valley floor leading to the mountains was flat desert broken by roads and strip malls and the backside of the Strip. I could see the billboard and neon sign for the Rio Hotel and Casino.

There was no place else on earth like Vegas. Even Disney couldn't compete with this. I'd been to Vegas twice before. Several years ago and then last year for the PBUS conference. I was always shocked at how fast Vegas grew. Trailer parks, McMansions, artificial lakes and fountains, bigger and more spectacular hotels and malls. They erupted overnight. It was magic. Good old-fashioned American capitalist magic.

It was close to nine when Lula came bustling in. "Just give me a minute to jump in the shower and get dressed and I'm ready to roll," Lula said. "This here's a shopping paradise. They got stuff here that I didn't even know existed. Everything's spandex and sequins. It's a retired ho's dream come true."

By ten we were in a rental Taurus, heading out of town. Lula was reading the map, directing me to the address Singh had given Califonte on his job application. I wasn't making the bust at Singh's house, but I wanted to see it anyway. I wanted to make sure nothing weird was going on.

Much of the sprawl in Vegas is given up to high-end gated golf course communities. We were deep into the sprawl, but we were on the wrong side of the tracks. We were driving past block after block of small dusty Southwest houses, not a ghetto situation of graffiti and uncollected trash, more an area of neglect by necessity. Screen doors were askew, yards were hardscrabble weed and desert dirt, cars had seen a lot of hot, dry miles.

Connie had checked on Singh's address before we left and found he was living with a woman named Susan Lu, a cocktail waitress at Caesars. So here was the Susan in Singh's life. I was guessing Singh met Lu on his business trip, communicated with her by email, and decided to move in.

The house was typical of the neighborhood. It was a modest single-story stucco bungalow. A Joshua tree grew in the front yard. The small backyard was fenced. I didn't see Boo, but then, most of the yard wasn't visible from the street.

"Sure would be tempting to knock on his door and drag his boney ass out here," Lula said. "Then we could lock him in the trunk and go shopping."

"We aren't that good," I said to Lula. "We don't even have handcuffs. I'm not taking a chance on screwing this up."

My cell phone rang. It was Lou Califonte. He was calling to tell me that he hadn't been able to get in touch with Singh. He'd spoken to Susan Lu and Lu told him Singh went out early this morning and hadn't yet returned. Lu expected Singh back by lunchtime. Califonte set up a tentative meeting for two o'clock.

"Don't you hate that?" Lula said. "Right in the middle of our time here. How are we supposed to have any fun like that? I hear Siegfried and Roy got their tigers on display. How many chances you think we're gonna get to see Siegfried's tiger?"

"Just help me get Singh back to the hotel room and you can go off for a couple hours. We don't have to leave for the airport until six-thirty."

"Yeah, it's not like I gotta check luggage."

We returned to the room a little after one. Connie was still asleep with the pillow over her face. There was a small sealed cardboard box on the coffee table. The delivery from Ranger. And there was a small floral arrangement next to it. Red roses and white carnations. The card with the flowers read: *You're one step behind me again. Singh's been eliminated. The game continues.*

I was totally dumbstruck.

"Hey," Lula said. "Are you okay?"

I took a step back, bumped into a chair, and sat down hard. I went lightheaded for a moment. I hadn't been expecting this. I'd been caught totally off guard. The killer knew I was in Vegas. Even worse, he had to be here, too. I was pretty sure he was telling me he'd killed Singh and, according to Susan Lu, Singh was alive this morning.

"I think he's dead," I said.

"Who's dead?"

"Singh."

I'd dropped the card on the floor. Lula picked it up and read it. "I don't get it," she said.

"Just give me a second and I'll explain it to you." I found my way to the bathroom and I stood there until I was sure I wasn't going to throw up. Lula was at the bathroom door, watching. I put a hand up. "I'm getting there," I said. "I was just caught by surprise and it knocked the air out of me." I left the bathroom, walked to the desk, and reread the card. The card

was standard hotel stock. The flowers had been sent
through the hotel.

I called the concierge and waited on hold while he
traced the flowers down. He returned to tell me the order had been phoned in and placed on Carl Rosen's
credit card. The hotel wasn't able to access the call orig-
ination number.

TEN

Lula was standing over Connie. "Do you think she's dead? She's not moving under the pillow."

"Take the pillow off her."

"Not me. I *hate* dead. If she's dead, I don't want to see."

I walked over and took the pillow off Connie's face.

Connie opened an eye and looked up at me. "Did you bring Singh in?"

"No. I think Singh might be dead."

"Dead or alive," Connie said. "It's all the same to me." She sat up in the bed. "I can't get any sleep in this hotel. People keep coming in and out delivering stuff. Did you see you got flowers?"

"About the flowers," I said. And I told them about the carnation killer.

"Holy crap," Lula said. "Why didn't you tell me sooner?"

"I didn't know what to say. The whole thing is so bizarre. And the police wanted the details kept from the public while they tried to match the photos to a victim."

"Hey, I can keep a secret. Look at me. My mouth is zipped," Lula said.

"You can't keep a secret, ever," I said. "You have no sense of secret."

"That's so not true. I didn't tell you about Joe and Terry Gilman, did I?"

For a couple beats no one in the room said anything. We just stared at each other with our mouths open.

"I didn't say that," Lula said.

I felt my eyebrows pull together. "What about Joe and Terry Gilman?"

"You keep doing that and you're going to need Botox," Lula said.

"Are you talking about the jumping out the window incident?"

"No. I'm talking about the coming out of the motel, looking chummy incident."

"When?"

"I guess it must have been about two weeks ago. It was a Saturday afternoon and I was going shopping at Quaker Bridge and you know how there are a couple motels on Route One that are mostly by the hour? Well, I saw them coming out of one of those skanky motels. It was the one with the blue trim and the wishing well in the front. I almost ran off the road."

"You're sure it was Joe and Terry?"

"I bet they were doing police business," Lula said. "That's why I didn't tell you. I knew you'd get that look that you got now. And you'd get all huffy and make a big thing for nothing."

I used my fingertips to smooth away the frown line in my forehead. "I don't get huffy. Do I look huffy?"

"Fuckin' A," Lula said.

At least she took my mind off the flower freak. It's always nice to have a choice of things to worry about.

"Open the box from Ranger," I said to Lula. "I have to call Morelli and tell him about the flowers."

Morelli answered on a sigh. "Yeah?"

I meant to start out with the facts about the flowers, but the wiring between my brain and my mouth got crossed and I started with Terry Gilman. "So," I said to Morelli as my opening line, "have you seen Terry Gilman lately?"

"I saw her yesterday. Why?"

"You are such a jerk."

There was a beat of silence where I figured Morelli was staring down at his shoe and counting his lucky stars he never married me. "That's what you called to tell me? I'm a jerk?"

"I called to tell you I just got a floral arrangement. Red roses and white carnations." I read the card to him. "The flowers were ordered through the hotel and placed on Carl Rosen's credit card. You might want to remind the Rosen family to cancel Carl's cards. It looks like the killer lifted Rosen's MasterCard."

"He's loving this," Morelli said. "This is like a chess game. And he's winning. He's taking your pieces one by one."

"This particular piece was with Susan Lu first thing this morning and hasn't been heard from since. I don't suppose you have Bart Cone in custody."

"Not in custody, but he's being watched. He's not in Vegas. I'm almost sure of it."

"What about the other Cones?"

"All three were in for questioning late yesterday afternoon. It's Saturday so they're not at work, but I'll make sure they're tracked down and accounted for."

"I'm going back out to talk to Susan Lu," I said to Morelli. "I'll call you if anything turns up."

"I'd feel better if you just stayed in your hotel room until your plane. Let the Vegas police talk to Susan Lu."

"I'll be fine. Ranger had a care package dropped

off for me. And I've got Lula and Connie to watch my back."

"Oh *shit*," Morelli said.

"This is like Christmas," Lula said, opening the box from Ranger. "I love getting presents. Look at this. Pepper spray. One for each of us. And handcuffs. Not the cheap-ass kind, either. These are good-quality cuffs. And leg shackles. And a thirty-eight Smith and Wesson snubby revolver. Guess that would be yours since I shoot a Glock. And here's a box of rounds for your thirty-eight." Lula pawed through the packing. "Hey, there's no Glock. Where's *my* gun?" She dumped the box upside down and a note and a stun gun fell out.

I took the note and left the stun gun for Lula.

Call if you need help. I'll come to your room at six to take you to the airport. Erik. His phone number was printed at the bottom of the note.

Lula was reading over my shoulder. "Who's Erik?"

"Ranger said he was sending hardware to replace what we lost in luggage. It looks like Erik comes with the hardware."

I loaded the .38 and slipped it into my purse. I stuffed the personal-size pepper spray canister into my jeans pocket, I stuck the cuffs half in and half out of the back of my pants, and then I shrugged into a lightweight zipper-front sweatshirt that was going to make me sweat, but it covered the cuffs. I called to ask that the car be brought around from valet parking.

"I'm going, too," Connie said. "Give me five minutes to jump in the shower."

A half hour later the three of us left the room for the lobby. Lula on one side of me, Connie on the other. Connie had made a phone call to a local bondsman and had arranged for a second arms delivery. As a result,

Connie and Lula now wore two guns apiece. They each had a gun at the small of their back and they each had one in their purse. My fear of getting shot by the carnation killer was considerably less than my fear that I'd get shot by Connie or Lula.

"You know what I think?" Lula said in the elevator. "I think we're an accident waiting to happen."

I could ask Erik to ride along with us, but I'd had some past experience with Ranger's men and there was no guarantee that Erik would be any less scary than the carnation killer. "Just keep your eyes open. We'll be fine."

Connie didn't say anything. Connie had some Mafia skeletons in her closet and Connie took soldiering seriously.

It was after noon when we pulled into Susan Lu's driveway. Lula, Connie, and I got out and went to Lu's front door.

Susan Lu was about five feet, four inches with a flat dish face and glossy straight black hair. She looked older than Singh. I placed her somewhere between forty and forty-five. She was surprised to find us on her porch and immediately bristled. Probably we looked like door-to-door missionaries, so I understood the bristle. I looked over her shoulder at a small curly white dog scratching at a baby gate that confined him to the kitchen. Boo.

I identified myself, introduced Lula and Connie, and I asked if we could come in. Lu said no and we went in anyway. Lu was a lightweight.

I already knew Singh wasn't in the house. The car still wasn't in the driveway. And besides, I was pretty sure he was dead. Still, I asked anyway.

"Is Samuel Singh here?" I asked Susan Lu.

"He isn't," Lu said. "He went out first thing this morning for a pack of cigarettes for me and he hasn't returned. He should have been back hours ago. And he isn't answering his cell phone. Men are such shits. Listen, I'd like to chat, but I have to get ready for work and I'm not feeling all that social without my goddamn cigarettes."

The dog was barking now. *Yap yap yap.* And every time it yapped its little front paws would come off the ground.

"Is that Samuel's dog?"

"Yeah, I don't know what's wrong with it. Usually the little turd just mopes in the corner. I've never seen it trying to get out like this."

Lula took a step back and nervously shifted foot to foot. God only knows what she had in her purse. Suckling pig, two dozen hamburgers, a twenty-pound turkey.

"Sammy brought the dog with him just to piss off some awful old woman and her daughter. He was boarding with them and he said the old woman was something out of a horror movie. He wanted to take a picture of himself with the dog and send it back to them, but he hasn't gotten around to it. After he gets his picture the dog's going to the pound. Nasty beast."

I gave Susan Lu my card. "Tell Samuel to call me when he comes in."

"Sure."

Lula, Connie, and I left Lu, got into the car, and I backed out of the driveway. I drove around the block and parked three doors down from Lu, behind a van so we could watch the house.

"You think Singh's gonna show up?" Lula wanted to know.

"Nope."

"Me, neither."

"You parking here so you can keep an eye on Lu?"

"Yep."

"You're waiting for her to leave and then you're gonna snatch the dog, aren't you?"

"Yep."

Connie was in the backseat, probably reviewing in her mind which of the local bondsmen she'd use to bail us out after we were arrested for breaking and entering.

After fifteen minutes of no air-conditioning, the car started to bake under the desert sun. Lula immediately fell asleep in the heat. She was head back, mouth open. And she was snoring. Loud.

"Holy mother," Connie said, "I've never heard anyone snore like this. It's like being locked in a car with a jet engine."

I gave Lula a shove. "Wake up. You're snoring."

"The hell I am," Lula said. "I don't snore." And she went back to snoring.

"I can't take it," Connie said. "I've got to get out of the car."

I joined her and we walked down the street. We were wearing baseball hats and dark glasses but no sunblock and I could feel the sun scorching the exposed skin on my arm.

"Let me run through this," Connie said. "Lillian Paressi, Howie at McDonald's, Carl Rosen, and possibly Samuel Singh are all tied to the same serial killer. And now he's targeted you."

"I don't know about Howie, Carl, or Samuel, but Lillian Paressi received red roses and white carnations and a note just before she was killed."

"Like the flowers and notes you've been getting."

"Yeah. So I'm guessing he likes to taunt his victims. Likes to get them afraid before he strikes. Some kind of game for him."

"Are you sure it's a *him?*"

"I'm not sure of anything. In the beginning I suspected Bart Cone, but the police are keeping a close watch on him. If Cone's still in Trenton and Singh turns up dead, that eliminates Cone from the suspect list."

When we got back to the car, Lula was still snoring

and there were two dogs patiently sitting on the curb by the passenger side door.

"I don't know what's more creepy," Connie said. "You getting stalked by a killer or Lula walking around with a purse filled with pork chops. I'm feeling like I'm in Stephen King land."

It was two o'clock so I called Califonte and asked if Singh was there. Califonte said no, sorry. I gave Califonte my cell number and asked him to call me if Singh showed up.

Connie and I got back into the car and put our fingers in our ears. After five minutes my shirt was soaked and sweat was running down the side of my face. This was the glorious life of a bounty hunter.

"Tell me again why we're sitting here, melting," Connie said.

"The dog."

"I need a better reason."

"There's something about that dog that gives me an estrogen attack. He's small and helpless looking. And those little button eyes! The eyes are so trusting. And he's going to the *pound*. How awful is that? I can't let that happen."

"So you have to save the dog."

"He's counting on me."

"Stephanie to the rescue," Connie said.

"I could call you a cab," I said. "And you could go back to the hotel."

"No way. I'd have to sit around the pool and get a tan and have half-naked waiters bring me cold drinks. Where's the fun in that when I could be sitting here listening to Lula?"

Susan Lu left the house a little after two. She walked to a bus stop on the far corner. After five minutes a bus appeared and Lu got on.

"Thank God," Connie said. "I'm at the end of the line with the snoring and the sweating."

I gave Lula a shove. "Wake up. Susan Lu left the house. We can get the dog now."

Lula squinted at me. "I feel like my eyes are fried. I'm not as young as I used to be. I can't do this all-night shit anymore. And this place is hotter than snot. How can anyone live here?"

I cranked the car over and pulled into Lu's driveway. Lula, Connie, and I got out and walked around to the back kitchen door.

"Door's locked," Lula said. "Too bad you have this thing about busting in."

"This is for a good cause," I said. "I suppose we could force the door if we did it really carefully."

"Hunh," Lula said. She swung her purse into the window beside the door and shattered the window. "Oops," Lula said. "Guess I accidentally broke a window." Then she reached in and opened the door.

"Cripes," Connie said. "Could you make more noise? Maybe there's someone left in the neighborhood who didn't hear that."

I tiptoed over the glass shards, scooped up Boo, and handed him to Lula. I quickly walked through the rest of the house. I took Singh's laptop, but found nothing else of interest. I wiped Lula's prints off the doorknob and we left.

"We're like Robin Hood or something," Lula said. "We rescued this cute little guy. I feel like singing the Robin Hood theme song."

We stopped and thought about that for a second.

"Damn," Lula said. "There's no Robin Hood theme song."

We got into the rental Taurus and hightailed it out of the neighborhood. Best not to delay, in case someone

confused us with dognappers and called the police.
The police might not understand about Robin Hood.

I stopped at a supermarket and bought a dog leash and
collar, and a small bag of dog food for Boo. I bought
Popsicles for Connie and me and two pounds of sliced
deli ham for Lula.

I didn't know if dogs were allowed at the Luxor and I
didn't think it was worth the hassle to check. I wrapped
the dog in my sweatshirt and smuggled him up to the
room.

"Isn't this a pisser," Lula said, going into the room.
"Look at what's here. My luggage. Came just in time to
lug it back home."

"Hopefully they won't lose it this time."

"Damn right they won't lose it. I'm not flying. I'm
done flying. I'm driving home."

"It'll take you days."

"I don't care. Nothing you could say would make me
get back on a plane. I got the rental car and I'm driving.
And I can take Boo. I don't like the idea of handing him
over to those airport people."

Boo was on the floor, snooping around.

"He's a cute little guy," Lula said. "I can see why
Nonnie wanted him back."

I had a problem now. There was a small chance that
the flowers were a hoax and something other than death
had kept Singh from showing for the job interview. I
didn't want to take off only to find out down the road
that Singh was alive and well in Vegas. I called Morelli
and Ranger. Neither had anything to report. I called my
family next.

"We're all fine," Grandma said. "Except for Albert,
who seems to be in labor. That isn't possible, is it?"

When I was a kid my family seemed so stable. I was
the flaky kid and my mom was always right, my sister

was perfect, my dad was the rock. It hasn't been until recently that I've come to realize nothing is that simple. People are complicated and chock full of problems. That said, my family's problems don't seem so huge. We're a family of plodders. We put one foot in front of the other and keep going forward. And eventually we get someplace. Maybe the place isn't spectacular, but it's a place all the same. And while we're plodding, sometimes the problems solve themselves, sometimes the problems get pushed low on the list of priorities and get forgotten, and sometimes the problems cause little pockets of irritation in our bowels.

Mostly we solve our problems with cake.

I was hungry and I would have liked to order room service, but I was afraid Boo would be discovered. Room service is third on my list of favorite things. Birthday cake is first. Sex is second. And then room service. Room service is better than having a mother. You order what you want and they bring it to your door, guilt-free, no strings attached. Pretty amazing, huh?

"I'm going out for something to eat," I said. "And I'm going to check on Susan Lu. I want to make sure she really did go to work."

"I'm with you," Lula said.

Connie was on her feet. "Count me in."

The three Mouseketeers.

We gave Boo a glass of water and told him to be a good dog. We put the *Do Not Disturb* sign on the door, locked up, and left.

According to Connie's information, Susan Lu worked at Caesars. Caesars was exactly the wrong distance from the Luxor. Too short to feel justified taking a cab. Too long to hoof it in the heat.

We stepped outside and sucked in blast furnace–quality air and Connie made the decision for us.

"I'm not walking," she said. "And I'll shoot anyone who tries to make me."

Caesars is everything a casino should be . . . noisy, smokey, gaudy, and bustling with people who can't wait to throw their money away. And if that isn't enough, it has a terrific shopping center. The waitresses servicing the game tables all wore little toga outfits. Some looked better in their togas than others. I suspected Lu would not look *wowie kazowie* in her toga. We did a casual walk around the room and didn't spot Susan Lu.

"This isn't gonna work," Lula said. "It's too big. There's too many of the toga women. And there are cocktail lounges on the sides, too. And restaurants."

"I don't know how to break this to you," Connie said, "but I think we're being followed. You see the guy in black over by the statue of Caesar?"

Lula and I turned and looked.

"Don't look!" Connie hissed.

Lula and I stopped looking.

"You have to be sneaky," Connie said.

Lula and I did a sneaky look.

"I don't recognize him," I said.

Connie slid him a sideways glance. "He was in the lobby of the Luxor when we came through."

"Probably just a coincidence," I said.

He was about five feet, ten inches and average build. He wore a black suit, black shirt, and black silk tie. His hair was dark and slicked back behind his ears.

"I bet he's got a purple car with a bobble-head doll on the dash," Lula said. "I bet he's a pimp. I guess I know a pimp when I see one. The question is, why would a pimp be following us?"

Connie and I looked at Lula.

"What?" Lula said.

Lula was wearing a skin-tight pink stretchy T-shirt

with *sexy* written across her boobs in silver sequins. It had a low scoop neck showing an acre of cleavage and it was tucked into a matching spandex miniskirt.

"Hey, I'm not the one wearing a shirt asking if you got crabs," Lula said.

I looked down at my shirt. "It's for the baseball team in Lakewood. Joe bought it for me."

"Hunh," Lula said.

I didn't think the guy in black looked like a pimp. I thought he looked like someone who bought *GQ* and took it seriously. Probably he was from L.A. and worked in the CAA mailroom.

"Let's go across the room and find a blackjack table," Connie said to me. "See if he follows you."

"Fine, but I can't play blackjack. I'll just stand and watch."

"That's ridiculous," Connie said. "Everyone can play blackjack. All you have to do is count to twenty-one." Connie was pulling me along by my purse strap. "I'll have Vinnie bankroll you."

"*You* play blackjack."

"That won't work," Connie said. "I want to see if he's after you. Maybe he's the carnation guy. This way, you sit down and Lula and I can sort of fade away, all the while keeping our eyes on you. Then we wait to see what he does."

"Here he comes," Lula said. "He's coming along with us. He's trying not to be noticed, but I'm on to him."

Connie tugged me toward an empty chair. "Sit," she said, "there's an opening at this table."

"This is a twenty-five-dollar table," I said. "Aren't there any loose change tables?"

There were two men and two women already playing at the table. They were drinking and smoking and their faces were without expression. They looked like they knew what they were doing. They'd look at the dealer and tap the table and obviously that meant something. One of the women wanted to double. She lost her chips after that, so I made a mental note not to double.

When the hand was done Connie dropped fifty dollars on the table. The dealer gave me two chips and the fifty bucks got whisked away by the dealer and stuffed into a slot on the table.

Everyone put chips out, so I put one out, too. I looked over my shoulder at Connie. Connie was gone. When I swung my attention back to the table I had two cards face up in front of me. A king and an ace.

"Twenty-one wins," the dealer said. And he gave me a bunch of chips.

Wow. I won. I didn't even have to do anything.

Everyone else played out their hands and then we all started again with new chips on the table. I put mine out, too. The dealer gave me two cards face up. A six and a jack. Panic. I had to add. A jack was worth what? Ten? Okay, ten seemed reasonable for a jack. So I had sixteen. I looked around. Everyone was waiting for me to say something.

The dealer asked me if I wanted a card. More panic. I didn't want to go over twenty-one. I had to subtract. I *hate* to subtract. "Sure," I said. "Give me another card."

The dealer asked me if I was *certain* I wanted another card. "You have a six showing and *the book* says not to take another card," the dealer said.

I didn't know what book he was talking about, but all the other players agreed with the dealer and *the book* so I decided not to take a card.

The dealer had a six and a ten on the table. He dealt himself another ten. "Dealer busts," he said.

And I got another chip. Hot damn. No wonder people liked to gamble. This was easy.

We started a new game and I got sixteen again with the first two cards. The dealer had a nine showing. I told him I didn't want any more cards. What the hell, it worked the first two times. Now he told me *the book* didn't like that decision. Well, God forbid I should go against *the book*. "Okeydokey," I said. "I'll go with the book and take another card."

I got dealt a king of hearts.

"Busts," the dealer said, and he took my chips and my cards.

So much for *the book*.

I played another hand. Lost another chip. Everyone played their hands out and we started over. Connie was nowhere to be seen. The guy in black was behind me, watching me. I could feel him back there. The photo images of shattered skulls popped into my head. The memory of the heat and numbing blackness that followed the hit from the dart washed over me. I felt a panic attack trying to get a toehold.

The dealer wanted to know if I was going to play.

"What?" I asked.

"You need to put a chip in to play."

I shoved a red chip into my circle.

"Red chips are worth five," the dealer said. "This table has a twenty-five-dollar minimum."

I pushed a different colored chip at him. The chips had numbers on them, but I was too flustered to make sense of it.

The dealer gave me a ten of spades and a two of hearts. This was easy to add. Twelve. A long way to go to twenty-one, right? I asked for another card. This started a lot of arguing. Apparently *the book* wasn't clear on this one. The dealer gave me a ten of diamonds. Damn! Busted again.

I didn't know exactly how much I had because I was having a hard time adding up all the different colored chips, but I knew I didn't have a lot. One more hand, maybe.

When the new game started I pushed a couple chips into my ring. The dealer gave me a nine of spades and a three of clubs. I bit into my lower lip, unsure what to do, and I felt a hand settle on my shoulder. I turned and looked. It was the guy in black.

"I'm going to help you," he said.

There was a lot of noise behind me. I heard Lula let out a shriek and the guy in black gasped in surprise, jerked away from me, and went over backward. Everyone at the table stood and gawked, including me.

Lula and the guy in black were on the floor. Lula was ass up, on top of the guy in black. You could hardly see him under the pink spandex. He was squashed spread eagle under Lula so that only his hands and feet stuck out. Connie was standing on one of his hands.

"Don't freakin' move," Connie yelled at the poor smushed guy in black.

From what I could see there wasn't much chance of him moving. I wasn't even sure he was still breathing.

Uniformed and plainclothes security instantly appeared and wrestled Lula off the guy in black.

"He was going for a gun," Lula said. "He's a killer."

The guy in black didn't move. He was still on his back, gasping for air. "I have identification in my inside jacket pocket," he said. "And I think I have a broken back."

"Can you move your toes?" one of the security guards asked him.

"Yeah."

"How about your fingers?"

He wiggled the fingers on one hand. Connie was still standing on the other hand.

"Ow," the guy in black said to Connie.

Connie stepped off his hand. "Sorry," she said.

One of the plainclothes men lifted the identification. "Erik Salvatora. Looks like he's a rent-a-cop."

"I'm a licensed private investigator and a security specialist," Salvatora said. "I'm employed by RangeMan LLC and I was asked to protect Ms. Plum while she's in town. God only knows why when she's got Big Bertha and the Bonecrusher with her."

He was Ranger's man. RangeMan was Ranger's corporate name.

"Hey," Lula said. "Watch who you're calling Big Bertha. Nobody tolerates that political incorrectness anymore, you little candy ass."

"This was a terrible misunderstanding," I told everyone. "My friends and I didn't realize he was assigned to guard me. My usual bodyguard missed his flight."

Now they were all wondering who the hell I was that I needed a bodyguard. And that was fine by me because I wanted this to go away. We were all carrying guns, probably illegally. I had no idea what the gun laws were in Nevada.

"I thought he was going for a gun," Lula said.

Erik struggled to get up. "I was going for my wallet. I was going to buy her some chips. I was supposed to keep my distance, but I couldn't stand watching her play anymore. She's the worst blackjack player I've ever seen."

"Really sorry," I said. "Can we take you to a hospital or something?"

"No! I'll be okay. Probably just a slipped disc and possibly a broken bone or two in my hand."

"Don't worry about six o'clock," I called after him. "I might not be going to the airport."

He looked at me blank faced. As if taking me to the airport was too terrible to contemplate right now. "Okay," he said. And he limped away.

"Sorry," I said to the security people. "I guess we'll be going now, too."

"We'll see you out," one of the uniforms said.

We were escorted out of Caesars, the doors closed behind us, and we stood blinking in the sun, waiting for our eyes to adjust to daylight.

"That was sort of embarrassing," Lula said.

I whipped my phone out and I called Morelli. "Reporting in," I told him. "Anything new?"

"I was just going to call you," Morelli said. "I know a guy on the Vegas police force. I gave him a call when I got off the phone with you and asked him to keep his eyes open for Singh. I just got a call back from him. They found Singh in his car in the airport parking lot about an hour ago. Shot twice in the back of the head, close range. We're checking the passenger lists on all Vegas flights in and out of LaGuardia, Newark, and Philadelphia."

I had a moment's pause where I didn't know what I felt. There was an emotion struggling around inside me. Relief that there was closure on the Singh hunt. Disappointment that I hadn't been able to save him. And dread. The killer's constant presence was wearing me down.

"The Cones?" I asked.

"All present and accounted for."

"Too bad. That would have been so easy. At least I can leave Vegas now. And I'm bringing something home with me that might be helpful . . . Singh's laptop."

Silence at the other end. "Susan Lu gave it to you?"

"I found it on the sidewalk. I think there might have been a break-in and the laptop got dropped and left behind somehow. And I found it."

I wasn't sure what was going on at the other end of the connection. Either Morelli was smiling or else he was banging his head against his desk. I was going to go with smiling.

"I'll pick you up at the airport," Morelli said. "Try to stay out of trouble. Do you need a police escort when you leave your hotel?"

"No. I've had enough police escorts for one day. Thanks anyway." I disconnected and relayed the information about Singh. "The Vegas police found Singh at the airport an hour ago. Two bullet holes in the back of his head," I told Connie and Lula.

"I was sort of hoping it was a bluff," Lula said. "That the killer wasn't really here and he sent you the flowers to get you to go home. Not that I'm scared or anything."

We all did some mental knuckle cracking and tried not to look nervous.

"We should go back to the hotel," I said. "If we're going to make the plane we need to pack."

Everyone agreed, so we flagged down a cab and we all piled in. I called Ranger on the way. I told him about Singh and then I told him about Salvatora.

"I already talked to Salvatora," Ranger said. "His hand is okay, but he said he needs a chiropractor for his back." Ranger paused and when he continued I could hear the laughter in his voice. "Salvatora said a fat woman in pink spandex and silver sequins fell on him."

"That would be Lula. And she didn't fall on him. She tackled him."

"She did a good job," Ranger said. "I'm sorry I missed it. Salvatora's partner will take you to the airport."

"How will I know him?"

"He looks like Salvatora . . . but more."

Five minutes later we were walking through the hotel to the elevators and we were being very vigilant. We didn't know what the killer looked like. It didn't seem likely that he would strike in a public place, but there was no guarantee.

We took the elevator to the eighteenth floor, walked halfway down the hall, and Connie unlocked our room door. She stepped in and muffled a scream. Lula and I were directly behind her and we had the same reaction.

The dog had destroyed the room. Pillows were chewed. The blanket was shredded. A corner of the mattress was missing. Toilet paper was everywhere.

Connie closed and locked the door behind us. "Don't anybody panic. It's probably not as bad as it looks. Cheap mattress, cheap blanket, right? How much could a pillow cost?"

"Uh-oh," Lula said. "I think he pissed on the cable wire and shorted the television. This here's like traveling with a metal band," Lula said.

Boo was on the bed, tail wagging.

"But look at him," I said. "He's so cute. And he looks sorry. Don't you think he looks sorry?"

"I think he looks happy," Lula said. "I think he's smiling. I'm glad we saved this little guy. That bag of monkey doody Mrs. Apusenja deserves him."

"We weren't gone that long," Connie said. "How could such a little dog do all this damage?"

"Guess he was feeling anxiety," Lula said. "Poor thing's been through a lot, what with getting dognapped and everything. And look at him, he's just a puppy. He might even be teething. At least he didn't eat the flowers. It's nice to come back to fresh flowers in the room."

"They were sent by a serial killer! *They're death flowers*," I said.

"Well, yeah, but they're still nice," Lula said.

I looked at my watch. I had to pack. "Not a lot of time to take care of this mess," I said.

"Here's the plan," Connie said. "We check out and it all goes on Vinnie's bill."

"See that," Lula said. "This dog's nothing but good luck. We get to stick it to Vinnie all because this dog was smart enough to eat the room. I think this here's been a positive experience. That's my new philosophy anyway. Nothing but positive experiences. That's why I'm driving home from here."

"You've got to be kidding," Connie said. "It'll take you days."

"Don't matter. I'm not getting back on a plane. I'm done with planes. They aren't any fun. All that searching and starving and standing around in lines. I don't do lines. That's another part of my new philosophy. No lines. And I can take Boo with me if I drive. Me and Boo can have a road trip. I'm starting to get real excited about this. I always wanted to have a dog when I was a kid, but I never had the chance. I was dog deprived."

"Works for me," Connie said. "If you take Boo we don't have the hassle of crating him and getting him on the plane."

I called valet parking and had the car brought around. I gave Lula the pepper spray and the stun gun and two hundred dollars. Connie contributed another hundred and fifty. It was all the money we had between us. We loaded Lula, Boo, and Lula's luggage into the car and waved good-bye.

"I'm not sure if she's the smart one or the dumb one," Connie said.

There were only two of us now and we each had a loaded gun in our pockets. We stopped at the snack bar, got a bag of food, and returned to the room to finish packing.

My packing was simple. Take all the little complimentary soaps and shampoos from the bathroom and put them in my carry-on bag. Connie's packing was more complicated.

"Oh shit," Connie said, "look at this."

She was holding up the wedding photo. It had a few dog tooth marks in the lower left corner.

"Do you suppose you actually got married?" I asked her.

"I don't know. I don't remember." She closed her eyes and groaned. "Sweet Jesus, please don't let me be married to an Elvis impersonator."

"There must be some way you can find out," I said. "There have to be records. Probably you can have it annulled."

There was a rap on the door and Connie and I went into panic mode for fear it was the maid. I looked out the security peephole and recognized Erik's partner from Ranger's description. The guy in the hall looked a lot like Erik, but bigger and weirder and scarier. He looked like a Vegas pit boss on steroids.

"It's our chauffeur," I said.

I opened the door and invited the big scary guy in. He was dark-skinned with slicked-back black hair and dark, heavy-lidded eyes. He was wearing black cowboy boots, black leather pants, a black leather jacket, and a shiny black silk shirt that was unbuttoned half down his chest. He had a colorful crucifixion tattooed onto the back of his left hand. And he had a gun at the small of his back, under the jacket.

"I'm Miguel," he said. "I'm Erik's partner."

"Jeez," I said. "We're all really sorry about Erik. I hope he's okay."

Miguel gave a brief nod, which I took to mean that Erik had his back straightened out and was recovering nicely.

"I'm ready to go," I told him, handing over the cuffs and shackles and guns. "My partner is driving back. She has the rest of the hardware."

Another small nod. Fine by him.

Connie was packed, but she was in the middle of the room with the photo in her hand and she was looking conflicted. "I need to get this straightened out," she said. "I'm going to stay and catch a later flight."

"I can stay with you," I said.

She shook her head. "Not necessary. You'll be safer in Trenton with Morelli."

And Connie would be safer in Vegas without *me*. I gave her a hug and my room key. Miguel shouldered my bag, stepped aside, and followed me wordlessly to the elevator.

This is the thing about men who never talk. It's easier to assume that they're strong and that they have the sort of wily cunning a woman wants in a bodyguard. I try not to be judgmental, but in all honesty, I'd feel less secure if Miguel had rambled on about how difficult it was to find a decent silk shirt. So no conversation was okay by me because I needed some help being brave. I wanted to think this guy could leap tall buildings in a single bound.

I left the hotel and slipped into the air-conditioned security of a new black Mercedes. "Your car?" I asked Miguel.

"More or less."

He walked me to the security check, waited watchfully while I went through. No hassle this time. And then I was on my own. In theory this was a safe zone. Still, I found a seat with my back to the wall and I boarded last, looking for familiar or suspicious faces.

I was in the last row with three empty seats next to me. Lula's seat, Connie's seat, and a seat reserved for Singh. If Singh had been with me, we would have boarded first and if at all possible through a side door. Walking a guy in chains down the aisle in front of the paying customers doesn't set the tone for a stress-free flight.

I was happy to once again have my back to the wall, but I felt naked without hardware. It was a creepy thought that the killer might be on the plane. He could be the preppy-looking guy across the aisle or the hairy guy three rows up. They'd watched me take my seat.

Hard to tell if they wanted to kill me or if they just didn't have anything better to do than to stare.

By the time I deplaned in Newark I was too tired to be afraid. God bless those lucky souls who can sleep while flying. I've never been one of them.

I'd arranged to meet Morelli at baggage claim. I didn't have any baggage to claim, but it was the easiest pickup point. It was seven in the morning, Jersey time. My teeth felt furry and my eyes ached.

I searched the crowd for Morelli and felt my heart skip a beat when I found him. Morelli never blended. He was movie-star handsome and looked like a man you'd avoid in a fight. Women always looked twice at Morelli, but seldom approached. With the possible exception of Terry Gilman.

Morelli's face softened when he saw me. He reached out and drew me to him, wrapping his arms around me. He kissed my neck and held me close for a moment. "You look beat," he said. He stepped back, took my bag, and smiled at me. "But pretty."

I gave him a sideways glance. "You want something."

"The computer for starters."

"Always a cop."

"Not always. It's Sunday. How tired are you?"

I was dog tired until I saw Morelli. Now that I was next to him I was having some non-sleeping thoughts. The nonsleeping thoughts lasted about thirty seconds into the ride home.

I opened my eyes and stared up at Morelli. He was out of the truck, trying to get me awake enough to get me into the house. He had my seat belt off and my bag slung over his shoulder.

"Jeez, Steph," he said, "didn't you sleep on the plane?"

"I never sleep on a plane. I have to be ready in case

it crashes." I heaved myself off the seat and shuffled up the sidewalk. Morelli opened the door and I braced myself for the Bob attack. We heard him thundering through the house, coming from the kitchen. He reached the small foyer and Morelli held up a giant dog biscuit. Bob's eyes got wide, Morelli threw the biscuit over Bob's head down the hallway, and Bob turned in mid-gallop and followed the biscuit.

"Pretty smart," I said.

"I should take him to obedience training, but I never seem to get to it."

What Morelli meant was that he should try obedience training *again*. Bob had flunked out twice before.

Morelli set the bag on the floor at the foot of the stairs and removed the computer. "I'm not going to open this. I'm going to turn it over to the experts first thing tomorrow."

That had been my thought, too. I hadn't fooled with the computer.

"Have you told Vinnie about Singh?" Morelli asked.

"I left that for Connie. She stayed behind to clean some things up."

"Vinnie'll put a good spin on it. You found Singh. That's the important part. The system worked."

"I need more sleep," I said. "Wake me up when it's time for dessert."

"Bad news," Morelli said. "Dessert will be too late. We're expected for dinner at my mom's house. We accepted this invitation two weeks ago. It's Mary Elizabeth's birthday."

I'd totally forgotten. Mary Elizabeth is Joe's great-aunt. She's a chain-smoking booze hound and she's a retired nun. And no party for Mary Elizabeth would be complete without Grandma Bella because Mary Elizabeth is Bella's younger sister. I got a sharp pain in my right temple and my blood ran cold. I was having dinner with Grandma Bella.

"Are you okay?" Morelli asked. "You look sort of white."

"I'm having dinner with Grandma Bella. My life is passing in front of my eyes. I'm as good as dead. I should just stand outside and let the carnation killer shoot me."

"You have to have the right attitude about Grandma Bella."

"And that would be what?"

Joe shrugged. "She's crazy."

I slept until late afternoon. When I woke I was in Joe's bed, still dressed in my travel clothes, partially tangled in a lightweight summer patchwork quilt. The sheets were rumpled under me and the pillowcase was damp with sweat and humidity. Aunt Rose's gauzy curtains hung limp against the open window. The air was heavy, but the light was soft. The room felt like Joe and good sex. There were mental imprints of time spent here that didn't get smoothed away with new sheets. If I closed my eyes in this room, even if I was alone, I could feel Morelli's hands on me.

And today the room smelled like popcorn.

The popcorn aroma was drifting up from the living room where Joe and Bob were watching a ball game. I shuffled downstairs and looked in the popcorn bowl. Empty. I checked out the game. Not interesting.

Joe looked over at me. "I could call and cancel."

"You can't do that. It's a birthday!"

"I'd come up with something good. I'd say you broke your leg. Or you had an appendix attack. Or you insisted we stay home and have a lot of sloppy sex."

"Thanks. I appreciate the thought, but I don't think any of those would work."

"The sex would work."

I smiled at him and took the empty popcorn bowl back to the kitchen. "Nice try."

I toasted a bagel, smeared it with too much butter, and ate it with the butter dripping down my arm. Do I know how to eat a bagel, or what? I went back upstairs, took a shower, and got dressed for dinner.

I was halfway through makeup when Morelli appeared in the bathroom doorway. He leaned a shoulder against the jamb, hands in pants pockets. "We're late," he said. "How's it going?"

It wasn't going good. Dinner with Joe's family had me in a state. I'd accidentally poked myself in the eye with the mascara wand and almost gone blind. "It's going great," I said. "Give me another minute."

"You have a big black blob on your eye."

"I know that. Go away!"

Ten minutes later I clattered down the stairs in my high-heeled strappy sandals, the swirly skirt, and a stretchy top. It was the best I could do under the circumstances. I didn't have a lot of clothes at Joe's house.

"Nice," Joe said, eyes on the skirt. "I'm going to have fun with this outfit when we get home. You have panties on, right?"

"Right."

"I don't suppose you'd want to take them off."

"I don't suppose."

"Doesn't hurt to ask," Morelli said with a grin. "It would make dinner more interesting."

Everyone was at the table when we arrived. Joe's mom was at the head. Grandma Bella was next to her, then Mary Elizabeth. Joe's sister, Cathy, was next to Mary Elizabeth. Joe's Uncle Mario was at the foot of the table. Cathy's husband was seated across from her.

Joe and I were seated across from Mary Elizabeth and Bella.

"Sorry we're late," Joe said. "Cop business."

Mary Elizabeth was looking very happy. She had an empty highball glass in front of her and a half-empty wineglass. "More like monkey business," she said.

Bella shook her finger at Joe. "All the Morelli men are sex fiends."

"Hey," Uncle Mario said, "how's that to talk?"

Mario was Bella's first cousin and the only male Morelli left from Bella's generation. Morelli men weren't especially long-lived. Mario was small and wrinkled, but still had a full head of wiry black hair. It was rumored he colored it with shoe polish.

Grandma Bella fixed an eye on Mario. "Are you telling me you're not a sex fiend?"

"There's a difference between an Italian stallion and a sex fiend. I'm an Italian stallion."

Joe filled our wineglasses. "Salute," he said.

Everyone held their glasses high. "Salute."

"I didn't see you in church today," Grandma Bella said to Joe.

"I had to miss today," Joe said.

And last week. And the week before that. And come to think of it, last time Joe was in church was Christmas.

"I prayed for you," Bella told him.

Joe took a sip of wine and looked at Bella over the rim of his glass. "Thanks."

"And I prayed that the bambinos would get over the death of their mother."

Joe's mother gripped her wineglass and narrowed her eyes at Bella. I stopped breathing. Everyone else slumped in their seat with an *Uh boy, here it comes* sigh.

"The bambinos?" Joe asked.

"You will have many bambinos. The mother will die. It will be very sad. I saw it in a vision."

I bit down hard on my lower lip. My poor little bambinos!

"Don't worry," Bella said to me. "It's not you. The woman in the vision was blond."

ELEVEN

Joe drank more wine and draped an arm around my shoulders. "At least you're not the dead woman in this vision."

Mrs. Morelli threw a dinner roll at him and hit him in the head. "That's a stupid thing to say to a woman. Sometimes you're just like your father." She crossed herself and looked penitent. "God rest his soul."

Everyone at the table crossed themselves except Joe. "God rest his soul," everyone said.

"And *you*," Mrs. Morelli said to her mother-in-law. "No more with the visions."

"I can't help I have visions," Grandma Bella said. "I'm an instrument of God."

This brought on a lot more crossing and Uncle Mario muttered something that I think included the words *devil woman*.

Bella turned on Mario. "You watch your step, old man. I'll put *the eye* on you."

The table went silent. No one wanted to mess with *the eye*. *The eye* was Italian voodoo.

While all this was going on, Mary Elizabeth had put away three glasses of wine. "I love a party," Mary Elizabeth said, her words slightly slurred, her eyes slightly crossed. She raised her wineglass. "Here's to me!"

We all raised our wineglasses. "To Mary Elizabeth!"

When we were all stuffed with chicken in red sauce and meatballs and macaroni casseroles, Mrs. Morelli brought out the desserts. Plates of Italian cookies from People's bakery, fresh-filled cannoli from Panorama Musicale, cheeses from Porfirio's, and the birthday cake from Little Italy.

By now it was sweltering in the Morelli dining room. All the windows were open and Mrs. Morelli had brought a fan in to circulate air. Sweat was running down my breastbone, soaking my shirt. My hair was stuck to my face and my mascara was not living up to its water-proof promise. No one cared about the heat. Everyone but Joe and his mom was shit-faced, me included.

Candles were lit on the cake, raising the room temperature by another ten degrees. We all sang "Happy Birthday," Mary Elizabeth blew out the candles, and Mrs. Morelli made the first cut in the cake.

Grandma Bella slammed her hands palms down on the table and tossed her head back. She was having a vision.

Everyone at the table groaned.

"I see death," Grandma Bella said. "A woman."

More groaning from around the table.

"I see white carnations."

"Don't worry about it, honey," Morelli whispered in my ear. "There are always white carnations."

"This woman who died," I asked Grandma Bella. "Is she a blonde?"

Grandma Bella opened her eyes and looked at me. "She has curly brown hair," Bella said. "Shoulder length."

My hair. Good thing I was too drunk to care.

"That's the vision," Bella said. "I'm tired now. I need to lay down."

Bella always got tired after a vision.

We watched her leave the table and go upstairs.

"Good riddance," Mary Elizabeth said. "She's such a downer."

And we all made the sign of the cross and had dessert.

Morelli poured me into his truck and drove me back to his house where he dragged me out of the truck and propped me against the passenger side door. "If you're going to throw up, it'd be good if you could do it out here," he said. "It's supposed to rain. It'll wash away."

I thought about that for a moment and decided I wasn't going to throw up. I took a step and went down to one knee. "Oops," I said. "The curb's in my way."

Morelli hauled me up, slung me over his shoulder, and carried me into the house and up the stairs. I flopped onto Morelli's bed and put one foot on the floor to stop the whirlies. "Wanna have sex?" I asked.

Morelli grinned. "I think I'll take a rain check on that one. I'm still worried you're going to be sick. Do you want me to help you get undressed?"

"No. But it'd be good if you could make the room stand still."

I was awake but I was afraid to open my eyes. I suspected hell was lurking just beyond my eyelids. My brain didn't fit in my head and the little devil guys were poking hot sticks in my eyeballs.

I cracked an eye and squinted up at Morelli. "Help," I whispered.

Morelli had a coffee cup in his hand. "You really tied one on last night."

"Did I make an idiot of myself?"

"Honey, you were at a dinner party with my family. On your best day you couldn't even *compete* in the idiot contest."

"Your mother isn't an idiot."

"My mother likes you."

"Really?" I eased myself into a sitting position, put both hands to my head, and applied pressure in an attempt to prevent my brain from exploding. "I'm never doing this again. Never. I'm done drinking. Okay, maybe a beer once in a while, but that's it!"

"I went out and got *the cure*," Morelli said. "I have to leave for work, but I want to make sure you're okay first."

I opened my other eye. I sniffed the air. "*The cure? Really?*"

"Downstairs," Morelli said. "I left them in the kitchen. Do you want me to bring them up?"

Not necessary. I was on my feet. I was moving. Slowly. I was at the stairs. One step at a time. I was going to make it. I put my hands over my eyes to keep my eyeballs from falling out of my head while I worked the stairs. Then I was on firm floor. I inched forward. I was in the kitchen. I squinted into the red haze and I saw it. It was sitting on the little wooden kitchen table. A large bag of McDonald's French fries and a large Coke.

I carefully eased myself onto a kitchen chair and took my first fry. "Ahhhh," I said.

Morelli was slouched in the chair opposite me, finishing his coffee. "Feeling better?"

I sipped some Coke and I ate more fries. "Much better."

"Are you ready for ketchup?"

"Definitely."

Morelli got the ketchup out of the fridge and dumped some on a plate for me. I mushed some fries in the ketchup and tested them out.

"I think the brain swelling is going down," I said to Morelli. "The pounding has stopped."

"Always a good sign," Morelli said. He rinsed his cup

and set it in the dish drain. "I'm out of here. I have to get the computer to the lab." He kissed me on the top of my head. "Be careful. Tank's outside, doing his thing. Try not to lose him."

"I owe you," I said.

"Yeah, I know. I already have plans."

And he was gone.

Bob was patiently sitting beside me, waiting for his share. I fed him a couple fries, finished up the rest, and drank the Coke. I gave a big burp and felt pretty decent.

I took a shower and got dressed in a short denim skirt, white sneakers, and a white T-shirt. I pulled my hair into a ponytail, applied some lipstick and a single swipe of mascara, and I was ready for the day.

I put a call in to Lula and got her at a truck stop.

"I'm fine," she said. "Me and Boo are having breakfast. We're making real good time. We're traveling straight along Route Forty all the way. This here's real interesting. I never drove through anything like this before. This is cowboys and Indians country."

I hung up, dropped a raisin and a small chunk of cheese into Rex's cage, gave Bob a hug, and told everybody I'd be back. I locked up after myself and waved to Tank. Tank gave me a nod back.

I drove the short distance to my parents' house and parked in the driveway. My grandmother was at the door, waiting for me, responding to some mysterious instinct embedded in Burg women . . . an early warning signal that a daughter or granddaughter was approaching.

"That big guy is following you again," Grandma said, opening the door to me.

"Tank."

"Yeah. I wouldn't mind spending some time with him. You think he could go for an older woman?"

Young women, old women, barnyard animals. "Hard to say with Tank."

"Your mother's at the store and the girls are off playing somewhere," Grandma said. "Valerie's in the kitchen eating us out of house and home."

"How's she doing?"

"Looks like she's going to explode."

I went in and took a chair across from Valerie. She was picking at a bowl of macaroni and chicken salad, not showing much enthusiasm for it.

"What's up?" I asked.

"I dunno. I'm not hungry. I think I'm in a slump. My life is same old, same old."

"You're having a baby. That's pretty exciting."

Valerie looked down at her stomach. "Yeah." She gently rubbed the baby bulge. "I'm excited about that. It's just that everything else is so unsettled. I'm living here with Mom and Dad and Gram. After the baby there'll be four of us in that one small bedroom. I feel like I'm swallowed up and there's no more Valerie. I was always perfect. I was the epitome of well-being and mental health. Remember how I was serene? Saint Valerie? And I adapted when I moved to California. I went from serene to perky. I was cute," Valerie said. "I was *really* cute. I made birthday cakes and pork tenderloins. I bought my jerkoff husband a grill. I had my teeth bleached."

"Your teeth look great, Val."

"I'm confused."

"About Albert?"

Valerie rested her elbow on the table and her chin in her hand. "Do you think he's boring?"

"He's too funny to be boring. He's like a puppy. Sort of floppy and goofy and wanting to be liked." He could be a little annoying, but that's different from boring, right?

"I feel like I need a hero. I feel like I need to be rescued."

"That's because you weigh four hundred pounds and you can't get out of a chair by yourself. After you have the baby you'll feel different." Okay, so I was being a big fat hypocrite again. I felt the same way as Val. I wanted to be rescued, too. I was tired of being brave and semicompetent. Difference was, I refused to say it aloud. I suspected it was a basic instinct, but it felt wrong somehow. For starters, it felt like a terrible burden to dump on a man.

"Do you think Albert is at all heroic?" Valerie asked me.

"He doesn't look like a hero, but he gave you a job when you needed one and he's stood by you. I guess that's sort of heroic. And I think he'd run into a burning building to save you." Whether he'd get her out of the building is another issue. Probably they'd both die a horrible death. "I think you're doing the right thing by not getting married, Val. I like Albert, but you don't want to marry him just because Mom's in favor of it, or because you need a second income. You should be in love and you should be sure he's the right man for you and the girls."

"Sometimes it's hard to tell what's love and what's only indigestion," Valerie said.

I left Valerie with the macaroni salad and drove to the office.

Connie looked around her computer screen at me when I walked in.

"Well?" I asked. "Are you married?"

"No. It turned out to be a joke photo. I caught the ten o'clock out of Vegas."

"And the room damage?"

"It all went on Vinnie's credit card. Vinnie almost popped a vein when he heard. But then the reporters started showing up and Vinnie was distracted. The room bill got pushed on a back burner. You saved

Vinnie's ass. You even made him look *good*. The visa bond worked. The guy fled. We found him."

"Actually, the Vegas cops found Singh."

"Not when Vinnie tells it. Vinnie's made some improvements on the story. So we all still have our jobs. Vinnie's not going to be selling used cars in Scottsdale. Everybody's happy."

Everybody except me. I was being stalked by a lunatic. And it was possible that I was indirectly responsible for causing three murders.

"Now that Singh is off the books, I've got a backlog of skips," Connie said. "What would you like . . . first-time rapist, repeat domestic violence, assault with a deadly weapon, or possession?"

"What's the possession?"

"Kilo of heroin."

"Whoa! That's a biggy. That's Ranger's. How about the deadly weapon."

"Butchy Salazar and Ryan Mott got into a fight over Candace Lalor. And Butchy ran over Ryan with his Jeep Cherokee. Three times."

"Butchy was drunk?"

"Yep."

"Give me Butchy." Sometimes a drunk is an easy catch if you can get him in the morning.

I took the papers from Connie. I didn't need a photo. I knew Butchy. Went to school with him. Didn't like him back then. Wasn't real crazy about him now.

"I'll give you the rapist, too. It's his first time around. Maybe he just forgot to show for court. I tried calling, but all I get is a machine."

"Have you tried his work number?"

"He's unemployed. Got fired when he got arrested."

I looked around. "It feels strange not to have Lula here."

"Quiet," Connie said.

"Empty."

"Glorious," Vinnie yelled from his inner office. "Freaking glorious."

I hefted my bag higher on my shoulder and I headed out. Tank was standing guard on the sidewalk, in front of my car.

"I have a couple FTAs," I said to Tank. "One's in the Burg and one's in Hamilton Township. I have to stop at my apartment first to get some clean clothes and stuff."

"It might be easier if we took one car for the busts," Tank said.

I agreed. "Do you want to drive or ride shotgun?"

Tank's eyebrows raised a fraction of an inch. Shocked that I would even consider driving. Tank only rode shotgun to Ranger.

"It's the twenty-first century," I told Tank. "Women drive."

"Only in my bed," Tank said. "Never in my car."

I didn't have a reply to that, but I thought it sounded like an okay philosophy. So I beeped the Escape locked, got into Tank's SUV, and we chugged off for my place.

We went through the standard routine at my apartment. Tank went in first and did a safety check. The photos were gone from the floor. Residue remained where the police had checked for prints. I gathered a few things together when Tank gave the all clear. Mostly what I wanted from my apartment was hardware. I took the cuffs and pepper spray from my bedside table and dropped them into my shoulder bag. I went to the cookie jar next and added the .38 to my bag of goodies. I knew Tank was fully armed and probably had fifty pairs of cuffs in the back of his truck, but I wanted my own. Am I a professional, or what?

I locked up and we took the elevator. Two-hundred-year-old Mrs. Bestler was in the elevator joy riding.

"Going down," she told us, pressing the button, leaning on her walker. "First floor, ladies' handbags, designer shoes." She looked up at Tank. "My goodness, you're a big one," she said.

Tank smiled at her. Big bad wolf reassures Grandma he's not going to eat her for lunch. The doors opened and we got out.

"Have a nice day, Mrs. Bestler," I said.

"Don't take any wooden nickels," Mrs. Bestler sang out.

According to Butchy Salazar's bond agreement, he was renting the top half of a two-family house on Allen Street. For years now, Butchy's worked nights tending bar at a dive on Front Street, so chances were good that he'd be at home.

Tank did a pass in front of the house. No activity. He returned and parked two houses down on the opposite side of the street. I called Butchy on my cell phone and got his machine. I didn't leave a message. Tank and I got out and approached the house. No back door to worry about, so we positioned ourselves to either side of the front door. I rang the bell for the upstairs apartment and waited. No response. I rang again.

The downstairs door opened and an older woman stuck her head out. "Butchy isn't home and my cats hate when people ring his bell," she said. "The bell scares my cats. They're very sensitive."

"Do you know where Butchy is?"

"It's his day off from work. I think he's gone out to do his grocery shopping and stuff. Not that he does a lot of cooking. Mostly he buys beer and filthy magazines. I tell you, this neighborhood's going to hell in a handbasket."

The woman closed her door and I looked up at Tank. It was strange being on a bust with him. I was used to Lula with her crazy clothes and smart mouth.

"Okay," I said, "let's go for the rapist, Steven We-gan. We can come back to Butchy later. Wegan lives in Hamilton Township in one of those apartment complexes off Klockner Boulevard."

Minutes later we were parked in the lot in front of Steven Wegan's apartment. We sat for a couple minutes, getting the feel of things. A woman left her apartment two doors down, got into her car, and drove off. Aside from that there was no activity.

"One of us should take the back door," I said.

"Can't do that," Tank said. "My first job is to protect you and I can't do that if I can't see you."

"No one followed us here. I was watching."

Tank went stony. An unmovable object.

"Fine," I said, "we'll both take the front door."

We left the truck, crossed the lot, and I rang Wegan's bell.

Wegan answered on the first ring. You've got to love first-time offenders. They don't know the drill. Next time around Wegan will be out the back door, hiding in the Dumpster.

He was a slim five feet, eight inches with close-cut brown hair and dark brown eyes. His papers listed his age as twenty-six. He was unmarried.

"Yes?" Wegan said, looking first to me, then up at Tank. The gears were turning in Wegan's head when he looked at Tank. Tank wasn't someone you wanted to unexpectedly find on your doorstep.

"Steven Wegan?" I asked.

Wegan swallowed. "Un-hunh."

I introduced myself and explained to Wegan that he missed his court date and needed to refile. Wegan bobbed his head yes, but his eyes were saying no, no, no.

I reached back and took hold of the cuffs secured under my skirt waistband. Wegan went white, turned,

and bolted. And before I could make a move, Tank ef-
fortlessly grabbed Wegan by the scruff of his neck and
held him two inches off the floor. Wegan kicked out
and then went limp. Tank gave Wegan a shake, causing Wegan's feet to flop around. "I'm going to put you
down now," Tank said. "And you're not going to try
anything stupid, right?"

"R-r-r-right," Wegan said.

I cuffed Wegan, we secured his apartment, and we
all marched over to Tank's SUV. We put Wegan in the
backseat, cuffed and shackled.

I couldn't help thinking it would have played out differently if Tank hadn't been along. Lula and I would have
chased Wegan all over his apartment, knocking over
lamps and chairs in the process. We would have snagged
him eventually, but the capture would have been total
Abbott and Costello.

"Do all your captures go like that?" I asked Tank.

"No," he said. "They don't always try to run."

It was midafternoon when we left the police station. Wegan
was back behind bars. Tomorrow morning he'd go before the judge who would once again set bail, higher
this time. Vinnie would get a call from a pleading Wegan, and for another bonding fee, Wegan would walk.

We stopped off at Cluck in a Bucket for a late lunch
and then motored over to the Burg to try our luck with
Butchy. We parked across the street and looked up at
Butchy's open windows. Television sounds drifted out
to us. Butchy was home. We crossed the street and took
our places on the small stoop that served as a front
porch.

"Do you know this guy?" Tank asked.

"Yeah."

"Is he going to shoot at us?"

"Depends how drunk he is."

Tank drew his gun and I rang the bell. No answer to the bell. I rang again. Still no answer.

"He's not coming down," Tank said.

I called Butchy on my cell phone.

"Yeah?" Butchy said.

"It's Stephanie Plum," I told him. "I'm downstairs with my partner and we need to talk to you."

"So go ahead and talk."

"You missed your court date and you need to reschedule."

"And?"

"And you need to do it now. Come downstairs and open the door."

"Suck my dick," Butchy said.

"Sure," I told him. "Just come down and open the door."

"Fuck off," Butchy said. "I don't feel like going to jail today. Why don't you come back next month? Maybe I'll feel like going to jail next month."

I told Tank to back up and stand on the sidewalk where Butchy could see him.

"Look out your window, Butchy," I said. "See the big guy standing on the sidewalk?"

"Yeah."

"That's my partner. If you don't open the door, he's going to put his foot through it. And then he's going to go upstairs and root you out like the rodent you are and put his foot up your ass."

"I've got a gun."

"Is it as big as Tank's?"

Tank was holding a .44 Magnum.

"I swear to God," Butchy said, "if you come in I'll blow your head off." And he disconnected.

"He's not coming down," I told Tank. "And he says he's armed."

Tank walked up to the door, put his boot to it just

left of the handle, and the door flipped open. "Wait here," Tank said.

I had my gun in hand, too. "No way. This is my bust."

Tank turned and looked at me. "Anything happens to you, I have to answer to Ranger. Frankly, I'd rather take a bullet from this moron."

Okay, that made sense to me. "I'll wait here," I told him.

"I'm coming up the stairs," Tank called to Butchy. "When I get to the top I want you unarmed, face down on the floor with your hands where I can see them."

I looked up and saw Butchy ass first, half out the window above me. He was waiting for Tank to get to the top of the stairs and then Butchy was going to go out the window, onto the small roof over the stoop, and drop to the ground.

I ducked into the doorway so Butchy wouldn't see me. I held my breath and waited to hear him on the roof. Tank got to the top of the stairs, Butchy's feet scuffed on the roof, and I jumped out. I had my gun two-handed and I yelled for Butchy to stop and freeze.

"I've got him," I yelled to Tank. "He's on the porch roof."

Tank jogged down the stairs and moved to join me on the small patch of front lawn. He cleared the porch just as Butchy catapulted himself off the roof, and the two of them crashed to the ground with Butchy on top of Tank.

I rushed in and grabbed Butchy by the arm, cuffing him behind his back while he still had the air knocked out of him. I rolled him off Tank and shoved him aside. Tank was on his back with his leg twisted at an impossible angle.

"Just shoot me," Tank said. "It'd be less painful."

I called EMS and then I called Ranger. A half hour

later, Tank was rolled into the EMS truck, his leg held stable by an inflated cast.

Ranger and I stood side by side and watched the truck disappear around the corner. A big, bald, jug-headed guy, neatly dressed in black jeans and T-shirt, stood by Tank's truck. He had his muscle-bound, bulging arms crossed over his massive chest and his tiny eyes fixed on Ranger and me.

"I need to go to the hospital and get Tank admitted," Ranger said. "I've asked Cal to follow you around."

"Cal has a flaming skull tattooed onto his forehead. And he has muscles in places muscles aren't supposed to grow. Cal looks like . . . Steroidasaurus."

"Don't underestimate him," Ranger said. "He can spell his name. He's not overly violent as long as he remembers to take his medication. And he gives good shade."

I did a grimace.

Ranger pulled me to him and kissed me on the forehead. "You two are going to get along just fine." Ranger stepped back and turned to Butchy, who was sitting cuffed and shackled on the curb. He grabbed Butchy, dragged him to his feet, and handed him over to Steroidasaurus.

It was almost six when we left the police station. Butchy was chained to a bench across from the docket lieutenant. Steven Wegan was in the lockup. I had body receipts for both of them. Not a bad day in terms of income. Not a great day in terms of Tank's leg. Definitely a weird day, having spent it in the company of Ranger's Merry Men.

Halfway through town my cell phone rang. "Your sister's in labor," Grandma said. "She was working her way through a Virginia baked ham when she started getting contractions."

"Is she going to the hospital?"

"She's trying to decide if it's time. Do you think I should call Albert?"

"Definitely call Albert. It's his baby, too. He's been going to the birthing classes with Valerie."

"It's just that she's not in a good mood. You know how it is when she gets disturbed in the middle of a ham."

TWELVE

Valerie was sitting on the couch in the living room when I arrived. She was doing her breathing exercises and rubbing her stomach. My mother and grandmother were standing beside her, watching. The two girls were on the floor, staring bug-eyed at Valerie. My father was in his chair in front of the television, channel surfing.

"So," I said. "What's up?"

The front door crashed open behind me and Albert stumbled in. "Am I too late? Did I miss anything? What's going on?"

"Mommy's having a baby," Angie said.

Mary Alice nodded her head in agreement.

Albert looked terrible. His shirt was untucked and his eyes were glassy. His face was chalk white with red spots high on his cheeks.

"You don't look so good," Grandma said to Albert. "How about a ham sandwich?"

"I've never had a baby before," Albert said. "I'm a little flub-a-dubbed."

"I'm having another contraction," Valerie said. "Is anyone timing? Aren't these coming awful close together?"

I didn't know anything about having a baby, but I knew it worked better if you delivered it in the hospital.

"Maybe we should go to St. Francis," I said. "Do you have a suitcase ready?"

Valerie went into the breathing and rubbing mode again and my mom ran upstairs for the suitcase.

"So what do you think, Valerie?" I asked when she stopped rubbing and puffing. "You've done this before. Are you ready to go to the hospital?"

"I was ready weeks ago," Valerie said. "Someone help me get up."

Albert and I each took an arm and pulled Valerie up.

She looked down. "I can't see my feet. Do I have shoes on?"

"Yep," I said. "Sneakers."

She felt around. "And I've got pants on, right?"

"Black stretchy shorts." Stretched to within an inch of their lives.

My mother came down the stairs with the overnight bag. "Are you sure you don't want to get married?" she asked Valerie. "I could call Father Gabriel. He could meet you at the hospital. People get married in the hospital all the time."

"Contraction!" Valerie said, huffing and puffing, holding Kloughn's hand in a death grip.

Kloughn went down to one knee. "Yow! You're breaking my hand!"

Valerie kept huffing.

"Okay," Kloughn said. "Okay, okay. It's not so bad now that the hand's gone numb. Besides, I got another one, right? And probably this one's not actually broken. It's just mashed. It'll be fine, right? Mashed isn't so bad. Mashed. Squished. Smushed. That's all okay. That's not like broken, right?"

The contraction passed and we propelled Valerie out the door, down the sidewalk to the driveway. While the rest of us were flub-a-dubbed, my father had slipped outside and started the car. Sometimes my father knocks me out. On the surface he's all meat and potatoes and television, but the truth is, he doesn't miss much.

We put Valerie in the front seat. Albert, my mom, and I got in the backseat. Grandma and the girls stayed behind, waving. The trip was only several blocks long. St. Francis was walking distance from my parents' house, if you wanted to take a good long walk. I called Morelli from the car and told him I wouldn't be home for dinner. Morelli said that was cool since there didn't seem to be any dinner anyway.

Even with our combined abilities, Morelli and I as a single entity didn't equal a bad housewife. Bob ate regularly because we scooped his food out of a big bag. After that it was all downhill to take-out.

Albert and I walked Valerie in through the emergency entrance and my mom and dad took off to park the car.

A nurse came forward. "Omigod!" she said. "Valerie Plum? I haven't seen you in years. It's Julie Singer. I'm Julie Wisneski now."

Valerie blinked at her. "You married Whiskey? I had a big crush on him when I was in high school."

This caught me by surprise. I was just a couple years behind Valerie, but I had no idea she'd had a crush on Whiskey. Whiskey was drop-dead cute but not a lot upstairs. If you talked cars with Whiskey you were on solid ground. Any topic other than cars, fugeddaboudit. Last I heard he was working in a garage in Ewing. Probably happy as a clam at high tide.

"Big contraction," Valerie said, her face turning red, her hands on her belly.

"So what do you think?" I asked Julie. "I don't know a lot about this stuff, but she looks like she's going to have a baby, right?"

"Yeah," Julie said. "Either that or forty-two puppies. What have you been feeding her?"

"Everything."

My mom and dad hustled in and went to Valerie.

"Julie Wisneski!" my mom said. "I didn't know you were working here."

"Two years now," Julie said. "I moved from Helene Fuld."

"How are the boys? And Whiskey?" my mom wanted to know.

Big smile from Julie. "Driving me nuts."

My dad was looking around. He didn't care about Whiskey and the boys. He was scoping out televisions and vending machines. Good to know where the essentials are in a new environment.

Julie wedged Valerie into a wheelchair and took her away. My parents went with Valerie. Kloughn and I were left to complete the admission ritual. From the corner of my eye I caught site of a black hulking mass, positioned against a wall. Steroidasaurus was still watching over me.

When we satisfied admissions that the bill would be paid, I sent Albert upstairs to be with Valerie and I went over to talk to Cal.

"It's not necessary for you to stay," I said. "I'm going to be here for a while. When I'm done at the hospital I'm going back to Morelli's house. I don't think I'm in any danger."

Cal didn't move. Didn't say anything.

I slipped out the emergency room door and called Ranger and filled him in. "So I thought it didn't make sense for Cal to stay here all night while I'm with Valerie."

"Hospitals don't screen for killers," Ranger said. "Keep Cal with you."

"He's scaring people."

"Yeah," Ranger said. "He's good at that."

I disconnected, returned to the emergency room

lobby, and went upstairs to look for Valerie. Cal followed close at my heels.

We found Valerie on a gurney, in a hospital gown under a sheet, her stomach a huge swollen mound on top of her. My mother and father were at her head. Albert was holding her hand. Julie was attaching an ID bracelet onto Valerie's wrist.

"Omigod," Valerie said. "*Unh!*" And her water broke.

It was an explosion of water. A tidal wave. We're talking Hoover Dam quantity water. Water everywhere . . . but mostly on Cal. Cal had been standing at the bottom of the gurney. Cal was totally slimed from the top of his head to his knees. It dripped off the end of his nose and ran in rivulets down his bald head.

Valerie drew her legs up, the sheet fell away, and Cal gaped at the sight in front of him.

Julie stuck her head around for a look. "Uh-oh," she said, "there's a foot sticking out. Guess this is going to be a breech baby."

That was when Cal fainted. *CRASH*. Cal went over like he was a giant redwood cut down by Paul Bunyan. Windows rattled and the building shook.

Everyone clustered around Cal.

"Hey," Valerie yelled. "I'm having a baby here!"

Julie went back to Valerie.

"Is it a girl or a boy?" Valerie wanted to know.

"I don't know," Julie said, "but it's got big feet. And it's not a puppy."

A doctor appeared and took charge of Valerie, wheeling her down the hall. Kloughn and my mom followed after Val and the doctor. My father wandered into a room that had a ball game going. And I watched a couple nurses pop ammonia capsules under Cal's snout.

Cal opened his eyes but it didn't look like anyone was home.

"He hit his head pretty hard when he fell," one of the nurses said. "We should get him checked out."

Good thing it was his head, I thought. Not a big loss there if it's broken.

It took six people to get Cal onto a stretcher and then they rolled him away in the opposite direction they'd gone with Valerie.

One of the nurses asked if I knew him. I said his name was Cal. That was about it. That was what I knew. I wasn't allowed to use my cell phone in that part of the hospital, so I went outside to call Ranger.

"About Cal . . ." I said. "He's sort of out of commission."

"Used to be you destroyed my cars," Ranger said.

"Yeah, those were the good old days."

"How bad is it?"

"Valerie's water sort of broke on him and he fainted. Bounced his head on the floor a couple times when he went down. Lucky he was in the hospital when it happened. He was looking a little dopey, so they took him somewhere for testing."

"St. Francis?"

"Yep."

Disconnect.

I was making a shambles of the Merry Men. I suspected Tank was somewhere in the hospital, too. I'd stop in to say hello, but I only knew him as Tank. Probably Tank wasn't the name listed on the chart.

Morelli called while I was still outside. "So?"

"I'm at the hospital with Valerie," I told him. "It's been pretty uneventful except for the birth and the concussion."

"What, no fires or explosions? No shoot-outs?"

"Like I said, it's been quiet, but it's still early."

"I hate to ruin my tough-guy image, but to tell you

the truth, I don't even like to kid about this stuff any-more."

I didn't know how to tell him . . . I wasn't kidding. "I should get back to Valerie," I said.

"Television sucks tonight. Maybe I'll come over to the hospital."

"That would be nice."

The sky was overcast and a fine mist was settling around me. Streetlights popped on in the gloom. A block away, headlights glowed golden on cars cruising Hamilton. I'd exited the emergency entrance on Bert Avenue to make the call. I'd walked toward the back of the building, going just far enough to avoid activity. I had my back pressed to the brick wall of the hospital while I talked, trying to stay dry, trying to keep my hair from frizzing. Used to be there were houses across the street, but several years ago the houses were torn down and a parking lot was created.

A kid walked out of emergency and turned toward me, moving with his head down against the light rain, hugging a small gym bag to his chest. From the brief look I'd caught of his face I'd put him somewhere in his late teens to early twenties. Not really a kid, I guess, but he dressed like a kid. Low-slung baggy homeboy pants, gym shoes, short-sleeved shirt unbuttoned over a black T-shirt, spikey green hair. Probably had multiple piercings and tattoos, but I couldn't see any from this distance.

I dropped my phone into my purse and headed back to emergency. The green-haired kid got a couple feet from me and staggered a little, bumping against me. He picked his head up, looked me in the eye, and raised a gun level with my nose.

"Turn and walk," he said, "I'm really good with this gun. I'll shoot you dead if you make a single false move."

Usually there were people hanging out around emergency, but the rain had driven everyone inside. The street was deserted. Not even car traffic. "Is this about money?" I asked him. "Just take my bag."

"Hah, you wish, sweetie pie. This is The Game and I'm the winner. Just me and the Web Master left. I get to go on to the next game after I do you."

I turned and gaped at him.

"What?" he asked. "You didn't know it was me? You didn't think the hunter had green hair?"

"Who *are* you?"

He jumped and slashed at the air. "I'm the Fisher Cat."

I'd never heard of a fisher cat. I was pretty sure we didn't have any in Trenton. "Is that a real animal or did you make it up?"

"It's a member of the weasel family. It moves along real quiet. You hardly know it's around. It's real sneaky. And it's ferocious."

"Have you ever seen one?"

"Well, no, not exactly. You know, like, in a book."

"If I was going to name myself after an animal I'd want to see it first."

"That's because you have no imagination. Gamers have imagination. We create stuff."

"What stuff?"

"The Game, stupid. And then we *transcend* the game. The game becomes the reality. Is that total whack, or what?"

"Yeah, total whack." It had been a long day with a lot of adrenaline expended. For that matter, it had been a long week that had brought a lot of terror and death. This kid was right about one thing. I hadn't expected the bearer of that terror and death to have green hair and a tongue stud. "So this is a game," I said. "With a Web Master?"

"Pretty cool, huh?"

"Did you pull wings off butterflies when you were a kid?"

"No. I was a total wimp kid. I was a wimp until I found the Web Master and got into The Game."

"Are there rules to The Game or do you just go around randomly killing people?"

"The Web Master runs The Game. He's the one who decides who can play. Not everyone gets to play, you know. There are always five players and a prize. This time you're the prize. I know you've been getting messages from the Web Master. That's part of his job. He's the one who keeps the rabbit running while the players are in the elimination stage. This is my second game. The first game was a couple years ago. I was last man standing on that one, too. I got to hunt a cop that time."

"What's with the flowers?"

"That's The Game designation. If you play the Web Master's game, you're a Red Roses and White Carnations player."

I couldn't believe I was standing on the sidewalk, talking to this kid who looked more like the Green Goblin than a Fisher Cat and was holding me at gunpoint . . . and not a car drove by. No one strolled through the emergency room doors, looking for a place to sneak a smoke. No emergency vehicles barreled down the street with lights flashing.

"You look kind of young to be killing people," I said. As if age mattered when you were insane.

"Yeah, so far as I know, I'm the youngest player. I was seventeen when I killed Lillian Paressi. I got so excited I did the deed on her after she was dead."

"That's sick and disgusting."

Fisher Cat giggled. "Maybe I'll do it on you, too, after I blow your head apart. I should have done it on Singh. The Web Master sent me to Vegas to get Singh.

Really nice of you to find the little jerk for us. You don't just walk out on a Game. The Game is everything."

I thought I was sounding pretty comfortable. My voice wasn't wobbling. My breathing appeared normal. I was asking questions. Deep inside there was bone-jarring fear. This was a seriously sick person. He had a gun. And it was going to ruin his night if he didn't kill me.

"The Fisher Cat has a real good sense of smell," he said. "I can smell your fear."

"I don't think that's fear you smell," I said. "My sister's water broke on me."

"Don't joke about it," he yelled. "This is serious. This is the *Game*."

Oh boy. Good going, Stephanie. Now he's mad.

He waved the gun at me. "Walk toward the garage."

I hesitated and he shoved the gun in my face. "I swear to God, I'll kill you right here if you don't start walking," he said, still agitated.

So maybe it was fear he smelled. I was putting out a lot of it. I walked toward the garage, thinking the garage might be helpful. It looked empty, but visiting hours were still going on and I knew there had to be people around. I'd never paid attention before, but there had to be security cameras. Whether they were working or anyone was watching was a whole other thing.

We were still on the sidewalk, almost to the back of the garage. I assumed we were going in through the rear exit and once we were inside I would make my move. My plan was to jump behind a car and then run like the wind, screaming my lungs out. Not real sophisticated, but it was all I had.

"Stop here," he said. "This is my truck."

It was a dark blue pickup parked at the curb. The paint was faded and there was rust showing around the tail pipe. The bed was covered with an old white fiber-glass cap. So much for escape plan A.

"Get in the back," Fisher Cat said. "We're going for a ride."

No way was I getting into the truck. The gun was scary. The truck was death. I rolled out and jerked away from him. He fired off a shot and I felt the bullet bite into my arm. I turned and ran and he ran after me, snagging the back of my shirt, throwing me off balance. I went down to one knee, pulling him down with me, and the gun dropped out of his hand.

And that's when I snapped. I was suddenly really pissed off. I whacked him with my purse, a good solid *whump* on the side of his head that jarred his mouth open and had his vision unfocused. I probably should have hit him with my bag again, but I wanted to get my hands on him. I wanted to gouge his stupid eyes out. This little creep killed people for a game. And one of them was a cop. My sister was in the hospital having a baby and this jerkoff was trying to kill me. How tacky is that?

I grabbed him by his ridiculous green hair and banged his head into the truck a couple times. He was flailing out with his arms, kicking at my legs. We both went down to the ground and rolled around, locked together like a couple squirrels, scratching and clawing and hissing. We weren't bitch slapping, trying to make a statement like Lula and Mrs. Apusenja. This was real life-or-death combat. Luckily, while we were rolling around, my knee connected with Fisher Cat's crotch and I shoved his gonads halfway up his throat.

Fisher Cat went dead still and, almost in slow motion, somebody's fist smashed Fisher Cat's nose. Looking back on it, I suppose it was my fist. At the time, the fist didn't seem to be connected to my brain. The nose gave with a sickening crunch and blood spurted out, killing my outrage.

"Oh crap!" I said. "I'm *really* sorry." I don't know why I said it because I wasn't all that sorry. It was one of those female reflex things.

His right hand blindly struck out at me, he made contact with my arm, and lights exploded behind my eyes.

When I came around I was on my back on the sidewalk. The misting rain felt good on my face. It was dark, but there were lights everywhere. Red and blue and white. The lights were haloed in the rain, giving them a surreal quality. The fog cleared from my head. I blinked and Ranger and Morelli swam into my field of vision. There were a lot of other people behind them. A lot of noise. Cops. Yellow crime scene tape, slick with rain.

"What happened?" I asked.

"It looks like you took a few volts," Morelli said. His lips were tight and his eyes were hard.

It took a beat for me to remember . . . Fisher Cat's arm reaching out to me. "Stun gun," I said. "I didn't see it until it was too late."

Morelli and Ranger each got a hand under an armpit and hauled me up to my feet. The first thing I saw was Fisher Cat, motionless on the grass beside his truck. A couple cops were in the process of setting lights to illuminate the body.

"Holy cow," I said. "He looks dead." I had a moment of panic that I'd killed him. Now that he'd zapped me, it was sort of satisfying to know I'd broken his nose, but I wasn't crazy about the idea that I might have beat him to death. I looked closer and saw the two bullet holes in his forehead. I let out a *whoosh* of relief. I was almost certain I didn't shoot him.

"Those aren't my bullet holes, are they?" I asked Morelli.

"No. We checked your gun. It hasn't been fired."

Ranger was grinning. "Somebody beat the shit out of this guy before he got shot."

"That would be me," I said.

"Babe," Ranger said, the grin widening.

My arm felt like it was on fire. The entire upper half was wrapped in gauze and a fine line of blood had begun to seep through the gauze. "I'm missing a chunk of time," I said. "What happened after I went lights out?"

"Ranger and I pulled in minutes apart and we got worried when we couldn't find you," Morelli said. "We knew you went outside to make some calls, so we went looking for you."

"And you found me laying here unconscious and the green-haired guy dead?"

"Yeah." Again, the tight lips and flat voice.

Morelli didn't like finding me unconscious. Morelli loved me. Ranger loved me, too, but Ranger was programmed differently.

"Your turn," Morelli said.

I told them everything I knew. I told them about the game. About Fisher Cat. About the webmaster. About the cop.

"We need to do this downtown," Morelli said. "We need to get this recorded."

It was raining harder. My hair was soaked. The bandage on my arm was soaked. I was streaked with mud and blood, my legs and arms were scratched from the scuffle. "How's Valerie?" I asked. "Is she okay? Did she have the baby?"

"I don't know," Morelli said. "We haven't checked on her."

The ME angled his truck into the curb just in front of the blue pickup. He got out and walked toward the body. He looked over and nodded to Morelli.

"I need to talk to him," Morelli said to me. "And

you need to go inside and get your arm looked at. It's not serious. The bullet just grazed you, but it probably needs stitches." He looked over at Ranger. "If anyone in her family sees her like this, they'll freak."

"No sweat," Ranger said. "I'll get her cleaned up before I get her stitched up."

Ranger loaded me into his truck and drove me to Morelli's house. He opened the front door, switched a light on, and Bob came running. Bob stopped when he saw Ranger and eyed him suspiciously.

"I can see this dog's a killer," Ranger said.

"Ferocious," I told him.

"I'm assuming you have clothes here," Ranger said. "Do you need any help?"

"I can manage."

His eyes darkened. "I'm good in the shower."

My temperature went up a couple notches. "I know. If I need help, I'll yell for you." Our eyes held. We both knew I'd jump out the bathroom window if I heard Ranger on the stairs.

I took a boiling hot shower, scrubbing away the dirt and blood and horror, being careful not to soak my slashed arm any more than was necessary. I toweled off and gasped when I looked in the mirror and saw my hair. A huge chunk of hair was missing. The left side was four inches shorter than the right side! How the hell did that happen? It had to have been Fisher Cat. Okay, that does it. I was glad I broke his nose. To tell you the truth, I wasn't sorry he was dead, either.

I got dressed in clean jeans, T-shirt, and sneakers. I tucked my wet hair behind my ears, covered it with a ball cap I found in Morelli's closet, and went downstairs.

Ranger was slouched on the couch, watching a ball game. Bob was beside him, his big shaggy orange Bob head resting on Ranger's leg.

"Looks like male bonding going on here," I said.

Ranger stood and clicked the television off. "Dogs love me." He slid an arm around my shoulders and herded me to the front door. "I called the hospital. Valerie had a baby girl. They're both doing great."

Happiness and relief rushed from the center of my chest clear to my fingertips, and there was a terrifying moment when I was afraid I was going to cry in front of Ranger. I ordered myself to get a grip and I steadied my voice. "What about Cal and Tank?" I asked.

"They've both been discharged. Tank's got his leg in a cast. Cal has a concussion. Not serious enough to keep him in the hospital."

Ranger drove me to the hospital and walked me into the emergency room. He waited while my arm was cleaned and stitched. Then he called Morelli.

"She's done," Ranger said. "Do you want to take over?"

Morelli arrived a couple minutes later and Ranger disappeared into the night. Some day when I had more time and emotional energy I was going to have to think about the odd dynamic that existed between Morelli and Ranger and me. Morelli and Ranger were able to work as a team when necessary, all hostility seemingly put aside. And at the same time, in an entirely different area of the brain, rivalry existed.

Morelli and I found our way to maternity and located Valerie. My parents were gone, but Kloughn was still there, sitting on the edge of a chair at bedside.

"Sorry I missed the big event," I said to Valerie. "I had a mishap with my arm here."

"She was great," Kloughn said. "She was amazing. I don't know how she did it. I've never seen anything like it. I don't know how she got that baby out of there. It was magic." Kloughn's face was still flushed and his surgical gown was sweat stained. He looked dazed and a little disbelieving. "I'm a father," he said. "I'm a father." His eyes filled and his smile wobbled. He swiped at his eyes and his nose. "I think I'm still flub-a-dubbed," he said.

Valerie smiled at Kloughn. "My hero," she said.

"I was good, wasn't I? I helped you, right?"

"You were very good," Valerie told him.

The baby was in the room with Valerie. She was wrapped in a blanket and she had a little knit cap on her head. She seemed impossibly small and at the same time too large to have exited through a vagina. When I was in school I'd taken all the usual courses in human reproduction and I knew the process . . . the cervical dilation, the flexibility of the pelvic bones, the muscle contractions. So I knew some of the biology, but it still looked to me like this was a case of threading a walrus through the eye of a needle. There were days when I wasn't sure how Morelli fit. I didn't want to contemplate trying to pass a baby.

"We've named her Lisa," Valerie said.

"Was it hard to pick out a name?" I asked.

"No," Valerie said. "We both agreed on Lisa. It's the family name that's giving us problems."

Valerie looked tired, so I gave her a hug and a kiss. And then I gave Kloughn a hug and a kiss. And then we left. I'm not a huggy-kissy person, but this was a huggy-kissy occasion.

Morelli and I left the hospital and went straight to Pino's. We ordered takeout and ten minutes later we walked into Morelli's house carrying a six-pack of Corona and a bag full of meatball subs. Bob was real happy to see us. Bob can smell a sub a quarter mile away.

I dragged myself into the living room, flopped onto the couch, opened the sub bag, and handed them out.

One for me. One for Morelli. And two for Bob. Morelli cracked open two beers. We each took a long pull and dug into the subs. Morelli channel surfed while he ate, finally settling on wrestling.

"I'm tired," Morelli said. "You scare the hell out of me and it makes me tired."

I was way beyond tired. I was numb. I had a lot of questions for Morelli, but I didn't want the answers tonight. I wasn't up to thinking. I could barely chew and swallow.

Tomorrow morning I had to go to the station and tell a recording machine everything I knew about Fisher Cat and the game. Tomorrow would be a big questions-and-answers day. Hopefully when I woke up my brain would be back in thinking mode.

Good thing wrestling was on. You don't need a brain to enjoy wrestling. Lance Storm was kicking the beejeezus out of some new guy who looked like King Kong's mutant brother. Storm was wearing little bright red panties that made him easy to find in my befuddled state. I opened a second beer and silently toasted Storm's panties.

THIRTEEN

Morelli nudged me awake. "Rise and shine," he said. "I need to get to work and you need to come with me."

"There's something poking me in my back."

He slid his arms around me. "Actually we have a couple minutes to spare."

"How many minutes?"

"Enough to get the job done."

"Are we talking about your job or mine?"

His hand skimmed the length of my belly and settled between my legs. "We're wasting valuable time."

Okay, here's the real difference between men and women. I wake up thinking about coffee and doughnuts and Morelli wakes up thinking about sex. Morelli kissed the back of my neck, did some really clever things with his fingers down there, and the thoughts of coffee drifted away. Truth is, the magic fingers had my full attention and the coffee thoughts were replaced by a fear that the fingers might stop.

The fear was groundless, of course. Morelli had learned a lot since our first time behind the éclair case in the Tasty Pastry bakery.

"So," Morelli said when we were done, "do you want to be first in the shower?"

I was face down on the bed, my heart rate was around

twelve beats per minute, and I was in a state of euphoric slobbering contentment. In fact, I think I might have been purring. "You go first," I said. "Take your time."

Morelli went downstairs and got the coffee going before taking his turn in the bathroom. After a couple minutes the coffee fumes penetrated my after-sex glow. I rolled out of bed, pulled on a pair of shorts and a T-shirt, and followed the fumes to the kitchen. I poured out a mug of coffee and padded to the front door to get the morning paper.

I opened the door and found a red rose and a white carnation wrapped in cellophane, sitting on the paper. So much for euphoria. I brought everything inside and locked the door behind me. I left the flowers on the sideboard and opened the small square white envelope that had accompanied the flowers. The envelope held a note written on card stock.

Are you pleased that I saved you for myself? Do you get hot when you think about me and all I've done for you? I could have killed you last night just as I could have killed you when I took you down with the dart, but that would have been too easy. Your death must be worthy of a hunter. It was signed, *Lovingly yours.*

And tucked into the envelope was a lock of my hair, tied together with a slim pink satin ribbon.

I got goose bumps on my arm and a chill ripped through my stomach. The shock was short-lived and I went back into bravado mode. Okay, I told myself, so that solves the mystery of the missing hair.

I was sitting in the living room with my coffee and the note when Morelli came down the stairs. He was freshly shaved and his hair was still damp. He was dressed in jeans and boots and a black T-shirt, and if I hadn't just had the mother of all orgasms I would have attacked him and lured him back to bed.

"I saw the flowers on the sideboard," Morelli said.

I handed him the card. "They were left on the porch this morning. They were on top of the paper, so the webmaster stopped around when it was daylight. Maybe someone saw him."

"He's taking chances," Morelli said. "He's glorying in his success and that's going to make him careless."

"Something to look forward to."

"I'll have the neighborhood canvassed." Morelli read the note. "Sick," he said.

I took a shower and did the best I could with my hair, pushing it behind my ears, lacquering it up with hair spray. I'd get a cut as soon as possible, but I hadn't a clue what could possibly be done with it. I looked close in the mirror. Extensions, maybe? Hairweave?

Morelli was on the phone when I came downstairs. He glanced at his watch and ended his conversation when he saw me. Morelli was ready to roll. The day had started without him. That's what happens when you're a sex fiend.

"I was talking to Ed Silver," Morelli said. "We just got the report back from the state techs. They were able to recover some email from Singh's computer. And the email corroborates what you learned last night. There were five players and the webmaster. We know Fisher Cat was last man standing, so we're missing a dead player."

"Do you know any more about how the game is played?"

"One of the emails spelled out the rules. The webmaster conducts the game. Players only use their game names and can communicate with each other only through the webmaster. So the webmaster always knows all. The webmaster gives out clues about the players' identities and the hunt begins. All players know from the beginning that there will only be one man standing at the end of the game. All players know there's no pulling out once the game has begun. Pulling out marks a player for assassination."

"Singh."

"Yeah. It looks like Singh was assassinated. The game began a full month before you got involved. You might have been the prize from the very beginning. Or the webmaster might have changed the prize midway. Or maybe the webmaster didn't feel any rush to designate a prize until the game was under way."

"And I happened along."

Morelli shrugged. "No way to know. You're a good prize. Bounty hunter. The webmaster had to come up with something to top the cop. The prize isn't mentioned in any of the emails to Singh. The rules were that the webmaster only gave up the prize to the last man standing."

"And the webmaster?"

"That's the bad news. No clue to the webmaster. His emails are, so far, untraceable. And he hasn't given away anything of himself. There were some messages to Singh about his disappearance, requesting that he return to finish the game, warning of the consequences. And there were a couple earlier messages that got the game going. Player names and hunt clues."

"Is Bart Cone still a suspect?"

"Everyone's a suspect. Cone is high up on the list."

"What about the other victims' computers?"

"We were never able to find Rosen's or Howie's computer."

"Fisher Cat's?"

"Fisher Cat's name is Steven Klein. Nineteen years old. Worked at Larry's video rental and lived with his parents. The state has a team going through the parents' house, but so far as I know the computer hasn't turned up yet."

I glanced at the newspaper I'd dropped onto the

coffee table. Klein's picture was on the front page. To be more precise, Klein's sneakers were on the front page because the rest of him was hidden behind a couple cops and a back shot of me, standing hands on hips, head down. My hair didn't look good.

"Crap," I said.

Morelli looked down at the photo. He raised his eyes and looked over at me. "Did you get a new haircut?"

"Yeah. Somewhere between getting shot and posing for this newspaper picture. I guess you didn't look in the envelope."

Morelli took the envelope off the coffee table and looked inside. Morelli's usually pretty good at hiding emotion, but the lock of hair pushed a button that was beyond his range of control. Color rose in his cheeks and he slashed out at a table lamp, hitting it with his closed fist, sending it flying across the room to smash against the wall.

Bob was curled into a big Bob ball at the end of the couch, sound asleep. He levitated six inches off the couch when the lamp crashed and he ran for the kitchen.

"Feel better?" I asked Morelli.

"No."

"Do you have anything else for me?"

"Klein, Rosen, Singh, Paressi were all shot at fairly close range. Howie was shot across a parking lot. Even using a laser scope, there's still a skill level required to put a twenty-two between someone's eyes at a distance. Someone in the carnations and roses group is a very good shot. I'm guessing it's the webmaster. A possible scenario is that you discovered Howie's identity and the webmaster had to take him out or risk having the game blown. And then maybe the webmaster discovered he liked killing and decided to insert himself into the game as a player."

"Was Bart Cone in the military? Does he belong to a gun club?"

"Never in the military. No gun club that we know of." Morelli did another watch check. "We have to roll."

I did a fast scan for Ranger's man when I got outside, but I couldn't spot any shiny new black cars.

Morelli beeped his truck unlocked. "If you're looking for your rent-a-thug, I told Ranger you'd be with me this morning."

"Did he make you take a blood oath that you'd protect me?"

"He asked me if I had adequate health insurance."

The rain had stopped and Jersey was steaming. Grass was growing and oil-slicked puddles were evaporating. Another hour and the sun would be bright in the sky, shimmering in the ozone haze.

It was a terrific day for sandals, but I was wearing sneakers because it's hard to run fast in sandals. And I thought there was a good possibility that I might have to run fast today. I wasn't sure if I would be running *from* the webmaster or running *after* the webmaster. No matter which, I was prepared.

Ranger wore the eye of the tiger. He was always in the zone. I felt like I was in the zone today. Of course, there was the possibility that I was just delusional after the phenomenal sex, but what the hell, whatever the reason, I felt okay. And I was hardly thinking about the lock of hair. Well, all right, maybe I was thinking about it a *little*.

The Trenton cop shop is located on Perry Street and will never be mistaken for Beverly Hills PD. No potted palms or stylish mauve carpet. Mauve carpet doesn't hold up under pepper spray–induced snot.

Morelli brought me into a small room with a table and two chairs. He plugged in a tape recorder and punched the on button. I looked around and was ready to confess to anything. Just being in the grim little room, under the flickering fluorescent lights, made me feel guilty.

I walked my way through the conversation with Steven Klein, giving as much detail as I could recall. When we got to the part where I was zapped unconscious, Morelli shut the machine off and called Ranger. "She's all yours," Morelli said to Ranger. Morelli disconnected and looked over at me. "That was a figure of speech."

Ranger was driving a black Porsche Carrera. He was wearing black cargo pants, a black T-shirt that looked like it was painted onto his biceps, black Bates boots, and a Glock in full view on his hip. Ranger was in body-guard mode.

"Couldn't coerce any of your men into baby-sitting me?" I asked him.

He cut his eyes to me and he didn't exactly smile, but he didn't look unhappy, either. "You're all mine today, babe."

It sounded different when Ranger said it.

"I don't know what your plans are for the day," I said to Ranger, "but my plan is to go to the mall and beg for hair help. I'm finding it hard to maintain the eye of the tiger when my hair is lopsided."

On the way to the mall, I filled Ranger in on the game. "It has to be Bart Cone," I said. "Someone sent Steven Klein to Vegas to eliminate Singh. And there were only a couple people who knew Singh was in Vegas. Cone was one of them."

"It could also be someone Cone's talking to," Ranger said. "There are three brothers and they all have friends and associates. I'm sure the police have cast a wide net around them, but it wouldn't hurt for you to talk to the

Cones. Sometimes a man will share information with a woman that he wouldn't think to give to a cop."

Ranger parked at a mall entrance and we walked through the mall to the salon. We passed a Victoria's Secret along the way and I couldn't resist giving Ranger the test.

"Suppose I wanted to look for a thong," I said to Ranger. "Would you come into the store with me?"

Ranger did the almost smile. "Are we cutting a deal?"

"Everything's a deal with you."

"I'm a mercenary," Ranger said. "What's your point?"

For a couple years now I've been getting my hair cut by Mr. Alexander. The guy's name is Alexander Dubkowski, but no one calls him Al or Alex or even Alexander. It's *Mr.* Alexander if you want a decent cut.

We walked into the salon and Mr. Alexander looked our way and sucked in some air. Not only did I have a hair disaster of biblical proportions, I was with the Man from SWAT. And the Man from SWAT made people nervous.

"I had a hair accident," I said to Mr. Alexander. "Do you have time to fix it?"

Mr. Alexander went pale under his tanning salon tan. Probably afraid Ranger would shoot up the place if I didn't get an immediate appointment. "I have a few minutes between clients," he said, motioning me into a chair, draping a cape around me. He did some hair fluffing with his fingers, he bit his lower lip. "I'm going to have to cut," he said.

Panic. "It's not going to be real short, is it? How about a weave, or something?"

"I'm good, but I'm not God," he said. "It's going to have to get cut."

I blew out a sigh of resignation. "Fine. Cut."

"Close your eyes," he said. "I'll tell you when it's done."

I opened an eye halfway through and he quickly turned the chair so I wasn't facing the mirror. "No cheating," he said. When he was done, he spun me around and we both stopped breathing.

It was short. Longer in the back, curling along the nape of my neck. Short enough on the sides to have my ear show. A few wispy bangs over my forehead. And the whole thing looking slightly mussed and wind tossed.

Ranger came and stood behind me, checking me out. "Cute," he said.

"Last time my hair was this short I was four years old."

When we were back in the car I turned to Ranger. "Is it really cute or were you just trying to keep me from shrieking?"

He ran a hand through my hair. "It's sexy," he said. And he kissed me. Tongue and everything.

"*Hey*," I said. "We're not supposed to be doing that."

A smile hovered at the edges of his mouth. "Morelli told me you were all mine today."

"That was a figure of speech. He trusts us."

Ranger turned the key in the ignition. "He trusts *you*. I haven't signed on to the *trust me* program."

"How about me? Can I trust you?"

"Are we talking about your life or your body?"

I already knew the answer so I moved on. "Where are we going?"

"TriBro."

Twenty minutes later, Ranger was in the industrial park where TriBro was located. He pulled into a parking lot for a moving and storage company and cut the engine.

I looked over. "What's up?"

He reached behind me and snagged a black molded-plastic box with a snap closure. "I'm going to wire you. I want to make sure you're safe in there."

"You're not going in?"

"No one will talk to you if I'm along."

I raised an eyebrow.

Ranger did the almost grin thing again. "Sometimes people find me to be a little scary."

"*No!* Shocking. You ever think about losing the gun? Or dressing normal?"

He opened the box and removed a matchbook-size recorder. "I have an image to maintain."

I was wearing a black tank top and jeans. The jeans were hot, but they covered the bruises and scratches on my legs. Not much I could do to hide the bandage on my arm. My heart did a once over, knowing where the wire was going to get taped. "I don't think I need a wire," I said.

Ranger pulled my shirt out of my jeans and slid his hands under the shirt. "You're not going to ruin this for me, are you? I've been looking forward to this." He secured the recorder against my breastbone, just below my bra, with two crisscrossed pieces of surgical tape. The wire with the pinhead microphone ran between my breasts. "Ready to rock 'n' roll," Ranger said. He spun the Porsche out of the moving and storage lot and into the TriBro lot.

Let's take stock here. I've got my *go fast, feet* sneakers on and I'm wired for sound. I've got pepper spray and a stun gun in my purse. And I'm cloaked in an invisible invincible protective shield. Okay, so I lied about the shield. Still, four out of five isn't too bad, right?

I crossed the lot and entered the building. I gave a big smile and hello to the receptionist and got waved through to Andrew.

Andrew gave me the hero's welcome. "Way to go! You found him. The office called about an hour ago."

"Yeah, but he was dead."

"Dead or alive makes no difference to me. All right, I know that's heartless, but I didn't really know him. And you saved me a lot of money. I would have been out the bond if it wasn't for you."

"Unfortunately, your problems aren't over. Singh was involved in a killing game. All game members are dead now with the exception of the game organizer. And I'm pretty sure the game organizer works at TriBro."

Andrew went perfectly still and the color drained from his face. "You're kidding, right?"

I shook my head. "I'm serious."

"The police have been around talking to us, but no one ever said anything about a killing game."

I shrugged.

Andrew got up and shut his office door. "Are you sure about this? This isn't another witch hunt like the one Bart went through? That was a nightmare and nothing ever came of it."

"Lillian Paressi was a player in a previous killing game."

"What?" Color was returning to his face, the shock morphing to disbelief and anger. "That's ridiculous. That's the most insane thing I've ever heard. Why wasn't any of this brought out by the police?"

"They didn't know at the time."

"But they know now?"

"Yes."

"Then why aren't *they* here?" he asked.

I did a palms-up. "Guess I got here first."

"When you say you suspect the *organizer* of this game works at TriBro, does that include me and my brothers in your list of suspects?"

Up to this point I hadn't considered the possibility that Andrew or Clyde might be involved, but what the hell, cast a wide net, right? I took a shallow breath and jumped in with both feet. "Yeah."

Even as I was saying this I was thinking to myself that I had a lot of nerve making such an accusation. There was a really good chance that the webmaster was Bart Cone. There was also a chance that the webmaster was someone entirely out of the loop. And there was pretty much *no* chance that the webmaster was Andrew or Clyde. "So," I said, doing some mental knuckle cracking. "It isn't you, is it?"

He was back in his chair and he was stunned. His mouth was open, his eyes were wide and blank, and a red scald rose up his neck into his cheeks. "Are you crazy?" he shouted. "Do I look like a killer?"

I had a vision of Ranger listening to this in the Porsche, laughing his ass off. "Just asking," I said. "No reason to get huffy."

"Get out. *Get out now!*"

I jumped out of my chair. "Okay, but you have my card and you'll give me a call if you want to talk, right?"

"I have your card. Here it is." He held the card up and tore it into tiny pieces. "That's what I think of your card."

I left Andrew and I scurried down the hall to Bart. The door to his office was open so I peeked inside. Bart was at his desk, eating lunch.

"Can we talk?"

"Is it important?"

"Life and death."

He had a sandwich, a bag of chips, and a can of Coke in front of him. He took a chip and watched me while he ate.

"And?" he asked.

I gave him the same suave spiel. "I know about Lillian Paressi," I said. "I know she was part of a killing game."

"Do you have proof of this?"

"Yes." Sort of. "I also know about the current game. And I think the game organizer works in this building."

Bart didn't say anything. His face showed no emotion. He selected another chip and chewed thoughtfully. "That's a serious accusation."

"It's you, isn't it? You're the webmaster."

"Sorry to disappoint. I have no knowledge of any of this. I'm not a webmaster. And I'm not involved in a killing game. You're going to have to leave now. And you can talk to my lawyer if you want to continue this conversation."

"All righty then. You have my card?"

"I do."

I backed out of Bart's office, turned, and was almost knocked off my feet by Clyde.

"Oh jeez," he said, grabbing for me. "I heard you were here and I came looking for you. I guess I wasn't watching where I was going. *Shit.*" He clapped a hand over his mouth. "Sorry. I meant to say *shoot!*"

I took a step back. "No problem. I'm fine."

"Have you had lunch? Would you want to go to lunch with me? I'd buy. It'd be my treat."

"Gee, thanks, but my partner's waiting for me."

"Maybe some other time," Clyde said, not looking the least discouraged.

"Yeah. Some other time."

I hustled out of the building, forcing myself to walk not run across the lot to the Porsche.

"Very smooth," Ranger said, smiling.

I ripped the wire off and threw it on the dash. "I'm *never* wearing one of these again. You make me nervous!"

"I wanted to make sure you didn't get abducted into the broom closet and snuffed with a toilet brush," Ranger said. "One of these days we should talk about interrogation methods."

"It sort of went in the wrong direction. I don't know how that happened." I slumped in my seat. "I need lunch. A bag of doughnuts would be good."

"Would you settle for pizza?"

"No! Last time you took me for pizza in this neighborhood there were bloodstains on the table."

Ranger rolled the engine over and cruised out of the lot. "You didn't talk to Clyde."

"I talked more than I wanted. I'm afraid I'm going to open the door for the paper some morning and find Clyde sleeping on the doormat."

We compromised and went to Pino's for pizza. We were on our way out when my cell phone rang.

"I have a problem here," Connie said. "The police notified the Apusenjas about Singh's death over the weekend and now I have them sitting in the office. They want to talk to you."

"Why me? You were in Vegas. Why can't they talk to you?"

"Mrs. Apusenja doesn't want to talk to me."

"Tell them I'm out of town. No, better yet, tell them I'm dead. Very tragic. Car crash. No wait, that would be in the paper. Flesh-eating virus! That's always a good one."

"How long will it take you to get here?"

"Couple minutes. We're at Pino's."

Five minutes later, Ranger parked in front of the office. "You're on your own with this one, babe."

"Coward."

"Calling me names isn't going to get me in there."

I looked through the large plate-glass window. Mrs.

Apusenja and Nonnie were sitting on the couch, bodies rigid. "What *would* get you in there?"

Ranger leaned an elbow on the steering wheel and turned in my direction. And there it was . . . the eye of the tiger, focused on me.

I blew out a sigh and shoved my door open. "Wait here."

Both women stood when I walked into the office.

"I'm very sorry," I said.

"I want to know everything," Mrs. Apusenja said. "I *demand* to know."

Connie rolled her eyes and I heard the lock click on Vinnie's inner sanctum.

I decided it was best to give everyone the abbreviated version. "We had a tip that Samuel was in Vegas," I said. "So Lula and Connie and I flew out."

"A tip. Who would tell you about Samuel?" Mrs. Apusenja wanted to know.

"He applied for a job and his previous employer was checked as a reference."

"This makes no sense," Mrs. Apusenja said.

"Samuel was living with a woman he met on a business trip," I said. "I spoke to the woman, but not to Samuel."

Nonnie and Mrs. Apusenja went perfectly still.

"What do you mean, living with a woman?" Nonnie asked.

"He listed her house as his residence. And he was living there. I can't be more specific than that."

"I never liked him," Mrs. Apusenja said, narrowing her eyes. "I always knew he was a little pisser."

Nonnie turned on her mother. "*You* were the one who thought he was *wonderful. You* were the one who *arranged* the engagement. I told you these things were not done in this country. I told you young women were allowed to choose their husbands here."

"At your age you can no longer be choosy," Mrs. Apusenja said. "You were lucky to have an arranged engagement."

Nonnie slid me a look under lowered lashes. "Lucky to have him disappear and die," she murmured.

Yikes. "Okay, then, moving along," I said. "We learned from the police that Samuel had been shot and killed at the airport, so we went back and got Boo." Okay, so I rearranged it a little. It made for easier telling.

"Boo!" Nonnie shouted. "Where is he?"

"We didn't want to put him on a plane, so he's driving back with Lula. I think they might be here tomorrow or maybe Thursday."

"Samuel Singh should rot in hell," Mrs. Apusenja said. "He is a dognapper and a philanderer. After all we did for him. Can you imagine such a terrible person?"

I turned and looked through the window at Ranger. He was in the car, watching with a bemused expression. Ranger found me amusing. He enjoyed watching The Stephanie Plum Show. I didn't usually mind. I'd decided his interest was a mixture of raw lust, curious disbelief, and affection. All good things. And all things that were mutual. Still, every now and then I felt his enjoyment required some payback. And this was one of those times. If I had to deal with Mrs. Apusenja, so did he. Okay, so I was escalating the game, and Ranger would probably take this as a challenge issued, but I deserved to have some fun, too, right?

"Do you see that man in the black Porsche?" I asked the women.

They squinted out at Ranger.

"Yes," they said. "Your partner."

"He's homeless. He's looking for a place to stay and he might be interested in renting Singh's room."

Mrs. Apusenja's eyes widened. "We could use the

income." She looked at Nonnie and then back at Ranger. "Is he married?"

"Nope. He's single. He's a real catch."

Connie did something between a gasp and a snort and buried her head back behind the computer.

"Thank you for everything," Mrs. Apusenja said. "I suppose you are not such a bad slut. I will go talk to your partner."

"Omigod," Connie said, when the door closed behind the Apusenjas. "Ranger's going to kill you."

The Apusenjas stood beside the Porsche, talking to Ranger for a few long minutes, giving him the big sales pitch. The pitch wound down, Ranger responded, and Mrs. Apusenja looked disappointed. The two women crossed the road and got into the burgundy Escort and quickly drove away.

Ranger turned his head in my direction and our eyes met. His expression was still bemused, but this time it was the sort of bemused expression a kid has when he's pulling the wings off a fly.

"Uh-oh," Connie said.

I whipped around and faced Connie. "Quick, give me an FTA. You're backed up, right? For God's sake, give me something fast. I need a reason to stand here until he calms down!"

Connie shoved a pile of folders at me. "Pick one. Any one! Oh shit, he's getting out of his car."

Connie looked like she was going to bolt for the bathroom. "You lift your ass out of that chair and I'll shoot you," I said.

"That's a bluff," Connie said. "Your gun's home in Morelli's cookie jar."

"Morelli doesn't have a cookie jar. And okay, maybe I won't shoot you, but I'll tell everyone you shave your mustache."

Connie's fingers flew to her upper lip. "Sometimes

I wax," she said. "Hey, give me a break. I'm Italian. What am I supposed to do?"

I heard the front door open and my heart started tap dancing. It wasn't exactly that I was afraid of Ranger. Okay, maybe at some level I *was* afraid of Ranger, but the fear wasn't that he'd hurt me. The fear was that he'd get even. I knew from past experience that Ranger was better at getting even than I was.

I grabbed a bond agreement and tried to force myself to read it. I wasn't making much sense of the words and it was only dumb luck that I wasn't holding the bond agreement upside down when I felt Ranger's hand on my neck. His touch was light and his hand was warm. I'd been expecting it. I'd steeled myself not to react. But I yelped and gave a startled jump anyway.

He leaned into me and his lips brushed the shell of my ear. "Feeling playful?"

"I don't know what you're talking about."

"Watch your back, babe. I *will* get even."

FOURTEEN

Ranger reached around me and took the bond agreement I'd been holding. "Roger Pitch," Ranger read aloud. "Charged with assault with a deadly weapon and attempted robbery. Tried to hold up a convenience store. Attempted to shoot the clerk. Fortunately for the clerk, Pitch's gun misfired and Pitch took out his own thumb."

I could feel Ranger laughing behind me as he turned to the second page. Connie and I were smiling, too. We all knew Roger Pitch. He deserved to have one less thumb.

"Vinnie wrote a five-figure bond that wasn't totally secured because there seemed to be a low risk of flight," Ranger said.

"Pitch was a local guy with only one thumb. What could go wrong?" Vinnie yelled from his inner office, his words muffled behind his closed door.

"Goddamnit," Connie said, opening drawers, looking under her desk. "He's got me wired again. I *hate* when he does that." She found the bug and dumped it into a cup of coffee.

"Pitch didn't flee," Connie said. "He's just refusing to show up for court. He's at home, watching television, beating on his wife when things get boring."

"He's only a couple blocks from here," Ranger said. "We can pick him up and I'll call someone in to shuttle him over to the station."

Roger Pitch was mean as a snake and twice as stupid. Not someone I wanted to tangle with. "Yeah, but Connie has other files. Maybe there's something more fun."

"Pitch is a fun guy," Ranger said.

"He's a shooter."

"Not anymore," Connie said. "He blew this thumb clear to Connecticut. His hand's going to be bandaged."

Connie was right about Pitch's hand being bandaged. The incident happened three weeks ago, but the hand was still wrapped in big wads of gauze.

Pitch answered the door when Ranger and I knocked and he calmly accepted that we were bond enforcement. "I guess I forgot my date," he said. "It's all these pain pills they got me on. Can't remember a damn thing. Lucky I don't put my pants on my head in the morning."

Ranger and I were both dressed for the visit in full Super Hero Utility Belts. Sidearms strapped to our legs, handcuffs tucked into the belt, pepper spray and stun gun at the ready. Plus Ranger had a two-pound Maglite, just in case we needed to see in the dark. The lite could also crack a head open like a walnut, but walnut cracking was a little illegal, so Ranger saved it for special occasions.

"Let me just shut the television off," Pitch said. And then he whirled around, slammed the door shut, and threw the lock.

"Fuck," Ranger said.

Ranger didn't often curse and he rarely raised his voice. The *fuck* had been entirely conversational. Like he was now mildly inconvenienced. He put his Bates boot to the door and the door popped open to reveal Pitch at the end of the hall with a gun in his *left* hand.

"You're just a couple amateur pussies," Pitch yelled.

Ranger gave me a hard shove to the shoulder that knocked me off the small front stoop into a scraggly hydrangea bush. Then he stepped to the side of the door and drew his gun.

Pitch squeezed one off, but he was shooting with his left hand and clearly he wasn't ambidextrous because the round hit the hall ceiling. The second round bit into the wall.

"Goddamn," Pitch shrieked. "Piece of shit gun!"

Pitch had destroyed his thumb with a semiautomatic. And I guess one misfire was enough for him because he was now holding a revolver. The revolver held six rounds and Pitch fired them all off at us.

Ranger and I were counting shots. I was counting while I was trying to disengage from the hydrangea. There was silence after the sixth shot. Ranger stepped into the doorway, gun drawn, and told Pitch to drop his weapon. I climbed onto the porch and saw that Pitch was trying to get another round into the chamber. Problem was, he couldn't do it with the bandaged hand, so he had the gun rammed between his legs and he was fumbling with his left hand.

Ranger gave his head a small disbelieving shake. Like Pitch was so pathetic he was an embarrassment to felons the world over.

Pitch gave up on the gun, threw it at Ranger, and ran into the kitchen.

Ranger turned to me and smiled. "And you said he wasn't going to be fun."

"Maybe you should shoot him or something," I said.

Ranger ambled into the kitchen where Pitch was rummaging in a junk drawer, presumably looking for a weapon. Pitch came up with a screwdriver and lunged at Ranger. Ranger grabbed Pitch by the front of his shirt and threw him about twelve feet across the room. Pitch hit the wall and slid to the floor like a glob of slime.

Ranger cuffed Pitch to the refrigerator and called Tank. "Send someone over," Ranger said. "I have a delivery."

We stayed to watch Pitch get taken away by yet another of the Merry Men, we secured the house, and we walked out to the car.

"You could have told me to move instead of dumping me in the bushes," I said to Ranger.

"It was one of those instinct things. Keeping you out of harm's way."

"Yeah, right. Maybe more like getting even with me for sending the Apusenjas out to talk to you."

Ranger opened the passenger side door for me. "When I get even it's going to be something much more rewarding than dumping you in the bushes."

I buckled myself in and looked at my watch. "My sister came home today with the baby. I should stop around and see how she's doing."

"Tank's going to be glad he broke his leg when he finds out how I spent my afternoon."

"You don't like babies?"

"I come from a big family. I'm used to babies."

"Well then?"

"My grandmother is a little Cuban woman who cooks all day and speaks Spanish. Your grandmother watches pay-per-view porn."

"She used to watch the Weather Channel, but she said there wasn't enough action."

"Maybe you should check the dose on her hormone replacement. Last time I saw her she was trying to imagine me naked."

I burst out laughing. "That's what happens when you're a hottie. Women imagine you naked. Lula imagines you naked. Connie imagines you naked. Two-hundred-year-old Mrs. Bestler imagines you naked."

"How about you?"

"I don't have to imagine. I've seen you naked. Your naked body's burned into my brain."

Ranger turned onto my parents' street. "I'm going to wait in the car. And if you send your grandma out to harass me, I swear . . ."

"Yeah?"

"I don't know what I swear. I can't think of anything awful enough to do to you that wouldn't leave you maimed or psychologically scarred."

"Nice to know there are boundaries."

Ranger parked in front of my parents' house and got out of the car.

"I thought you weren't coming in," I said.

"I'm not. I'm going to stay out here. I can't see the entire street if I sit in the car."

Grandma Mazur opened the front door for me. "Is that Ranger with you? Isn't he coming in?"

"He thinks he's coming down with a cold. Doesn't want to infect everyone."

"Isn't that thoughtful! He's such a nice young man. Lots of times men aren't nice like that when they're hot-looking. Maybe I'll bring him something from the kitchen."

"No! He just ate. He's not hungry. And you can't take a chance on getting infected. What if you got sick and gave the cold to the baby?"

"Oh yeah. Well, you tell him I was asking about him."

"You bet."

Valerie was on the couch, nursing the baby. The girls were watching Valerie. My father was in his chair, concentrating on CNN.

My mother came in from the kitchen, took a look at

me, and made the sign of the cross. "Your arm is bandaged, you have grass stains on your pants, and pieces of some sort of bush are stuck in your hair. And Ranger is outside, wearing a gun." She looked more closely. "Is that a wig?"

"It's my real hair. I got it cut."

With the exception of the baby, everyone stopped what they were doing and looked at me.

"Sometimes it's fun to change things," I said. "Right? What do you think?"

"It's . . . cute," Valerie said.

"I wouldn't mind wearing my hair like that," Grandma said. "I bet it'd look real good if it was pink."

The phone rang.

"It's Lois Kelner across the street," Grandma Mazur said. "She wants to know if we're being invaded. She said it looks to her like there's one of them terrorists in our driveway."

"It's just Ranger," I said.

"I know that," Grandma said, "but Lois is calling the army."

My mother did another sign of the cross.

"Maybe you should get Ranger out of the driveway," Valerie said. "Paratroopers landing on the roof would upset the baby."

Grandma's eyes lit. "Paratroopers! Wouldn't that be something."

"I'll try to get back later," I told everyone. I stopped in front of the hall mirror to pick the branches out of my hair and to take a close look at the cut. I'd never before thought of myself as *cute*. Sometimes I felt sexy. And sometimes I felt downright fat and stupid. Cute was a new one.

I opened the front door and waved at Ranger. "Visit's over."

"That was fast."

"The woman who lives across the street thinks you're a terrorist. She said she was calling the army."

"You have plenty of time then," Ranger said. "It'll take the army a while to mobilize."

Ranger drove me back to Morelli's house. We clipped Bob to his leash, I stuffed a couple plastic sandwich bags into my jeans pocket, and we ambled down the street after Bob. Me and the terrorist out for a stroll with the dog.

"I feel like I should be doing something to find the carnation killer," I said.

"You have state and local police working on it now. They have a lot of resources and they have some good stuff to trace back. The photos, the emails, the flowers. And now they have interrelated murders. They can re-examine them and look for commonality. And they'll go back through case histories to see if they can find other victims of the game. Your job right now is to stay alive."

I glanced over at Ranger. He'd gone through three of the victims' apartments. Plus Bart's townhouse. "Have you been through Klein's house?"

"I went through last night while the police were there."

"The police allowed you access?"

"I have friends."

"Morelli?"

"Juniak."

Joe Juniak used to be police chief. He was elected mayor of Trenton and now was running for governor.

"Klein lived with his parents," Ranger said. "His room was a typical kid's room. Messy, posters of rock bands, small arsenal under his bed, and a personal stash of pot in his underwear drawer."

"You think that's a typical kid's room?"

"It was in my neighborhood."

"What about a computer?"

"Klein had a laptop. His parents said he took it everywhere with him. It wasn't in his room and it wasn't in his truck. Probably the webmaster took the computer after he shot Klein. Paressi's computer was missing. Rosen's computer was missing. By the time the police got to Howie's apartment, his computer was missing."

"Klein slipped up somehow when he took out Singh. He didn't get Singh's computer," I said.

"He was probably waiting for Lu to leave, but you and Connie and Lula were in place by then."

Bob stopped, hunched in front of old Mr. Galucci's house, and conversation was momentarily suspended while we watched Bob poop. How embarrassing is this? Poop is not something I feel comfortable sharing with Ranger. Actually, I'm not comfortable sharing poop with *anyone*. I'm not even comfortable with it when I'm alone.

When Bob was done I scooped the poop up in a sandwich bag. And now the horror continued because I had a bag of poop and no place to put it.

"Babe," Ranger said.

Hard to tell if he was horrified or impressed by my poop scooping. "I don't suppose you have a dog in the Bat Cave?" I asked him.

"The Bat Cave is dog free."

Bob pulled at the leash and we continued walking.

"Everyone involved had a laptop," I said. "Did they have anything else in common?"

"Singh, Howie, Rosen, and Klein were all computer geeks and loners. Paressi doesn't entirely fit the profile, but she became a computer junkie when she broke up with Scrugs. Probably there's a connection between her and Rosen. Maybe Paressi talked to Rosen about the game and Rosen came on board after Paressi was killed. They were all between the ages of nineteen and twenty-seven. Rosen was the oldest. None were especially successful."

"Bart Cone doesn't fit the profile, does he?"

Ranger was looking ahead at houses and cars. "Not entirely, but he fits better than Andrew." Ranger turned at the sound of a car a block behind us, traveling in our direction. He had his hand resting on his gun and his eyes stayed steady on the car. The car passed without incident and Ranger dropped his hand off the gun.

"Andrew lives in a nice mid-range house with his wife. It's a stable relationship. They like to cook. They vacation at the Jersey shore. They have two kids.

"Clyde lives in a rental house on State Street. He shares the house with two other guys. I'm guessing he's known them forever. I found a photo of the three of them when they were in high school. The house is pretty much a wreck inside and out. Thrift shop furniture, broken blinds, refrigerator filled with beer and take-out boxes."

"So Andrew and Clyde aren't loner computer geeks."

"They aren't loners. I don't know how much time they spend on the computer."

We turned the corner and headed for home. "You've been busy using your breaking and entering skills," I said.

"I just enter. I don't usually break."

"You broke down Pitch's door."

"Lost my temper."

Bob hunched again.

"Oh, for crissake," I said.

Morelli was sitting on his front step when we got back with Bob. "Lucky you," he said. "A two-bag day."

"I think we should stop feeding him."

"Yeah," Morelli said. "That would work." He stood and took Bob's leash and looked over at Ranger.

"It's been quiet," Ranger said. "No shooting. No one tailing us. No death threats or poison darts."

Morelli nodded.

"Your watch," Ranger said to Morelli. And he left.

"The bodyguard thing is getting old," I told Morelli.

"Did you tell that to Ranger?"

"Would it do any good?"

Morelli followed me into the house. "I have some bad news and then I have some bad news," Morelli said.

"Let's start with the bad news first."

"I checked your email account this afternoon just before I left work. You have another carnation letter. It's on the sideboard. I printed it out for you."

I looked at the email.

It will happen soon. Nothing can stop it. Are you excited?

"This guy's turning out to be a real pain in the ass," I said. "Now what's the bad news?"

"Grandma Bella's on her way over."

"What?"

"She called just as you were coming down the street with Bob. She said she had another vision and she had to tell you."

"You're kidding!"

"I'm not kidding."

"Why didn't you tell her not to come? Why didn't you tell her I wasn't home?" All right, maybe I sounded a little whiney, but this was Grandma Bella we were expecting. And whiney was better than flat-out hysteria, right?

"She's coming with a dish of my mother's manicotti. Have you ever tasted my mother's manicotti?"

"You sold me out for manicotti!"

Morelli grinned and kissed me on the forehead. "You can have some, too. And by the way, your hair is cute."

I narrowed my eyes at him. I wasn't feeling cute. In

fact, I'd decided I didn't like cute. *Cute* wasn't a word anyone would use to describe Morelli or Ranger. Cute implied a degree of helplessness. Kittens were cute.

A car stopped in front of the house and I took a deep breath. Calm down, I thought. Don't want to be rude. Don't want to let them sense fear. There was a knock at the door and Joe reached for the handle.

"Touch that handle and you die," I said. "She's coming here to see me. *I'll* let her in."

The grin returned. "Woman in charge," Morelli said.

I opened the door and smiled at the two women. "How nice to see you again," I said. "Come in."

"We can't stay," Joe's mother said. "We're on our way to church. We just wanted to drop this manicotti off."

I took the casserole and Grandma Bella fixed her scary eye on me.

"I had a vision," Bella said.

I looked down at her and screwed my face into an expression that I hoped conveyed mild interest. "Really?"

"It was you. You were dead. Just like the last time. You went into the ground."

"Uh-hunh."

"I saw you in the box."

"Mahogany? The model with the scroll work?"

"Top of the line," Bella said.

I turned to Joe. "Nice to know."

"A comfort," Joe said.

"So was there anything different about the vision this time?" I asked Bella.

"It was the same vision. But last time I forgot to tell you . . . you were old."

"How old?"

"*Real* old."

"We have to go now," Joe's mother said. "It wouldn't hurt you to come to church once in a while, Joseph."

Joe smiled and gave her and Bella a kiss on the cheek.

"Be careful." He closed the door after them and took the manicotti from me. "Way to go. That was impressive."

"I'm fearless."

"Cupcake, you are *not* fearless. But you can bluff with the best of them."

"What gave me away?"

"You had a death grip on the manicotti. Your knuckles were turning white."

Bob and I followed Morelli into the kitchen.

"I was old in Bella's vision," I said to Morelli. "I guess I can stop worrying about the carnation killer now. And I definitely don't need a bodyguard."

"I can hardly wait for you to explain this to Ranger," Morelli said.

I woke up to sun streaming in through Morelli's bedroom window. Morelli was long gone and Bob was asleep in his place, head on the pillow, one eye open and watching me.

I got up, went to the window, and looked out. There was a shiny black Ford Explorer parked two houses away on the opposite side of the street. Not Ranger. Ranger never drove the Explorer. Not Tank. Tank was sitting somewhere in the Bat Cave with his leg elevated. Probably Cal. Hard to tell at this distance.

I took a shower, dressed in a tank top, jeans, and sneakers and wrinkled my nose at my hair. I had a tube of hair gunk that was a combination of wallpaper paste and mustache wax. I pulled a big glob of it through my hair with my fingers and my curls stood up at attention. I was a couple inches taller with the gunk in my hair and I wasn't a real good judge, but I suspected I was no longer cute.

A half hour later, I rolled into the office.

"Whoa," Connie said at my hair. "What happened to you?"

"I got a haircut."

"I hope you didn't give him a tip."

"Am I cute?"

"That's not the first word that comes to mind."

Vinnie stuck his head out and grimaced at me. "Holy shit. What'd you do, tag yourself with the stun gun? I wouldn't show that hairdo to your mother if I was you." And he went back into his office.

"I didn't think it was *that* bad," I said to Connie.

"You look like you soaked your head in liquid starch and then stood in a wind tunnel."

Vinnie jumped out of his office. "I got it! I know who it is that you look like . . . Don King!" And Vinnie jumped back inside and slammed and locked his door.

I felt my hair. It was pretty stiff. Maybe I overdid the hair gunk.

"Omigod," Connie said, looking out the big front window. "It's Lula!"

Sure enough, the red Firebird was parked at the curb and Lula was at the door with Boo under her arm.

"What did I miss?" Lula wanted to know, coming over to the desk. "What's going on? Did I miss anything?"

I didn't know where to begin. There'd been death, birth, sex, and hair loss.

Lula shifted Boo on her hip. "Are you still looking for that carnation guy?"

"Yep," I said. "Haven't found him yet. I tried calling you, but your phone wasn't working."

"I stopped to take a break, got out of the car, the phone fell on the ground, and the dog peed on it."

"You made good time," Connie said.

"That is one motherfucker long trip," Lula said. "I was in the car for eight hours and my ass was asleep when I hit Little Rock and I said, 'Stick a fork in me, 'cause I'm done.' So I handed the rental car in and I hooked up with a couple truckers who drove day and night. And here I am. They dropped me off late last night."

Connie took a closer look at Lula. "Did you lose weight?"

"I lost ten pounds. Can you believe it? All you gotta do is eat meat all day. I've eaten so much meat in the last five days I can't remember ever eating anything else. I got meat oozing out my ears. And to tell you the truth, I'm starting to feel funny about all this meat. You don't think I could turn into like a *meat vampire* or something, do you?"

"I never heard of a meat vampire," I said.

"For the last couple days my teeth have been feeling funny. You know, like they're growing. Just these two ones in front. What do they call them . . . canines. And then I was looking at myself in the mirror this morning when I was brushing my teeth and I was thinking they looked bigger. Like vampire teeth. Like I'm eating so much meat I'm turning into a carnivore. And I'm getting dog teeth."

Connie and I were speechless.

"What happened to your hair?" Lula asked me. "You look like Don King."

"Yes, but I'm not cute," I said.

"Fuckin' A," Lula said.

Lula and I packed off in my car and headed for the Apusenjas'. Boo was on Lula's lap, ears up, eyes bright.

"Look at him," Lula said. "He knows he's going home. Isn't it something the way dogs know these things? I tell you, I'm going to miss this little guy." Lula cut her eyes to the rearview mirror. "Looks like you still got a bodyguard."

I turned and squinted back at the Explorer. Cal was behind the wheel. And he had someone riding shotgun. Great. Now I had two baby-sitters.

I whipped out my cell phone and called Ranger.

"Lula's back," I told him. "So, thanks anyway, but I don't need Cal."

"He's staying," Ranger said.

"I can take care of myself. I want you to tell Cal to stop following me."

"The carnation killer isn't going to move on you when you're so obviously guarded. He doesn't want to shoot you in the head from a distance. He wants to play with you."

"Yeah, but this is really annoying and it could go on forever."

"Not forever," Ranger said. "Just long enough for the police to do their thing. They have some leads. Having Cal in place buys them some time."

"Grandma Bella said I wasn't going to die until I was real old."

"That makes me feel so much better," Ranger said. And he disconnected.

I parked in front of the Apusenjas' house. Lula leaned forward and adjusted the rearview mirror and checked out her teeth.

"You're starting to creep me out with this teeth stuff," I said.

"How do you think I feel? I'm the one turning into a . . . creature. I feel like Michael J. Fox in that werewolf movie. Remember when he started growing hair all over? It was like he was turning into Connie."

Lula gave up on the teeth and looked over at the house. "I'm bringing this dog back because that's the right thing to do, but the bride of Frankenstein better not start on me."

"The bride of Frankenstein likes us now. She said she guessed I wasn't such a bad slut."

"Bet you got all excited over that." Lula levered herself out of the Escape, holding tight to Boo. She set him down on the ground. Boo ran to the Apusenjas' front door and started yapping to be let in.

Mrs. Apusenja opened the door and let out a shriek. She scooped up Boo and held him close and got a lot of sloppy Boo kisses.

"Isn't that nice," Lula said. "A family reunited. It almost makes me want to get a dog. Except for the peeing and pooping part."

Tell me about it.

FIFTEEN

I was on my way back to the office when Grandma Mazur called.

"We got a situation here," she said. "I don't suppose you're in the neighborhood?"

"What kind of a situation?"

"Valerie decided she's going to marry Albert."

"That's great."

"Yeah, except Albert's been living with his mom and his mom isn't happy that Albert's not marrying in his faith. Albert's mom wants him to marry a Jewish girl and so she's kicked him out of the house. That means everyone's going to be living here. Albert just showed up with a couple boxes of his stuff and he's moving it into that little room upstairs with Valerie and the girls."

"Oh boy."

"Exactly. We need to put rubber walls on this house. We don't all fit in it anymore. Your father says he's moving in with Harry Farnsworth. He's upstairs packing and your mother's all upset."

"My dad's moving out?"

"I can sort of see his point on this. He had to drive to the gas station on Hamilton to use the bathroom this morning. So I don't exactly blame him, but what's your mother going to do if your father moves out permanent? Where's she going to find another man? It's not like she's a live wire."

I did a large mental sigh. "I'll be right there."

"Don't tell nobody I called you," Grandma said.

I made a U-turn on Hamilton and smiled, knowing Cal was scrambling to follow me in the big Explorer.

Lula leaned over the seat, watching him. "Good to keep a man on his toes," Lula said. "I bet he's all worried back there, cursing you out. He can't find a place to wheel that SUV around. Uh-oh, he just jumped the curb and knocked over a garbage can. Ranger won't be happy to see a scratch on that shiny new car."

I pulled into the driveway, blocking my father's car so he couldn't make a getaway. Then I ran back to Cal, who was parking in front of the house. His face was red and a trickle of sweat traced a path down his temple.

"It's okay if you park here," I said to Cal and Junior, "but don't get out of the car. Both of you stay here and try to look normal." Even as I said it, I knew it was an impossible request. "And don't worry about that big gash in the right front fender. It's really not all that bad," I said.

The red in Cal's face kicked up a notch.

Lula was waiting for me on my parents' front porch. "You are *so evil*," she said. "There's no gash in the right front fender."

Grandma Mazur opened the door to me. "What a surprise," she said, real loud. "Look everyone, Stephanie's here."

Mary Alice was back to being a horse, galloping around the house, making horse sounds. The baby was screaming surprisingly loud for a newborn and Valerie was furiously rocking it in the rocking chair. Angie was drawing on a pad in the dining room. She had cotton wads stuck in her ears and she was singing, trying to drown out the noise. Albert Kloughn was pacing in front of Valerie.

"Maybe there's something wrong with her," Kloughn said to Valerie. "Maybe we should take her back to the hospital. Maybe she's hungry. Maybe she's wet."

"Maybe she's got gas," Grandma Mazur said. "I know I do. This family's getting on my nerves. I can't stand all this noise and commotion. It gives me indigestion. I gotta get some Maalox."

"I'm outta here," Lula said. "Nice seeing you all, but I'm going to wait in the car. I'm not good with crying babies. I've been locked in a truck cab with a dog and two horny truck drivers for the last couple days and on top of that I'm worried I'm turning into a carnivore."

"I wouldn't mind hearing about the two horny truck drivers," Grandma said.

I went into the kitchen where my mother was ironing. She always irons when she's upset. Ordinarily no one would approach my mother when she's got an iron in her hand, but I thought I should say something. "This house is bedlam," I said to her.

"I got a nice almond ring from the bakery," my mother said. "Help yourself. And there's fresh coffee."

Even when my mother was in a state, she was still a mother.

"What do you think of my hair?" I asked her.

She looked at me and made the sign of the cross. "Holy Mary, mother of God," she said. Then she smiled. "I can always count on you to top anything we have going on here."

"I hear Val's getting married."

"Thank goodness."

"And I hear they're all going to live here."

"What can I do?" my mother said. "They have to live someplace. Am I going to turn my daughter out on the street? They're going to buy a house as soon as Albert gets a little more established."

There were heavy footsteps on the stairs.

"Your father," my mother said. "He's moving out. We've been married for over thirty years and now he's moving out."

Only if he pushed my car out of the driveway.

I went back to Val in the living room and shouted over the baby. "I'm living with Morelli these days," I said. "Why don't you and the kids and Albert move into my apartment?" This was right up there with poking myself in the eye with a hot stick. I didn't really want to turn my apartment over to Valerie, but it was the only way I could immediately get her out of my parents' house.

"It would just be temporary," Kloughn said. "Just until we find a place of our own. Boy, that's really nice of you. Valerie, isn't that nice of Stephanie?"

"It is," Valerie said, shifting the baby so it could nurse.

Lisa stopped crying and Valerie looked like she was morphing back to the serene Saint Valerie. I was thinking that there was probably a lot of my mother in Valerie.

"There's nothing like a baby," Grandma said.

Mary Alice galloped by and stopped to look. "I'd rather have a horse," she said.

"When she gets older you'll be able to help feed her," Valerie said. "And she'll be as much fun as a horse."

"Horses have nice silky tails," Mary Alice said.

"Maybe we'll let Lisa grow her hair long into a ponytail," Valerie said. "Would you like to take the little cap off her head so you can see her hair?"

Mary Alice took the cap off Lisa's head and we were all transfixed by the wispy dark hair that swirled from Lisa's crown and framed her face. Lisa's tiny hands were balled into fists, her eyes were open, and fixed on Valerie.

And just like that, as of that instant, I wanted a baby. I didn't care if it had to come out of my vagina.

"I'll tell your father about the apartment," Kloughn said. "I don't think he really wanted to move in with Harry Farnsworth."

"I'll go over and box my stuff so you have room in the closet. You can move in anytime. Only thing, if there are any flower deliveries you should be sure to call me right away."

"Thanks," Valerie said. "You're a good sister. I'll make it up to you. And we'll start looking for a place of our own right away."

I yelled good-bye to my mom and I went out to Lula.

Lula was in the car, looking antsy. "I don't know what's wrong with me," Lula said. "I just feel all jumpy. I'm just not myself."

"You're not still worried about your teeth, are you?"

"I know they're growing. I can feel it. It's unnatural. And I got these cravings. I want to bite down on something. I want to feel it crunch in my mouth."

"Jeez. You mean like a bone?"

"Like an apple. Or a Cheez Doodle. Nothing crunches on this diet. Meat doesn't crunch. I'm crunch deprived."

I was a baton twirler when I was in high school. And that's how I felt now . . . like I was leading a parade. I pulled away from the curb and Cal pulled away from the curb. I drove to my apartment building. Cal followed me to my apartment building. We all parked in the lot. We all got out of our cars. We all took the elevator to the second floor. Then everyone followed me down the hall to my apartment. First Lula, then Cal, and then Junior. Junior was a clone of Cal, except for the tattoo. Junior was tattoo free. At least what I could see of him was tattoo free, and that was more than enough for me.

Cal opened the door to my apartment and took a look inside. Nothing out of the ordinary popped up, so we all trooped in. I filled a laundry basket with clothes and personal stuff and moved some things around to free up space for Valerie. While I was freeing space I could hear Lula trying to make conversation with Cal.

"Hey," Lula said, "what's going on?"

"What do you mean?" Cal asked.

"I don't mean anything," Lula said. "That's one of those things you say when you're trying to be friendly. That's an opening line."

"Oh."

"I heard you hit your head when you fainted in the hospital," Lula said.

"Yeah."

"Are you okay now?"

"Yeah."

"I could be wrong here," Lula said, "but I think you're dumb as a box of rocks."

"Sticks and stones," Cal said.

There was a moment of silence where I figured Lula was regrouping.

"So," Lula finally said to Cal. "Are you married?"

The whole packing process took less than ten minutes. I'd been moving clothes piece by piece to Morelli's house over the last couple days and there wasn't a lot left. I handed the laundry basket over to Junior and everyone marched out to the hall and waited while I locked up. I took a last look at the closed door and had to choke back a panic attack. I was turning my apartment over to my sister. I was homeless. What if I had a fight with Morelli? What then?

Junior put the laundry basket in the back of the Escape and we all got into our cars.

"Where are we going?" Lula wanted to know.

"We're going to TriBro. I'm not sure what I'm going to do once I get there. I guess I'll figure it out then."

I cut across town and picked up Route 1. It was the middle of the day and traffic was light. Cal had no problem following me. I took the off-ramp that led to the industrial park and wound through the park to TriBro. I parked toward the back of the lot and I sat there, watching.

"The killer's in that building," I said to Lula.

"You think it's Bart?"

"I don't know. I just know it has to be someone at TriBro."

After a half hour Lula was restless. "I gotta get something to eat," she said. "I gotta stretch my legs. I'm all cramped up in this car."

I was hungry, too. I didn't know what I was doing in the lot anyway. Waiting for divine intervention, I supposed. A message from God. A sign. A clue!

I put the car in gear and left the lot with the Steroidapods following close behind. I drove down Route 1 for a couple miles, took the turnoff to the mall, and parked at the Macy's entrance. This is always a good place to park because you hit the shoe department first thing while you still have lots of energy.

Lula pushed through the double glass doors and stood in the middle of the aisle. "They're having a sale!" she said. "Look at all those racks of shoes on sale."

I looked at the racks and for the first time in Plum history, I didn't want to shop. My mind wouldn't move off the carnation killer. I was thinking of Lillian Paressi and Fisher Cat and Singh and Howie. And probably there were a lot of others. I knew of two games, but there might have been more. I was thinking of my sister's baby and the fact that I didn't have one. And maybe never would.

"Look at those sandals with the four-inch heels and rhinestones," Lula said. "You can't go wrong with rhinestones. And heels always make your legs look real shapely. I read that in a magazine."

Lula had her shoes off, looking for a pair of the sandals in her size. She was wearing a poison green spandex tube top and yellow stretch pants that matched my car and came to mid-calf. She found the sandals, slipped them on and paraded in front of the mirror.

Cal and Junior were at the edge of the aisle, looking uncomfortable. They probably had expected to follow me around and catch some scofflaws when they got their marching orders from Ranger. And here they were in the Macy's shoe department, gaping at Lula, who was all boobs and booty in the rhinestone shoes.

"What do you think?" Lula wanted to know. "Should I get these shoes?"

"Sure," I said. "They'll go with the pink outfit you got in Vegas."

What if Ranger's wrong? I thought. What if the carnation killer is tired of the game and doesn't want to play with me? What if he just wants to kill me? He could be watching me now. Lining me up in his sights.

Lula paid for the shoes and we hit the food court next. Lula got a chicken. I got a cheeseburger. Cal and Junior got nothing. Guess they didn't eat while working. Didn't want to have a burger in their hand if they had to go for their guns. That was fine by me. I was scanning the mall and my eyes were rolling around in my head so fast I was getting a headache.

I watched Lula tear into her food and I had a creepy thought that she might be right about her teeth. She could really rip apart a chicken.

"What are you staring at?" Lula wanted to know. "Are you staring at my teeth?"

"No! Swear to God. I was just . . . daydreaming."

After we ate we went back to the cars. I drove about a half mile down Route 1 and Lula and I turned our attention to the motel coming up on the right. It was the Morelli and Gilman motel.

"Probably I didn't see what I thought I saw that day," Lula said. "Probably I was just imagining . . ."

Lula stopped talking because Morelli's truck was parked in front of one of the units.

"Uh-oh," Lula said.

I'd been doing eighty and I was a quarter mile past the hotel by the time I screeched to a stop. Cal and Junior went flying past me, utter surprise and horror on their faces. I put the Escape into reverse, backed up on the shoulder at a modest fifty miles per hour, and turned into the motel parking lot. No sign of Cal and Junior.

"Suppose it's police business?" Lula wanted to know. "Like maybe it's a sting."

"He's not working vice anymore. And this isn't even in Trenton."

"You aren't going to do something stupid like beat down the door, are you?"

I parked at the far end of the lot, behind a tan van. "Do you have a better idea?"

"We could sneak around back and listen in. Then if we hear them doing the deed we can beat down the door."

I'd rather knock and have Morelli answer the door half-dressed than catch Morelli and Gilman in the act. I couldn't think of too many things that would be more depressing than hearing or seeing Morelli playing hide the salami with someone other than me. On the other hand, I didn't want to make a false accusation. "Okay," I said, "we'll go around back."

We walked around the side of the motel and began counting off units. Each unit had two windows on the back side. I was guessing one window was in the bathroom and one in the bedroom. There were twelve units in the first building. All were at ground level. A strip of grass hugged the back of the building. Beyond the grass was a chunk of overgrown woods filled with refuse. A plastic milk crate. Soda cans. A torn mattress. I had no idea what was on the other side of the wooded area.

Curtains were drawn on all the units. We listened briefly at each window, hearing nothing. We got to the seventh unit and heard voices. Lula and I pressed closer to the window. The voices were muted, difficult to hear. The back window was closed. The air-conditioner was running in the front window. There was a slight break in the curtain halfway up the back window. Lula tippytoed to the woods and got the milk crate. She put the milk crate under the window and motioned that I should get on the crate and look in the window.

No way was I going to look in the window. I didn't want to see what was going on inside. I whispered to Lula that she should look.

Lula got up on the milk crate, pressed her nose to the window . . . and her phone rang. Lula grabbed at the phone hooked onto her stretch pants and stopped the ringing, but it was too late. *Everyone* heard the phone.

Shouting erupted from inside the motel room. A gunshot rang out. And a large man in a tan suit crashed through the window and knocked Lula off the milk crate.

"What the hell?" Lula said, sprawled on the ground in a tangle of curtain, sprinkled with window glass.

I wasn't sure what any of this was about, but I'd heard the shot and the guy who came through the window wasn't Joe, so I roundhoused him with my purse and sent him to his knees. I had him at gunpoint when Morelli stuck his head out the broken window.

"Oh Christ," Morelli said when he saw me. And he ducked back inside.

Guys came running from either side of the building. Obviously cops, but I didn't know any of them. Two were in FBI T-shirts. Morelli joined them. I didn't see anything of Terry Gilman.

Morelli grabbed me by the arm and pulled me aside. "What the hell are you doing here?"

"I saw your truck."

"And?"

"I thought I'd stop by to say hello."

"I'm working!"

I was getting annoyed. He was just a notch below yelling at me. "How was I to know? This isn't Trenton. You're not driving your crappy cop car. And a couple weeks ago Lula saw you coming out of this motel with Terry Gilman."

Morelli's eyes narrowed. "You went around back to spy on me and Gilman?"

"Actually, Lula was going to do the spying. I didn't want to look."

The guy in the suit was getting dragged away in bracelets.

"Isn't that Tommy Galucci?" I asked Morelli.

Tommy Galucci was famous in the Burg. Everyone knew he was a Mob boss, but the police had never been able to get anything to stick on him. Maybe because in the past the police never really cared all that much. Being a Mob boss in Trenton didn't get you on *America's Most Wanted*. Trenton was just a midsize pothole in the organized crime highway. And Galucci was a good citizen. He gave to the church. He kept his yard nice. He went out of town to cheat on his wife. But lately it was rumored Galucci was having a midlife crisis, wanting to make more of a name for himself, pushing his associates around.

"Yes, it's Tommy Galucci. Some of his *business partners* aren't happy with him and want to see him removed some way other than a one-way ticket to the landfill. They decided it would be a good thing for everyone if Tommy got to spend a couple years relaxing on a farm."

"Like a federal-run farm surrounded by razor wire?"

"Yeah, something like that. The *business partners* decided they wanted me to run the operation. Probably that was Uncle Spud's suggestion. And Gilman was acting as the go-between. People see me and Gilman together and the first thought isn't *sting*."

"It wasn't my first thought. Why this motel?"

"It's owned by Galucci's brother-in-law. Galucci did a lot of business here. Felt safe to him."

"Guess I screwed things up."

"I don't know what it is with you. You fall into a hole filled with shit and you come up smelling like a rose. Galucci wasn't cooperating. I wasn't getting anywhere with him. When he heard the phone he freaked, thinking he was set up. He shot the fed who was in the room with me and then he tried to escape by going out the window. The fed in the room with me just got a superficial flesh wound, but now we have Galucci on assault with a deadly weapon."

I looked beyond Morelli and saw two suits grilling Lula.

"You better rescue Lula," I said. "Probably it's not a good idea to let those guys look in her purse."

Morelli did some negotiating with the feds involved in the bust and it was suggested that Lula and I should leave the scene immediately and never return. Lula and I were happy to comply with the suggestion.

Cal and Junior had backtracked and found me and were parked two cars down in the motel lot. Their faces were red and they had deodorant failure. Ranger wouldn't have been happy if they'd lost me.

"See that," Lula said when we were all heading south on Route 1. "I told you Morelli was there on account of work. You should be more trusting of Morelli."

"If you'd been in my shoes, would you have trusted him?"

"Hell no," Lula said.

Truth is, I did trust Morelli. But there's a limit to trust. Even the most trusting woman who saw her boyfriend's truck at a motel in the middle of the day, *twice,* would have doubts. There's a difference between being trusting and being stupid.

Traffic was heavy and slow going in and out of Trenton. It was coming up on rush hour. Drivers looked sweaty and impatient. Men drummed their fingers. Women chewed on their cheeks.

I was still feeling the pull from TriBro. I turned off Route 1 and found my place in the TriBro lot.

"I don't get it," Lula said. "What's with this parking thing? What are you waiting for?"

I didn't know. Instinct kept dragging me here today. I half expected to see ominous dark clouds boiling over the building. Ghostbuster clouds. Portents of danger.

We sat there for a while and employees started to leave. The lot was almost empty and my phone rang.

It was Clyde. "Hey, Stephanie Plum," he said. "Is that you out in the lot? I see a yellow car and it looks like you inside. I'm watching you with binoculars. Wave to me."

I waved to Clyde.

"What are you doing in the lot?" he wanted to know.

"Just sitting," I said. "Watching."

"Is that your partner with you?"

"Yeah. That's Lula."

"It's quitting time," he said. "Do you and Lula want to go to dinner? We could all get a burger someplace."

"I don't think so."

"Okay," Clyde said. "Call me if you change your mind."

"Pretty soon we're gonna be in this lot all by ourselves," Lula said. "You and me and the two big dummies over there. You aren't planning on breaking in, are you? Maybe see if Bart Cone left his computer on?"

"Bart's smarter than that. He's not going to leave anything incriminating on his computer. Even if he did, I'm not that good at computers to be able to find it. And I'm sure the building has an alarm system."

The idea was tempting, though. Just not practical. And it was out of my league. It was a Ranger escapade.

"Okay, then how about the guy who just called you? The goofy Cone brother that doesn't do anything and wants to be a junior G-man. He's always wanting to take you out, right? I bet you could get him to let you in. I bet he doesn't even like his brother."

"*No*. I'll never get rid of him. It would be like feeding a stray cat. Once you give it a bowl of food you're stuck with the cat for life. I don't even *talk* to Clyde Cone."

"Too bad," Lula said, "because I bet he'd let you in and you could go snooping through ol' Bart's files and drawers and everything. You couldn't get into his email, but you could take a look at the desktop on his computer."

Truth is, I didn't want to go into the building. Not even with Cal and Junior doing backup. There was something bad in the building. The monster was there. He was waiting for me.

I got a call from Morelli wondering where I was. I didn't know what to say. I was sitting in an empty parking lot. Waiting for the mystery to be resolved. "I'll be home soon," I told him. "Don't worry."

The *Don't worry* message was insincere. I was worried. I was really, really worried.

"Steph," Lula finally said. "Maybe we should go home."

She was right, of course. So I cranked my yellow Escape over and drove out of the lot. I dropped Lula off at her car at the office and then I went home to Morelli.

I made peanut butter and olive sandwiches for supper and we ate in silence in front of the television. Probably we should have talked about the motel thing, but neither of us knew how to begin. Maybe it wasn't important anyway. We seemed to still like each other.

At nine o'clock Morelli was glued to the television and I was still fighting the fear or dread or whatever the hell it was that had its grip on me. I went to the kitchen and got a beer and took it out to the back porch. The air was soft and smelled nice, like fresh dirt and new grass. Joe didn't do much with his backyard, but his next-door neighbor, Mrs. Lukach, had flower beds and a dogwood tree. Joe and I had gardening skills that were almost as good as our housekeeping and cooking skills.

I finished my beer and stood. I turned toward the house and I felt a familiar piercing pain in my back. In my mind I called for Morelli, but either he didn't hear over the drone of the television or else it was only a mental plea for help, because the blackness came and there was no Morelli.

Even before I opened my eyes I knew I was in trouble. Fear filled every part of me. The fear was a hard knot in my chest. The fear clogged my throat. The fear slid in a greasy wave through my stomach. I forced my eyes open and I looked around. I was on the floor, in the dark.

I didn't seem to be hurt. I wasn't restrained. I moved my leg and realized I had a chain padlocked around my ankle. There were jingle bells attached to the chain. The potential significance of the ankle chain took my breath away.

I had a dull throbbing ache behind my eyes. It was from the drug, I thought. Like last time, when I was shot with a dart in the parking lot.

The only source of light was a single candle burning on a desk to my right. The light was dim, but I knew where I was. I was at TriBro. I was in Clyde's office. I could make out the action figures in the bookcase to my left.

I pushed myself up so I was sitting and realized someone was slouched in a chair, lost in shadow, watching me from across the room. The shadowed figure leaned forward into the candlelight and I saw that it was Clyde.

"You're awake," he said. "And you look scared. Sometimes when I get scared I get sexually excited. Do you get excited when you get scared? Are you hot?"

The words sent a new rush of cold fear into my chest. I looked into Clyde's eyes and I saw the monster emerging.

"Get up," Clyde said. "Go around the desk and open the drawer. I have a surprise for you."

I steadied myself on the desk and got to my feet, swallowing back nausea from the drug. I inched around the desk, carefully opened the drawer, and looked down at another lock of my hair, tied with the slim pink ribbon.

I looked up and my eyes met Clyde's. "Now you know," Clyde said. "You're surprised, right? I bet you never thought it was me."

Everything fell into place. Web Master wasn't a computer term as we'd all assumed. It was a Spider-Man reference. Days ago, I asked Clyde what he wanted to do, and he said he wanted to be Spider-Man. Spider-Man was known as *the webslinger* and Clyde's game name was the Web Master.

"Spider-Man didn't kill innocent people," I said. "Spider-Man was a good guy."

"I'm not the web*slinger*," Clyde said. "I'm the Web *Master*. There's a difference. And I don't kill innocent people. I run a game so people can kill each other. How cool is that?"

"What about the prey? Aren't they innocent?"

"I pick the prey out real careful. And they're never innocent. The cop killed a guy in the line of duty. And so have you. As soon as I saw you at the plant that day I knew you had to be the next prize. Bart tried to warn you away, but you wouldn't listen. It wouldn't have mattered. I had my mind made up right away."

"Bart knows about the game?"

Clyde was smiling, rocking back on his heels, enjoying his moment. "Bart's confused. I got careless with the game two years ago and Bart got to read an email. Paressi and Fisher Cat were left in the game and I was giving them the kill clue. Bart didn't know it was a game. He thought I was involved with Paressi and he went to the kill spot to stop me from a crime of passion. Problem was, he got there too late. Paressi was dead and Fisher Cat was gone."

"And Bart was accused of the crime."

"Yeah. And he was being a hero, protecting me. What a moron. Then when the DNA came back he was totally confused. It wasn't his DNA, of course. And Bart knows enough science to know that the DNA couldn't have been mine, either. It had the wrong structure. It was Fisher Cat's DNA."

"Didn't Bart ask you about the email?"

"Yeah. I gave him some bullshit story about unrequited love. And he wanted to believe it. He wasn't warning you off because of the game. He was worried I'd go gonzo for you and write another nutcase letter."

"What about Andrew? Did Andrew know about the game?"

"Andrew? You gotta be kidding. Andrew's got his perfect office, and his perfect family, and his freaking perfect house. Andrew doesn't see bad things. Doesn't allow them into his life. Doesn't ask questions that might have troubling answers. Andrew lives in Denial Land.

"Everyone always thinks Andrew's so perfect and everyone always underestimates me. Silly, lazy Clyde. Poor, dumb Clyde."

"And?"

"I'm not dumb. I'm smarter than everybody. Ask any of the people who play my game."

"They're all dead," I said.

"Oh yeah," Clyde said on a giggle. "I forgot."

"Why did Singh take off?"

"He was scared. He went after Bag Man, who you know as Howie. Somehow, Singh managed to screw up the kill and then his cover was blown. He turned chicken and ran."

"Now what?"

"Now we play. I've got a new game I thought up just for you. It's sort of a treasure hunt. And the grand prize is death. It's going to be a real good death, too. Scary and sexy and bloody."

This guy was so crazy. He'd been letting the insanity leak out little by little over the years and no one had noticed. Or maybe his family had noticed and chose not to recognize it for what it was.

"Okay, here we go," Clyde said. "I'm going to tell you about the game."

Morelli would have discovered I was gone by now. He'd call Ranger and they'd be out looking for me. If

I dragged this on long enough, they might find me in time.

"I can't think," I said. "I have a headache and nausea from the drug."

"That should be passing. I gave you a small dose. Just enough to have you unconscious for the capture. Probably what you're experiencing is a blood pressure rise from the fear. You're scared, right?"

I looked at Clyde. I didn't say anything.

"Yeah," Clyde said. "You're scared big time. I can feel it. I'm very sensitive to these things."

I raised an eyebrow.

"I *am*," Clyde said. "I have heightened senses . . . like a superhero or a werewolf."

"I understand pigs have a superior sense of smell. Maybe you're part pig." I was relieved not to have stuttered. I was so scared my mouth felt detached from my face.

"Here's the game plan," Clyde said. "All the doors are locked. You can't get out. Your only hope is to find a weapon and eliminate me before I get tired of playing with you. I have a loaded gun, a stun gun, and a big sharp knife hidden somewhere in the plant. Plus, there are things you'd naturally find here . . . like acid and hammers and shit like that.

"I've got two of your buddies hanging out here, waiting for you to find them. If you die, they die, too. In fact, if you don't find them soon enough, they'll die. You have a half hour to find the first one."

"Who are they?"

"That's for you to discover. Oh yeah, and I forgot to tell you . . . you'll be doing this in the dark. You can take the candle if you want. Romantic, right?"

He was smiling again. I guess this was his idea of a date.

"I've disconnected the alarm system," he said. "If

you trip the smoke detectors the signal won't get sent out anywhere. The sprinklers will go off and we'll all get wet, but nobody'll come to save you. That might be fun . . . seeing you in a wet T-shirt."

Clyde stood so I could see he was armed. "I have a twenty-two for the kill," he said. "And I have a paint-ball gun and a pellet gun for the rabbit in the shooting gallery. That's you. You're the rabbit. Oh yeah, and I have a taser. It's new. I always wanted to use a taser." He pointed the taser at me. "This is the start of play-time. I'm going to give you a chance to run. I'm gonna count to twenty and then I'm going to shoot you with the taser. *Go!*"

He started counting and I took off, forgetting the candle. Halfway down the hall I had to stop running. It was pitch black and I had no idea what was in front of me. I put my hand to the wall, feeling my way, jingling with every step. The hall led to the front foyer and I was prepared to crash through the glass door if necessary. I needed to get out of the building. Crazy Clyde was going to kill me and he wasn't going to spare his hos-tages. It didn't matter who I found. We were all going to die unless I could escape and get help. Clyde wasn't going to leave witnesses.

I saw the ambient light from the foyer and broke into a run. I turned the corner, heard gunshot, and felt the sting of impact. I felt blood run down my side, down my leg. I cried out and put my hand to my side. Paint. I was hit with a paintball.

"I'm right behind you," Clyde said. "If you go toward the door I'll shoot you with the taser. I'm dying to use the taser. Sometimes they use these things for tor-ture. The electric lead stays hooked into you with a barb and you can keep getting shocked. How cool is that?"

I was in the middle of the floor and I was breathing heavy. "What do you want me to do?"

"I want you to run, rabbit. Run *away* from the door."

I took a step and stumbled down to one knee. I was too scared to run. Too scared to think. Not good, I told myself. I had to try to stay calm. I managed to get myself to my feet and I ran in blind panic down the other side of the hall, toward Andrew's and Bart's offices.

There was a faint bar of light under a doorjamb in front of me. I pushed the door and it swung open. It was Bart's office. The office was lit by a single candle on the desk. Albert Kloughn was duct-taped to the desk chair behind the desk. He had duct tape across his mouth and wrapped around his ankles. His eyes were huge and tears rolled down his cheeks.

I ripped the tape off his mouth and was about to go for the tape around his torso when I saw the bomb.

"Don't touch me," he said. "I'm b-b-b-booby-trapped."

I snatched at the desk phone. No dial tone. I locked the door from the inside and pawed through the junk on Bart's desk, looking for something helpful. My hands were shaking and my heart was thundering in my chest. "I *hate* this," I said. "I *hate* this game. And I *hate* the pathetic excuse for a human being who's out there stalking me."

"You have to get help," Kloughn said. "This guy is crazy. He's going to kill us."

"There are just nuts and bolts on this desk," I said. "I need something I can use as a weapon."

"I know where there's a weapon," Kloughn said. "I can swivel myself in this chair and I was looking out the window into the warehouse when the crazy guy was hiding things. There's a room off to the side with glass windows all along."

"The quality control area."

"I don't know, but there's a workstation just by the door to that room. And he hid a gun there. It's right on top of the table part of the machine."

There was a knock on the door. "You're not allowed to lock yourself in Bart's office," Clyde said. "It doesn't matter anyway, I've got a key. But now you're gonna have to get punished before we can go on with the playtime."

I heard the key scrape in the lock and I grabbed a wooden crate half-filled with gears and threw it at the window that led to the warehouse. The glass shattered and I dove through the window. If I got cut it wasn't going to be any worse than what was going to happen to me at Clyde's hands.

I hit the ground and rolled. I'd seen the roll done in the movies and it seemed like a good idea. Problem was, in the movies they weren't usually landing on two thousand metal gears. Still, I wasn't decapitated from the glass shards when I pitched myself through the broken window, so that was a point in my favor. I scrambled to my feet, sliding on the debris, and ran for the first workstation. Beyond the first workstation the room blacked out and I was going to have to feel my way to the side room where the quality control people worked.

I was almost to the workstation when I was hit by another paintball. Thank God, I must have been beyond the reach of the taser. The paintball hit square in my upper back. If I lived to see another day, I'd be bruised. I dropped to the floor and put the workstation between me and Clyde. I heard Kloughn give an unearthly blood-curdling shriek, the candlelight went out, and then everything was quiet.

I was guessing that Clyde didn't want to chance going through the broken window. He was going to have to go back to the hall and enter the warehouse through the door at the end of the adjoining corridor. That gave me some time.

I crossed the room as fast as I could, creeping along low to the ground, my hands outstretched to keep from smashing into a workstation. I found the wall with the windows and knew I was in the right place. I followed the wall to the door and then paced off to the workstation. Sure enough, there was the gun just like Kloughn said. I couldn't see the gun even when I held it inches from my face, but I could feel that it was a six-shot revolver and it was loaded.

I backed myself into the test room and closed the door. I took up a position behind a desk, kneeling with my forearms resting on the desk, two-handing the gun to keep it from shaking. I was doing deep controlled breaths, telling myself to focus, to be a professional.

I heard the door open and I shouted for Clyde to stop. There was a gunshot and I felt the hit to my shoulder. And in that instant, I unloaded everything I had. I squeezed off all six rounds, shooting blind. The last shot was followed by silence. It was solid black in the office. I couldn't see my hand in front of my face. Either Clyde was dead or else he'd retreated. I wasn't willing to leave the desk to find out. It was Dolly Freedman's desk. I reached into her top drawer and got her pepper spray. Then I ducked under the desk and waited.

I heard something scuff in the direction of the door and my heart stuttered. He wasn't dead! The monster wasn't dead. A sob caught in my throat and I blinked back tears. There was the rustle of clothing directly in front of me and I covered my face with my arm and hit the trigger on the pepper spray.

"Oh shit. *Fuck!*" A man's voice. Not Clyde.

The spray was knocked out of my grasp, a hand grabbed me by the front of my shirt, hauled me out from under the desk and dragged me to my feet, moving me out of the area, away from the spray.

I was told to hold still. I knew this voice. I was held tight to Ranger. He slid goggles over my head and I was able to see in the dark. Ranger had two men with him.

Cal and Junior. And Junior was bent at the waist, gagging. That was the one I got with the spray.

"Sorry," I said.

He made a dismissive gesture with his hand.

I looked to the door and saw feet. Clyde's. The feet weren't moving. Clyde hadn't jumped away fast enough. Turned out Clyde wasn't as smart as he thought.

"Dead?" I asked.

"Looks that way. From what I can see, he took three in the upper body."

"I was shooting blind in the dark," I said. "I didn't know if I hit him."

"Anyone else in the building?"

"He has Albert Kloughn tied up with a bomb strapped to his chest in one of the offices. He said he had another hostage. I don't know who that is. I didn't find the other hostage." My knees gave out and I sort of sunk into Ranger and dissolved into tears. He had his arms tight around me, holding me to him. He sent Junior in search of the mechanical room to get the lights back on. He sent Cal to search for the second hostage. Then he called Morelli.

"I've got Stephanie," Ranger said. "She's safe, but there's a hostage unfound and a hostage potentially carrying a bomb. I haven't seen the bomb. I'm going to check it out now."

"Where's Joe?" I asked, wiping my nose with the back of my hand, trying to regain some control.

"We split up. I got the factory and he went to Clyde's house."

"How did you know it was Clyde?"

"Cal saw the truck tear past him. He didn't know what the truck driver was up to, but he thought it was suspicious enough to check with Morelli. Cal got part of the plate and Morelli ran it through the system, checking it against the principals."

The lights flickered and we took our goggles off. Every light flashed on at full power and we got a better look at Clyde. He was lying face up. The monster was gone and Clyde looked very ordinary in death. In fact, he looked oddly peaceful. Maybe it had been a relief to give up the game.

"Help," Albert Kloughn said. His voice was barely a whisper.

We all turned and stared at him, strapped to his chair on the other side of the warehouse. His face was red and mottled and he looked like he wasn't going to live long enough for the bomb to explode.

Ranger jogged across the room. "Try not to move," Ranger said to Kloughn. "I'm coming around to take a closer look."

We all followed after Ranger, watching from the hall while Ranger went into the office.

"I think it's a dummy," Ranger said, "but I'm not an expert." He took out a pocketknife and cut the duct tape away from Kloughn's ankles. He sliced into the tape binding Kloughn to the chair. "I'm not going to touch the device you've got strapped to your chest," Ranger said. "Stay here in the chair until the police get here with a demolition team."

Ranger's walkie-talkie chirped.

It was Cal. "You have to see this," he said. "I think I found the second hostage. I'm in the lunchroom."

We left Junior with Kloughn and we followed the hall to the lunchroom. Cal was standing hands on hips, smiling up at Lula. She was swinging like a giant piñata from a rope attached to a ceiling fan. She was still wearing the poison green top and the yellow stretch pants and her feet were treading air about fifteen feet off the ground. Her arms were duct-taped to her sides and she had duct tape across her mouth. A thick rope was wrapped around and threaded through the duct tape on her body and then looped around the fan. She had the beady little charging bull eyes, she was making angry *mmmmrf mmrff* sounds under the duct tape, and she was kicking her feet. Plaster dust was sifting down on her head from the ceiling fixture.

Ranger's face creased into a smile. "I love my job," he said.

"He must have gotten her up there with a forklift," Cal said. "There's one parked down the hall. Do you want me to drive it down here?"

"Don't need it," Ranger said, shoving a table under Lula, and climbing onto it.

Her feet were still swinging in the air and she was still kicking.

"You kick me and I'm leaving you here," Ranger said.

"Hmmph," Lula said under the duct tape.

Ranger worked at the rope with his knife, the rope gave, and Lula dropped onto the table. Cal reached out to support her and the two of them went to the floor.

I ripped the tape off Lula's mouth and Ranger cut the tape that was binding her arms.

"I was drugged!" Lula said. "Do you believe it? I was taking the garbage out and he shot me in the ass with a dart. That little shit, Clyde. Next thing I know I'm swinging around from the ceiling. I'm beside myself. I'm in a state. I didn't know what to think. I saw some kinky shit when I was a ho, but I never did anything like this." She looked around, wild-eyed. "I need something to eat. This here's an eating situation." She spied the vending machine and stormed across the room. "I need money. I need quarters or dollars, or something. Omigod, they got Twinkies in here. I need a Twinkie real bad."

"What about the supermodel diet?" I asked Lula.

"Fuck that. I hate those boney-ass supermodels anyway. I don't know what I was thinking." Lula was shaking the vending machine. "Who's got a hammer?" she asked. "Somebody help me out here."

Ranger slid a dollar into the machine and Lula punched the button.

"Hello, Twinkie," she said. "I'm coming home. Lula's back in town."

It was way after midnight when Morelli and I got back to his house. He dragged me up the stairs, stripped my clothes off, and shoved me into the shower. I had paint everywhere. Yellow, red, blue.

"You're a disaster," Morelli said, standing to one side, watching me.

"Is it coming out of my hair?"

"It's out of your hair, but I think you might have a permanent blue stain down the back of your neck. You're not going to believe this," Morelli said, "but I'm too tired for sex. I'm beat. I'm not even forty and you've turned me into a burnout. I'm standing here, looking at you naked in the shower, and nothing's happening."

The soap slid from my fingers, I bent to retrieve it and Morelli changed his mind on the burnout.

"Move over," Morelli said, peeling his clothes off. "I can see you need help here."

I woke up feeling great. I opened my eyes and I knew it was over. No more red roses and white carnations. The sun was shining. Birds were chirping. Albert Kloughn didn't explode with the bomb. Morelli was beside me, still sleeping. Life was good. Okay, so I was slightly homeless and I had a blue stain down the back of my neck. Ranger was still at large, waiting to get even for the Apusenja event, but that was in the future. It could be worse. Eventually I'd get my apartment back. And in the meantime I was with Morelli. Who knows, maybe I'll just stay here. Then again . . .

The doorbell rang. I propped myself up on an elbow and looked at the bedside clock. Eight-thirty.

Joe put his hands to his face and groaned. "Was that the doorbell?"

I got out of bed and went to the window. Joe's mother and Grandmother Bella were on the front porch. They looked up at me and smiled.

Shit.

"It's your mom and Bella," I said. "You'd better go see what they want."

"I can't go," Joe said. "My mother would fall off the porch if she saw me like this."

I looked under the sheet. He was right. His mother would fall off the porch. "Fine!" I said, rolling my eyes. "I'll go. But you'd better throw some cold water on yourself and come down and rescue me."

I wrapped a robe around myself and ran a hand through my hair on the way down the stairs. I opened the door and tried my best to smile, but my mouth only partly cooperated.

"Coffee cake," Joe's mother said, handing me the bakery bag. "Fresh-made today. And Bella has something to tell you." Joe's mother elbowed Bella.

"It's about the vision," Bella said. "I was wrong about the dead blond wife and the babies. It wasn't Joseph in the vision. It was Bobby Bartalucci."

"That's a relief," I said. "But poor Mrs. Bartalucci."

"I could have been wrong about the dead part, too," Bella said. "Maybe she was just sleeping."

I heard Morelli on the stairs behind me. Felt his hand rest on my shoulder. "Morning," he said to his mother and grandmother.

"And one more thing," Bella said to me. "It's about your car. It's going to be blown up. *Kaboom*. There's going to be nothing left of it, but don't worry, you won't be in it. I had a vision."

Bella and Joe's mom drove away and Joe and I stood in the open doorway, staring at my car.

"Something to look forward to," Joe said. And then he kissed me and took the bakery bag into the kitchen.